FILTHY SCORE

KENNA KING

CONTENTS

The Hawkeyes Hockey Series

Check out **www.kennakingbooks.com** for more books and information.

SCAN ME

CHAPTER ONE

Tessa

"Uh oh..." My friend Autumn, and fake girlfriend to the Hawkeyes right-wing Briggs Conley, elbows me and then smirks. "Someone's in trouble."

"Who, me?" I ask, following her gaze to see a familiar large, brooding blond-haired hockey player who just entered the bar.

His eyes search the large, dimly lit club from right to left until his gaze catches on mine. Something dark flickers in them as he finds his target and heads directly toward our table from across the room.

Lake Powers.

Jersey #12 and left-wing superstar for the Hawkeyes.

We're coworkers, I guess you could say. Although it rarely feels like it. The word 'coworkers' hints at the idea that Lake and I share some kind of commonality or camaraderie.

We don't.

He plays a game in front of hundreds of thousands of adoring fans and gets paid millions. Meanwhile, I'm holed up in the belly of the stadium, babysitting a bunch of grown men's social media accounts for one percent of the same pay.

He's the talent on the ice, and I handle putting out the media dumpster fires he likes to set ablaze and leave for me to extinguish.

That makes me sound a little bitter, but I'm not. I love my job. It's just that Lake and I have massively different roles, and that difference put us at odds the first day I stepped into the Hawkeyes locker room while Sam Roberts, the general manager, introduced me to the guy.

As the PR manager for the Seattle Hawkeyes, it's my job to virtually follow all the players and clean up any media messes they get into as well as find ways to boost their public image. By doing so, it helps boost the image of the Hawkeyes franchise too.

My stomach flutters at the look in his eyes as he heads straight for our table. I remind myself that irritation is causing this reaction... Lake and I are far from friendly.

Figures he'd finally find me.

He overheard me tell Penelope a few days ago, during a private conversation between her and me in my office, that my great-uncle taught me to pickpocket one summer when I was a kid. As a magician for a traveling circus, it was a part of his schtick, and he was exceptional at it. The audience loved it, and it came in handy for me as a party trick I'd do in college occasionally.

So when Lake bet me that I couldn't lift his wallet off him because "I'm as quiet as a freight train," I knew I couldn't pass up a chance to knock Lake down a peg or two. Besides, I never turn down a bet.

So unbeknownst to him, Lake's unlimited black card is currently holding open a tab that's paid for the past couple of rounds of drinks for our girls' night. He must have finally figured it out and tracked me and his high-limit credit card down.

I might have also bought a drink or two for a girl who had been crying after a bad breakup. She needed a little pick-me-up, and Lake is just the man to pay for it since I'd imagine a girl in every bar across town right now is crying because of him anyway.

Karma, baby.

I watch as Lake keeps coming closer.

Practically every man and woman he passes tries to talk to him, women throwing themselves at him, but he doesn't take his slitted eyes off me.

Goosebumps shoot down my arms at his focused and intense stare, and a rogue shiver rolls through my shoulders and down my back as he inches nearer.

Unconsciously, I check the distance to the back exit. A small part of me wants to get up and make a run for the back door. I fidget in my seat with every step he takes that eats up the space between us, but I cram that weakness down further in my gut. I'm not that woman anymore; I don't let attractive hockey players intimidate me.

Did I just say attractive?

I mean... Lake's okay if you like the blond-haired, icy-blue-eyed California surfer guy vibe... even though he's from Colorado. Still, he looks like he should be on an early 2000's Abercrombie clothing bag.

But even if I thought he was attractive in that dominant hockey player way with piercing blue eyes and a smile that could instantly incinerate a pair of panties, we're enemies... or at the very least, we're not friends. I've done my fair share of dating lying, cheating hockey players in high school, college, and even more recently, to know they aren't worth the lay.

I have a type, or rather, I *had* a type.

Never again.

I'm done with the whole bunch of them. And even so, we work together.

The throng of people dancing in the middle of the room part for him as if he's Moses from the Bible parting the Red Sea. I roll my eyes. He must be eating this up that I get to witness his glory even though this should be my moment.

Gross, gag me... and I don't mean the good kind.

"Welp, that's my cue to go." Autumn smirks again. "This was fun. Another night next week?"

Penelope and Isla pull their eyes off Lake for a second to nod in agreement at Autumn, and I do my best to focus on them too and pretend I didn't see Lake headed this way even though he watched me stare back at him for the last few heartbeats.

He already knows that I know he's here. And, unfortunately, he's smarter than that pretty-boy face makes him seem.

A zing of excitement takes me by surprise as Lake walks up to the side of my chair, his smoldering hockey stare beating down on me. If the bar wasn't so loud, he'd be close enough that I'd be able to hear his breathing. Isla and Penelope stare up at him from across the table.

"Hi, Lake," Penelope says in her usual sweet voice.

"Hi, Penelope," he says quickly, barely offering her a glance. He might be mad at her, too, since she played a small part in the bet... mostly just by hearing it. "The card, Tessa," he says, his hand outstretched toward me as if waiting for me to hand over his limitless credit card.

Honestly, having a black card in my purse always leaves me a little uneasy, and I'm looking forward to the end of the night when I can give Lake his card back.

Whenever my brother, Brent, who also plays for the Hawkeyes, right behind Lake as a left defenseman, has given me his card to book flights or send our grandmother a birthday gift, I'm always suspicious of any random stranger who walks too close to me. I'm always relieved to give my brother his card back and no longer be responsible for it.

So I'll give Lake his card back. He's learned his lesson...

Don't bet me that I can't pick-pocket your wallet because I don't back down from a bet. And I don't make a bet I can't win.

"I don't have it," I tell him, giving him as little interest as possible.

Isla leans forward over the table and closer toward me. "Didn't you buy our burgers and our drinks with it?" she asks in a whisper as if Lake might not hear her.

"Oh, you're an accessory to theft?" he asks her, leaning on the table.

Her eyes dart up to Lake and then go wide.

I can already tell from Lake's body language and the glint in his eye that he's enjoying screwing with her. He gets a better reaction from her than he'll get from me.

"Uh..." Isla says hesitantly.

She gives me a pleading look to save her.

The barstool that I'm sitting on doesn't swivel so I have to swing my legs to the right in order to face him. I glare up at him slightly but not enough to make it seem as though I want to have a long conversation about this.

"I told you I'd get your wallet, and I told you that I'd take it on a shopping spree," I say smugly.

"And this is your idea of a shopping spree? You're spending my money on burgers and booze?" he asks with a bit of amusement in his voice.

"So... what if it is? What did you expect I'd buy?" I ask, casually leaning my arm over the chair's backrest and leaning sideways into it as I face Lake.

I'm intrigued to find out what he thinks my spending habits would look like.

"I don't know. Don't women want designer clothes, shoes, handbags, and jewelry?"

Sure, those things are nice, but I'm more of a laptop, coffee gift card, and random lotions and bath salts kind of a girl.

I wasn't going to spend tens of thousands of dollars on a new wardrobe with Lake's money. I might have won the bet, but that kind of money would make me feel like I owed him something in return, and I don't want to owe Lake anything.

"You assumed she would take your card out around town?" Penelope asks in surprise, leaning in over the table toward us.

She knows me well enough to know I wouldn't spend someone else's money like that, even if it was my wager.

"I figured she'd probably run up my card a hundred thousand or more," he says without flinching. "Shit, I don't know. I thought I might find a Mercedes G-Wagon out front of the stadium tomorrow with her name on the license plate."

"A hundred thousand and a car?!" I practically shout, my eyes widening at his comment. "You think I'd do that?" I ask, almost a little insulted that he thinks I'm the kind of person to take advantage of someone else.

His eyes settle back on mine again, leaning in closer so we can hear each other over the loud music.

"It was a bet, and I lost, evidently, and that's what we agreed on, didn't we?" he asks, his eyes darting back and forth between mine like he's trying to read me.

He sets his hand on the back of my chair, his thumb just barely grazing over my arm as he does.

It wasn't on purpose, that I'm sure of, and I shake off the light tingles that surface on my shoulder where he touched me.

It's not Lake that has my body reacting this way. Absolutely not! I'd never touch a man with that many "miles" on him... or at least, not anymore.

I've been going through a dry spell lately, having to use my trusty vibrator and porn to get me through, but it's just not the same. However, what else is a girl to do when you're on a permanent hockey dick hiatus, and that's all you meet because you work for a hockey team as the in-house social media manager?

Hand to forehead.

Dating sites have proven to be a cesspool of men only looking to get their own rocks off with zero care for making sure the female counterpart reaches her final destination as well.

It's almost as if they figure they'll never see you again, so why even pretend to care whether or not they can satisfy you.

Disappointing... on every level.

The dating apps need a better rating system that only the women who click on the guy's profile can see, but none of the men are aware of. A hidden referral guide, if you will...

1 Star = Be prepared that he'll "forget" his wallet.

2 Star = Don't expect foreplay because you're not getting any.

3 Star = It was mediocre, but you might have better luck.

4 Star = Worth a second go-around.

5 Star = Would refer to a friend.

"I'd never take advantage of you like that, Lake."

He looks at me like he's trying to figure me out; like what I just said doesn't fully compute. Then he finally speaks as if he's ready for this conversation to end so he can be back on his way.

"Okay then, if you don't have it, who does?" his thick raspy voice asks while he surveys the bar.

"The bartender. He has our tab open. Be a doll would you, and close it for us." I finally turn in my chair and raise my glass at him, giving him my least give-a-fucks expression.

My eyes lock with his, and a devilish smirk stretches across his face.

Okay, I lied.

He's gorgeous.

But so full of himself.

I probably just got a venereal disease standing this close to him.

"How did you find out that she had it?" Penelope asks, excitement in her voice as if she's been waiting patiently for the moment when Lake found out about me winning the bet.

"I have alerts on my card. It tells me when something gets charged to it," he tells her.

"And it told you we were here?" Isla asks him.

"It said that there was a three-hundred-dollar charge at this club but that didn't make sense since my wallet was still in my back pocket. So imagine my surprise when I searched through my wallet to find that my black card was missing," he says, leaning in closer to me again and speaking in my direction.

"I told you not to take the bet," I remind him.

"How did you take only the one card? It's usually tucked under several other cards. I never use it."

"I lifted your wallet, took the card, then returned the wallet right back where it was before," I tell him, pride bursting out of me.

His perfect lips pull into another smirk, and I bite down on the inside of my mouth to stop myself from licking my lips.

"You touched my ass twice? Too good the first time, had to cop another feel?" he asks, a twinkle in his eye.

Isla and Penelope start snickering on their side of the table. I flash them a serious brow, asking non-verbally, *"Whose side are you on?"*

I turn back to Lake after their snickers die down at my *almost* glare.

"I have no interest in your ass, Lake. And I have to be honest... it was a little doughier than I expected," I lie.

I hear Isla just about spit take and Penelope gasps in amusement.

Doughier? Only in the sense that taking a bite out of it would probably be sinfully delicious since I'm on a diet... a hockey player diet.

Lake's expression goes flat, but it only takes a second for him to recover... like a true professional fuck-boy.

"Is that right?" he asks, his left hand still on the back of my chair and now his right settles on the bar table as he faces me straight on and leans down, his spicy deodorant wafting across my nose. "Well, you could have fooled me. Sure seems like you liked it if you touched it twice."

That's another bet I'd take if I could prove it—I have no interest in touching Lake's toned professional athlete ass ever again.

Hell no!

"I think you're just trying to deflect from the fact that I won yet another bet. What does that make us... 3-0? Are you feeling emasculated yet?" I ask, straightening my spine in my chair to show I'm not backing down.

The added length in my posture pushes my mouth closer to his, not that there is any way I'd kiss him.

"Not a chance, Tessie," he says, shifting his weight from his left leg to his right. "Anytime I feel like that, I look over at the women in my cheering section, or I throw a punch out on the ice at a rival player, and then the whole world rights itself again."

Tessie.

God, I hate it when he uses that nickname.

It's what my brother has called me since I was a kid, and because Lake and my brother are close, both on the ice and off, Lake thinks that gives him license to use it. He knows how mad it makes me too... that's probably the real reason he uses it.

"Don't call me Tessie... I've told you at least a hundred times," I say, pulling my arm back off the backrest and setting my hands in my lap, my shoulder now farther away from his touch against the chairback.

"Oh... I'm sorry." He fakes an apology and places a hand on his heart condescendingly. "I'd offer to make it right by buying you a drink, but you've already helped yourself to my credit card and bought drinks for the entire bar."

"I didn't buy drinks for everyone in the bar, but that's not a bad idea," I say and then lift my hand to flag down the bartender.

Lake's fingers wrap around my wrist as he pushes my hand back down.

I laugh to deflect from the fact that his touch made my stomach flip... or maybe I'll get lucky, and instead, it's the onset of the stomach flu and *not* a chemical reaction to his skin on my skin.

"You have the money, cheapskate, or have you blown all of your millions already? Buy your fans a round," I say, looking over at the crowd of women waiting for Lake to turn around with the hope they can snag his attention.

It's always the same thing when I see him at bars, restaurants, and especially outside of the Hawkeyes stadium; women want Lake, and men want to be Lake's best friend.

It's probably a cliché statement, but nothing could be closer to the truth in this case.

I've seen it with my own eyes.

Lake

Getting the credit card alert earlier today had me shaking my head. I didn't have to guess who had my card when I saw the charge for over a hundred dollars at Wally's Burgers and Shakes. It's Tessa's go-to after-club place for food since they're open until two o'clock.

I only know this since Brent Tomlin, her older brother and the guy who has my back out on the ice, has asked me to drive him to pick her up from the burger joint a small handful of times when he was already a couple of beers in and lived at The Commons apartment building like most of the guys on the team.

Now that he's bought a house in suburbia Washington, he doesn't ask me for late-night trips to burger restaurants to pick up his infuriating sister.

The second I saw the charge, I realized that Wally's must also be her pre-game snack spot too before hitting the clubs.

I knew by the time I saw the charge she'd already be gone, so I waited for the credit card company to send me another alert. It was tough to wait another hour for a hit, but I got it. Ground

Zero is a club downtown with dancing, overpriced drinks, and rude staff... something that people come here to experience, which is fucking weird.

The second I saw the alert, I already had my keys in my hand. I walked out of my penthouse at The Commons on a mission to find the girl with my high-limit credit card.

I knew better than to keep it in my wallet, but I've had it in there for over six years and have never used it once. I sort of forgot about it.

I guess it only takes a smart-mouthed little brunette to remind you that nothing is sacred in this world.

Of course, she won the bet, but I'm not sure how she did it. I suspect she cheated and went through my locker yesterday during drills. She would have had to figure out the combination to my locker, though... I'm not sure how she could have done that, but the woman is resourceful.

She could have spent a hell of a lot more money. And her telling me that she'd never take advantage and spend an exponential amount of my money has me wondering if that's true. Because the majority of women I come into contact with are looking for just that—an unlimited spending lifestyle.

My eyes trail over Tessa's face; her long dark eyelashes and full lips are still in full view, but it's too dark in the club to get a good view of those eyes. They're usually light in color, like gold, but they turn to a dark amber when she's mad.

I bet in the right lighting, I could see the blazing fire in them directed at me.

"I'm not a cheapskate. My bank account has no trouble handling the tab. I just think it might be bad business for the

Hawkeyes' best and most good-looking player to be paying to overserve patrons only to have one of them drive home tonight and wrap their car around a lamp post... or worse. You'd have a shitstorm on your hands, and I don't want you saddling me with a fake girlfriend like Briggs to fix my reputation."

Tessa looks over at Penelope and Isla, and they all share a frown of concern. Do they think I don't know that Briggs and Autumn are faking it? Give me some credit... I'm not the dumb jock they make me out to be.

"Oh please..." Tessa scoffs, looking back at me. "There's no number of fake girlfriends in this world that could save your reputation. You're too far gone," she says, and then pulls her martini to her mouth and takes a sip.

"If you mean too far gone because my reputation is out of this universe and into another dimension of awesomeness? Well, then I'd have to humbly agree with you."

Tessa rolls her eyes.

Isla isn't sure what to say—probably because we don't know each other well—and Penelope snickers. She's always a good sport and the franchise's unofficial little sister. I know for a fact that any of us on the team would beat the life out of anyone who hurt Penelope Roberts. And her dad, the Hawkeyes' general manager, would expect nothing less from us. He'd also kill any one of us if we ever made a pass at his pretty daughter.

"Your head is so big, I can't believe you made it through the door," Tessa says.

"I've been told that my head is the eighth wonder of the world... want to see it?" I ask, knowing full well that Tessa will tell me to shove my head up my ass, but fuck it... I'm here for whatever she wants to throw at me.

I should dislike Tessa for all the shit she's sent my way. All the times I've been sent to our GM, Sam Robert's office, to answer for not keeping my social media in line with the franchise's "family clean" image, but I can't help enjoying the banter.

"Sure, whip it out. I'm sure the gaggle of women behind you would like to see it. And maybe I'll get lucky, and you'll get arrested for public indecency, and the Hawkeyes will drop you for yet another infringement on your contract. Then you can be someone else's problem," Tessa says, and then takes another sip of her girly pink drink.

"You'd miss me," I tell her.

"Don't bet on it."

CHAPTER TWO

Tessa

It's been almost a week since Lake lost our bet and came to find me at Ground Zero, but I haven't had the chance to bump into him in the halls to sport my "I told you so" swagger like I usually do. Lake coming down to confront me at the club, though? Making him come all the way out to find me was a pretty great start.

The only real reason I bet anyone in the first place is for bragging rights. Who cares about the spoils? When it comes to betting millionaire hockey players, betting a hundred dollars or a thousand dollars, or even a shopping spree, barely makes a dent in their bank account. I prefer to go for something these cocky boys don't give up without a fight.

Pride.

They don't like losing, that's indisputable.

With all of their away games lately, the players haven't been around except for a few weekdays for practice, but then they're back on buses or planes to their next game.

I hate the hollowness of these walls when they aren't echoing with players. I may give these guys a ton of crap, but at the end of the day, I love my job. It's always something new, there's always a challenge to conquer, and the energy of a pro hockey team is contagious. Plus, I get to watch every home game from the owner's box seats, and I get to work for the same team as my brother.

Sure, the last one doesn't always seem like a pro, but I love my brother, Brent, even if he's a pain in my butt most days.

I head to the break room just as I get in for work to make myself a cup of coffee. I didn't have time to stop at Serendipity's Coffee Shop this morning for a coffee and a sticky bun.

The single-serve machine wakes up complaining about needing more water to start. I turn to the sink and fill the plastic reserve with tap water and then set the container back in place. The machine begins hissing after I fill it, and the water heats. I open the Hawkeyes social media account to see what the wide web is discussing about the team that signs my paycheck... and that has also become a real family for Brent and me. Something neither he nor I have really had since our parents passed away in a plane accident when I was in high school. Our dad was flying his little Cessna personal aircraft when it went down in the hills of Southern California, where we grew up. Ever since then, it's been me and Brent.

Our grandmother and great-uncle offered to take us in, but Brent had already turned eighteen and was considered an adult. Brent didn't want us separated so he petitioned the courts to be my legal guardian. We've been each other's family ever since.

A picture hits me right away. A player that the Hawkeyes account follows was tagged in a photo.

An indecent photo.

I just about scream out loud, but I hold it together. I know how to handle this, and I'm going to do it as quickly as possible before anyone else sees it.

I power walk out of the break room, deciding to come back for my delicious coffee after I handle this nuisance.

I won't let Lake ruin the best part of my morning.

My coffee.

The first few sips should be savored, met with a light breathing exercise and a couple of minutes of meditation before I dive into the day. I'm sure Lake would love nothing more than to get my day off track, but I won't let that happen.

Tessa: Where are you?

Lake: At your mom's house.

What the hell?

Tessa: My mom has been dead for fifteen years, asshole.

He knows this. He's been Brent's best friend ever since he got traded from the San Diego Blue Devils to the Seattle Hawkeyes four years ago.

His number lights up on my phone.

Lake calling...

"What?" I bark into the receiver.

"Fuck... Tessa, I'm sorry. It was just a stupid thing that the guys say... shit... never mind what stupid stuff they say, I didn't mean—"

"Just forget it," I bite out.

"It was thoughtless. I forgot. Sometimes I forget that you and Brent had the same parents—"

I wish he'd just stop apologizing. Or rather, stop talking altogether.

"Lake, where are you?" I ask, not bothering to get into this with him.

It's been fifteen years since it happened, but I'm not hashing it out with Lake. He's probably the last living soul I'd choose to talk to about the most painful thing that has ever happened to me.

I don't like talking about my parent's passing with anyone other than Brent, and he and I barely ever discuss it. Neither one of us wants to relive it.

"I'm in the locker room," he finally says.

"Good," I say as I push through the locker room door, hanging up on him as I enter. "Tessa in the house. Hide whatever family jewels you don't want value assessed," I yell out with barely any warning.

But who am I kidding? They're a filthy bunch. Every single last one of these men are proud of their packages and would be happy to bare it all. If the shoe was on the other foot, their asses would be canned if they ever walked in on me without warning, so I give it even though they don't care.

"Lake!" I call out.

He walks around a corner, coming into full view, all the sharp edges of his brawny body still dripping from the shower. I might as well have been dropped in a bathtub of ice-cold water with the way my body shudders and my eyes can't look away.

All I see are bulging muscles, damp hair, and a thin white cotton towel wrapped low around the waist of the hottest player in the league.

That's per the gossip blogs... not my personal observation.

Despite the distraction of G.I. Joe, a special hockey edition, action figure standing in front of me, I won't be distracted from the reason for my visit. This online picture has to come down before the public or Phil Carlton sees it.

"What can I do for you, Tessa?" he says, scratching the back of his neck, resulting in his bicep flexing.

Dear God, give me the strength not to either throttle this man to death... or push him to the ground and straddle him.

I avert my eyes from any of his body parts. I'm not going to let Lake and his statuesque body get me off track today.

I pull my phone back up, scrolling back to my social media app, and then lift my phone for him to see the half-naked woman on my screen with Lake's hand plastered to her toned, bronzed butt cheek.

He gives a small chuckle as he looks at the screen and then looks back at me.

"What's wrong with it?" he asks, giving me a low brow as if I'm the crazy one.

Of course, that's his reaction, and he even seems as though he truly doesn't see the issue.

"She's practically naked, and your hand is on her ass," I say, staring back at him through my eyelashes.

"Naked? No way. She's wearing a tasteful... thong... thing," he says, struggling to come up with a description for the dental floss-sized strip of material smashed between her globe-shaped rear end.

"Tasteful and thong don't belong in the same sentence," I tell him, fluttering my eyelashes in annoyance. "We've already been over this. You can't post pictures on your social media with this type of content. Phil Carlton made sure it was in all of your contracts before you signed that the team has full say in what it deems as appropriate image content for a family-friendly franchise and its players. This is not it," I say, pointing at the image. "We need big endorsements to keep this building and this team running."

"I didn't post it," he defends.

He pinches his hands on his hips just above the white cotton towel that hangs below the V of his pelvis. I swallow hard, embarrassed at how much saliva has gathered from the image of a half-naked Lake Powers.

He stares down at me like he can't understand why I'm down here bugging him over a photo. His eyebrows knit together, and his lips purse on the left side of his mouth.

"The Hawkeyes have already had you doing charity work before. We had to clean up your image from the last picture that got posted to your social media of you taking a body shot off a woman who had to have emojis covering her bare breasts during last offseason. Do you want a repeat?"

"I only had to do the charity work because *you* suggested it," he says, his eyes narrowing.

"And you're lucky it was effective. The signed jerseys that they auctioned off to help the local women's shelter worked to bury the story and replace it with a better one. It got people talking about something else and softened your image toward women. It dislodges the idea that you're a womanizer and instead shows that you support them in their darkest hour of need," I tell him, recalling how I sold it to Sam.

But it worked, and Lake got a huge endorsement after that.

"I don't need a softer image, Tessa. I'm a goddamn hockey player, not a dirty politician trying to cover up my past offenses. Who gives a shit if I lick salt off her naked chest and took a lime slice off her—"

"Don't finish that!" I snap, throwing up my hand toward his face to shush him. "I saw the unedited shots too," I say, shaking my head at the imagery.

And who the hell puts a lime near her cooch? Wouldn't that burn like a motherfucker?

Lake is a filthy hockey player, and back when I was a glutton for punishment, he would have been exactly the type of pro athlete I would have been interested in. But I've wised up over the years of dating exactly Lake Powers' type.

Lake smirks and then leans into his left leg even farther. "Shit, half my fan base probably became bigger fans after those pictures surfaced. But just like this one, I didn't even post the picture. She tagged me in it."

Somehow, he thinks this gives him a get-out-of-jail-free card.

"Take it down, Lake... now," I say, crossing my arms over my chest and tapping the toe of my four-inch heels. "And set your account so that people can't tag you. This was a part of your agreement with Sam Roberts last time."

Lake knows better and was already asked to make his account untaggable. He must have decided not to listen even after his charity punishment, which turned into an endorsement deal for him by a patron of the event.

Somehow, nothing bad ever happens to Lake.

He shows up for a charity event and gets a million-dollar endorsement from an athletic wear company.

It's infuriating, especially because he makes my job the hardest.

This argument is dumb. How hard would it be to just take the stupid picture down?

He didn't even post it, so why does he care?

The answer is that he doesn't... he just likes pushing my buttons and being combative with me, unlike he is with any of the other staff around here.

"I'm sure as hell not going to do it if you ask like that." He crosses his arms over his chest to match my stance, bringing his biceps and forearms closer to my personal space. His pecs flex at the strain.

I don't look down at his arms, but it's impossible to miss in my periphery.

I hate how curious I am about how those arms would feel holding me up against him.

No, Tessa!

Bad girl!

"Are you joking? You're going to be a child about this?" My eyes drill into him.

"Ask nicely, and I'll think about it."

"I'm the head of public relations. I'm telling you that this is bad for your image, and for the Hawkeyes. It needs to come down immediately before everyone sees it." I try to reason with him instead, although it's not a promising option.

"That didn't sound like a please," he singsongs with a bright white toothy grin.

Not that I'm impressed. I know a couple of those teeth are fake. Knocked out in fights over his long hockey career.

"Please? Are you kidding me? I'm not asking you to move my couch up three flights of stairs. I'm telling you that this is going to cause undue issues and you will bear the brunt of it," I say, unwrapping my crossed arms and planting my hands on my hips. "And stop being so confrontational with me."

He looks to his right to see if any other players are coming back from the showers. Then I look, too. I don't want to end up with a "Free Willy" epidemic on my hands. If the guys are all taking showers, then this is a bad time for this standoff, but I know there can't be many since morning skate was over an hour ago.

When we both see that the coast is clear, we face each other again, and Lake shakes his head.

"I'm not being confrontational. Just say please, Tessa," he says, bending down closer to eye level with me with a challenge in his eyes.

I hate the way he's asking me to say please because he's not asking—he's ordering. It's condescending and irritating. I hate that he's demanding such a small price. I should just swallow my pride and say please, but I already decided a year and a half ago when I left San Diego and headed to Seattle that I wouldn't *swallow* down anything from these hockey players ever again.

No more infidelity.

No more puck bunnies calling late at night.

No more accepting being manipulated and intimidated.

No more accepting the bruises left on my arm when he squeezes it too tight when I don't want to play by his rules, or he drank too much after losing a game.

"You know what? Forget it! I can't wait for Sam to see these," I tell him, waving my cell phone up at my eye level.

Just then, Reeve Aisa walks by, yanks down Lake's towel, and then keeps walking with a snicker. Lake's towel pools down at his feet. I guess the coast wasn't clear after all.

Lake barely reacts, but his hands move to cover his cock. I quickly spin around, giving Lake my back... but not before I get an accidental eyeful of his "hockey stick." These guys are known to play pranks on each other, and I guess today I get to witness one.

It figures that he'd have a freaking torpedo hanging between his two muscular thighs with a nickname like Magic Stick.

Is it really too much to ask for Lake Powers to have a micropenis?

"Fuck, Aisa...you're going to get me an appointment with HR!" Lake yells, watching Reeve who's already halfway toward the lockers by now.

Reeve looks over, just now realizing I'm here. How did he miss me?

"Shit. Sorry, Tessa," Reeve says but laughs anyway and keeps walking. "Don't tell Brent I gave you a peep show of the Magic Stick... He might kill me."

The Magic Stick... the nickname that the puck bunnies have for Lake. I always thought it was a farce, but the rumors might be true now that I've seen it in person. Not that I care. I've been hockey player free for over a year, and I plan to stay that way.

Regarding Reeve thinking that Brent would kill him for flashing me Lake's goods, it wouldn't happen. Over the years, I've dated enough of Brent's hockey friends that it doesn't bother him like it did the first time I dated a teammate of his in high school.

The kid did get beaten to a pulp the next day at practice, but after that, Brent started ignoring who I was dating. Seemed better that way.

Besides, the only reason he might have a problem with it is if Lake and I started messing around, which will never happen as long as I have any dignity left in my sex-starved body.

Lake

"Aren't you going to pick up your towel?" she asks after she spins back around and looks down at the white cotton towel still on the floor where it fell.

"Aren't you enjoying the view? I've heard it's spectacular."

She gives a dramatic eye roll, and I suck in my lower lip to keep from smiling at her reaction.

I can't bring myself to bend down and pick up the towel. It would feel too much like bowing down to her. I don't know why, but it would. And fuck it, I put in the hours on this body, so someone ought to appreciate it. Although if Tessa wasn't always out on a witch hunt for me, worshipping her while on my knees with my head between her thighs could be fun. But sleeping with Tessa wouldn't be a one-night type of thing. Not that I think she's only the relationship type but because she's Brent's little sister. If you're going to chase a teammate's sister, you'd at least be ready for the whole fucking dating thing, and I don't do serious relationships... not anymore.

"Reeve is right about HR. I'm sure they'd at least take an interest in that last comment," Tessa says.

I shake off her empty threat. She wouldn't file anything against me, or at least I don't think she would. Either way, she's the one that came into the men's locker room.

"Are you going to say please, or am I going to keep the photo up?" I ask again, my hands still cradling my cock and balls, but I won't back down.

The locker room is heated, but today, it was conditioning on the ice. My heart's still pounding from the intense workout, so I'm not cold in the least. The towel can stay on the ground for all I care.

Besides, I like the cold. I would have been a pro snowboarder if I could have picked a profession, but I'm a better hockey player.

I can't complain... I get to play a game to pay my bills. If only I didn't have the Hawkeyes PR Manager out for my head, things around the Hawkeyes stadium would be pretty cush. Tessa's starting to think she runs my image, but she doesn't.

Do I give a flying shit about the picture of me touching that girl's ass?

Nope.

I was so drunk at that pool party that I barely remember who she was, and touching her ass wasn't intentional. If anything, I think I was trying to get around her and head toward the barbecue to help out my buddy. I don't even remember what happened to warrant my hand on it anyway, nor do I think we even shared more than a word or two that entire day, but someone who was watching at the party got the shot and sent it to her.

Probably a friend of hers. I swear, these social media climbers are working in pairs like sheepdogs trying to corral you into doing something to make their post go viral, all clamoring for that coveted blue check mark.

She's getting her ten minutes of fame, and I'm getting my ass chewed out by the pint-sized media dictator that Sam Roberts hired when he heard that Brent Tomlin's sister moved to Seattle to live with Brent. She used to work for the San Diego Blue Devils hockey team, the same team I got drafted with and where I spent my first eight years. I was traded to the Hawkeyes four years ago and landed myself, thankfully, here instead. San Diego is a great team, but I had a few issues with one of the players, and I'm grateful to be with the Hawkeyes now. This is where I belong... with this team and this group of guys.

From what I've heard, Tessa knows her stuff, and Phil Carlton seems to be enamored with her ability to change the public's perspective of his team.

It was when Tessa moved here that Brent bought the house and moved out of The Commons... and that's when Captain No-fun got her office next to the locker room and started busting my chops about anything and everything that I say or do that any media outlets get ahold of to boost viewership.

Tessa Tomlin is like a tiny little grizzly bear, and when coming face-to-face with this predator, it's best to stand your ground, stare it directly in the eye, and make yourself look as big as possible so it doesn't fuck with you. But if it attacks, you go straight into the fetal position and cover your head and face until she gets bored with you and moves on.

Standing here butt naked with my dick in my hands... I'm not exactly sure which position I'm currently in. Standing my ground or cowering in the fetal position?

"You have until you leave the stadium campus to untag her post from your social media account and block future users from tagging you."

Then she spins around to leave in a pair of tall black stilettos and a black pencil skirt that reaches down to her slender legs. Her long dark locks lightly wave and sway down to her lower back.

I'll give her one thing. She has a nice full backside that would look fucking amazing with my red handprint on it.

"Or else what?" I yell after her.

But she doesn't respond.

I watch her ass sway from side to side as she leaves in that hot as fuck skirt that shows off every curve of her long legs.

Damn, that's a nice ass.

"Or else what, Tessie?" I call out one last time before she pushes through the locker room door and exits.

I chuckle.

I'm glad she didn't say please because leaving the photo up will eat at her all day, and something about that does something for me.

But I sure as shit have no intention of digging into those urges.

CHAPTER THREE

Lake

"You've got impeccable timing," I tell Reeve, walking toward the lockers after I've pulled my towel back around my waist.

I waited to bend over and reach for my towel until after Tessa walked out of the locker room a little more infuriated than when she walked in.

The woman frustrates the fuck out of me... but I couldn't have pulled my eyes off her ass, even if they offered me double my contract salary.

Reeve looks over his shoulder, a white towel still wrapped around his waist and hair wet from the showers. We were the last two to get through stretches with the physical therapist today after practice.

"Shit, sorry," he says, pulling a T-shirt over his head. "I didn't see Tessa in the locker room."

"Yeah, well next time, just make sure it isn't someone like Phil Carlton's wife or some shit. I like all those zeros on my contract," I tell him, reaching into my duffel bag and pulling out a T-shirt of my own. "And I'd like to keep playing for this team."

"What was she doing in here anyway?" he asks.

He reaches into his duffel bag and grabs a pair of boxer briefs, pulling them on under his towel.

I don't blame him for taking a little more precaution with a rogue Tessa still in the building.

I turn toward my locker and wide-open duffel.

"Her usual shit."

He chuckles.

"You two ever just going to fuck and get it over with?"

What the hell did he just say?

I whip my head to look at him. "Jesus, did you hit your head in practice today? Where the hell did that come from?"

He puts his palms up as a surrender.

"Never mind, man, I thought it was common knowledge. Forget I said anything."

I shake my head. He's lost me.

"What? Whose common knowledge?"

"Forget it, Lake," he says, pulling on his black sweats and zipping up his duffel bag. He swings the duffel bag over his shoulder and walks over, patting my shoulder. "Good luck with that."

Then he walks toward the exit.

I turn to watch him leave.

"Reeve! Whose common knowledge?" I yell out to him.

He doesn't answer, and within seconds, he's out the locker room door.

"Fuck and get it over with..." What the hell?

Tessa

Hours after my confrontation with Lake, where I saw more than I bargained for, he still hasn't untagged himself from the photo. My blood pressure must be through the roof, and no amount of breathing exercises have helped me manage my irritation at the way we left things.

> Tessa: Lunch at Serendipity's Coffee Shop?

> Penelope: I'm free for lunch.

> Isla: I've got Berkeley, but we're free.

I watch as text bubbles from Autumn start coming up.

> Autumn: Packing to go to Walla Walla with Briggs to see his dad.

> Tessa: Oh yeah. I forgot. Update us when you can.

She texted me early today to tell me that they were leaving at the last minute to see Briggs's dad who's really sick.

Autumn: Thanks girls.

Penelope: Also, where are you staying?
Is this a one-bed type situation?

Tessa: Oh my God, Penelope, not everything is a romance novel.

Autumn: I'm not sure yet, but I just quit
my job, so we'll see what happens.

Tessa: What! Now you have to meet us
for lunch.

Isla: You can't drop a bomb like that!

Penelope: Knew it! Go get your man.
Love ya

An hour later, Penelope comes downstairs to get me so we can meet Isla and Berkeley. She's the two-year-old little girl Isla nannies for who belongs to another player on the team, Kaenan Altman.

We pull up to the curb of the quaint little shop, lucky to find a close parking spot. It started drizzling the minute we pulled out of the underground staff parking of the stadium, and now, with the car turned off, the rain makes it virtually impossible without the intermittent wipers to see out of the windshield. We open our doors to climb out and make a dash for the building.

I'm envious of Penelope's polka-dot rainboots as I try not to sprain my ankle while running in a skirt and heels in the pouring rain.

The tiny stone building that houses Serendipity's Coffee Shop seems almost smashed between two other larger brick-built ones. Its bright red apple door and cheery signage beckon you to come in out of the Washington rain and sit awhile, enjoying a warm cup of coffee, one of their delicious bakery items, or something on their lunch menu.

Although the building looks small from the outside, it's a long building with nooks and crannies for coming here with a group, laptop, or book and getting a warm, snuggly spot to curl up in.

When Penelope and I walk into Serendipity's Coffee Shop, the smell of coffee and freshly baked bread instantly makes me hungry. My tongue jets out to wet my lower lip, and my mouth waters at the faint hint of onion and garlic in the air from the lunch rush.

I see Isla and Berkeley have already reserved a table. Berkeley sits with her dark brown curls in high pigtails, a juice box in one hand, and a sticky bun on a little plate just for her. Isla smiles and waves us over.

"We got here as fast as we could," Isla says. "What's the emergency?"

"I wouldn't call it an emergency, but I'm about to kill Lake, and I'll need a foolproof alibi," I tell her, flopping into one of the other chairs with a dramatic huff. Penelope trails just behind me, but she doesn't sit. She hovers over the table instead.

"I'll get your order because I can't be an accessory to this conversation... I'm too soft for prison," Penelope teases. "Plus, I'm the one who has to notify family if a player gets injured on the ice and gets transported... or worse. I have no poker voice to speak of. They'd be on to me in a second."

I nod in understanding. "A hazelnut latte please and make it a double." I wish this place made something stronger like a hot toddy or Bailey's Irish cream, but since they don't, I'll go for the next best thing: a double shot of espresso to keep me wired enough to make it through my day.

"And I can't help you either. I'm too ticklish," Isla adds, lifting her large white porcelain coffee cup to her lips before Penelope turns away to make our order.

Penelope swings back around lightning-fast, and we look at each other for a second.

"Huh?" I ask, looking back at Isla.

Isla adjusts the toddler's tablet covered in a Barbie-pink foam case, currently playing some alphabet memory song for Berkeley. She's enthralled, unwilling to take her eyes off the screen to make sure the juice box straw makes it to her mouth.

"I'm just warning you, if they try to torture the information out of me by way of tickling, I'll give you up before they ever lay a single finger on my feet. That's how bad it is," she says, her eyes on the tablet, still adjusting it.

"Good to know," Penelope says, pretending to write it down on imaginary stationery for future use.

Penelope and I both laugh and then Isla joins in.

"Then what in the hell is the point of having best girlfriends if it's not to kill each other's enemies and then use it as group blackmail to keep all of us in a lifelong blood pact that only ends with us all taking the murders to our graves?" I ask.

Penelope leans in over the table. "You mean that all of us will take it to our graves, except for the last living friend, who will write a tell-all book about it, become a best-selling author and get mega rich, and then live out her last best days on a mega yacht near a country with no extradition laws with her sugar baby boyfriends who are all a quarter of her age," Penelope points out.

I knew there was a reason Penelope, and I became such fast friends when I started working for the Hawkeyes. We think the same.

"Wait! Who gets to be the last one alive?" Isla asks, leaning in now too, seeming interested all of a sudden.

"How the heck should I know? I guess we'd have to draw straws?" Penelope suggests.

"I don't think that's how death works," I offer. "Do either of you even have someone you'd like off'd?"

"Sure, but mine currently lives in Canada and plays for the Hawkeyes farm team. I haven't seen him since college, and I'll probably never see him again," Penelope says, still standing, waiting to go make our order but the conversation got too good.

Understandable.

"Mine is my ex-fiancé who's trying to guilt trip me into coming back to Colorado to run our business while he screws his new girlfriend who used to be our warehouse manager," Isla blurts out.

"Wow, what?!" I ask, and Penelope instantly pulls a chair back from the table and sits her ass down. There is no way she's leaving now, and I don't blame her. Coffee and sticky rolls be damned. Things just got interesting.

"It's a long story, and this lunch is about you, Tessa," Isla says, looking over at me. "Plus, I don't want to talk about it too much around..." Isla nods her head toward Berkeley.

"Well, since neither of you will reenact the 'Earl's Got To Die' Dixie Chicks music video with me... I guess I'll have to wait for Autumn to get back. She'll do it with me. She's a ride-or-die kind of friend. Thanks for nothing," I tease the two women sitting around the table with me giggling and shaking their heads.

"I suppose Lake gets to live another couple of days," Isla says, taking a sip of her coffee that I'm now becoming jealous of.

"No rush. He'll still be there to snuff out in a couple of days. I mean, it's not as if he's going to somehow get in your good graces all of a sudden," Penelope adds.

"True. A couple more days will hurt, but it won't kill me. I don't think," I say, and then stand because I'm going to need coffee and one of their delicious deli cashew chicken salad sandwiches before I dive into what transpired between him and me, and the social media pictures.

He still hasn't taken the photo down, and now I don't think I have a choice but to go to Sam and tell him what's going on. It feels a lot like I'm having to run to the principal's office and tattle on Lake for doing something naughty at recess.

After a good hour of me explaining exactly what happened in the locker room earlier today while filling my belly with yummy carbs and caffeine, I know what I have to do. Both girls convinced me that going to Sam is the only way to let Lake know I'm serious. I hate that it's come to this, and I hate that I seem to hold zero authority in Lake's eye if he thinks he can just blow me off like he did. Especially since he knows that the player's images are important to Phil Carlton, and when issues like this arise within the team's franchise, Phil and Sam look at me and ask why I haven't remedied the situation.

Sooner or later, they're going to see this post and ask why I didn't make sure it got taken down.

What am I supposed to tell them? "Oh yeah, about that... Uh, Lake doesn't respect my authority and refused to take down the photo after he flashed me his penis and then proceeded to hold his dick in his hands." That'll go over well.

Say goodbye to your Christmas bonus this year because Lake is making you look bad and won't let you do your job.

CHAPTER FOUR

Lake

It's been twenty-four hours since Tessa came through the locker room like a damn tornado demanding I do whatever she wants. I would have done it if she'd asked nicely, but I'm glad she didn't because I get far more enjoyment from pissing off Tessa than I should.

I stand in the large kitchen of the penthouse I rent during the hockey season and dial my agent, putting my phone on speaker as I walk to the commercial grade stainless-steel fridge. The fridge is as wide as it is tall and provides way more refrigerator space than a bachelor like me needs... but it looks cool.

I pull the long cylinder stainless-steel handle and open the fridge door, reaching inside to grab the steak I've been marinating in a brine of soy sauce, lemon juice, and minced garlic since this morning before practice.

"Lake! My favorite client," Josh, my agent, says when he answers the phone.

For the money I make him, I probably am.

I hear the sound of his chair sliding around on the wood floors of his office and then the groaning of the leather chair as he leans back in it. It's the usual way he relaxes in his chair when I come into the office as if I'm an old buddy instead of a multimillion-dollar client. Like the magic is dead in our professional relationship, and he doesn't have to try anymore.

"You mean your highest paid client," I poke.

"Same thing, isn't it?" he teases back with a chuckle. "So... what did you call for? I know you're not calling to ask about the wife and kids," he says.

The take-home he gets from his percentage of my contract paid him enough to go out on his own ten years ago and pays for his expensive office and support staff. But that doesn't give him enough credit. He does a good job for me so I shouldn't complain.

I shake my head and smirk, grabbing the plate with the T-bone steak, and head for the balcony of my penthouse. I can see the smoke starting to billow out from underneath the barbecue's hood.

"I had a conversation with a coworker yesterday, and I'm curious about it. It's about something in my contract."

"What about your contract?" he asks, a slight edge to his voice.

I hear Josh's chair snap back. His reaction time and concern make me feel a little better. I have him alarmed, and I'm happy to hear that when it comes to the potential of a contract dispute, Josh is on alert.

"It's nothing big, but I'm curious how much control the Hawkeyes have over my media presence."

"Whoa, what? Why?"

I push open the sliding door with my pinky that I left ajar after I lit the pilot light earlier on the outdoor grill. I hold the plate with the raw steak in one hand and my cell phone in the other, trying to balance everything.

The second I walk out onto the balcony, the sound of a drizzly busy city fills my eardrums.

Droplets of rain drum on every surface they can reach, and traffic driving through the puddles and over the wet asphalt amplifies the background noise. I set down the steak on the side table of the grill, then press the side button on my phone to turn up the volume to hear Josh over the sounds of a wet winter in Seattle.

"Nothing. Really. I just got my ass chewed by their PR manager who didn't like a picture I got tagged in. It's nothing big, but she mentioned my contract."

"Dammit... I knew I should have fought over that one," Josh says, and I can hear his jaw clench on the other line.

"Fought what?" I ask, lifting the barbecue lid and waving out the smoke that rises out of it... it's hot and ready.

He sighs dramatically. "Fought their control over our image on social media. That's something that the agency should have full control over. I didn't like it when I read it, and it was on my take-off list in the first round of negotiations, but..."

"But what?" I ask.

"But then they tacked on another million to your yearly contract, I didn't want to make any waves. It seemed like one of the stipulations that companies add to their contracts that they never really flex their control over."

"Well, they're flexing... and flexing hard," I tell him, using a set of tongues to grip the steak on the plate and set it on the barbecue.

Loud sizzling and popping sounds break out as the steak hits the hot barbecue grill, putting a nice crispy bark on the steak. My mouth waters at the smell of charred meat. Today was a hard practice and I burned enough calories to eat ten of these things, in addition to a good hearty carb load to keep up my energy this week.

"What exactly is going on?" he asks.

I hear his suit rustle and then a buzz as he hits the intercom on his landline to call his assistant.

"Yes, sir?" I hear his female assistant say over the intercom.

She's about my age, early thirties, or maybe she's a few years older than me. She's friendly enough when I come into the office but not the chatty type. She seems a little too serious for that and always seems to be reading through a contract with a highlighter whenever I come in.

"Jody, I need you to pull up Lake's current contract on your tablet and come into my office. We're looking for the media clause."

"You got it, sir," she says, and the line seems to go dead.

Not more than thirty seconds later, the large wooden door to Josh's office opens, and footsteps approach Josh's desk.

"I'm going to put you on speaker, Lake," he tells me.

The echo through his office says he did it before announcing it to me, but I don't care if I'm on speaker.

There isn't any company that I keep that would prompt me to clean up or hold back from saying something if the thought came to me. Well, all except my mom... and my nieces. Other than that, I am who I am and people have to deal with the vulgarity of that on occasion. I've even heard of some finding my fluid conversation "refreshing."

"Ok, Jody. Whatcha got?" he asks, his voice sounding like he's hovering over his desk, likely placing his phone in the middle of his large table so that I can hear him and Jody.

I flip my steak over, nodding when I see the perfect grill marks on it. I listen to her over the sound of sizzling from the other side of my steak and the light drizzling of rain on a dreary Seattle evening.

I tune out part of the legal jargon until she gets to the meat of the contract rules.

"'Anything deemed inappropriate or off-brand with the Hawkeyes Clean Family Fun image must be corrected or altered to fit within the parameters set forth and advised by the Public Relations team.'"

Shit.

I have no leg to stand on, but she still could have said please. Even though I would hate to have untagged the photo because Tessa would have felt vindicated, I would have honored the deal I made her. She couldn't say something as easy as please.

Surely, if Sam or Phil get word of this, and I tell them that all she had to do was say please, they'll side with me.

The following morning, I go to the fridge to pull out a carton of eggs, cheese, and a few other things for a quick egg scramble. I start guzzling down a protein shake as I start making breakfast. I have practice in about two hours, but I need food beforehand, or I'll play like shit. I don't do well on an empty stomach.

My phone flashes with a text.

> **Sam GM: I need to see you in my office. Come in early.**

> **Lake: Sure thing, boss.**

Would she have ratted me out?

Sure, she would, she's done it before.

I consider swiping into my app and untagging the photo now so it's no longer available to see, but that will only make me look more guilty, won't it?

Best just to see how this goes.

Worst-case scenario, Sam makes me sign a few autographed jerseys again like last time and sends me on my way with a slap on the wrist.

I head for the stadium as soon as I finish my food, opting to walk the two blocks instead of driving. It takes less time to walk than to pull out of our secure underground parking and then check into the stadium parking, which means I have to take an additional elevator to get to Sam's office.

Most of the guys who live here walk except for a couple of guys who live elsewhere.

Since I'm leaving early, I don't see any of my teammates headed in yet, so I walk by myself in the light mist of the Washington weather. The ocean breeze picks up a little, and the salty smell of it has me taking in a deep inhale. I love the smell of living by the ocean.

I grew up in Colorado, and although there is almost nothing as beautiful as the Rocky Mountains I was raised under, living near the ocean certainly holds its appeal.

I walk through the stadium doors and wave hello to the usual security guys on in the mornings.

"Morning, Clint," I say to my favorite security guard, who I bullshit with the most. He's in his eighties and retired from the Seattle police force but says he's too bored living in the over fifty-five community center, so he got a job here to get himself out of the house.

"Did you propose to Rosie yet?" I ask him about the seventy-year-old girlfriend he said he bought a ring for a few months ago but has been too nervous to ask.

"I finally did. Last weekend. I had her great-granddaughter help me." He smiles proudly.

"Yeah? Did she turn you down when she realized she and I are a better match?"

"HA! Nice try, Mr. Powers. She said that you're too inexperienced for the kind of lovemaking she's interested in."

My eyebrows shoot to my hairline.

"Excuse me?" I ask with a chuckle.

"Yep. She wants a man she doesn't have to teach new tricks to. She wants a man with miles on him."

I grin as Clint straightens his spine, walking with extra confidence.

"New tricks, huh? She has a few things she thinks she can teach me?" I ask.

Sure, Clint and Rosie have lived more life than me, but it's hard to believe she's done things I haven't done yet. I've cleaned off the bucket list... well, mostly.

But that last bucket list item was something I added over four years ago, and it was a mistake to add it even though I didn't realize it at the time. Now, there's no way in hell that item's getting checked off.

That was back when I saw a woman in the stands during our first home game, and I swore I'd sleep with her... then I learned her name the second Brent put his arm around her and pulled her in for a kiss on the top of her head after post-game media.

Tessa Tomlin.

"Well, congratulations, Clint. Make her happy, or else I will," I tease and then turn to head for the elevator.

"I got the doctor prescribed stuff now Lake... you can't compete."

When I look back, Clint has already turned and headed in the opposite direction, whistling as he goes.

Funny bastard. Somedays he's the highlight of my day, especially today since I know I'm about to get my ass chewed by Sam Roberts while Tessa watches with a gratified smile, knowing she got what she wants... forcing me to bend to her will.

But I could bend her will into a much better position that would leave a different kind of gratified smile on her face.

Goddammit.

Someday I'll have to stop thinking about fucking Tessa. It's not healthy. Or at least what I deem as healthy, which is to never have an infatuation with a woman, never let a fling go on past a week, and never give her more than your cock, fingers, or mouth.

A heart isn't safe outside of your body, and I know that better than anyone.

I step off the elevator and onto the third floor of the Hawkeyes corporate offices where our general manager, the owner, and the legal team have their offices.

I look to my right where Phil Carlton's assistant, Adele, sits at her desk. The desk is about bar height, and the dark espresso color matches the wide plank wood flooring throughout the office space.

"Hi, Adele. Headed to see Sam," I tell her.

She nods. "Tessa mentioned you'd be coming in. Good to see you, sir."

"You too," I say, giving her a nod as I walk past and head down the hallway. I've given up trying to get her to call me Lake instead of Sir. I know most of the other players have tried to do the same and failed as well. But the fact that she calls Tessa by her first name makes me think Tessa must have broken down the wall.

I walk down the hallway. My boots echo against the wooden floors throughout the corridor as I glance over at the shadow boxes filled with the Hawkeyes memorabilia and the retired jerseys that hang on the wall.

As I near Sam's office door, I can hear the sound of a female voice.

Tessa's.

Yep, figures she'd be here too.

I walk through the first door that leads into the reception space for Sam's office. Penelope, his assistant, and daughter, isn't sitting at her desk. Instead, she's standing in the doorframe of Sam's office as the three of them—Sam, Tessa, and Penelope—chat about something.

I clear my throat as I walk through the first door and farther into the reception area. Penelope hears me and turns around.

I see Sam standing at his desk, but I can't see Tessa, who's probably standing off to the right since Sam's attention seems to be pointed in that direction as he nods to something she says that I can't hear.

"Hi, Lake. They're ready for you," she beams, her long blonde hair in some fancy-looking braid that lies over her shoulder against the turquoise Hawkeyes company-issued polos with a black Hawkeyes logo.

She steps out of the doorframe and starts walking toward me, turning to her left and around her desk that sits just past Sam's office door.

I take a few more steps until I'm now standing in the doorframe of Sam's office. Sam looks over at me. Tessa looks too, but the turning of her head to see me seems as though it took a second longer than it could have.

If she didn't want this meeting, she didn't have to rat me out to Sam. She could have just said please, and we could be past this already. I'm sure Sam will see that Tessa is being unprofessional and petty.

"Lake, come in," Sam says in his typically calm demeanor, his hands resting on his hips, his black Hawkeyes ball cap low on his head with signs of his hair graying along his ears.

"Hey, boss," I say. "Tessa," I acknowledge.

I take the steps necessary to bring myself to the end of his large ebony lacquered desk next to where Tessa stands.

She's not sitting, which bodes well for this being a quick conversation and a hand cramp later from all the autographs I'll probably have to sign.

He looks at both of us and starts.

"Lake, I know you have a long day of practice, along with physical therapy and a long list of other stuff... just like the rest of us, so I'm going to make this short so we can all get on with our day."

I nod in response.

Maybe this is what Tessa needs to see. That this social media watchdog shit she's pulling isn't important.

Find a damn hobby to fill your time.

"First of all, I want to address the fact that you don't seem to take Tessa's authority in matters of public relations very seriously."

"Hey, hold on just a minute. She—"

But he doesn't. He keeps on going. "Do you think the Hawkeyes pay Tessa a salary and give her an arbitrary title just because Phil Carlton likes blowing money?" Sam asks.

Oh shit. This isn't going the way I thought.

"No, sir."

"That's right. He doesn't. And we are all well aware that Phil is courting a big-name sponsor that wants their name in big lights on a pro hockey team stadium, but they don't give a shit which pro team," he says, looking straight at me. "However, Phil Carlton cares what team... and so should you."

A set of stern steely-blue eyes stares back at me under his Hawkeyes ball cap.

"I understand, sir."

I nod, breaking eye contact to glance over at Tessa whose eyes just settled on me. She averts her eyes, so I give Sam back my attention.

"I don't think you do, which is why I'm telling you now," he says. "This is the kind of money that gets our stadium a new state-of-the-art locker room and a Ferrari leather seat viewing room to watch reels and go over plays as a team. The kind of money that gets us therapy lap pools, brand-new saunas, and cold plunge pools for after practice."

I nod again because nothing I can say will help me at this point.

"The list is longer, but I'm listing the first few things that you would care about because your actions are selfish, so it would seem I should go with the stuff on the list that you would care about for yourself," he says, his usual cool and calm demeanor heated to a level I don't see often.

Sam is a hell of a good general manager, and he's usually on our side when it comes down to the health of the hockey franchise. Even last year, when he made me sign jerseys for the charity to cover up the last social media incident, he barely slapped my hand. It seemed more like a nuisance than anything.

"My actions were incorrect. I see that now," I say, plunging my hands into my athletic pants.

"Are you seeing that girl?" he asks.

"Seeing who?" My confusion is evident from my scrunched expression.

I don't *see* anyone.

"The half-naked woman in the picture you were tagged in?"

"No. No, sir, I'm not. I don't even know who she is," I say honestly.

He shakes his head.

"So why in the hell is this the damn hill you want to die on?" he asks, stepping forward toward his desk and hitting his phone to wake it up.

I see the tagged photo on Sam's phone from the Hawkeyes' social media account.

"It's not, sir."

He looks back up at me. His eyes lock with mine.

"Untag the woman's photo and make your account untaggable like I asked last time your social media was a problem. This continued issue is a reason Phil could see trading you. We have a player he wants to bring up from the farm team, and we might make a trade to do it. I suggest you prove you're not the ass headed somewhere else."

What the hell? They'd trade me for a rookie on the farm team?

I pull my hands out of my pockets and take a step toward his desk.

"Someone's getting traded?"

My eyes flash to Tessa, but she looks like this is news to her too, although she's doing a better job of hiding her surprise.

"It's possible, but no decisions have been made yet."

"Okay, I get it. I'll be on my best behavior. Do you have some posters or jerseys for me to sign before I leave for Colorado next week for vacation?"

"No jersey to sign, Lake…"

Sweet! I got my ass handed to me, but all in all, this turned out okay.

"Instead, you're going to stay behind for your bye week, and Tessa has a dog rescue you will volunteer for during adoption week."

He's making me stay home?

I glance over at Tessa, and ideas to make the rest of her life miserable flash through my mind.

Reeve's idea that she and I need to fuck and get it over with was crazy.

I settle my eyes back on Sam.

"I'll do it a different week. I already have plans," I argue.

Tessa turns to me, and I turn my head toward her. "With your schedule for the next couple of weeks after your bye week, you'll be out of town. This is the best week to do it," Tessa says, flashing a sweet-as-pie smile, but I know those devil horns are hiding under that silky dark hair.

This is beyond being bossy. Tessa has crossed a line, but I won't go down without a fight. I'm supposed to go home to Aspen, Colorado, to see my family and to finalize some decisions with my cousin Bobby. I can't miss this.

Living on the West Coast means I miss out on pretty much everything. I was looking forward to this week. No... more than that, I need this.

This is also the time I go back every year for the annual music festival, Snow Dayz. It's like spring break in Cancun but colder with a shit ton of snow. I already told one of the event organizers that I'd be there to make an appearance at some of the events.

I'm not letting Tessa derail my plans.

I have to think of something.

"Sir, I've already given my word to another charity that I'd be in Aspen to emcee one of their events. Not showing up now would look bad on me and, potentially, on the franchise. This is a big event, and the local radio stations have already announced that I'll be there," I tell him.

Snow Dayz is as far from a charitable event as you can get, but I'm still volunteering my time and it's good exposure for the Hawkeyes. I already agreed to emcee the wet T-shirt contest at the festival, and the radio stations have announced my attendance for the event. As long as Tessa and Sam think that this could be bad PR for the franchise, they won't be able to fight me on it.

"Mr. Roberts, he's trying to wiggle out of this. He'll just keep finding excuses not to do the charity work," she practically whines.

So she wants a fight, does she?

"I *am* doing charity work... just while on vacation," I tell Sam, trying to play on his soft spot for his players.

He's been in our shoes before as a player many years ago, so he understands.

Tessa darts her eyes back from me and looks at Sam.

"As if he's going to do anything on vacation. He's going to blow this whole thing off." She huffs.

Well, she's not stupid. I'll give her that.

"If you're so worried he's going to blow off the charity work, are you planning on staying here during bye week to make sure he does it?"

Tessa looks at him as if she's not sure whether or not to speak.

"I...I wasn't planning on it."

I turn toward her, a smile planted on my face and an idea to ruin something of hers too.

"Really? Where are you going on vacation?" I ask.

I can see her teeth clench just slightly. She's not happy that I'm asking.

"Cabo, if you must know," she says, her eyes on Sam and not on me.

Cabo? With bikinis and booze and dudes out on the prowl for casual vacation hookup sex.

Something about that makes my fists clench and that feels like a dangerous sign.

"With who?" I spit out, thinking I said that in my head and not out loud.

She glares back up at me, dark amber eyes looking like daggers ready to cut me wide open.

"Someone I used to know from college."

That's code word for a dude.

If it was a woman, she would have said something like "a good friend from college," but she didn't.

"What's his name?"

"None of your business," she shoots back.

Bingo.

"Okay, I think we're getting off track here," Sam interjects. "I have real work to do, and I want this resolved before you leave my office. How do we settle this?"

"Easy," I say as the perfect solution comes to mind. "I go to Colorado and do my charity work, and Tessa comes with me to make sure I do it."

Tessa turns to me lightning-fast and crosses her arms over her chest.

"No way. I have plans—"

"Done," Sam says, and then sits back in his seat, glancing at the paperwork in front of him.

No doubt what he was working on when Tessa came in this morning and dumped this shit on him.

"Mr. Roberts, I have non-refundable tickets and someone expecting me," she argues.

"Ms. Tomlin," Sam says, looking up from his desk, his face barely visible under his cap. He's already checked out of this issue. I can see it in his eyes that this issue is now resolved. "You wanted the dog adoption charity requirement on his one week off all season when he should be resting and recouping. You're the one worried he can't self-monitor the charity event on his own, as well as he has told us he has a previous engagement for charity work in Aspen."

"The dog adoption photos would soften his image. It's a win-win with this big sponsorship coming up. And with Autumn doing so much for Briggs, the top players are looking like altar boys right now. We need this."

She takes two steps forward, inching closer toward Sam's desk, her arms outstretched at her sides trying to petition her case.

"Then I think Lake's idea makes the most sense. Lake will have to manage both charity events while in Aspen." He looks at me, and I nod.

I'll agree to doing Snow Dayz and her dog adoption thing next week... as long as her trip to Cabo is ruined, and we do the charity work in Aspen.

"Good," he nods back to me and then turns to Tessa. "I'm sure you can find a dog rescue in the Aspen area for Lake to help out. Then you can be sure that the right photos and content are getting put out for the public. And you're right, this sponsorship means a lot to this franchise. We all need to do what we can to reel in this sponsor."

My phone buzzes in my pocket, and I pull it out, even though this might not be the best time.

"But my trip..." she pleads.

I look down at my phone and see the name flash over my phone.

Chelsea calling...

Tessa leans slightly toward me, and when she sees the name on my screen, she gives a faint huff of annoyance. I tuck my phone in my back pocket. I'll have to call her back because now isn't a good time.

Sam speaks up. "Give Penelope the price for the non-refundable expenses and the Hawkeyes will reimburse you for the lost funds. The Hawkeyes will also fund this entire trip to Aspen to make sure everything goes off without a hitch. As you said, this is important to cleaning up Lake's image and getting us that sponsorship."

"But…" She tries one more time, and I bite back a chuckle.

"That will be all," he says without looking back up. "Lake, you're about to be late for practice."

I look down at my phone.

"Oh fuck," I mutter and then rush out of Sam's office and head for the lockers. I wish I could have walked Tessa down to her office and gloated the entire way, but I have some time between practice and physical therapy to rub it in a little. I'll be sure to stop by her office after drills.

Now Tessa gets a little taste of her own medicine for trying to ruin my vacation. At least I'll still get to do most of the things I want to do in Aspen: seeing my family, taking part in the festival, and meeting with Bobby and the realtor… Tessa doesn't get to do any.

Only a few moments ago, Tessa was looking forward to sand, sun, and the beach with some dude who's probably wanted to bang her since college. But things just changed, and she'll have to cancel on his ass to come with me to snow, ice, and more snow.

And the best part?

This music festival books out all of the accommodations in town months in advance.

Tessa is about to show up to the vacation from hell with no hotel vacancies or rental cars to speak of.

But I'll let her figure that out when she gets there.

Tessa

How the hell am I being punished for this? None of this seems fair.

I send out a text to the girls.

> Tessa: Plan backfired. Please bring booze.

> Isla: Oh no! Okay. I'll ask Kaenan for a night off. I have a feeling there will be too much cursing and boozing to bring Berkeley.

> Tessa: Good foresight.

> Penelope: I left to go down to the copier, and when I got back, you and Lake were already gone. What happened?

> Penelope: I swear I just saw my dad pull out a whiskey bottle from his bottom drawer and take a swig. I didn't know he had booze in his office. Was it really that bad?

> Tessa: Too long of a story to tell via text.

Tessa: Side note: I can take the lingerie and bikinis I bought for Cabo back to the store. I'm not getting laid now.

Autumn: Holy crap! What did I miss? Briggs and I come home tomorrow. Tell me when and where.

Penelope: Okay, girls. My apartment, tomorrow night. I'll pick up charcoal face masks, Isla will bring the booze, Autumn… can you do your famous chocolate chip cookies? We'll order Chinese food. Bring your jammies and pillows. We're having a sleepover, girls!

Isla: Kaenan has poker night at Lake's penthouse tomorrow night, but his mom is in town and said I deserve a girls' night. See you girls tomorrow.

Autumn: Yeah. Briggs is going to poker night too. Can't wait to see you all!

CHAPTER FIVE

Lake

"I heard something interesting yesterday," Briggs says, flopping open the pizza box on top of a stack of eight other boxes.

Steam comes billowing out as the smell of pepperoni, spicy sausage, and pizza dough fills my large penthouse kitchen. He grabs half the pie and pulls it onto a plate that can barely contain the contents. Strings of cheese still attached to the rest of the pizza are left behind to be devoured by another hungry hockey player looking to score some cheat meal pizza. Consuming large amounts of complex carbohydrates is high on the dietician's meal plan for the amount of calories we burn a day... but greasy pizza isn't usually the recommended way to get it.

"Oh yeah? What's that?" I ask, grabbing a beer out of the commercial grade fridge and popping off the top before taking a long pull of it.

I head back toward the large island where Briggs stands while he grabs a handful of chips and takes a scoop of the seven-layer dip that his fake girlfriend turned real fiancée made for him to bring and plops it on a second plate for himself.

"Autumn said she's going with Tessa tomorrow to take back a bunch of clothes that she bought for her trip to Cabo because she's not going anymore. Instead, she's going to Aspen..." He smirks, then licks the pizza sauce from his thumb after filling his plates. "With you."

Brent's eyes flash to mine from far off in the living room. He's sitting at one of the poker tables I set up with his plate of food.

Is he pissed about this? I don't know, but from our limited conversations about Tessa, I know that she's dated some of his hockey teammates in the past, and as far as I know, they're all still alive to talk about it.

It must not bother him as much as it would bother me if any of my friends tried to date either of my older sisters. I'd do what Autumn's brother did to Briggs. Coldcock him in the parking lot of his place of employment when he thought he was safe.

"That makes a hell of a lot more sense," Ryker says, walking up to the island and interjecting himself into the conversation. He grabs a chip and then scoops up some of the homemade dip. "I had a meeting with Sam earlier today, and Penelope was arguing with the airlines over the phone trying to get Tessa's plane ticket changed from Cabo to Aspen. That sounds like a strange change of itinerary. What the hell is she going to do in Aspen with you?"

I don't like the feeling of Briggs and Ryker standing by the snacks together while I'm getting a look from Brent on the other side of the living room. Even with the casual conversation, I already feel outnumbered, and no one even knows what's going on.

Kaenan walks into the apartment and catches the end of the conversation. "Hold the fuck on. You're taking Tessa to meet your parents?"

The rest of the guys who weren't listening or were barely interested all turn around and stare back at me. Now I'm outnumbered. This was not what I had in mind.

Not all the players on the team have the same hate/hate relationship that Tessa and I have. Many of them are starting to treat Tessa like they treat Penelope... an unofficial Hawkeyes sister. Not just because she's Brent's little sister but also because she's helped boost the media attention for a lot of these guys and facilitates endorsement money for them.

I'm pretty well alone on an island when it comes to my feelings about Tessa Tomlin.

And now that Briggs spilled the beans that Tessa is coming to Aspen with me... and I've got a correctly labeled reputation of never fucking the same girl twice, people are interested to see how this unfolds. But it won't unfold in any way except that I'm single-handedly giving Tessa a taste of her own medicine. I have no intention of trying anything with Tessa in Aspen.

When it comes to dating, no woman could convince me into an exclusive relationship. Not to mention that all the guys in this room have a vague understanding of my history and know that the last time I brought a girl home was fifteen years ago. I swore after everything that happened, I'd never get that serious about anyone else again. I understand their reactions and the dropped jaws, but they don't know what's going on between Tessa and me.

Brent stands up from the poker table and heads my way.

The rest of the guys see him, and they all fake having something else important to do and walk out of the kitchen.

Traitors.

I watch Brent move toward me in the kitchen.

"It's not what you think," I tell him once he passes through the threshold of the kitchen opening.

He's not buying it because when you say "It's not what you think," it's usually *exactly* what you think. The only problem is, telling him the truth might be worse than where his mind is going.

How do I tell my good buddy that I'm basically forcing his little sister to come home with me to Aspen in order to ruin her vacation to Cabo and cockblock her from a week with some dick having hot, bikini vacation sex with her? As well as the fact that now that she's being forced to come to Aspen, practically against her will, she'll probably end up sleeping in the airport all week because there's no fucking way she'll find a hotel vacancy this close to our departure tomorrow. Not with the music festival coming into town.

He comes over to my side of the island and stops by the chip bag, right where Ryker stood less than a minute ago.

He leans a hip against the countertop, all casual, and grabs a chip out of the bag, his eyes fixed on the snacks instead of me.

I don't know if the fact that he's not giving me eye contact is more or less unnerving, but he did abandon his dinner to come in here to talk to me. This isn't exactly a social call.

"My sister is a big girl, and she can make her own decisions. But what's this about her canceling her Cabo trip with Elliot?" he asks.

"His name's Elliot?" I ask... and I shouldn't have.

That's when his eyes flash back up to mine. My interest got his attention.

Dammit.

It doesn't sit well with me that Brent knows the asshole's name, either. This isn't some random Poindexter dude who couldn't pull Tessa in college and now has some software start-up business and a gym membership and all of a sudden has money to entice her with. Not that using men for money seems to be Tessa's game. Otherwise, she could have maxed out my card when she lifted it.

"I have to do some charity work in Aspen for some shit Sam wants me to do. He decided that Tessa needs to go to make sure we get the media right on it."

It's not a lie, but it's not one hundred percent accurate either.

Brent is a solid friend and a hell of a hockey player, but I know he feels responsible for Tessa since becoming her legal guardian after their parents died. So if I told him my plans are to ruin his sister's week in an effort to scare her away from ever fucking with me again, I don't think it would fly with him.

"Oh... good..." he says, finally scooping a healthy amount of dip on his chip and crunching down on it. "I didn't want her to go to Cabo anyway. Elliot's nice enough, but he's a safe choice."

I knew it.

Now I feel even better about sabotaging her trip.

"So you're cool with it?" I ask.

"Yeah," he says, grabbing another chip and taking another swipe of the tasty dip. He chews for a second and stares back at me, his eyebrows knitting together.

A thought just came to him.

"Unless I should be concerned about her going to Aspen with you—" he asks, mid-scoop and an eyebrow cocked.

"No, no... it's just something Sam is making us do together. That's it," I reassure him.

"She's not staying with you?" he asks, grabbing another chip, but his eyes remain locked on mine.

I don't need the answer key to score one hundred percent on this pop quiz... I know the correct answer.

"No. I'm not sure where she's staying," I tell him honestly.

But wherever she finds a spot to stay, it won't be comfortable since I already checked, and the hotels and rental cars are booked out for Snow Dayz.

"Hey! Are we going to play or what?" Kaenan yells from across the large living room where I laid out three separate poker tables.

The background TV noise of the sports channel and the clanking of beer bottles fill the space around us.

Brent and I both swivel our attention in that direction to see all the guys seated and eating, talking among one another and waiting for the game to start.

"Let's get back to it," Brent says, pushing his hip off the countertop and heading for the living room.

I follow him. I hope fucking with Tessa isn't worse than actually just fucking Tessa.

Brent might be more pissed about the first one.

Tessa

"What a dickhole!" Autumn says.

She leans over from where she is on the couch while Penelope sits on the floor painting Autumn's toenails a robin's egg blue. Her hair is up in a pink towel with a thick hair conditioning mask, and her face is covered in a black charcoal face paste that has now dried, not allowing her to open her mouth as wide.

In fact, all four of us look the same with matching pink towels wrapped around our heads and charcoal face masks plastered to our faces.

We all sound a little weird now that our face masks have dried, making it a little uncomfortable to get too animated with our facial expressions.

"I know. Elliot told me to quit and come work for his family." I chuckle.

I'd never consider it, but it was sweet that he offered. Working for the man I'm dating would just get too complicated. What if I wanted to quit the job... or what if I wanted to quit him?

Not that we're technically dating. This Cabo trip was supposed to be a chance for us to figure out whether or not now was finally the time to see if being more than friends is viable.

"Oh yeah, yuck. Working with your significant other is bad news. Don't do it," Isla chips in.

Her history with her ex-fiancé is a cautionary tale.

"I won't," I assure her, leaning into the couch more and lifting my right foot to admire the pretty coral nail polish that Penelope put on my feet and hands.

It looks so good with this tan I've been working on at the tanning salon so that I'd look good in Cabo. What a pity this golden-bronzed skin will be covered up with a parka for all of next week.

There goes a hundred dollars for the elite month tanning package I bought. I really should send a bill to Lake for reimbursement.

"You still want to take everything back tomorrow?" Autumn asks.

"Yeah. I don't need three hundred dollars' worth of lingerie for Lake."

The second I let out the words, a flip happens in my stomach as I imagine taking the lingerie with me to Aspen. A start-up corny porno image of me showing up at Lake's home in nothing but a skippy cosplay costume from the adult store flashes in my imagination.

I clamp down my eyes in an effort to wash them of the image, but it takes a minute for the idea to melt away.

"Are you sure you don't?" Penelope asks, wiggling her eyebrows at me.

I reach over to the coffee table and grab one of Autumn's cookies off the plate to distract my fingers from fidgeting at the question.

"Positive. Lake is the last Hawkeyes player I'd ever consider," I say.

I take a bite, then pretend to watch the ending to *Pitch Perfect 2* that we all voted on. It took us all of the first *Pitch Perfect* to eat our Chinese takeout and then most of *Pitch Perfect 2* to get our hair and face masks on, along with our toes and fingers painted.

"Ohhh, the last player, huh?" Autumn says. "I think it's time for a game of kiss, marry, kill."

"Yes!" Penelope squeals. "Ouch!" she says and then rubs the side of her mouth where she ripped a little of her face mask.

"You ok?" Autumn bends down closer to her.

"Yeah, I'm fine. Continue," Penelope says, getting back to painting Autumn's toes.

"This could be fun," Isla adds.

All three of them look back at me.

"Ok fine, but Autumn gets to go first since she suggested it, and you can't pick Briggs to marry because you already are, you lucky B," I tease.

We all giggle, as much as we can with these torturous masks plastered on our faces.

"Wait, I have to go first?" Autumn asks.

"I'll go," Penelope says, lifting her arm with the nail polish paintbrush still in her hand.

"The floor is yours," Autumn tells her with a little relief. "I think we should keep it open to staff too. The physical therapist we just got is kind of cute, and Bex has that daddy vibe... you know?"

"Daddy vibe?" Isla asks.

"Yeah, you should know. Kaenan's got that daddy vibe too... but he's actually a daddy. Hot," I tease, knowing it will get Isla to blush a little.

"All staff included, dully noted. Okay Penelope, let 'er rip tater chip."

She hums, indecisive for a second as she starts painting the second coat on Autumn's right foot.

"I'm going to go with.... Marry Reeve... Kiss Seven... Kill... Bex."

We all laugh.

"Why kill Bex?" I ask.

"Because he scares me a little. He's so intense, and he never smiles."

I admire Coach Bex's work ethic, but I get where she's coming from. He can be a bit intimidating.

"Autumn, you're up," I tell her.

"I had it before I even suggested it. Here we go... Marry Seven... Kiss Ryker... Kill Briggs."

"Kill Briggs? Why?" Isla asks with wide eyes.

We all watch Autumn. Penelope even stops her painting to look up at her.

"Because he drank all of the milk in the carton yesterday... and get this... he put it *back* in the fridge... empty!"

We all give a uniform, "Ooohhh."

"Rookie mistake," I say. "But must he die for it?"

"I've considered all of the alternative options, and this is the best course of action," she says, her face straight as an arrow.

We all shake our heads at her.

"Isla, it's your turn," Penelope says.

"Can't I go last?" she whines.

"Nope," I tell her.

"Fine. Okay, um. I would kill... I don't want to kill anyone," she says, her hands slapping against her thighs like she wants to give up.

"Come on, fake kill someone... it's liberating," Autumn encourages.

"I guess I'd kill Lake because he just killed my friend's vacation..." I smile over at her, then give her leg a quick pat. "I'd kiss Ryker... and I'd marry..." We all practically lean forward waiting for her answer. "Kaenan."

I toss my hands up in victory. It's about damn time she came to the conclusion.

We whoop and holler for a second as Isla's cheeks go bright red.

"You're up, missy." Autumn elbows me in the right arm.

"I'm taking Brent off the list for obvious reasons, and that goes for Briggs and Kaenan too because they're already taken, and that's just straight-up girl code." I wink at Isla, but she pretends not to see it. "But it's still the same three I would have anyway. I'd marry Ryker because he's the team captain, and that's sexy. Plus, his jersey number 19 is my lucky number... it's fated." Penelope chokes out a laugh. "I'd kiss Coach Bex because of how dominant he is on and off the ice... Even with a twenty-year age gap, I bet he'd melt my panties off. And we all know who I'd kill... Lake Powers because he's just the freaking worst!"

The alarm goes off on our time for the face masks, and we all stand from the couch. Autumn pulls on Penelope's hand to pull her up off the ground into a standing position. We all head to the kitchen to wash these off.

I consider the fact that Lake is only a floor above me right now, and I fight the urge to take the elevator up to the penthouse floor and give him a piece of my mind.

But this is girls' night.

And you don't fuck with girls' night.

CHAPTER SIX

Tessa

I asked Isla and Berkeley to drop me off at the airport earlier this morning for my flight. Brent, Ryker, and Seven left yesterday to head for Playa Del Carmen, and I wish I could have stashed myself in my brother's suitcase instead.

Before he left, he walked into my room while I was packing and gave me one small warning—not to get involved with Lake.

He didn't need to waste his breath while sitting on the baby-blue duvet covering my king-size bed in the room that he rents me in his mansion. There is zero chance of Lake and I hooking up.

He watches me pack jackets and pants for a freezing Aspen instead of bikinis and sundresses for Cabo.

He sits there staring at the contents of my luggage with his left leg up on my bed and his right foot down on the plush off-white carpeting that all the bedrooms in this house have, minus the master, which has the same matching wood floors throughout the rest of the house.

"He's my best friend, Tessie, so I hate to say this about the guy behind his back... but you can do better than him, a lot better," he says, locking eyes with mine for a second.

I hate when people say that. "You can do better" always feels like a cliché. Like it's not you, it's me... or you're marriage material. If either of those things were true, wouldn't you do anything you could to keep me?

"I thought you didn't care who I date?" I ask, since he's never stopped me from dating his teammates before.

Brent has given parental-type responsibility a wide berth since our parents died. Even though maybe he should have been stricter. He's always let me get away with murder, and I think it's because he feels bad that I was so young when they died. He's played the brother role so he doesn't try to fill my parents' shoes. He was just a kid himself at eighteen... trying to raise another kid.

He let me date asshole hockey players and kept his thoughts to himself. He let me pick one of the biggest party schools for college because I promised him that I'd still get good grades and that I would be smart about where and with whom I partied with and he paid my tuition without a lecture.

"I don't. But if you're going to date one of them, date Seven or Reeve... neither of them are the equivalent to an overused, never sanitized subway seat."

Oh, gross.

"You're one to talk." Giving him my little sister's snark, I finish folding a sweater and place it in my luggage.

"Yeah well, I'm not trying to pull someone as put together and smart as you, and Lake shouldn't be either. He's not in the right headspace."

I think that was a compliment, but also... Lake isn't in the right headspace?

"What does that mean? 'He's not in the right headspace?'" I ask.

Brent looks down at the carpet on the other side of the bed where he's sitting and blinks a few times as he considers his next words.

"I don't know much about it. I just know that he had a traumatic event years back that made him the way he is."

My eyebrows scrunch together as I look back at him.

"The way he is?" I ask.

That's as cryptic as it gets.

"That's all I know. He doesn't talk about it, and I don't ask. Until this very moment, I've never given a shit about Lake's swinging door policy. I just don't want to see you get hurt. You've been through enough."

I head for my walk-in closet and pull out the biggest down jacket I own, then walk back to my luggage and cram it in with a little resentment toward its fluffy feathers. It's not the cute crochet bathing suit coverup I bought and then promptly returned after my tropical vacation got canceled.

"He's a job. Nothing else. I'm going to get in, get the content I need for media, and then get the hell out of there."

I turn toward my dresser, open the top drawer, and grab the first ten pairs of clean underwear sitting on top. I don't give a crap if they're granny panties, lacy thongs, or my "period" undies stained from prior use. No man in Aspen will catch me with my pants down on this trip, so I don't care what I wear.

I drop the wad of underwear into the large black hard case.

"Even if he tries to pull something on you while you're in Aspen?" he asks with a lifted eyebrow.

I turn and look him dead in the eye.

"Even if Thor himself descends from the heavens and demands that I sleep with Lake to save all of humankind from complete and utter destruction, I'll tell him to let the world sink to the bottom of the ocean... Lake's not worth it."

Brent blinks a couple of times. "That was dramatic... but okay, I'm glad we're on the same page," he says, his left hand pushing down on my mattress as he lifts himself off my cushy bed. "Just be careful, okay?"

I nod as I pretend to fiddle with the items in my luggage.

He walks out of my room and into the hallway of the huge house he bought when I moved from San Diego to Seattle after breaking up with my boyfriend. Yet another hockey player who turned out to be just like all the others... except worse. Something I've never told my brother about, but he already knows that my luck with pro-NHL players has been 0-6... a losing streak of depressing proportions.

The flight to Aspen, all four legs of it since changing my ticket from Cabo to Aspen has been a complete shit show, and even worse than I could ever have imagined.

I ended up in the middle seat next to the lavatory on the first flight, which contained a passenger who had eaten either Mexican food or something very spicy before takeoff that did not agree with them.

During the second flight, I got a window seat, which would have been nice if I wasn't stuck next to a handsy old man who seemed to continue to bump into my boob every time he put his tray table away—over a dozen times.

On my third flight, I ended up in an aisle seat, but the stewardess rammed the drink cart into the back of my elbow only thirty minutes into the flight. I figured I'd have luck on flight four, but wouldn't you know that I'd get stuck next to a sweet little baby who turned to me and puked on my shirt during takeoff.

I could have endured it all. I could have painted a smile on my face and called it just one long shit day that won't repeat itself tomorrow. I could have... until I stood at the baggage carousel for over an hour, waiting as every last piece of luggage was taken off the moving conveyor.

My luggage isn't here.

I want to break down in tears, but I won't. At least not in front of the conveyor belts in the middle of an airport at almost eleven o'clock at night.

And who knows, since I basically flew across this entire continent, maybe my luggage decided to take a more direct route and has been waiting for me for half a day. I'm not usually a glass-half-full kind of girl, although I wouldn't consider myself a Debbie Downer either. But I put on my best Penelope Roberts optimism and head for the luggage counter.

"Hello," I say with a half-hearted smile when the attendant doesn't even bother to acknowledge me as he continues to stare at his computer screen, clicking away.

He's barely an inch taller than me, slender with short brown hair, thin lips, and lackluster chocolate-brown eyes. The skin peeking out from his thick navy-blue airline hoodie is paler than most people in Seattle.

"Luggage tag?" he practically barks, rolling his eyes.

"Uh... what?"

"Do you have your luggage tag?" he asks slowly as if I'm not smart enough to understand him.

What an ass.

I didn't do shit to him.

"Oh... yeah, I think so," I say, reaching inside my purse for my wallet. "I started in Seattle, and I have four layovers so hopefully it's just sitting in the back," I tell him while digging for my wallet that has my luggage tags tucked inside where I put them when they handed them to me in Seattle.

Motherfucker!

My wallet... where the hell is my wallet?

Then it dawns on me. Absolute dread and irritation coat my throat almost making it hard to speak but also making me want to scream and throw something.

I left it after picking up some snacks and earplugs on the last leg of my journey.

Puke covered with no luggage and now no wallet. I just about decide to throw in the towel and call Sam to tell him I quit. He can take his adult babysitting job and shove it. This isn't worth it anymore, and Lake wins!

An overreaction?

Maybe.

But right now, that would feel pretty damn incredible compared to how I feel.

Instead, I take a cleansing breath and remember that Sam didn't do this, and he's not the enemy. Lake is, and I should go straight to his house and TP it tonight. Except I have no wallet and therefore no money to buy said TP. Nor am I sure how I would get there considering Penelope couldn't find a single car rental in this town. Luckily, the one thing I do have is my rideshare app, which is connected to my bank account. At the very least, I'll be able to pay to get myself a ride to the only motel Penelope could get me.

The attendant at the counter starts tapping his toe, or at least it sounds like he is, as he watches me continue digging through my bag as though the wallet is suddenly going to do a Houdini trick and reappear out of nowhere.

No such luck.

"Shit. I left my wallet back in the Dallas airport."

"You started in Seattle? Why did they route you through Dallas?" he asks.

"It's a long story—"

"You know what," he says, putting his palm up to stop me. "I'm off in fifteen minutes and I don't actually care. What's your last name and the flight number that you just got off?"

Wow, this guy. I look around to see if there is any supervisor looking person around but I don't see another soul. The airport looks closed down for the night. No outbound flights left for takeoff.

I give him my last boarding pass which has all of my information on it and he begins typing away instantly. No doubt hoping to get me out of his sights.

He makes a long sighing noise as if I am the biggest nuisance to his sad, little decrepit life.

"Your luggage is stuck in Salt Lake City." My first leg. "And all flights are currently grounded due to a snowstorm you just missed."

Just my luck again... I could have been stuck in a snowstorm in Salt Lake City instead of stuck in Aspen with Lake. A far better option.

I rub my index finger gently across my right eyebrow trying to keep myself from a nervous breakdown.

Breathe Tessa.

"Crap, what does that mean? It will get here sometime tomorrow, right?"

"It's a snowstorm. I'm not God," he says, typing quickly on his computer screen again.

And thank the powers that be for that because I can't imagine how shitty the world would be if you were the one in charge.

"I understand that but—"

"I just opened a claim for you and your information is in here. Someone will contact you when your luggage gets here," he says, his voice almost monotone.

"Ok but when—"

"I'm off the clock. Wait for someone to call you," he says, stepping back and turning toward the door behind him.

"You said you have fifteen more minutes!" I say, but it's too late, he's gone.

I blow out a frustrated breath. So much for trying to be nice. That got me nowhere and with no wallet, now I get to smell like baby vomit all night.

I pull up the app on my phone and order a rideshare. With the time difference, I know Penelope is still awake and I call her after the rideshare shows that someone is on their way but she doesn't answer on the first ring.

I hope she's doing something fun.

One of us should be.

I debate calling Autumn or Isla next but I know this is around Berkeley's bedtime, so I don't want to disturb Isla, and Autumn and Briggs went home to Walla Walla for Briggs's bye week to see how Briggs's dad's treatment went. I don't want to disturb her during this time.

Instead of calling anyone else, I head to the bathroom and shoot off a text to Brent.

> Tessa: Just landed

> Brent: Text me again when you get to your hotel.

> Tessa: How's Playa Del Carmen?

> Brent: It's a fucking fishing hut. Ryker's trying to convince me to go in on a suite

> down the road at one of the all-inclusive resorts in Cancun with a lazy river.

What I wouldn't give for a lazy river right about now.

> Tessa: Didn't Wrenley tell you his place down there was exactly five stars? I mean, it's Wrenley after all.

Seven Wrenley, aka Lucky to the fans, has a house... or rather a "fishing hut" in Playa Del Carmen. My brother and Ryker invited themselves down to Seven's little getaway spot in Mexico to do a little fishing during their bye week. What I wouldn't give to be in a fishing hut on the warm beaches of Mexico instead of here.

> Brent: Yeah, but I thought he was under-selling it. Like when I tell people we live in suburbia land.

> Tessa: But we technically do.

> Brent: Sure, but most suburbia houses aren't over six thousand square feet with an indoor pool.

> Tessa: You're kind of being a prima donna.

> Brent: Shut up.

Tessa: YOU shut up.

Brent: Text me. Don't forget.

Tessa: K, love you.

Brent: Love you.

With only a hoodie that I brought on the plane because I didn't want to carry around something large with me on the plane, and all of my warm gear in my bag that's hundreds of miles away from me, I walk into the airport bathroom and pull off the only shirt I have with me. I stuff the soiled shirt in my laptop bag and pull my hoodie over my head, covering the coral pink lace bra with embroidered cherry blossoms on it. It was the one article of clothing I couldn't bring myself to return. The bra was too dang pretty.

If this hoodie is the only clean thing I have right now, I certainly don't need to soil it by pulling it over the vomit. Hopefully, there is a laundromat at this motel, although Penelope said that it was showing 2-stars and "mixed" reviews.

Just what I need to top off my night.

I'm not that bougie, I don't need five stars but a solid 3+ star would have been nice.

I stand outside the airport as I watch the last of the passengers from my flight embracing people coming by to pick them up. Everyone seems so happy to see one another. I cross my arms over one another and rub each side to try to warm my upper arms.

I watch my breath as billows of steam from my hot mouth push out away from me and into the cold, late January night in Colorado.

My mind wanders, unsupervised, to what Lake is doing right now.

Probably sitting in his massive mansion, having a raging party with all his friends and half-naked woman in every corner of the house. Why my mind goes straight to there being an active game of naked twister in the middle of his huge living room, which I've never seen and I'm making up in my head, is beyond me. The point is, Lake probably isn't standing out in the cold, with only a single hoodie to keep warm, a soiled shirt covered in formula stuffed in his laptop bag, and a purse void of any actual funds to buy anything.

I check my app again and the driver from the rideshare is only a few minutes away.

A call comes through.

Autumn calling...

"Hello?" I ask, a little nervous she's calling to give me bad news.

I hate that that's where my mind goes but with Briggs's dad's health I'm not sure what to expect.

Maybe that's what happens when you lose your parents so young. You barely remember a time in your life when you lived in a world with false security thinking that nothing bad will happen to you. That everything will work itself out because there was a time in your life when the worst thing actually happened and nothing ever truly righted itself back after that.

"Hi," she says.

"What's wrong?" I say, my voice on edge.

"What? Nothing. Everything's fine here. The doctors are really happy with Mr. Conley's progress so far. I just wanted to call and see how your flight went."

Phew. I blow out a breath.

Thank God.

"Good, you scared me. It seemed late for you to be calling. I thought something happened," I tell her, my eyes fixed on the red taillights of the last car pulling off the curb.

"I'm sorry. I didn't mean to worry you. Did you make it to Aspen?"

"Yeah... I guess you could say that. It was an absolute shit show. I also have no wallet and no luggage," I tell her, trying to keep my teeth from chattering in the cold.

"Oh! That's awful. Do you need me to Western Union you some money or send funds through a cash app?" she asks.

"That's sweet, but I'm sure there's a bank here where I can pull out funds tomorrow," I tell her, even though I also don't have a driver's license to prove identification, and no one knows me here at these banks to vouch for me like they would at home at the bank I frequent.

"If you need something tonight, I'm sure Lake can help too. He's somewhere in town, right?"

You mean the man I've been daydreaming about murdering in his sleep for the past sixteen hours of flight time?

"Hell no. I'm not asking him for anything," I say, my eyebrows scrunching together and a deep frown forming across my lips.

I see the lights of the only vehicle left headed my way. This must be my rideshare.

I run my free left hand up and down my right bicep to warm it. Hopefully, this driver has the heat on blast.

"It's his fault that this is happening. You're supposed to be in Cabo getting wined and dined—"

"And poked from behind. I know," I tell her.

I hear Autumn start giggling. "That's not what I was going to say. Just because it rhymes doesn't mean it works in this scenario."

"Your giggles suggest it worked just fine," I say to make my point.

She attempts to clear the giggles from her throat. "Okay, well, moving on. Has Elliot said anything since you last talked to him?"

"Yep, he said he wants a rain check. He asked me to see if my boss will give me next week off to go to Cabo with him before he has to crack down on signing some new talent for endorsements."

"That sounds promising, right? The cute guy whose family owns one of the biggest athletic shoe brands in the world. And major bonus points, he isn't a hockey player."

"You had me at, *isn't a hockey player.*"

We both chuckle.

Autumn had her struggles with Briggs in the beginning when they were fake dating, so she knows a thing or two about it, but now they're happily engaged.

"Well, this stupid assignment will be over in a week. Perk up, buttercup. Phil Carlton is going to worship the ground you walk on when you get Lake Powers looking like a shiny copper penny. Then you can ride off into the sunset with the billionaire heir."

I don't care about his billion-dollar family money. I just want what I was promised. A beach vacation with hot sex and a guy who cares enough about me to want to take me there. Now, because of Lake, I'm not getting either.

"Yeah, we'll see. I was just hoping to dust off the cobwebs down there while getting a *real* tan. Elliot offered me both. But hey, I have to go, my ride is here."

I like Elliot, but I'm not one hundred percent sure how much yet. I don't want to lead him on, especially since his company is in negotiations with Lake's agent to get him to endorse their sports gear.

I was open to heading to Cabo for a fun weekend, but I've been concerned that Elliot might want more than that from the beginning. And then it gets me thinking... maybe Elliot is exactly what I need.

"Ok," Autumn says.

"I'll call you tomorrow to hear about how Mr. Conley is doing," I tell her.

"Sure thing. Talk tomorrow."

"Bye."

"Bye."

My rideshare arrives, and I open the back passenger door and slide in. I can't see his face since he's in the driver's seat and staring back at his cell phone app. He lists off the motel address to confirm my destination.

"Are you sure this is where you're staying?" he asks.

"Yep," I say, looking down at my screen to verify the address Penelope gave me.

"Are you sure it's not a different motel?"

"Nope. It's the Royal Inn outside of town."

He hesitates for a second. "Uh, ok," he says and then doesn't say another word to me after.

When he pulls up to the motel, I see exactly why he asked more than once about the motel.

He seems ready to drop me off and leave once he enters the parking lot.

I glance up at the lit-up sign and read it as half the sign glitches like a bug zapper every time a mosquito gets electrocuted.

Hourly rates $15

Only one kind of motel offers hourly rates—the kind I have no place staying in.

Great. So, the day can still get worse.

"Ok, this is the last time I'm going to ask. Are you positive this is the right motel?" he asks again, looking over his shoulder at me.

He's a young guy. Not much older than my twenty-nine years. But it's dark and I can't make out much of his features, especially with his big jacket and beanie.

Nonetheless, his eyes seem kind, and the squinty look of concern doesn't have me feeling great about getting out of his car.

"Yep. But if I disappear and people start coming looking for me, please make sure that Lake Powers is held responsible for my demise," I instruct.

"Lake Powers? Why, are you here for him?" He turns toward me like something just dawned on him. "Are you a reporter doing a story on the accident because that happened a really long time ago, and it should just stay in the past where it belongs," he says a little defensively.

Accident? What accident?

But I don't know this guy, and my job is to make Lake look good, not stir up questions and old drama.

"Absolutely not. I work for the team."

"Oh, I see." He nods. "Well, I don't really like leaving you here, but there's not much I can do if you refuse to try somewhere else, and I think everything is booked up because I've been moving people all day into the hotels around town." He shrugs. "But... there's a woman's shelter nearby, and it might be safer than here."

"I'll be okay," I tell him, not loving the idea of either option, but I'm here now, and there's a door and a lock on this place, plus twenty-four-hour surveillance and someone always manning the check-in desk.

"You have my information, so call if you need me to come back and get you. I wouldn't consider this place unsafe, just gross, so get to your room, and I wouldn't open your door until morning light, and you'll be fine."

So reassuring.

"Great... thanks," I tell him, then open the door to climb out. Looking left to right, I wait to see if any sketchy people are lurking around. Luckily, no one is in sight... it's too damn cold to be outdoors.

Armed with my purse, heavy laptop bag, and my pick-pocketing skills... I grip my phone in my hand and remember that little tidbit I learned on social media.

If you push down on all of the side buttons at once, your phone will call 911... right?

Shoot, I wish I'd paid more attention to that little phone hack.

Lake

When I pull into my driveway, I see my middle sister Harmony and my two nieces Sadie and Lana waiting at my front door with balloons in one hand and a homemade banner they're hanging onto at opposite sides that reads:

Welcome Home, Uncle Lake

I've been waiting all month to wrap my arms around these two sweet little girls since I left after visiting for Christmas. I'm not home enough, and that hits me when I'm barely in the driveway of my house and I already feel like the real me is starting to charge back to one hundred percent.

The physical exertion of what I do isn't even a quarter of the energy spent. It's all the other bullshit.

I'd skate for free.

Out on the stadium, ice is where all my past mistakes can't get to me.

My oldest sister Chelsea picked me up from the airport, so I hop out of the passenger side of her car and race up the paved jet-black driveway. I sail up the pebbled concrete staircase that leads up to the three-story house with a double wooden entry door I bought in this gated community. I also bought the house next door for my sister Chelsea and her girls to live in. I might be the youngest brother but protecting my sister and my nieces is my top priority and I want Chelsea and the girls close. They watch over my house during the season when I'm living in Seattle so it works out.

I paid off my sister Harmony's house too, which is farther down the drive, and purchased a house for my parents on this same street. They could have purchased their own homes with the lucrative women's clothing store in town that they own together but it felt good to do it.

Now that my parents are retired, their house just sits empty most of the time anyway. They probably stay in Seattle in my penthouse to see my home games more than they stay in the mansion I bought them down the street.

"Did you girls make this sign for me?" I ask, pulling them in for a big group hug.

"We stayed up all night, Uncle Lake," Lana says, with her two missing front teeth.

Lana is six while Sadie is eight. Even though I've sworn to never get married, thus never planning to have kids of my own, coming home to these two gives me a quick glimpse into what that would feel like, racing home on my days off to be with my own family.

I shake the idea loose. I made a promise to myself that I'd never consider a life like that again.

"Do you like it?" Sadie asks.

"Do I like it? I love it!" I say, squeezing them a little tighter.

"We never get to come to your games like Nanna and Pappa do and make you a sign, so we wanted to make you one for coming home," Lana says.

"Sounds like we need to convince your mom to bring you to a game soon, huh?"

"Yes!" they both squeal.

After a delicious home-cooked meal at my sister's house next door, I head back to my place, up the small cobblestone walkway that I had installed by a landscaper for easy access between the two houses through a side entrance.

I thought I would enjoy knowing that Tessa might be having a hard time finding a place to stay tonight. Initially, the idea of her sleeping in the airport entertained my thirst for revenge. But now, as the sun sets, the idea of her out there and me not completely sure if she's safe is making it hard not to text her to make sure she landed somewhere in one of the downtown hotels.

The thought came to me after my last beer while catching up with Chelsea and Harmony out on the deck of Chelsea's house, and I've been avoiding it for the past thirty minutes. I walk through the side door of my house that opens up into the massive kitchen, even bigger than the penthouse kitchen I have in Seattle. The temptation to text her is building.

Fuck it.

I'm doing it.

Lake: Did you find a place to stay?

Ice Queen: Yep

Relief hits me instantly, but I'm a little annoyed she didn't volunteer more information.

> Lake: Oh yeah? Where?

> Ice Queen: The Royal Inn.

No.

Hell no!

There's no way she can stay at the pay-by-the-hour motel, but maybe there's more than one motel with a similar name.

> Lake: Outside of town?

> Ice Queen: How many Royal Inns can there be?

Goddammit.

This should feel good. This should be the payback I wanted. But all I feel is this building need coursing through my veins to get her out of that place as fast as I can. My feet are practically moving on their own, heading straight for the garage, and they won't stop until I'm standing at Tessa's motel room door.

I don't even bother to respond. I just grab my keys off the key rack and head for my six-car garage.

I start one of the two cars I keep here year-round, a red Jeep Wrangler, and roll out of the garage without the loud engine waking up my nieces... or my nosy sister who will ask questions when she looks out the window on my return to find me bringing back a woman.

Despite my reputation as Lake Powers the Magic Stick in Seattle and anywhere I'm playing during the season, I'm not that guy here at home. I don't do that in Aspen.

This is a small community of people who know me and my family... and know my past. I don't have the same reputation here as I do everywhere else. In Aspen, I don't take women home.

I'm protective of this place, and I've done my fair share of causing this place pain. Now all I want to do is make it up to the people who made me who I am in this town.

It's a small enough town that I get to the motel in record time. The guy at the front desk gives up Tessa's location easily and that pisses me off even more. What would have happened if I had been a stalker or something?

I'm feeling more vindicated for showing up unannounced. She can't stay here. She's not safe.

CHAPTER SEVEN

Tessa

Checking in was easier than it should have been. He didn't ask for ID or to verify the credit card put on hold for this reservation. I just told him my name, and he gave me a key. That simple.

Thank God, considering I have no form of identification or credit card to pay for this room.

I walk out of the motel office and down the first story of the two-story motel. I walk up the flight of stairs to the second story and find my room number 212. Even with the cold weather, a few people are still scattered around the building outside smoking, and a couple is making out in the parking lot against a car.

I get into my room as fast as I can and close the door behind me, locking the deadbolt and securing the chain and the other two locks on this door. The extra locks don't make me feel any safer, but I guess I'm glad they're here.

After about thirty minutes of looking for hidden Peeping Tom cameras, I finally relax and strip the bed of the nasty top cover, leaving only a sheet and a thick, scratchy orange wool blanket. I doubt I'll get great sleep, but right now I'm too wound up to sleep anyway.

I turn on the TV and start scrolling after I take a disinfectant wipe from my laptop bag and wipe the remote control down.

This chaotic energy from today is hard to wind down from without a good release, but my vibrator is sadly in my checked luggage. My body keeps reminding me that I should be getting railed by Elliot in Cabo right about now.

I could kill Lake with my bare hands.

Or better yet, smother him as I sit on his face. That's one man I wouldn't mind suffocating under me.

Wow!

Where did that come from?

I'm so damn horny I'm coming up with a fantasy starring Lake, and that's exactly why I need to get rid of this toxic energy.

My thumb continues to scroll until I hit the pay-per-view screen. An old seventies porno displays on the screen, and my thumb stalls. It wouldn't be my first pick, but with how pent-up I am right now and the fact that I'm going to need some distraction like a porno to help me forget for a second what kind of nasty motel I'm stuck in because of Lake, it might be just what I need.

It isn't until after I hit play that I realize this charge will probably show up when Penelope gets the bill for this.

Oh well.

I'll just say that I accidentally sat on the remote, and it ordered pay-per-view without my knowledge.

A text comes through from Lake, and I type off a quick response.

The movie is grainier than I'd like and certainly from the seventies as advertised, but the plot of a mailman coming to deliver mail to a woman while her husband is away on business is working for me in a way I wasn't expecting.

Another text comes through from Lake and now I'm annoyed. He's throwing off my game, but I respond without thinking too much about it and quickly get back to the task at hand.

The film pulls no punches, and we're quickly into the nitty-gritty of the sex scene. I'm surprised at how quickly I get wet for this, and before I know it, my hand snakes down my torso and dips below my panties.

I'm wet as the mailman bends the woman over her mailbox in what appears to be, broad daylight. I dip my middle finger between my folds to test out my slickness. Yep, this is working for me. Then, when the female next-door neighbor walks out, seemingly appalled at first but then joins them, I'm biting down on my lower lip and pressing a finger through my center.

Knock! Knock!

I jump almost completely off the bed.

My heart sprints and I feel so light-headed that I might pass out.

I reach for the first thing I see to use as a weapon. A landline telephone, my hand barely steady enough to hold it as I shake like a leaf from the adrenaline kick of having someone pound on the door.

"Who is it?!" I yell, my voice shaking.

"It's me." A gravelly low voice that sounds oddly familiar.

"It's me who?!" I yell back.

This better not be a damn knock-knock joke.

It must be some pimp with the wrong door number.

I consider calling 911 with the telephone in my hand, but I swear, I'm not even sure I know how to use a landline anymore.

"It's Lake. Now open up," the voice on the other side says with annoyance.

Oh... you're annoyed?! Let's compare which one of us is more annoyed with the other.

What is Lake doing at my door?

Confusion and then instant relief hits me.

Lake's here with his strong arms and ability to knock a grown man flat on his ass out on the ice. I let out the breath I was holding.

It's the first time since the rideshare pulled into the parking lot that I've felt safe. I hate how it feels like my knight in shining armor just showed up because I hate him. The only reason this day is awful and that I'm even here, in Aspen, and in this motel, is because of this man.

I walk up to the door cautiously and look through the peephole.

"What do you want?" I grumble.

"For you to open the door," he says, taking a step closer and staring back at the peephole.

I unlock the many locks that I had engaged before he showed up. I wasn't really scared until he beat down on the door, but now that he has, I realize I must have been suppressing it as a survival tactic.

I open the door just a little to poke my head out.

"Why are you here?" I demand.

"Because..." he starts, but then his eyebrows furrow. "Are you not alone?"

The TV... shit balls!

Lake takes a step closer and tries to peek his head over me and through the door.

"I'm alone," I say, closing the door quickly to block his view so he can't see past me at the TV... even though he's a good foot taller than me. "But you didn't answer my question... why are you here?"

He abandons his mission to find the sound, and his eyes meet mine.

"I'm here because you can't stay here," he says, licking his lips, probably from the cold, and then takes another step toward me.

"Well, that's too bad because I'm already settled in for the night and there are no other vacancies at other hotels tonight. So go home."

Please don't leave me here.

"You're coming home with me," he says, and then he must hear the moaning of the two women being taken at the same time by the mailman because he looks over my head again, trying to find the human he thinks I'm hiding in this room. He pushes up on his tiptoes and glances over my head past the door. "Are you watching porn?" he asks, his eyes twinkling with the idea that he caught me in the act.

"What! How dare you barge in here and make accusations!" I bark.

Lake pushes the door, and I wasn't ready for it. The door swings open as I tumble one step backward along with it. Lake's quick reflexes instantly wrap a protective arm around me to keep me from falling. I guess his speed is useful for more than just ice hockey. He barely looks down at me secured in his arm as if catching falling women comes second nature and doesn't faze him in the least.

Charming.

Instead, his eyes glue to the dated TV located at the back left corner of the room.

"Holy fuck you are." He beams like a kid who just found the Christmas gift stash his parents were hiding.

With the mixture of the porno, my buzzing center from the scare of Lake banging on the door, and the fact that there's a bed within three feet of us, the temptation to knock Lake down on the bed and straddle him and use his body to get rid of the female version of blue balls is ever growing.

I need to make a move now!

One way or the other.

Thankfully, the cringe-worthy duvet lying on the ground and the burnt orange scratchy blanket acting as the only barrier between me and God-only-knows-what stains on the mattress sober up any ideas of wanting to get naked.

"Get out! Get out! Get out!" I yell, pulling myself out of his arm and shooing him backward with my hands, my entire body getting into the rhythm.

His eyes abandon the TV and stare down at me next.

"You dirty little girl." He smirks. "Never mind, I'm moving in," he says, trying to sidestep around me and head for the bed.

"Lake, I'm going to kill you if you don't leave right now."

He chuckles a little like he knows how mortified I am that he caught me in this situation. I'm not mortified that he knows I watch porn but because he caught me in a pay-by-the-hour motel, not only watching porn but masturbating to a film our parents could have watched years before either of us were ever conceived.

Something about the entire ordeal is just a little too embarrassing for me, and I need him the hell out of here. Knight in shining armor, my ass. I wish he never knocked on this door.

"Okay, fine, I'll leave, but you're coming with me." He steps back toward the open motel room door and then steps outside into the second-story corridor.

"No, I'm not. I'm fine here," I huff, crossing my arms in an attempt to create a barrier that will keep him out in case he changes his mind and barges back into my motel room.

Both of our attentions dart over to an older man with a graying beard and a woman half his age walking up the stairs. He's barely able to walk straight, seemingly drunk off his ass. He has his arm wrapped around her and she tries to keep him upright while she's dressed in less than I would wear to the beach, let alone wear in almost freezing temperatures.

"So how much did you say for one go?" the man asks her in a drunken stupor.

I barely make out his words with how much he slurs them.

"Just the tip? Or the whole thing?"

Lake's eyes jet back to mine. "You're leaving with me now."

I nod this time. I know when I've been beaten.

The woman fumbles with his room key, and they finally disappear into the motel room as Lake takes a step forward, almost as if to block the opening of my door so no one has access without going through him first.

My heart squeezes at his protective stance at my door.

I've never seen this side of Lake... the protective side. I guess that's not totally true. He's a fiercely loyal and protective teammate on the ice. I've just never seen him be this protective with a woman, especially not with me.

"Okay, I'll meet you downstairs," I tell him, not that I have much to grab besides my cell phone, purse, and laptop bag.

His eyes finally break away from the closed door to his left as we listen for the neighbor's door to lock and the chain to engage. Then his eyes lock onto mine and the intensity of the way he's looking at me, I've only seen during game day.

A set of shivers cascade down my spine, leaving goose bumps on my arms and legs.

"Like hell I'm leaving you here. I'll wait," he says, crossing his arms over his chest, making a stand, and continuing to block the door with his imposingly large frame.

I hate that I feel safer with him looking so menacing at my door. I hate that I like that he's staying until I'm ready. I hate that with all the men I've ever dated in my life, none of them would have stayed and waited. They all would have gone down-stairs and sat in the car, not considering for a second the kind of danger I could be in or the inappropriate scenarios that I could be exposed to by being in this motel. They'd probably just head downstairs, climb into their vehicles, and use the time to secretly talk with other women behind my back.

Lake wouldn't be any different, I have to remind myself of that fact. He has a worse reputation than any of the men I've dated. I mean for goodness' sake; his nickname is Magic Stick among the puck bunnies.

So he's a little more protective than the others. That doesn't mean he'd be loyal if he ever actually decided to date anyone instead of one-night stands. Word on the street is that he hasn't dated a woman in over fifteen years, so loyalty toward a monog-amous relationship is not currently in practice.

These facts are a moot point anyway because he and I are coworkers and enemies, and I am on a strict, no-hockey-player dating diet, and Lake is off the menu.

Lake

I feel relief the second Tessa is safely tucked inside my Jeep, and we're off the motel's property. I can't fucking believe she checked into that place. That place makes me want to take a boiling hot shower and scrub myself down with bleach after.

The second I heard the conversation between that man and the prostitute, I had to cross my arms over my chest to keep myself from grabbing Tessa and tossing her over my shoulder to haul her out of there kicking and screaming.

If she hadn't finally agreed to come with me, I would have done just that too. She could hate me after she was safely sitting in my car for all I care.

Now, forcing Tessa to come to Aspen without a place to lay her head is starting to feel like a shitty thing to do to someone. Especially a woman in a town she doesn't know, who just about stayed the night in a brothel.

I'm sure as hell not going to apologize or take any blame for this—Tessa brought this whole 'ruin her trip and make her spend it with me' on herself—but I'll at least make it up to her by putting her up in my house until we can find an opening at another hotel.

After a few minutes, I'm feeling back to myself. There's no way in hell I'm letting the fact I caught her watching a porno go.

I keep my eyes on the road and both my hands on the steering wheel as I ask a question that will have Tessa squirming in her seat uncomfortably. I said I would make the motel situation up to her, but I have zero plans for letting up and not continuing to punish her for all the shit she's gotten me in with Sam and Phil.

"So... what's your kink?" I ask, unable to hide the devilish smile forming across my lips but keeping my eyes on the road as I drive.

"My kink?" she says, turning to me quickly.

I take my eyes off the road just briefly, trying not to notice how beautiful she looks in a fucking hoodie and messy bun after what I presumed was a long-ass day of flying. And is it me or does she smell like sour milk? Still, she's naturally beautiful. Not like the made-up women I see every day.

"Porn, Tessie. What's your kink?"

Her jaw drops as if I didn't just catch her diddling off in front of an old porno where the stars are probably in their late eighties by now, if even alive at all. She has some nerve to fake surprise to my question.

"You're the last person I would ever tell. And I've told you several times, you can't call me Tessie... we're not friends."

Tessie is what Brent always calls her, but I already know she hates it when I use it.

"Out with it, Tessaaa." I hold out the A to annoy her, and it works.

She rolls her eyes and growls in her chair, turning away from me and staring out the window as she speaks.

"We're coworkers, and you're my brother's teammate, so this conversation is highly inappropriate. I'm not telling you what kind of porn I watch," she says, still looking out the window at the pitch darkness.

"We've got a week together because you couldn't let one picture that I didn't even post not ruffle your feathers, so we might as well use this time to our advantage and learn blackmail-worthy information about one another." I look over at her, and her head spins toward me at my suggestions. Her scowl increases, and I know I'm enjoying this too much.

"You want me to give you information that could humiliate me and let you hold it over my head while I live in fear for the moment when you decide to release the information?" she asks, tilting her head at me and blinking a few times as if to say *"not in your damn dreams."*

I grin, putting my sights back on the asphalt in front of us.

Now that she puts it that way, it sounds even better. I don't care if she knows what I'm into. There's some unknown energy surrounding this entire conversation that I'm enjoying, and I'm looking forward to answering the question when it comes back to my turn.

Do I want Tessa to know what I'm into?

It's a new revelation just now seeing the light, but yeah, I think I might like her to know.

"Would it help if I told you mine first?" I glance off the road for a split second to see that she's thinking about it. That's promising. Since she stalls, I decide to go for it. "I'm really into—"

"Stop! Stop!" She squeezes her eyes shut and waves her hands out toward me. "I'm not sharing what I watch, and I sure as hell don't want to know what you like either," she blurts out, taking me by surprise. I didn't take her as the timid kind when talking about sex. I've walked by her open-door office when she's talking with Penelope to know that Tessa isn't shy about sharing her "preferences" with her friends.

Although I never thought she and I would be sitting in my car, thousands of miles from Seattle in my hometown, and discussing how we like our porn, but here we are, and I plan to capitalize on the opportunity.

"I'm unsubscribing from this conversation. How do I opt out of future correspondence?" she asks, her eyes forced onto the road and not looking at me at all.

"You can't. This trip binds us for life," I tease.

In my peripheral, I can see her stare back at me for a second and she doesn't seem amused.

I shouldn't find that fucking cute, but damn me... I do.

"If you try to physically bind our wrists together, I swear to God, I'll gnaw off my own hand if that's what it takes to escape you," she says, looking me dead in the eye when I glance over at her quickly.

That's a first. I've never suggested a form of bondage to a woman and had her not offer up herself for me to do whatever I want with her.

"Ouch, that hurt my feelings. And here I was, thinking we were close to drafting a treaty between us. I did save you from an STD-infested motel room," I remind her.

"You're delusional. We hate each other. And besides," she says, pulling her left leg up a little like she just realized she sat in something disgusting. "This seat is probably covered in STDs left behind from panty-less puck bunnies from days past." She grimaces.

I take my eyes off the road and glance down quickly at the spot where she's lifted her leg off the Jeep's red leather captain's chair.

The Jeep was the first purchase I made when I moved back to Aspen after moving away for a while, and then I tricked it out with as many extra safety features as I could. I lifted it, added a full steel brush guard on the front, and studded tires.

I can feel her eyes on me as she watches me react. I look back up and meet her eyes, and then I center my vision back on the road ahead before I speak.

"There's never been a puck bunny in this rig. There's never been a non-blood-related female in the Jeep. Ever," I tell her, scanning the road in front of us, grateful it's a clear night with a bright moon lighting the way, peeking through the massive jagged mountain range of the Rocky Mountains.

The roads are free of snow and ice. The temperatures have been too uncharacteristically warm for it to snow, but the forecast is calling for it soon.

"HA!" she yells as if she doesn't believe me. "What a load. You think I'd buy that?"

I keep myself level and calm, but my hands tighten around the steering wheel. I don't like that she thinks I'd straight-up lie to her face.

I'm many things, but a liar isn't one of them.

"Have I ever given you a reason to believe I won't tell you the truth?" I ask.

She goes quiet for a second. In my peripheral vision, I can see her turn from me and stare out at the moon in front of us.

"No... not you, I guess"—she takes a deep sigh—"but someone like you."

Perfect, I get to fight against the stigma of the asshole players before me.

"The hockey player?" I say, remembering overhearing Tessa tell Penelope in her office once that Tessa won't date hockey players anymore.

Her face stretches as she flashes me a look like she thinks I might know more than I do.

I don't know anything... but now I'm curious.

"We're not all the same, you know," I tell her, my eyes back on the road.

"I've heard that before," she says, almost under her breath.

"But not from me," I add quickly in an attempt to separate myself from whatever dick treated her so badly that she's taken it out on me.

She pulls her purse onto her lap, as if ignoring my rebuttal, and plucks a small pink ChapStick tube from it. She slathers on the strawberry flavor. The cab in the Jeep fills with a sweet, fruity fragrance.

"Does it matter?" she asks, dropping her ChapStick back in her purse and then turning to look out at the dark mountains only illuminated by the moon, her arms crossing over her chest like a sulking teenager.

"It does if we want to be friends."

Goddammit, now she's got me trying to be friends. I'm not looking to date her, and I've never had to worry about being friend-zoned my whole life, but still, that isn't something I'd usually say if Tessa wasn't stonewalling me.

"Friends?!" she asks with a chuckle to her voice like my comment was a joke.

Now I sort of feel like a chump for my choice of words, but I need to find some way in, and if friendship is my trojan horse, then so be it.

Being at war with the Hawkeyes' public relations manager isn't doing me any favors. It pretty much stands for pain in my rectum.

"We're on the same team. Shouldn't we be at least... friend-ly?"

"We're enemies, Lake."

Enemies? That's the second time she's said that.

Yeah, maybe I didn't give her the warmest of welcomes the day she got a job at the Hawkeyes. I never thought we'd end up having to see each other more than a couple times a year back when she was only Brent's sister who lived in San Deigo.

"We are?" I ask, glancing over at her quickly, one eyebrow cocked in question.

"Of course we are," she says, tossing up her hands like she's done with me. "How many concussions have you had because the evidence is starting to show."

Have we had our issues? Hell yeah.

Do I hate Tessa...? Hate's a strong word. However, if she got fired, and I was only connected to her by way of Brent's little sister, I'd like her a lot more.

But either way, we're on this trip together, and now she's coming to stay at my house. I can't exactly ignore her while we are cohabitating, and my sister and nieces are about to meet her and see the way I treat her...

Oh shit.

My nieces...

I ease the steering wheel to the right and pull off the road onto the shoulder slowly.

"What are you doing?" she asks nervously, gripping the oh-shit handle above her window on the ceiling of the Jeep. The shoulder turns from asphalt to mud from the heavy rainfall over the last few weeks. Even with the way I eased off to the side of the road, the air freshener swings erratically back and forth while the beams of the Jeep's lights shine into the pitch-dark wooded area out in front of us. The heat from the Jeep rises off the hood and billows on the cold January night.

I look over at her and lean over the armrest a bit to get her attention.

"I want to forge a truce."

"A truce?" she asks, leaning farther away from me as I encroach in her space. I see her right hand down by her knee as it flattens.

She's ready to slap me if I try anything funny, and I want to laugh at the absurdity of the situation I find myself in. I've never incited a strong feeling in a woman to want to hit me for trying to kiss her.

Sure, I've been slapped plenty when they decided I misled them when I said one night only, and they chose to believe instead that I led them on. But not at the start of things heating.

Not that I plan to kiss Tessa anyway.

I need her on my side for what I'm about to ask her for next.

"Yeah," I say.

"After the shitty sixteen-hour flight, the baby puke, the lost luggage, the lost wallet, and the motel?" she asks, still trying to plaster herself against the Jeep's passenger door to stay as far away from me as possible.

"You lost your luggage and your wallet?" I ask, but she only stares back at me.

She looks at me like I'm not the same Lake Powers who was duking it out with her in Sam's office. The guy who ruined her vacation plans with some chump from college who finally thinks he can pull a chick who looks like Tessa, and intentionally requires her to come on a work trip knowing full well she'd end up without a place to stay.

I get her skepticism to the truce.

However, the sixteen-hour flight, the baby puke, which now makes sense from the smell, the luggage, and the missing wallet... which I only am now hearing about, none of those things are my fault. I can't take credit for Murphy's Law hitting Tessa on one fateful day.

"Even though I'm screwing up your vacation and making you do charity work?" she asks with even more suspicion.

"Yep," I tell her, and then I lean back off the armrest, which causes her shoulders to drop a little. She's backed off the defense now that I'm out of her personal space.

"I don't get it. You seem to have the upper hand here. Why offer me a truce? What's in it for you?" she asks, her eyes squinting at me.

She thinks something's amiss.

I'd love to get past this part without giving this all away, but Tessa won't agree without a thorough explanation and Tessa has a pretty accurate bullshit meter. I've seen her call out enough players on the team when they tell a tall tale in the break room or try to embellish a story at any level.

"Did I ever tell you that I have two older sisters?"

"Hmm... " she says, looking down at the floorboards of the Jeep trying to pull up a memory. "I think your mom mentioned it once."

When did Tessa meet my parents?

"My mom told you? When?"

Tessa stares out the window, not matching my surprise about the fact that she's talked to my mom. Where the hell was I during this?

"Phil Carlton brought your parents up to the owner's box once, and she and I chatted at the bar," she says nonchalantly. "Your parents are really sweet... is it possible the stork dropped you at the wrong house?"

Funny, she thinks she's a comedian.

My parents are nice, though. She has that right.

I bypass even commenting on her dig.

"My eldest sister has two daughters," I tell her.

"What does this have to do with a truce?"

How do I tell her I don't want my little six- and eight-year-old nieces seeing me fight with Tessa?

"They live next door, and the girls will be over every day... and I want them to be. I don't see them near enough, but if we're fighting, my sister won't let them come over."

"Oh..."

"She got divorced a few years ago. She and her ex used to fight a lot. She won't let the girls come over if she thinks we'll fight in front of them."

The girls have never seen me interact with women besides my sisters, mother, and female friends from Aspen that I grew up with.

"You'll stop making this trip a living hell if I agree to pretend to be nice to you?" she asks.

I meant being nice to each other, but whatever, I'll take it.

"Sure... yeah."

She thinks for a second. What the hell does she have to think about? This is good for both of us.

"Okay. I agree to your terms," she says, putting out her hand for us to shake on it.

I put my hand in hers, and we seal the deal.

Her hand feels soft and small in mine. I don't think I've ever touched her hand before.

I turn back to the steering wheel, put the Jeep back in drive, and pull back onto the highway.

This isn't how my sinister plan to teach Tessa a lesson was supposed to go, but I might like this scenario better.

"I have you scheduled for two days at the local dog rescue at the end of this week," she informs me.

"Ok," I say simply.

"When is your charity event? I have calls to make this week with players, but I'll make sure to be there to get photos for social media."

Shit... I didn't consider how tough it would be to keep her from finding out about Snow Dayz now that she's in town and staying at my house.

"Don't worry about it. Do your work instead. There will be professional photographers there and I will ask them to email you the best shots."

She seems to shrug it off.

Maybe she's too tired to fight me on this but I can't expect nosy Tessa not to try to pry again.

I'll have to think of a better excuse in case she asks again.

CHAPTER EIGHT

Tessa

Lake drives up a long winding road through tall trees covered in snow that must have fallen a few days ago since the roads are wet and muddy but clear of snow.

The high moon shines down on the wet asphalt, giving a reflection that we'll never catch, no matter how fast Lake drives. I sit on the passenger side, staring out the window while soft music plays from the radio station that's been playing in the background since I got in with Lake back at the motel.

His cinnamon-apple car freshener bobs and sways with the road's condition and gives a nice seasonal smell to the beautiful scenery out in front of me. It's so beautiful here.

I think about the truce Lake and I just entered into.

How long will this last?

A day?

A week?

It can't possibly last past the day we leave here. Lake doesn't respect what I'm trying to do for this hockey franchise, and I can't force him to want to follow the guidelines that I've outlined for the players in order to keep within the goals that Phil Carlton has given me to turn his team into the family-friendly franchise he wants.

His phone buzzes in the console.

> Harmony I heard you're in town. Better not forget to come see me. Miss you.

I roll my eyes. Chelsea... and now Harmony... Of course, he has a damn fan club here... why wouldn't he?

I readjust in my seat, and Lake doesn't even seem to be in the least bit of a hurry to respond. Probably because he doesn't want me to see the request he'll send for nudes.

Uck, guys.

I immediately want to call off the truce, but the fact I don't like that women are sending booty texts while I'm riding in the passenger seat of Lake's Jeep right now isn't a mature reason.

Lake takes a right, and the road turns between two large river rock structures that probably stand taller than me with two massive bronze elks almost the size of this Jeep perched on top.

"Where are we?" I ask, watching in the rearview mirror until the taillights from the Jeep are no longer bright enough to see the bronze statues as we leave them behind us.

"My house is in this subdivision," he tells me, keeping his eyes on the road.

A subdivision? I haven't even seen a single house yet. This certainly isn't like any kind of subdivision I'm familiar with.

Soon enough, a large house comes into view on the right, and then farther down the road, another large house shows to my left. Both are huge and built off the road a ways. Both were built to look more like a ski lodge than a house with large wood beams along with two-story floor-to-ceiling windows.

Lake continues to drive a little farther up the road until finally he slows and takes another right down a private drive.

We pull up to a massive house. Garden spotlights shine up against the house in the darkness of the night falling all around it. The warm amber lighting from the spotlights makes the mansion look as though it's glowing and so inviting.

The house features two stories and a walk-out basement, making the house three stories altogether. Its massive windows and two gigantic solid wood doors give it grandeur. Huge rough-cut timber and large stacked rocks make up the motif of the house, and a six-bay garage sits back a little farther from the front of the house.

Lake hits a button on the garage door opener and the first bay door lifts.

He points to the house on his left. It looks similar but more of a typical log house like the homes we passed on the street.

It's almost as big as this home but not quite, and it doesn't have the same grandeur that this one does.

"That's my sister's house," Lake says, looking back toward the garage as he pulls in.

I lean forward to look over him at the house as he pulls into the garage. I get a good enough look before Lake tucks us and the car slowly and safely into the garage bay.

"Seems like your two houses are closer together than most people's in this community," I say, unbuckling myself and reaching for the few things I have in my possession.

I notice another car in the garage now as well, parked on the other side of Lake. A shiny jet-black Porsche sedan that looks new and fast, but I know nothing about cars so that's all I can make out from here.

"It is," he says, unbuckling his seat as well. "I bought this place seven years ago. It was a double lot with two houses approved but had only one house built on it... this one," he says of the house we're currently inside. "When my sister divorced, she needed somewhere to go. I wanted her close, and I wanted the girls safe so I built her the house next door."

Was that my heart skipping a beat?

No way.

Absolutely not!

He opens his door after offering the answer and slides off his seat. I do the same, and we both close our doors.

"That was nice of you. Building her a home," I tell him.

It's something I imagine Brent would do for me.

I wait for him to walk in front of the Jeep and lead the way into the house. I have no idea what I'm in for tonight since it's so late. I look down at my phone, and I'm surprised to see the time reads just after one in the morning. I think it's safe to assume that the girls are asleep, and there will not be an impromptu meeting of Lake's family tonight.

"My sister needed support when she went through her divorce, and I was in a financial place to help her. I wouldn't want them anywhere else than right here next to me."

Who the hell is this guy, and what did he do with Playboy Lake Powers? Did he leave him in Seattle? I doubt it.

"You wouldn't?"

This new information doesn't line up with what I knew of Lake. He's known as the charming one-night-stand-only player of the Hawkeyes league.

Lake the family man just does not compute.

"Nowhere else," he says over his shoulder as I follow him to the garage door that I assume leads to the inside of the house.

"The code is #1212 to get into the house from any of the doors."

Really? That's easy?

It's not a number I'll forget.

"Your jersey number twice?" I ask, my eyebrows furrowed in confusion. "Isn't that... like... the first thing someone would try to break into your house?"

Lake just shrugs. "Maybe." And then he pushes the garage door open.

He hooks the Jeep key to the key ring hanging to the left of the door as we walk into a large mudroom. A row of beautifully laid-out wooden locker-style cabinets takes up the entire right side, a washer and dryer, and a big sink with a countertop to the left with upper cabinets. Dark onyx-colored slate tiles cover the floor. Smart for a mudroom in the winter.

"The Jeep is yours this week. I'll drive the Porsche," he says, walking through the mudroom and hooking a left. I follow, looking back behind us to see where a right turn would have taken us. Looks like a hallway that wraps around the entry of the front of the house and a powder room tucked in the corner. The door is just a little ajar, but I can see the toilet from here.

I turn my head to stare at the back of Lake's wide shoulders and follow him until the hallway opens up into the great room.

A huge room opens up to the top of the two-story ceiling. A floor-to-ceiling river rock fireplace takes over most of the wall to the left of the room. It's the biggest fireplace I've ever seen, and I'm pretty sure if I duck just a little, I could walk inside the damn thing. A big screen TV is mounted to the right of the fireplace, and a U-shaped couch that could probably seat twenty faces the fireplace and TV. A baby grand sits against the right side of the vast living room. Beyond it, large glass windows display the stunning scenery outside of this mansion with the moon casting down blue light like a halo on everything it touches.

"Wow," I whisper.

"It's a good view, huh? It's why I bought the house. You can see the Colorado River and the Rocky Mountains from here," Lake says proudly.

"It's... it's breathtaking," I say, completely mesmerized by the stunning view in front of me.

I want to run to the big windows and smash my hands against the glass and stare out at the mountains, trees, and river, but it's late, and Lake already took time to come all the way out to get me from that motel.

I'll never admit it, but I'm relieved he showed up and refused to let me stay. Even if it's one hundred percent his fault that I ended up there to begin with.

Lake gives me a small elbow nudge. "Come on. It'll be easier to see everything in the morning. You've had a long day, and we both need some sleep. Come with me, and I'll get you something to sleep in that's not covered in baby puke." He chuckles.

The reminder of the past twenty-four hours breaks me from my spell. I want to glare at him for taking enjoyment from my pain, but we made a pact to try to be nice to one another for the duration of this trip or at least for as long as I'm staying in the house.

Instead, I turn and follow him. After only a few steps, the large open-concept kitchen is now in view, and I swear it's the size of a damn cruise ship's kitchen.

It's the biggest kitchen I've ever seen in person.

"Who even cooks in this thing? You'd get lost in here."

"I do," he says, looking back over his shoulder at me as I continue to follow him.

I stop in front of the kitchen for a second. I pull out my phone to take a quick snapshot and fire the photo off to Autumn. I know it's after one in the morning, but no one will appreciate this more than her.

She must still be awake because I hear my phone buzz as Lake leads me farther away, headed for a flight of stairs.

> **Autumn:** Oh my God. Who do I have to marry for that?

> **Tessa:** Lake Powers

> **Autumn:** Never mind. Not worth it.

My instant reaction is to disagree with her... and not because I want the kitchen.

I stop dead in my tracks.

There is no way I just had that thought. I must be delusional from lack of sleep.

That could be it. Or this thinner air up here in the mountains is keeping my brain from working properly.

Sure, that's it.

> Tessa: Totally! Could you even imagine? An absolute nightmare!!!

Okay, that might be overselling it, but it's fine. She's probably half asleep anyway.

"You okay over there?" Lake asks.

I look up from my phone to see that he's over ten feet ahead of me.

"Yeah. Just fine," I tell him, tucking my phone into my back pocket and taking steps to catch up with him.

We both climb the stairs to the second story, and he leads me down the hallway.

The high ceilings carry up even to the second story, and I love the open feeling of it. The walls are mostly comprised of drywall with river rock or rough-cut lumber as an accent.

The deep gray colors of the walls have burnt orange and indigo blue accents around the house. The color palette is masculine, but the beauty of the place this house is set in gives it a feminine touch. Like it's touched by Mother Nature. I don't know... it just works.

Large pieces of artwork hang in every room that we've walked past. Pictures painted of the large elk, buffalo, the Rocky Mountains, and Native American paintings.

"The artwork here is incredible," I tell him, nearing the top of the staircase.

"They're good, right? I commissioned a local artist to do everything for me. I told him to come into the house and make as many pieces as he wanted, whatever size, whatever theme. I just wanted it to feel like Aspen."

"And this is what he came up with?" I ask.

Lake nods. "What do you think?"

"It's worth every penny. The artwork makes this house," I say.

"I agree," Lake says.

He turns back to make sure I'm right behind him and then turns left to head down the hall.

A large painting down the hallway catches my eye. A giant canvas against the right side of the hallway.

It takes my breath away.

It's a painting of a Native American woman cloaked in off-white furs and leathers. Tresses of her dark hair drift over her face as the wind sweeps over her. She's holding a bundled baby in her arms, wrapped in furs. You can't see the baby's face, only a tiny bit of its short black baby curls, but she holds the infant protectively as the deepness of her eyes stares back at you.

Chills run over my arms and down my spine.

I've never been moved by a painting before, but I can't stop looking at her.

There's something about the strength of her, the idea of this land being her home where she raises her children. In the peaceful views of Aspen and the quiet serenity.

I've never felt this way before. Almost a kinship to a place so quickly.

The drive up to Lake's house was so peaceful and his home is so inviting.

San Diego, where Brent and I grew up, is sunny and warm but vacant in a way I can't describe. Maybe it's because that's the place where we lost our parents? Lost our family. I can't be sure.

And Seattle is busy. People tell you that you get used to the dreary rain, but that still hasn't happened to me. I'm beginning to think after a year and a half, that those people lied to either me... or themselves.

Is it weird to want to feel a sense of closeness to a painting? Why is this feeling of wanting to follow in her footsteps and raise a child in this place rising out of nowhere?

I always assumed I'd want a family someday, but with all of my failed relationships and the fact that my mother and father won't be around to see me become a mother myself, I guess I've pushed down those desires for a long time.

So why are they stirring up now?

I turn to follow Lake and see him down at the end of the hallway.

Double wood doors, the same color as the floors that run throughout the entire house, stand tall and proud at the end of the hall. They look hand carved and expensive, just like every other door in this house. Their protective stance makes it seem as though they protect the contents of the primary bedroom beyond it.

We walk down the hall, and I take note of three additional single doors that match the thick-cut master bedroom doors.

He opens the door and walks through. I hesitate for a second, but he doesn't turn around to see it.

I'm a grown-ass woman who can certainly walk through another man's bedroom. Especially a man I'm not even fond of.

The truth is, I'm not worried about Lake... it's me I have to be concerned about.

I'm a woman who has a type... hot hockey players.

And now, not only am I alone in a room with one of the hottest players in the league but my body is primed for a release.

Lake might have foiled my plans to get laid out all week in Mexico by the billionaire heir to the Copeland Athletic brand, but my body doesn't seem to know the difference between Cabo, Mexico, and Aspen, Colorado. She is ready for action and horny as hell.

And the man walking in front of me has a reputation that suggests he knows exactly what to do with my body and how to pull multiple orgasms from it.

I try to coach my body to suck it up as I walk through Lake's bedroom, but I swear to God, his Fiji deodorant that he wears daily smells like a tropical vacation like coconut and palm trees, with a dash of spicy cinnamon. My body is completely confused as to why I'm not already jumping his bones.

Cinnamon... more like Sin-a-man. And hooking up with Lake would be nothing short of sinful.

Lake's bedroom continues the medium-stained wide-plank flooring. His room is painted an even more masculine dark blue color with a dark espresso wood bed frame and a dark leather padded headboard that has me wondering what it would feel like to have Lake rail me against it over and over again.

I shake the idea out and keep my eyes on the back of Lake.

I'm trying to ignore the matching side tables where only one side currently looks as though it's ever been used. The other side looks lonely and forgotten. Why does that make me smile on the inside, that no woman seems to have staked her claim?

There's no TV in the bedroom, and I have to say that seems rare for a bachelor.

I follow him through his beautiful bathroom, which features a rainfall shower. It looks like it was ripped from a damn forest waterfall. River rocks bulge out from the corner of the shower walls, and I can imagine that the effect of the water trickling down the rocks has got to sound like the rainforest when you're inside. A huge freestanding copper soak-in tub sits along the opposite side of the shower, and the door to what I presume is his walk-in closet is located just beyond.

Lake heads for it and opens the door. I have to see the floor-to-ceiling closet, but Lake's things take up less than a fourth of the room.

My jaw drops once I finally step inside.

It's a huge room with an enormous island in the middle for accessories. The closet is as big as the room I have at Brent's house in Seattle, and I can't imagine having this much space for everything.

"Are you planning on filling this thing up one day?" I tease, looking around at everything.

"No," he says simply, with a stern look on his face but doesn't give any more.

"Oh…" I say, looking back at him, but then avert my eyes when his warning look tells me not to ask any follow-up questions.

That's not like him. He's always sporting a cocky smirk or a charm-your-panties-off smile.

He shakes off whatever has come over him.

Whatever he was feeling, it's obvious he didn't want to show me that part of him.

Lake walks over to the back corner where most of his things are and reaches into a drawer.

I almost cringe when I wonder if he has a drawer of outfits for women to wear who stay over… maybe even leftover stuff that a puck bunny or two left behind.

I groan at the idea, but he's too far away to hear me.

If he hands me that, the treaty is over. I'm ripping it up, burning it, and then dancing on its ashes.

"Here. I don't have anything your size. You're too tiny to wear anything I own, but these should fit," he says, and then hands me what looks like his middle school gym shirt and matching shorts.

Did he keep these? Is he the sentimental type?

I would never have pegged him as such.

But there's one thing I can't let go, and my heart is galloping a mile a minute.

"Did you just call me tiny?" I ask, trying to keep my smile from beaming like the scorching brightness of the sun.

Sure to melt Lake's face right off.

I'm not tiny. Not in the slightest.

At five foot nine, and the weight of a girl who encourages girls' night once a week, I have an excuse for fast food, hard ciders, and Autumn's newest culinary confections. I'm not the stick figure puck bunny Lake is used to.

"Yeah," he says, and then takes a quick scan of me in assessment, but it doesn't stop little goose bumps from raising at his perusal. "You're like what... a hundred and five... a hundred and ten, maybe?"

My jaw drops, and I'm about to claw my way up this man and plant a kiss right on his damn mouth.

"Uh... yeah... sure, something like that," I say, sure as hell not about to tell him my real weight.

If that's his guess, then that's now cemented for all eternity, just like how I'll never be older than twenty-nine.

"If these don't work, I can—" he says, handing them over.

"No, this is fine. This should be great," I say, taking the two articles of clothing from him as my fingers brush against his.

I try not to let myself think about the touch as I quickly move on, laying the shirt and shorts he gave me on the walk-in closet island and then crossing my arms over my hoodie and lifting in an attempt to quickly put on the shirt to prove to him that what he gave me will work.

Why am I so excited to wear Lake's middle school gym shirt? I have no freaking idea, but I am.

The second the coolness of the closet and the bareness of my skin collide, I know what I've just done, and I freeze in position. Not the best reaction when you're only wearing a blush-pink scalloped lace bra that you were supposed to be wearing for Elliot in Cabo.

I hear Lake clear his throat. He can see my practically bare tits in my see-through bra… there's no way around it. My sweater works to cover my face from view and my complete and utter embarrassment.

My cheeks are probably as red as a tomato.

I pull my sweater back down immediately and clear my voice, reaching over and quickly grabbing the clothes that Lake gave me off the closet island.

I need to get out of here and bury my head in a pillow to scream.

"Okay, well thanks for this," I say.

I make the mistake of looking back up at Lake before I turn around and run out of the closet.

He's still staring at my chest even though my sweater is back over my breasts. Then his eyes reach back up to mine, and I can see his pupils have dilated, and an almost savage look creeps over his face. The look of pure desire and now I know I need to move.

Get out of this room before you end up under him.

"I'm a… I'm going to head for bed," I say, starting to back up.

Lake takes a step toward me. "Here, I haven't shown you where your room is yet. Let me take you."

"No, no!" I shake out my free hand, the one without the gym clothes in it. "It's fine. I'm sure I can find it," I assure him, backing out quickly. "Which room?" I say as I'm already free and clear of the closet and halfway through the bathroom.

He starts taking slow steps out of the closet, following me but letting me get farther and farther away from him. He knows I'm mortified. I can see it as his face changes from a man with an instant feral reaction to my practically bare breasts to now a man feeling a little sorry for me.

"It's the first one on your left, down the hall. It has an en suite for you," he says.

I don't look back, keeping my head down and staying on course.

"Okay, thanks. Good night."

"Night. Let me know if you need anything," he says, stepping out of the bathroom and into his bedroom as he watches me hightail it past his master bedroom doors.

I pull his door shut behind me with a loud thud, showing him that this night is over by physically closing the door on any more conversation.

CHAPTER NINE

Lake

The morning couldn't come soon enough. I walk down to the large kitchen and pull out two pans, a carton of eggs, and a package of bacon from the fridge. A few things I asked my sister to pick up for me at the grocery store before I got here yesterday.

I like doing my own grocery shopping, so I only asked for the bare minimum.

I place the two black pans, one small for eggs and one square in shape for the bacon, on the gas range stove under the big copper hammered range hood that is the centerpiece of the mahogany dark stained cabinets and black marble countertops. The designer insisted on the copper metal to break up the dark finishes of the rest of the kitchen... she was right.

I begin to break open the eggs over the pan, adding a little milk, a dash of salt and pepper, and a handful of cheese. I don't usually add cheese to my eggs; the hockey team's dietitian wouldn't like it, but I don't know how Tessa likes her eggs. By how much milk she pours into her coffee when I've seen her in the break room, she's not lactose intolerant.

Speaking of coffee...

I walk over quickly and pull down the K-Cups and set them next to the single-serve coffee maker, along with the sugar.

I'd make myself a cup if I liked coffee. A little caffeine hit would help since I never reached REM sleep last night, not knowing that Tessa was sleeping right down the hall from me. Barely more than a wall separated us.

I push a K-Cup into the machine and then lock it down and hit the middle button to brew a cup for her, then walk back over to the eggs.

The memory of last night flashes through my mind again.

Holy shit, those tits are something else.

My cock sprang to full mast the second she lifted her sweater.

I wasn't expecting her to be wearing a sexy as fuck bra under that Hawkeyes sweatshirt. I wasn't expecting to see Tessa's perfect breasts and mauve-colored nipples saluting me through the see-through lace from across my walk-in closet.

If she had waited even another second before pulling down her sweatshirt and covering up those perfect mounds, I would have been on her and bent down, pulling her nipple into my mouth and sucking down on her; tasting her and pulling moans from her lips. We would have never made it out of my closet last night.

And to think, the nerd she went to college with almost ended up with that imagery instead of me. My jaw tightens, and my hand grips the panhandle a little tighter as I stir the eggs.

I ended up flipping the comforter off me before five o'clock, finally giving in to the fact that I wasn't going to sleep with Tessa's nipples dancing around behind my eyelids and this boner I couldn't seem to shake.

I jumped into the shower and rubbed one out to the fantasy of what I would have done to Tessa if I thought I wouldn't have been greeted with a slap from her and a plexiglass check from her brother when I got home for fucking his sister and keeping to my rules of only one night.

Then I went down to my daylight basement gym and worked out until I was too tired to think of Tessa anymore while I looked out over the view that does its job to reenergize me and get me back out on the ice.

My workout didn't work to tire out my cock though. While taking a second shower in the downstairs gym, my cock just stared back up at me letting me know that this weird infatuation with Tessa isn't going anywhere anytime soon.

I should just fuck her and get it over with like Reeve said, but I know that's a bad idea. First, because I don't think she'll let me anywhere near her, and second, I'm not convinced one time with her will work based on the fact that my cock still doesn't feel sated after yanking off to the thought of her twice.

Finally, I hear the sound of a heavy door opening on the second floor. It's faint since this place is practically soundproof. I hold my breath and listen closely, willing the bacon sizzle to shut the fuck up, but it doesn't listen.

Soon, I hear the telling signs of a small, beautiful human with a great rack making her way down the staircase from the second floor.

I don't look behind me when I hear Tessa enter the kitchen. I let out a small sigh that the wait to be back in her presence is over.

What the fuck is wrong with me?

"You hungry?" I ask, flipping the six strips of marbled bacon in the flat pan.

I glance over my shoulder. I can't fucking stop myself.

I catch her giving my shirtless body a full scan and her tongue darting out to wet her bottom lip as she picks a stool at the large island designed to seat ten and slides up onto it.

Her eyes break away the second she sees that I caught her, and she looks down at the countertop as if she needs to focus on seating herself.

Bullshit.

I smile to myself. Maybe I'm not the only one affected by last night.

Cooking shirtless might be a little reckless with hot pans nearby but with her reaction to my body, I'm glad I'm taking the risk.

"Yes... please," she says.

Well, now she knows how to say please. It would have been a hell of a lot more convenient if she could have said that a few days ago, and then I wouldn't have forced Sam's hand to make her come with me to Aspen.

... and then she'd be standing on the beach right now with barely anything on while some tool who doesn't deserve to touch her would be pinning her down every night.

I flip a piece of bacon with a little more vigor than I mean to at the thought of her in a hotel room alone with that cock.

The bacon grease spits out at me and lands on my stomach and hand.

I hiss at the quick pain while jumping back.

"Are you okay?" Tessa asks.

I hear her jump off her stool and race over. Her hand pushes on my left arm to push me back farther from the range so she can see.

"Where did it get you?" she asks, her eyes quickly glancing over at my stomach, where my right hand wipes away at the grease with a dish towel that I already had sitting on the countertop in case of a spill. A little hit my thumb and wrist as well, and I put the grease spot to my mouth, sucking it off and soothing the burn with a flick of my tongue.

"I'm fine. It just got me a little on my stomach and hand, but I'm fine," I assure her.

Her eyes assess my abs, and I automatically flex at her notice.

Her fingertips reach out for me and brush softly over the area I had just wiped clean of the grease. My cock jolts at her touch, and now I have a goddamn half-chub.

It was barely even a touch.

What the fuck are you doing to me, Tessie?

"It looks a little red," she says, looking at the spot where the hot bacon juices hit me. "Here, let me get you an ice pack," she says, turning toward the fridge down against the wall to my right and next to the coffee maker.

An ice pack?

For a little burn?

"Tessa, it's fine. I promise," I tell her, still stirring the eggs to make sure they don't burn.

She ignores me and heads for the commercial-grade stainless-steel fridge, looking over at the setup I have for her next to the coffee maker. She smiles, glancing back at me with an inquisitive look on her face.

"Did you make me coffee?" she asks, continuing to the freezer.

"What if the coffee is for me?" I shoot the question back.

"You don't drink coffee," she says simply, giving the heavy commercial freezer door a good yank to open it.

She just unconsciously let out a little secret... She's been watching me and just now admitted to it. And I too just proved to her that I've been watching her the same.

I know she can't start her day without coffee, and she knows... I won't drink that shit.

"Okay, you caught me," I admit.

She sends out a little giggle and my ears perk up. Tessa Tomlin has never giggled at anything I have ever said. She usually just scowls at me.

How do I know that she likes coffee? Because I've seen her make a new coffee or reheat an old one over a hundred times in the break room at the Hawkeyes stadium, but with how many times I've been in the break room, could I tell you how many other Hawkeyes employees drink coffee?

Fuck no.

But plenty of the times I've seen her drinking coffee, I've thought about spiking it with a laxative. Especially after the last charity event she made me do for the last social media post she got me in trouble for.

She plucks an ice pack from the freezer and then shuts the door. I haven't seen an ice pack since my offseason when I spent my days in Aspen, soaking up a normal life in the town I grew up in with my nieces running around my house and Chelsea nagging at me about one thing or the other as sisters do.

Most people don't get it, but to me, it's fucking heaven after spending months keeping the Lake Powers brand going.

It's exhausting work to always be "on," but that's exactly what it feels like these days... work.

I watch her every move, trying like hell to make sure she doesn't catch me, but she seems a little in her own world as she saunters back over.

She looks up at my shoulder, and now I know what's coming. I'm surprised she didn't ask in the locker room back when this whole thing about the tagged photo came up, but I think she was so pissed off at me that she didn't give a shit about it. Or maybe she was too busy admiring my cock when Reeve yanked down my towel.

"Where did that come from?" she asks, pointing at the scar over my left pec.

This is the last thing I want to fucking talk about. This is a part of my life I don't want anyone to see, especially not her.

"It's nothing," I say, and then toss the long hand towel over my shoulder, covering up most of the scar, and then move closer to the range to cut her out and busy myself with moving the bacon off the pan and onto a plate with paper towels to soak up the leftover grease.

I got a tattoo a year after the accident in an attempt to cover most of it up.

You can't see it from far away or in the dark with the ink covering its long-jagged outline. And I do my best not to walk around without a shirt on in large groups, although pool parties and boating at the lake make it tough. Luckily, most people are too drunk at that point to notice a covered-up scar.

Unfortunately, it's daylight, she's standing close, and Tessa is too aware of everything around her not to notice it.

"Was it from a fight on the ice?" she asks.

Nosy woman.

I turn to her with a sharp brow lifted. "I don't want to talk about it. Do you understand?" I try to ask as softly as I can. I don't want to scare her away, but I need her to know that she is the very last person on this planet I'm going to tell my story to.

She'll never look at me the same way, and that shouldn't bother me, but it does. It's the reason I'm incapable of giving her a future.

"Okay." She nods somberly, and then I turn back and offload the eggs onto an awaiting plate with a spatula. "Here." She presses the ice pack to my stomach, which catches me off guard.

The cold burst travels down to my balls, and they tighten and make a run for the warmth of the insides of my stomach.

"Shit!" I yell and drop the spatula on the ground.

I swear to God my balls lodge into my throat as I try to take an inhale but can't.

Tessa jumps at my raised voice and then bends down quickly to recover the spatula.

Just then, the side door to the kitchen opens.

My sister, probably.

I look over the island countertop and smile as she walks in but then remember that I didn't tell her I brought a woman home.

I've never brought a woman home to this house, and I can't imagine what my sister's reaction will be, but I'm about to find out.

I want to hold Tessa's head down as she bends over in front of me to retrieve the falling spatula so that my sister doesn't see her, and I can shoo Chelsea off, but goddammit, the imagery of holding Tessa's head down has my cock hardening.

Fuck!

Instead, Tessa straightens up quickly at the sound of our morning guest... not to be confused with my morning wood, which won't fucking die, and Tessa's eyes widen as she sees my sister standing in the kitchen side door.

My sister looks like a kid who just walked in on her mom and dad doing the dirty on the family kitchen dinner table. Her cheeks turn pink, and her jaw drops open.

"Oh! I... I didn't know you had..." my sister stutters as she immediately starts backing up toward the door, giving the top half of Tessa a quick scan.

She can see that Tessa is in my old gym shirt, and I'm sure she's making instant assumptions.

I can hear my nieces' chipper voices as they come up the walkway along the house, headed for the door.

My sister barricades the side door, using her arms and body to block the view of my house from my nieces as they try to enter.

"Chelsea, it's not what you think," I tell her, taking a step toward her and then remembering I'm shirtless with an erection and Tessa's wearing my clothes to sleep in.

Ok, I'll admit it looks bad.

Dammit!

I hope she won't stop the girls from coming over here now.

"Momma, let us in!" Sadie yells, banging against the door.

"We want to see Uncle Lake. We made him pictures!" Lana wails.

"I swear, Chelsea, nothing's going on. We work together," I tell her, covering up my insatiable hard-on.

That's not helping, buddy.

I take a couple of steps back and move to cover myself up behind the island.

I didn't tell my sister about the fact that I tricked a woman from work to come out to Aspen so I could teach her a lesson. She wouldn't have been happy with me about it, and I figured I could keep my two worlds separate.... the way I have been for years.

If Tessa had found a safe place to stay, I might have pulled it off.

In hindsight, I realize I set myself up for this.

"Mom!" the girls scream in unison.

Tessa looks at me, reading the situation.

"He's telling the truth. We work together, and we can't stand each other," she adds.

"That's not what we discussed," I whisper to her.

Tessa throws up her hands as if she's done helping me if I can't be grateful for her trying to bail me out.

"Then why are you here?" Chelsea asks Tessa.

"Because I was staying at the Royal Inn—"

"Oh God!" my sister cuts her off and looks over at me as if to say "Could you imagine this pretty little thing spending the night in that filth?"

"Yeah, I know." I confirm my sister's nonverbal comment.

"So..." Tessa looks back up at me to her left. "Your brother came and got me last night and let me stay here." She looks back at Chelsea. "And my clothes are taking a separate holiday in Salt Lake City where the airlines left them, so I had to wear your brother's clothes last night."

"Oh," my sister says, taking one more glance over Tessa's outfit. "Do you need something to wear until your stuff gets here?" she asks, finally moving aside just slightly as my nieces see their opening and bum-rush through the small gap my sister gives them.

They both immediately jump up on a stool at the island, allowing me to stay safely tucked behind it, and slap pieces of white printer paper with drawings that look slightly like one big blob holding hands with two other smaller blobs.

Luckily, with my sister and nieces in my kitchen, my cock has gotten the message that it's not going to get any action with Tessa and is dying a quick death.

Thank fuck.

"Tessa, these are my nieces Sadie and Lana... and my sister Chelsea," I tell her.

The second I say the name Chelsea, Tessa's eyes jet up to mine. I smirk down at her... turns out that look in Sam's office might have been what I thought it was after all. She wasn't happy that an unknown woman was texting me.

I like that she thought it was some puck bunny from Aspen. I also like that she was wrong.

But most of all... I like that she was jealous.

Tessa

Now that the issues with Lake's sister are defused, and I know Chelsea isn't some woman who will be coming over late at night to keep me up while Lake thrusts her against his headboard, I walk over to the coffee machine while Lake fawns over the pictures his nieces drew for him.

This isn't the first time I've seen Lake with kids. He's always been good with them whenever I see him interact with them during player signings, meet and greets, and anytime a kid stops him and asks for a selfie outside of the stadium, but that's his job. Kid fans turn into adult fans, and every fan makes the team and the company Lake endorses money, so it's job security.

Even still, my ovaries twitch at the sight of him with them.

Seeing him with his nieces is completely different and completely the same. He's just as sweet, just as patient, just as interested in conversing with them, whether they are a fan he doesn't know or a sweet little girl who he shares DNA with.

My heart pumps a little faster as I watch Lake leaning over the island, his elbows and forearms propped against the countertop, taking on part of his weight, his right ankle crossed over the back of his left as he listens intently to the girls who fill any possible silence with gibber gabber. Lake doesn't even bother to try to slide in a word edgewise. He just leans in with a genuine smile across his lips as the girls tell him all about the drawings they made for him, Sadie's piano recital, and Lana's dance camp.

I look over at the forgotten breakfast, realizing that he's too enthralled with the girls to remember to eat.

I slide my coffee cup into the microwave to heat it a little since it's no longer piping hot like I like it, and then I walk over and dish up Lake a plate.

In my peripheral, I see Chelsea watching me, and then she wanders over to me while I add eggs and bacon to Lake's plate.

"So you work for the Hawkeyes?" she asks.

I glance up quickly at her to make eye contact and then focus back on the food I'm scooping up for him.

"Yeah. I'm the public relations manager. I'm in charge of making sure the franchise and the players' media presence looks good, and I deal with letting media outlets know what questions they can and can't ask in pre and post-game interviews."

I see Lake glance at us for a quick second and then focus on the girls.

I walk over to the fridge and pull on the thick stainless steel handle. I grab the ketchup bottle from the side door of the refrigerator. I know he has a strict diet, but who can eat eggs without ketchup? I walk back over to the plate and squeeze a circle blob of ketchup for him to dip his egg in the condiment if he wants to.

"Isn't bye week usually a vacation week for the team? Did you pull the short straw having to follow my brother out here or something?" she asks with a glint in her eye as the idea amuses her.

Short straw? There's nothing short about Lake's straw, but pulling on it is the last thing I plan to do.

"Something like that," I say, giving side-eye to Lake when he turns and gives me a cocky smirk.

Punk.

I pull open three drawers in search of a fork but come up empty until Chelsea opens the drawer next to her and hands it to me.

"Thanks," I tell her, and then set the plate of food that Lake made and I assembled in front of him.

Chelsea looks at me with her lip pulling up on one side like she's trying to hide her smile. Lake looks down at the food and then up at me from his hunched-over position, talking to the girls.

"You didn't have to do that," he says softly with the girl's chatter continuing without his observation.

I just shrug in response.

"I didn't know if you like ketchup, but..." I say, pointing at the pile of red goop on his plate.

"I do, thanks," he says, then glances back at the range with all food sitting next to it on plates from where he set it all. "Have you gotten any?" he asks, his eyes searching mine.

"Not yet, but I'm getting some now."

I turn away from him and walk back over to the range, and I hear his fork clink with the plate.

He's eating.

I smile to myself that he didn't refuse it, not that he would. We agreed to a truce for now, but old habits die hard.

"Lake," Chelsea says, looking down at her phone. "Don't you have a meeting with—"

"Shit!" Lake looks down at his watch like Chelsea reminded him of something he was about to miss. "I mean, shoot. Sorry, girls," he says, apologizing to Sadie and Lana for his language.

Neither girl seems to notice as they compare their pictures while sitting side by side on the barstools.

He turns to Chelsea. "I need to be there in thirty minutes."

"What meeting?" I walk over to the microwave and pull out my coffee and then begin to add the contents to make it delicious.

"He's meeting with—"

"No one important," Lake says, quickly cutting off Chelsea.

Her eyebrows furrow, and she stares at the back of his head in confusion.

"If she's the one who helps you with charity stuff to boost your image—"

"e it, Chelsea," he warns, giving her a long stare to make sure she doesn't plan to say anymore.

What the hell is that look for?

She looks at me and then back at him and gives a knowing nod like a puzzle piece finally fit into place for her.

What the hell does she know? And what did she just realize?

Lake turns and looks back at me. "I'll be back in a couple of hours, but you'll have the Jeep if you want to go anywhere."

"I have work to do here anyway. I won't likely leave," I tell him.

"Okay." He nods. "My cousin Bobby is getting some people I know together tonight at the pizza parlor... if you want to go?" he asks.

Is that hope twinkling in his eye?

"Sounds interesting. I'm in," I say, taking a sip of my coffee to check that it's yummy enough to consume.

"Good. I'll see you later," Lake says.

He walks over to the sink, rinses off his plate quickly, and sets it in the deep copper basin.

Then he walks over to Sadie and Lana on the island and kisses the tops of their heads. On his way out of the kitchen, he bends down and kisses the top of Chelsea's head while she stays seated at the kitchen table, and then he's gone.

The warmness of this man who seems so considerate and sweet, without the cocky swagger he carries around whenever I see him in Seattle. But here in Aspen with his family, he's a different man.

I hear him take two steps at a time as he ascends the stairs.

Chelsea finally stands from the chair she was sitting in. "Tessa, come over later if you want and borrow some clothes. I think we're about the same size, and the perk of owning a clothing store is that I have a ton of cute stuff for you to pick from," she offers.

"Thanks, that would be great," I say, taking another sip after stirring my coffee a little more to get the granulated sugar to dissolve.

It needs cream. Milk isn't cutting the acid of the coffee, but it will do until we go into town, and I can stop at the grocery store.

"Come on, girls. Let's go back to the house," Chelsea tells Sadie and Lana.

After Chelsea and the girls leave, I find the laptop bag that I set in the mudroom last night and carry it to the table. Then I pull out the card with the phone number and claim number the airline employee gave me last night, and I dial the number.

"Thank you for traveling with us. If you're looking to locate your lost luggage, please press 1 to be routed to our automated system…"

Great… not a real person.

I press 1 and follow the prompts.

"We've located your luggage using the claim number you provided," the automated voice says. "Your luggage doesn't have a set date of arrival at this time due to weather conditions. Please contact your local airport for further assistance. Thank you, goodbye." And the system hangs up on me.

Are you kidding me!?

"You suck!" I yell at the phone when loud footsteps echo down the staircase and through the hallway.

A gorgeous Lake comes into view in a long-sleeved dark Henley and a pair of intentionally distressed jeans that hug his ass and glutes in all the right places. I try not to stare, but it's a tough feat to accomplish.

"What happened?" he asks, twisting a watch he wasn't wearing earlier.

"The airline still has no idea when I'm going to get my stuff."

I flop my phone on the table with a bang. Frustration is getting the best of me. And where exactly is he going looking like a freaking snack?

Somewhere he doesn't want me to know about, and now my curiosity builds. Chelsea's reaction to him not wanting me to know has me wanting to go over and get the information from her while I peruse her closet.

A covert mission.

Maybe it was the other woman who texted him last night while I was in his Jeep. Harmony, I think it was?

"Shit, really? What about your wallet?" he asks.

"Penelope already texted me this morning before I got out of bed." The poor thing sat on hold with the airport while someone rummaged through the lost and found... while on her vacation. She didn't need to do that, but I appreciate her for helping out. She knew I was up until after two in the morning with all the chaos last night. "They found it, but the airline policy is that they have to send it back to the address on the driver's license inside the wallet, so it's headed to my brother's in Seattle."

"At least they found it. Trying to get all that shit reissued is a pain," he says, double-checking the time. He walks over to the fridge and pulls out a couple of bottled waters. "I'm out of here, but I'll see you later." He walks over to me as my head is down, typing in the code to my password on my laptop, and kisses the top of my head.

My fingers freeze on the keypad, and he doesn't make a single movement after that kiss either.

We're both holding our breath, I can feel it.

I finally look up at him, not sure what to say.

He looks flabbergasted too, his eyes wider than usual and that sharp brow has turned down as he looks at me.

"Sorry... I, uh... I don't know why I just did that," he admits.

"Force of habit?" I offer as a suggestion.

"Yeah... I think so," he says, not taking his eyes off mine.

My phone dings at a text.

> Autumn: What's this about a nip slip?! Did you flash Lake? What the hell is going on in Aspen? Tell me everything!!!

Lake sees the text... I know he does, and I could die of mortification that he knows I told the girls about our incident last night.

I guess we're even for embarrassing moments at the present.

"You're going to be late," I tell him, looking forward to the moment that Lake leaves, and we no longer have this weirdness between us.

"Right... okay... see you in a few hours."

And then he's out of the kitchen and headed down the hallway toward the mudroom and then the garage.

I listen for the Porsche's engine to come to life and the garage door to open.

The second the garage door closes after he pulls out of it, I breathe a sigh of relief.

CHAPTER TEN

Lake

"I like the layout of this building more. I think we can fit twice as many cots than in the other two buildings that the real estate agent sent," my cousin Bobby says.

We're both leaning over the light oak conference table set to seat twelve at least, inside the real estate agent's office.

Bobby places his left hand down on the conference table to steady himself as he stretches his right arm over the blueprints to point out a feature.

"And a bonus, it already has plumbing for the showers we'll need the contractor to install."

Bobby points at the bathroom area on the building's blueprints, splayed out for us to look over.

"Have you shown the contractor these yet?" I ask, leaning further over the blueprints.

The bathrooms aren't in place yet, but having the plumbing already in position will save money and time to get this shelter up and running.

"Are you sure this is the best of the three options?" I ask Bobby, and then glance over at the real estate agent who's standing opposite us around the conference table.

"I can still keep my eyes open," she says, her green eyes shifting between us. "Something else might come up. I have my feelers out there in Denver." Emma, Bobby's ex-girlfriend from high school, is now our real estate agent.

She knows her shit, and she's made a big name for herself in the commercial space of Denver. She flew in to have this meeting with us as a courtesy and to finalize the building and get signatures.

The real estate firm she's with has offices all over the country and opened their Aspen doors for us to use their conference room to go over the three sets of blueprints.

"What does your gut say? You've seen all three in person," I ask, turning to Bobby.

"This one. It has a commercial-grade kitchen, an easy way to divide spaces as we need for men's and women's shelters respectively. And the location is easy to access for anyone needing help."

I nod at him. After going over each building and its pro/con list, I think Bobby's right.

"Okay. Do whatever you need to do to make this happen. You have my approval to move forward." I look at both of them and turn to Bobby. "I'm heading out. You can take it from here?"

"Sure thing. I'll see you tonight at RockHouse?" He's referring to the local pizza and brew restaurant that we frequent when I'm home.

They have good food, good beer on tap, and plenty of pool tables and large-screen TVs with all the games playing. What more could a guy want?

"Just a heads-up, it might get crowded tonight. Word got out that you're home," Bobby tells me with a crooked frown like he knows I won't like it, but not much can soil my good mood right now.

I'm not sure if it's finally seeing the fruits of our labor coming to fruition with the buying of a building to start the largest shelter we've committed to thus far, or if it's the pain-in-the-ass woman currently hanging out at my kitchen table texting the girls about what happened last night... not that anything did. But she sure as hell thought it was something if Autumn heard from someone else about the nip slip.

Either Isla or Penelope got the information first, which means it's circulating.

I don't know if that's good news for me or not, but I'm about to find out.

"It'll all be fine. I'll see you tonight," I tell him, taking one more glance at the building that's about to cost me the biggest chunk of money I've ever spent, and that includes the houses I bought for myself and the houses for my family... combined.

A dream is finally coming true, and I wish the person who first dreamed it was here to witness it.

Tessa

The garage door opens a few minutes after I get back from Chelsea's house, dressed and ready for tonight, although the woman is a freaking fortress and wouldn't give up a single inch of information as to where Lake went or who he was meeting with.

I hear the sound of a vehicle rev its engine as it pulls into the garage bay. Likely it's a Porsche with a handsome hockey player inside, a hockey player I've sworn to myself I'll never touch.

As the garage door closes, I wait impatiently for the heavy door to the mudroom to open.

When it does, I jump slightly and then shake my head at myself. How embarrassing. I'm glad Lake can't see me right now.

"Tessa, you here?" Lake's deep voice echoes through the mudroom and reaches me in the kitchen, where I'm loading the dishwasher from today's breakfast.

The clanking of dishes fills the background noise.

I meant to have it done already, but with the pre-scheduled meeting with players over the Internet and then going over to Chelsea's, I didn't have time.

"Yeah, I'm in the kitchen," I say back.

Soon, Lake's footsteps get close enough that I see him emerge from the hallway.

"You look nice," he says, giving my outfit a full top-to-bottom scan. "Did you go over to my sister's?"

It's the first time he's seeing me in something other than his childhood gym wear since last night.

"Yep, she let me borrow this outfit, a pair of pajamas, and some clothes for tomorrow. Hopefully, my stuff will be here by then," I say.

Otherwise, at this point, they might as well send my stuff back to Seattle. I'll be home before I even get my luggage.

"Grab whatever you're going to need for dinner tonight. We're leaving." He turns toward the hallway and walks back out of the kitchen, leaving me behind.

"Wait, what?" I ask, bending down quickly, slamming the dishwasher closed, hitting the cycle button, and then heading for the kitchen table.

I grab my phone off the kitchen table. It's the only thing I'll need besides the shoes that I took off by the side door when I came back from Chelsea's.

I chase him down the hallway, his calm steps allowing me to catch up.

"I'm taking you shopping. Looks like you're going to get that shopping spree we bet on after all." His voice echoes through the large house. I follow him until we reach the mudroom, and he grabs the keys back off the key chain.

Oh... we are going.

"A shopping spree? I don't need that."

He doesn't answer as he opens the door to the garage and heads out without me. I'm about to miss my ride.

I run to my shoes and slip them on. I have no idea why he's in such a damn rush.

Twenty minutes later, Lake pulls up to a beautiful boutique with a sparkling chandelier in the entryway and a big pretty sign with the name JUNIPER on the front.

"This seems a bit too fancy for a few outfits to get me by. I'm sure your sister will let me borrow whatever I need, and I washed my shirt and pants from the flight. I'm fine... I don't need this," I tell him, looking in at the clothes that scream "your entire paycheck for one Burberry jacket."

It's not like I don't make enough money to afford a store like this. The Hawkeyes pay me well for what I do, but when I say "well," I mean more like I could afford to shop here once in a while and pick up one wardrobe staple piece, like a nice jacket to go out to the bar with the girls for my birthday, or a killer dress I'd wear to a charity event ...that one of my exes was attending... to make them eat their heart out for not appreciating what they had.

I sure as hell wouldn't be walking into a store like this to buy a week's worth of outfits and dropping the money like I'm buying a candy bar at the quicky-stop, like Lake's acting.

"You're here because of me, so the least I can do is make good on the bet I lost," he says, killing the engine and then pulling his keys from the ignition.

I hear his side of the Jeep door open as the car shifts from his weight leaving the vehicle.

"Come on, Tomlin, don't make me pull you out of this Jeep and toss you over my shoulder, kicking and screaming."

Why does the idea of Lake flinging me over his shoulder sound so appealing?

Because he's strong and being picked up and carried like I weigh nothing by an attractive hockey player has my panties dampening? Or is it because the idea of having Lake's hands on me has shivers cascading down my spine?

I debate pretending to refuse his command... just to see what he'll do, but then I remember... putting myself in a position to fall for Lake Powers is a really, really bad idea. I turn to the Jeep door and open it, obeying his orders to keep my libido from flaring up, but I slam the door once I exit to remind him that I don't like being told what to do.

I'm nothing if not consistent.

CHAPTER ELEVEN

Lake

"Hello... welcome," my sister Harmony says not looking up yet to see who's in her and Chelsea's shop.

Juniper's Boutique.

We take a few steps further into the store and then Harmony's eyes flash up to mine.

"Lake! You're here?" She beams, her smile bright and her smile wide with full red painted lips.

She jogs around the front desk in a pair of heels, long trouser pants, and a peach blouse.

Her strawberry-blonde hair is up in a professional-looking bun, her makeup thick, and her blue eyes that match mine staring back at me through black-rimmed glasses that I assume she uses to make herself look older and more serious than she is because she's never worn glasses in the thirty-two years I've known her.

Finally, her eyes drift over to Tessa.

"Oh... hi," Harmony says, greeting Tessa.

I'm not surprised that Harmony is taken off guard by Tessa. Harmony hasn't seen me with anyone since high school, minus the women who want selfies with me and tag me in their posts—not that anyone can do that now, thanks for nothing Tessa—or the one-night stands I get photographed with leaving the bar or restaurant.

"Tessa, this is my sister, Harmony," I introduce.

"You're Harmony? His sister?" Tessa's eyebrows furrow together. "Oh, I thought you were... never mind," Tessa says quickly, casting her eyes away.

Oh yeah... I almost forgot the side-eye she made in the car when she saw Harmony's text. Now it's confirmed. First Chelsea and now Harmony. Tessa isn't fond of females that aren't blood-related texting me.

How do I want to use this information to my advantage?

"I don't like owning up to it... but yes. We share DNA, believe it or not, but I got all the good looks, and Chelsea got the brain... Lake got..." She gives me a once-over and a longer than necessary pause. "Good hair." She gives me a teasing sister wink.

Nice, sis.

"Is this your shop? It's beautiful," Tessa says as her eyes glimmer at anything that sparkles.

I knew she'd like this place, even if she says she doesn't want to spend my money. I have a plan to get around that. Tessa isn't leaving here without at least a week's worth of clothing to get her through this trip.

I might have meant to torture her a little, but I didn't plan for her to be without her luggage.

"Thanks, we just did some renovations." Harmony beams, looking around the shop she and Chelsea have put a lot of work into since taking it over years ago after our mom retired, and our parents started traveling.

I take a fresh look at the place. They had a contractor come in and do several things after I returned to Seattle before the start of this season.

Rows of long-sleeved shirts start on the first row that lines up from the front of the small store and runs to the back wall. Next are jackets, then long-sleeved dresses, and then the right wall is decorated with dark-stained shelves that display jeans from different designer brands.

Accessories like shoes and purses have their shelving along the back wall, and to the left are dressing rooms.

Then she turns back to us. "What can I help you two with?" she asks me and then looks at Tessa.

We are, after all, standing in a woman's boutique with zero men's clothing.

Tessa pipes up.

"My luggage is throwing a tantrum and decided to stay in Salt Lake City. It's mad because it thinks it should be soaking up the sunshine," Tessa says, looking around the shop. "Which means,

I am without clothing due to this guy." Tessa tosses a thumb in my direction.

Harmony chuckles at Tessa's bluntness and flashes a wide-eyed look at me like "Where did you pick up this girl" and "I like her."

It figures Harmony would like her.

"A tantrum? Where are your clothes *supposed* to be?" Harmony asks with a little snicker.

"Cabo," Tessa tells her with an eye roll meant for me.

Harmony's eyebrows furrow quickly. "Then why in the hell did you come to Aspen? It's freezing here!"

Tessa glares up at me.

"Lake forced me here against my will," she says with a straight face.

I give an uncomfortable chuckle, trying to defuse the fact that Tessa just made me sound like I kidnapped her.

Harmony's eyes dart between Tessa and me. "He did?" She's my middle sister who has known me since my birth yet she's well on her way to believing Tessa's story.

Come on...

"No... No, I didn't." I shake out my hands at Harmony to dissolve whatever misconceptions are forming.

This small town is the perfect size for gossip to move at rapid speed, and since the other shop assistant is clearly eavesdropping from where she's neatening the jeans, I need to bury this tall tale.

As if my reputation around here isn't bad enough to have kept me away for years. I probably wouldn't have come back if Bobby hadn't finally convinced me, and Chelsea hadn't needed me during her divorce from Sadie and Lana's dad.

"I wouldn't peg Lake for the kidnapping type, but I've been waiting for Mom to get a call from Sam Roberts that you were abducted by a crazed female fan and locked in a basement dungeon for weeks on end. Forced to watch replays of all of your games since you were a young kid while she brushes your hair."

Jesus Christ.

Harmony's always been the sister with the sick sense of humor. It's probably why we get along so well. I'm not as protective of her as I am of Chelsea because Harmony can dish it out with the best of them.

Although, I think it might be a good time for my sister to stop watching those crime shows.

"That's some fucked-up imagery, sis," I tell her.

"Not as fucked up as some of the things I've seen women write about you in the comment section of those fan blogs I've stumbled upon," she says, giving me a sideways look.

I look over to see Tessa's scrunched facial expression at what my sister just said. I need to get this thing turned around, and fast.

"Here..." I tell her, pulling out my wallet and handing Harmony my black card.

"What's this?" Harmony asks, looking down at the card and flipping it over once to see both sides.

"It's me paying off old debts for a bet I lost," I say, nodding at the card.

Tessa shifts her weight from side to side and huffs, angling her body away from our conversation like she doesn't want any part of this.

"She can buy anything she wants. One day only," I tell Harmony.

"Anything she wants?" Harmony's eyebrows rise to almost her hairline.

In my periphery, Tessa shakes her head in disagreement, but at least she's not making a verbal disagreement anymore.

"Anything she wants," I repeat and nod.

I look out of the large shop windows to see the bright neon open sign for a coffee shop across the street and a window red marker that says Free Wi-fi. Bobby sent me the quote that the contractor already worked up. Making these changes will bring everything up to code and earn us sign-off from the city to accommodate the number of people we want to shelter on any night.

I need to look at it and give Bobby the second approval from me that he's waiting for.

The sooner we close on this place and get the contractor in there, the sooner we can have the location available to start helping people.

My mind drifts to Shawna for a minute until Tessa clears her throat. "This is unnecessary..."

"Psht, don't look a gift horse in the mouth," Harmony says, swiping Tessa's words away with her hand. "Lake Powers wants to spoil you with his gobs of money, then that's what we're going to do. I have no problem with spending my brother's millions." Harmony links her arm with Tessa's and pulls a hesitant Tessa toward the rows of tops.

Soon enough, I see Tessa soften to my sister's more aggressive relationship-building skills. I'm not sure exactly how close I

want these two to get, but knowing Chelsea and Harmony...
I might not have a choice. I wouldn't be surprised if they try
to turn Tessa into an honorary Powers sister and invite her to
family holidays.

"I'm going to head across the street," I tell both of them...
or whichever one is listening to me anymore, which feels like
neither. "Harmony, can I have a minute?" I ask softly. Tessa
doesn't bother to look up, but Harmony does and nods in
response.

She turns to Tessa first. "Here. Start looking through this rack
and pull whatever you like." Harmony waves a hand at the other
saleswoman across the store to signal her to come over. "We'll
start a changing room for you," she tells Tessa, and then turns
to head in my direction.

"Anything else you need to tell me about your Stockholm
syndrome girlfriend?" Harmony says, jutting out her hip and
placing a hand on it as if impatient that I'm taking her from her
life's work.

"Just that she won't buy anything if she can get away with it."
I check to make sure Tessa isn't listening.

She's not. She's standing at the rack flipping through the
clothes, seeming to like something, and then discreetly looking
at the price tag and pretending she's not interested in it. I know
this place isn't cheap. It affords to give several members of my
family a good living, along with a handful of employees. I know
it will cost a small fortune, but I don't care, and the more she
refuses it and turns away expensive items... the more I want to
buy out the whole damn store for her.

"I have to say, Tessa not wanting to spend your money is highly unusual. I've never seen a woman come into this boutique with her boyfriend's money and not go hog wild." She looks back at Tessa and then back at me, her face seeming like she wants to ask what the hell is wrong with her.

Damned if I know.

But fuck am I becoming increasingly curious about it.

I think to correct her assumption about our dating status. She's made the reference twice now that we're together, but I don't want to get into it with Harmony. The less anyone knows, the better, probably.

I'm tired of people knowing my business. That's why I spend my free time in Aspen instead of Seattle. I want a break from the paparazzi and everything else that comes with the fame and reputation of being Lake Powers, a pro player, on and off the ice.

I look up to make sure Tessa isn't reading my lips. The other saleswoman is holding up a shirt against Tessa and nodding as they discuss something... color, size, I'm not sure, and I don't care, as long as she buys something. I need to make good on our last bet.

I don't want her to think she can wiggle out of hers should I ever win one of our bets. And dammit, my odds may look bad, but I won't lose the next one.

"She's not going to make your job easy, so stash all the stuff that looks good on her and charge my card for whatever you think she should have."

"Whatever I think she should have?" Harmony's smile widens. "Chelsea and I have a sales quota we wanted to hit this quarter," she hints.

"Then knock it out of the park. Can you drop the bags by my house after you close up tonight? And whatever you do, don't tell Tessa about it," I tell Harmony, and then turn around quickly when I see Tessa notice that I haven't left yet.

I almost turn back and warn Harmony not to say anything about Shawna to Tessa but even bringing up her name to Harmony, who was her best friend in high school, just feels uncomfortable.

I exit the full glass door to the boutique, the bell chiming again when I walk out. I cross the concrete sidewalk and then check up and down the two-lane road that takes you through town.

When an opening comes between cars, I bolt for the other sidewalk and the coffee shop perched on the other side.

I walk through the door of the little café. The smell of strong dark roast coffee and muffins fills the air instantly, and I take a deep inhale. I don't drink coffee, but it smells like someone I know, and the second I realize how addicted I am to her smell, the alarm bells go off.

I need to get my head back on straight. Forcing Tessa on this trip was a bad idea, but there's nothing I can do about it now. I have to stay the course and keep my ever-growing desire for her to myself until I can suppress it with one-night stands back in Seattle; no way in hell I'm living out that reputation here.

I order a bagel and bottled water and then take a seat at the long wood bar-like seating that runs along the front window of the café so you can stare out at passersby.

I'll do a little people-watching once I agree to the cost that the contractor proposed and electronically sign the docs.

The glare of the afternoon sun makes it hard to see Tessa in the back of the store, but as Harmony leads her around to different spots, I get little glimpses of her as I scroll through the contractor's contract and quote.

If I could focus on anything other than Tessa, that would be great.

Tessa

"I think we've got a good idea at this point of what you like," Harmony says, and the saleswoman helping us nods in agreement. "Let's get you back to the changing room, and we'll just start feeding you things we think you'll like."

"Oh... uh, okay," I tell her.

I'm not completely comfortable with the idea of them handing me something before I see the price tag.

What if I fall in love with it?

Harmony is already leading me toward the wall with four floor-to-ceiling built glossy white changing rooms. The structure almost looks like it's made of acrylic and keeps with her modern take. The dark stained woods mix with crystal chandeliers and white acrylic changing rooms. It's a gorgeous boutique—Lake's sisters have done a great job.

I walk through the first door to find a decent-sized room. A small bench sits in the corner with a faux fur pink pillow on top of it and a long mirror secured to the wall in front of me.

On the left wall, three silver hooks are screwed in at even distances, a plaque above each one.

Keep – Toss – Burn.

I chuckle for a second at the uniqueness. I have to give it to the girls, they put a lot of thought into this place.

"Okay, here come the first few things," the other saleswoman says, opening the door slightly and then pushing more like twenty things into my arms.

I struggle to get a grip on everything, but she doesn't let go until I nod that I have it under control.

I try on the first few shirts, and I love them, but they seem a little too nice for casual day use.

"What's taking so long?" Harmony asks.

"The ones I tried on didn't work."

"You're supposed to show us!" she hollers. "Try them back on and come out here."

I do as she demands, and for the next forty-five minutes Harmony dresses me like her personal Barbie. Harmony has incredible taste, and I struggle to find a single thing I don't like. She also knows my body better than I do, and everything I try on is flattering.

As I start getting dressed back in the clothing that Chelsea let me borrow, I can hear Harmony on the other side talking to me.

"It's great to see Lake happy again after so long. We've been worried about him."

Huh?

Worried about him?

"Oh... well we're not—" I attempt to correct her thinking that Lake and I are an item even though Lake didn't bother to correct her when she said it while he was still in the store.

"The accident really changed him, and I thought he might never come home after he got signed as a walk-on rookie. It wasn't even his fault, but he took all the blame on himself."

The accident? Not his fault?

The scars along his left shoulder and pec come to mind.

He was in an accident... and before he made it to the NHL.

"The accident?" I ask, opening the door and peering out at her.

She freezes like she just said something horribly wrong.

"I thought maybe you already... you know what, forget I said anything. We're just all happy he's home. That's all," Harmony backtracks quickly with a plastered-on smile.

She takes the shirt and pants I agreed to let Lake purchase for me and then moves to the cashier's island in the middle of the store.

"I'll just ring this up and have you and Lake on your way," she says across the store.

I grab my phone off the acrylic bench, tuck it in my back pocket, and head straight for her.

"What accident made Lake not want to return to Aspen?"

Harmony doesn't look back up at me as she scans the clothing tags into the system.

"I'm sorry I said anything. Please don't tell Lake I mentioned it. I don't want him to be mad at me," she says, her eyes reaching up to mine with a plea in her puppy dog eyes.

I'm stuck now. She asked me not to say anything to Lake, so how am I supposed to ask the question without bringing up Harmony?

Lake won't tell me.

Harmony won't tell me.

But I know someone who will sing like a jailbird... the internet!

I know I don't have time to look it up right now. I'll have to wait to do my great detective work when I'm alone in my room.

Then the thought dawns on me. This must have been the thing Brent mentioned that he doesn't know the details about. Does Penelope know? Maybe I have other resources. But if they don't know and I start bringing up information that Lake doesn't want out in the open, could that cause a greater backlash against me?

Likely, and right now, Lake and I are getting along... kind of.

"Please don't tell him I said anything," Harmony begs again when I don't answer.

I nod, and my eyes catch on the other saleswoman who is looking over at us with concern that she might get in trouble too. Holy crap, does everyone know about this accident but me?

"I won't say anything. I promise," I assure her.

"Okay, thank you," Harmony says, handing me the bag of items and Lake's card. "I hope to see you around more. He may not believe this... but he deserves to be happy again."

What the—what? I want to ask so badly.

Why does she have to be so freaking cryptic?

I'm not sure if I'll be able to wait until tonight in my room to internet stalk Lake, but I have to. I'm not sure what I'm about to find, but it doesn't feel like something I should read about at a pizza parlor with a bunch of his friends nearby.

I spin around, and head for the door, my head feeling fuzzy and unsure about what I just learned—or rather, didn't learn—and how I am going to handle the next few hours with my phone burning a hole in my pocket.

Chapter Twelve

Lake

The second Tessa walked out of the boutique, she seemed different. I don't know if Harmony ratted me out about buying Tessa an entire wardrobe behind her back or if something else is going on. With Tessa, it could be anything, but I haven't had time to dig into it with her since we loaded up into the Jeep and headed down to the pizza parlor to meet the friends that Bobby invited to hang out tonight.

Bobby has his own fame-in-a-small-town too. He races for his family's Formula 1 race team, but he's been home for the past four months recouping before he hits the road again. Bobby and I both command large crowds wherever we go, but tonight, with both of us in one bar, it's sure to be a packed house of old friends.

The second Tessa and I walk through the doors, the scent of pizza and IPA beer wafts past my nose. I love this place and its smell. It's been here since I was a kid, but it's been through a massive remodel and new ownership now that Aspen continues to grow in popularity as a ski resort destination. The wide-open floor plan and the exposed A-line roof with its thick original beams, several pool tables, and booming music make this a cool place to hang out.

A mob of friends from high school and a group of locals all make a beeline for me and form a circle engulfing me. Tessa steps away from me, only allowing for more people to add more space between us.

Something in me wants to reach out and clothesline a half dozen people to get to her and pull her closer, but then I see something catch Tessa's eye, and she waves toward the bar with a smile.

My vision follows her line of sight to find Chelsea and Bobby sitting at the bar. Chelsea smiles and waves her over. Tessa makes her way over and I watch every step she takes, barely listening to the people around me asking questions and introducing themselves to me as if I forgot who they are since last summer when I was living here off-season.

The questions come too fast to answer as my vision jets back and forth between people hurdling them at me.

"How does it feel to be back in town?"

It would be better if I could spend it with my friends at the bar.

"Do you like living in Seattle?"

Most days, but I could do with less rain.

"Is the ice rink really cold?"

What?

"Can you get me a date with Ryker Haynes?"

I glance over to see a high school girl in a Ryker jersey. So much for this being *my* town. Besides, Ryker has to be at least twice her age.

I can't be rude and blow past them all. I need to spend a socially acceptable amount of time mingling. After all, they came here to see me, but the timer in my head starts ticking down until I can safely exit this mob and head to the bar to insert myself into the conversation.

My curiosity gets the best of me again, and I glance over to where Tessa is at the bar. I watch as my sister, who's sitting with Tessa to her right, introduces our cousin Bobby on Tessa's left. I don't like the smile that crosses Bobby's face when he reaches over and shakes Tessa's hand.

So help me, if that motherfucker tries to pick up my girl...

Wow, what?

My girl?

Shit, I mean *this* girl.

I run my hands through my hair trying to get a handle on how complicated things are getting.

My feet itch to run toward the bar and wedge myself into their conversation. To make sure they both know I'm still here. As if somehow, I'm a contender, still in the game. But I'm not.

I can't do long-term relationships. I promised I'd never be happy with anyone else.

I take selfies with fans and sign shirts, hats, a power bill... I hope that doesn't put me on the hook for it. Whatever, my agent will take care of it. I sign anything they ask me to sign.

When I look back up, I find my sister is gone, probably in the restroom, and Bobby is now in my sister's spot, turned on the barstool with his knees pointed toward Tessa, who is still facing the bar but laughing at something he said.

Her eyes find one of the large TVs mounted in the top right-hand corner of the bar, and it just so happens that the announcer is talking about my old team and the team she used to work for, the San Diego Blue Devils.

Her shoulders shrug together like she's grimacing, but since her back is to me, I can't be sure, and then she excuses herself, slipping off the barstool, and heads for the bathroom.

My eyes dart up to the TV to see what could have been the matter. I know she left the team in a hurry, but everyone in management was always cool with me and most of the group, aside from one player I shared a few choice words with. He even shoved me once in practice.

I could have beat the shit out of that punk-ass kid, but I restrained myself. I don't get in fights with teammates, and at the time, I figured Sinclair was just young and cocky... he'd grow out of it.

He didn't.

Bobby watches Tessa leave, and I feel my fists clench as he surveys her backside, though I can't blame him.

I have no reason to be pissed off that he's admiring Tessa, fuck... someone should since the only thing I can offer her is a one-night stand.

Bobby scans the room and then sees me staring at him. No doubt noticing the deep scowl on my face.

He jumps off the barstool and takes long steps, headed in my direction, his longneck beer bottle in one hand, his other dug deep in his blue jeans. He's wearing a black athletic brand hoodie and a thick down vest over top.

He passes by the five pool tables all lined up next to the bar, with three of the pool tables already in use, and then weaves through round tables laid out in the large space. The echo of voices fills the pizza parlor, along with the sound of sports games playing on large TVs mounted against the large ducting that fills the restaurant with heat. With the temperatures starting to drop back down again, a storm is supposed to hit us in another couple of days.

"Lake, got a minute?" he says, walking up.

"Yeah, sure. Hold on," I tell him.

The crowd sees Bobby, giving me my first opportunity for an out. I slip between a wall of people to my right and out of the claustrophobic mob pit.

I'm honored to have people wanting to come to see me and wish me well and a kick-ass season. I do appreciate them.

Bobby reaches me and the group finally disperses, a few people lingering close by for when they see their opening again.

"Thanks for that," I tell him.

Bobby looks over at the people still walking away, finding a pool table to play at or a table to sit at.

"No problem," he says, taking a sip of his beer. "I got your approval for the changes and sent them off to the contractor.

He'll work with the real estate agent until the property closes, and then he'll get to work."

"Perfect," I say simply.

The sooner this thing gets up and running, the better. Then I can finally say that Bobby and I delivered on what we set out to do.

"So Tessa..." Bobby says, his eyes locked on mine.

He's serious, but Bobby has that way of looking casual about everything. I guess that's what you get for having nerves of steel driving a tin box at 220mph.

"Yeah, what about her?" I ask. I dart a glance toward the bathrooms to see if she's exited yet, but she hasn't.

"I figured with how you described her that she'd be covered in dragon scales or have claws for fingernails."

"Doesn't she?" I tease.

He shakes his head, the right side of his lip turning up and he takes another swig of his beer.

"You seeing the same thing I am, right? I know you said you hate her and brought her here to punish her, but she's a goddamn smoke show."

Shit, maybe I shouldn't have told him about intentionally ruining her vacation. He told me it was a shit plan to begin with... and it turns out he was right. I wish now I had listened.

"That's just her daytime human disguise as a normal woman. It unzips in the back," I tell him.

He snickers at my stupid comment about Tessa being a large reptile under her skin, but the idea of unzipping anything off Tessa stays with me for a minute. I can practically feel the cool metal zipper between my thumb and my index finger as I roll the zipper down her back and the teeth come undone, exposing her bare back. The soft curvature of her spine... the two small dimples that I imagine are there just above her ass cheeks.

"That brings me to my next question. How exactly do you know where her zipper is?" he says, an eyebrow cocked.

"None of your damn business," I tease again.

"So she's giving you the cold shoulder now since you kept to your one-night-stand rule with her?" he asks, watching me carefully.

"No. Fuck no. I haven't touched her," I say.

Not that I don't want to.

Shit, I've wanted to since I added her to my bucket list four years ago. The first night I played a home game in Seattle and saw her in the stands. I didn't know she was Brent's sister at the time. Not until I walked out of post-game interviews and saw her standing in the hallway. I thought it was fate that she had come to find me... right up until Brent pushed past me and hugged her, thanking her for flying in from San Diego to see him play.

I don't add puck bunnies to a bucket list, but Tessa was different. She is different... and I knew it from the bottom of an ice rink with thirty pounds of hockey gear and a face mask to distract me.

The bucket list item:

Take that girl to dinner and listen to anything and everything she's willing to tell me for as long as she's willing to talk.

Did I plan on fucking her after?

Hell yeah, because I wanted to know everything there is to know about Tessa Tomlin, including how she sounds when she comes.

Then I found out that she's my new teammate's little sister and that option closed, especially now that she works for our team.

"You mind if I ask her out, then?" he asks.

What am I supposed to say to that?

"Hell no, stay the fuck away from her even though you and I both know that I swore I'd never date anyone seriously again... but I'm keeping Tessa anyway even though I can never make her happy."

This is the first time in my life that I've wanted to lie to a buddy and tell them I'm fucking someone who I'm not just so that I can pull the bro code and he can't touch her. But I have to fight the urge to do it.

"Shit. Yeah... I don't care, man," I tell him, lying to us both.

A hand touches the middle of my back, and I look quickly behind me to find three women, two brunettes, and a blonde, all with overflowing cleavage and fuck-me grins. Their makeup is overdone, and their expectations for tonight are way too high. I don't fuck in Aspen.

If this had been a week ago, and I was back in Seattle looking for a nameless, faceless woman to add to my one-night-only rule, I'd maybe consider it, but the snarky, pain-in-my-ass who's sitting alone at the bar is the only thing that has my attention.

I stare at her backside as she sits there sipping on her drink. I don't break my stare as I give him the green light. "Knock yourself out."

Her gaze drifts back up to the TV. I can't see her face with her back to me, but I can see the subtle headshake that she's not happy the Blue Devils are still being talked about.

"Thanks, man." He pats my shoulder and takes another swig of his beer like he needs liquid courage and then heads for the girl we both want.

What the fuck is wrong with me?

The air is thinner up here... that's what it is. As soon as we get back to Seattle, it will all go back to normal.

It has to.

CHAPTER THIRTEEN

Tessa

I thought the break to the bathroom would be enough time for the sports newscaster to move on to a new story or a new team.

Must be a slow news week.

I take a long drink of the Midori Sour that the guy made up for me. It's usually a little too sweet for me, but they make all of their sweet and sour mix in-house, so I knew I had to give it a go.

It's freaking delicious in its short glass with hot pink sugar around the rim and a metal skewer with three blueberries as the garnish.

And so is the smell of the yummy pizzas getting baked in the massive stone pizza oven that sits just within view of the customers so they can watch the pizzas bake from anywhere in the large open dining room.

I already put in my order for a meat lovers pizza with extra cheese and put it on Lake's tab... along with the drink.

He didn't have a tab open when I first sat down, but he sure as heck does now, and it's going to be a doozy because I am starving, and everything on the menu looks amazing.

A San Diego Blue Devils team picture of the man I despise comes up on the TV.

Noah Sinclair.

Bobby takes a seat again next to me while Chelsea seems to have been stopped by a friend chatting in the corner by the booth seating against the left wall.

I could use a distraction from the man I left San Diego to avoid. To start a new life that wouldn't result in me bumping into him daily.

"So, you've heard of me?" I ask, turning away from the TV toward Bobby.

I saw him walking back from talking to Lake, and I can only imagine what Lake told his cousin about me.

"Heard of you?" he asks, leaning an arm over the thick wooden countertop of the bar.

"Yeah," I say, licking a little of the sugared rim of my drink. Bobby watches intently as my tongue darts out. Oops.

"You seemed like you already knew my name when Chelsea introduced us. I'm guessing you've heard of me from Lake. That can't be good news for me," I say, glancing over my shoulder at Lake, who I catch watching us.

It's the third time my vision has traveled to find Lake in this room, only to catch him already watching me.

I grin inwardly at the thought that Lake is keeping tabs on me as if he truly wants to know where I am.

Does it matter that much to him?

And why?

"Nah, all I've heard is that you're good at your job, and you're keeping Lake in check," he says.

But I don't believe him.

He's covering for Lake. Although what would be the benefit of him coming clean and telling me all the dirty laundry of what Lake truly thinks of me behind my back?

I doubt it would make our working relationship any more bearable.

"Plus, I like a strong woman who can knock a pro hockey player around a little bit," he says, a sparkle in his eye.

"Oh, do you?" I smirk.

He shrugs and then holds up his empty beer when the bartender looks our way.

The bartender nods that he'll get Bobby a new one.

"So... you're here because of Lake." He leans in over the bar top.

He might not have the instant sex appeal that Lake does, but he still has the boy-next-door look down pat. And that single dimple to the right of his smile is really cute. I'm sure as a race car driver he cleans up just fine too.

"Yep, Lake is job security for me."

"He's that bad, huh?"

I just give him a side-eye look and he laughs, with a full beautiful smile and stunning emerald eyes.

"I don't know what version of Lake he lets you see but based on what you're telling me, it's not the real one."

That surprises me.

"It's fine, we only work together. I have to deal with him from 9-5 and then I get to clock out," I say, swirling my drink, and then pull one of the blueberries off with my teeth.

Yum! They're soaked in some kind of liquor and it's really good.

"You have a much harder job than mine. You've had to be friends with him since birth."

He smiles and looks at the empty beer bottle, his thumb picking at the corner of the label. He almost seems nervous all of a sudden. He rubs the back of his neck next. Yeah... I think he is. It's such a breath of fresh air after dealing with cocky player after cocky player in the NHL.

As a Formula 1 driver, he probably pulls as many women as Lake, but he just seems so down to earth that it's hard to imagine him like that.

"So... is it safe to say that you two aren't..."

My head shoots over to him. Is he asking what I think he is? One of his eyebrows raises as if to say, "Do I need to say the rest?"

I really wish you wouldn't.

He's either referring to dating or sleeping together, but because I have more self-respect than the women currently throwing themselves at Lake right now around the pool tables, neither is on the horizon.

I'm about to answer when I feel the nearness of an intrusive presence, one I know all too well.

I glance back quickly to see Lake watching me again, barely a few feet away and within earshot even in a loud pizza parlor, as if he's waiting for my answer.

How long has he been standing there?

I look back at Bobby.

"God, no. I don't date hockey players," I say, emptying the rest of my drink down my throat and practically slamming my drink on the countertop.

That was a little dramatic, but he didn't seem to take note and with Lake listening in to this conversation, I need something to keep me from telling him to buzz off and go back to the women interested in him hovering over them.

Bobby seems intrigued by the statement of facts that I just dropped on him.

"As in, you haven't ever dated them or…?"

"As in, I've dated them in the past and will never date another one for as long as I live," I proclaim.

I see Lake fidget slightly behind me after I say it.

"That bad, huh?"

I shrug. I don't want to get into the emotional and physical roller coaster of my last relationship, which was one too many of the same brand of bad men. This one just so happened to cross a line that none of the others had and after I got free, I promised myself I'd never fall for the muscles and the hockey stick again. It never leads to a happily ever after.

"Okay." He nods. "Well, now that I know I'm not step-ping on Lake's toes… and I'm not a hockey player." He winks.

"Would it be okay for me to ask to take you out? I know you're not here for long, but you have to eat right?"

Lake takes half a step closer. Does it make him uncomfortable?

I'm only here for a few more days and I have no other reason to come back to Aspen after this and he drives race cars for a living with an eight-month schedule that's far worse than a hockey player's season. I know what he's angling for and even though I could go for some skin-on-skin after such a long drought, having a one-night stand with a coworker's cousin while on a work trip with him, seems too weird for me.

"I should be honest with you, I'm not interested in a random hookup," I say, nibbling down on my lower lip.

He is cute and I hate to pass on the opportunity.

"Shit, sorry." He scratches the side of his neck quickly." I didn't mean... I just meant... I'm only asking about dinner. I didn't assume anything else. I just thought it would be nice to get to know you a little more in a different setting. And I travel to Seattle a few times a year. If I'm not half as mean as Lake, maybe I could call you when I'm in town. If we hit it off, that is."

I laugh when he suggests Lake is mean. He's funny and he took the pressure off instantly when I mentioned that I'm not interested in a one-night stand.

Ah, communication. How lovely... and how rare.

See, this is what I need.

Not those meatheads whose toxic over usage of steroids built their muscles but shrank their brains... along with their balls. Maybe that's why some of them are so damn cranky.

Lake is still standing behind us and I wonder if he's ever planning on interjecting into the conversation or just eavesdropping like a creeper.

CHAPTER
FOURTEEN

Lake

I should be a good cousin and a good friend and let Bobby shoot his shot with the ice queen, but fuck it, I don't care at this point.

I've had worse odds, like when I scored two goals skating with a sprained wrist in the playoffs for San Diego years ago, before the Hawkeyes offered a shit ton of money for me and a trade of a couple of their players.

I was happy to be off that team. Another teammate and I weren't getting along very well. He was a prick, and I was just about done with his shit. Then I got traded with a massive pay raise and a team who are like family to me now.

"Room for one more?" I ask, walking up between them on the barstools, but before Bobby can say anything, I ram in next to him, which causes him to practically slide off the barstool.

We're wedged together three deep against the bar as I attempt to become a physical wall between them.

"What the hell, Lake," Bobby grumbles.

"Quit your whining, you're fine," I say under my breath to him.

"Order for Tessa?" a young server says, standing at the order pickup at the far end of the kitchen.

Tessa gets up from the barstool.

"Here, I'll come with you in case you need someone to carry it."

I move back from the bar, preparing to walk with her.

"Hey, looks like Chelsea got us a booth," Bobby says, slipping off his barstool as well.

I look over, and my sister is waving us all to come sit with her.

"I'll grab my pizza and be over in a minute. Should I order a pitcher of beer?" Tessa asks Bobby... and not me.

"Sure, want me to get it, though? Your hands will be full—"

"We got it," I interject quickly. "You'd better go sit by Chelsea to hold our spot."

Bobby's eyebrows knit together. I get it doesn't take two people to hold a booth, but it's the only excuse I have.

"Wave me over if you need help," he tells her, and then heads for Chelsea and the booth.

Over her shoulder, she sends me a downturned eyebrow like she doesn't know why I'd do that.

I've finally got Tessa alone for a minute, and I'm not planning on wasting it, even if I'll look like an idiot carrying back a tiny personal-size pizza for her that she could easily do without my help.

I follow her closely as she walks up to the counter.

"Order for Tessa?" she asks the kid who called it out, waiting for them to hand her the order.

"Do you want any parmesan cheese or ranch for dipping?" the server asks, handing her the family-size meat lovers pizza she ordered.

The large pizza is enough to feed all four of us.

"Sure, can I have a little of each? That would be great, thanks."

"You ordered that entire pizza for you?" I ask in surprise.

"No, I ordered it for us... when I thought you were going to be nice. Now I wish I hadn't." She frowns.

"Where did you get the money?" I ask.

"I put it on your tab. My wallet is on its way back to Seattle, remember?"

"Right. I know," I say.

I pull my wallet from my back pocket and slide my black card out of its spot, handing it to Tessa.

"Here, take this," I tell her, taking the pizza from her so she doesn't have to carry it. It's still piping hot.

She grips the card and looks down at it.

"This is your black card. I'm not taking this," she refuses, handing it back to me.

"Yes, you are," I demand.

"What if I lose it?" she asks, trying to make up an excuse for me not to trust her with it, but that's not going to work either.

"I get text notifications when something gets charged to it. I'll just cancel it, and the credit card company will reverse the charges," I explain, looking beyond her at the server gathering the things she requested.

"I don't need the card, Lake," she says, slapping the card and her palm against my right pec.

Her fingertips' blazing heat reaches just beyond the edge of the cold metal card, and I swear I can feel the blueprint of her fingertips against my skin through my shirt.

I look down at her, the hot pizza balancing on my left hand, and lift my right hand to wrap around her wrist, gently but firm enough to anchor her there, keeping her from pulling her touch away from me.

Her bright eyes flash up into mine. I can feel her heart beating rapidly through the pulse point on her wrist. It matches the same rapid heartbeat of mine.

"Keep the card, Tessa. I'll be gone all day tomorrow, and I want to know that you can get whatever you need." I finally break from the stern demanding stance I usually have with her; it never fucking works.

Instead, this time I plead with her to put my mind at ease. I don't want the Royal Inn incident happening again where she's out of choices. I don't want her without clothes or anything else. My card can get her out of trouble if she needs it.

"I don't want to carry it on me but you can leave it at the house in case I need it." She's meeting me halfway, although her eyes turn to slits for a brief second like she thinks something's up with me not fighting her but instead begging her. "Where are you going?"

She starts to slide her hand down my pec, leaving the card against me. I take it—reluctantly and slide it into my back pocket. I'll leave it at the house for her as she requested if that's the only option she's leaving me with.

"I have that charity event at the ski lodge I told you about. I told Bobby I'd help out all day. He knows one of the people putting it on and they want me to emcee an event tomorrow night," I tell her, trying not to give any more away than I have to.

I look just beyond Tessa to find a small group of old friends from school watching us. I wish I could scoop her up and haul her back to my house in the mountains and have this conversation all to ourselves, but I have to stay a little longer. I can't leave before we've even eaten after Bobby keeps trying to ease me back into this community.

"Oh right... the blessed charity event that you absolutely could not miss, and that's why I'm here instead of sitting in salt-filtered crystal-blue water, poolside, drinking Mai Tais and gaining a stunning bronzed glow ...while I get rubbed down with tanning oils by the hot lifeguard on duty," she says, scowling at me and popping a hip out. "What is this charity even for?" she asks but I see the server walking back to us.

Saved by parmesan.

"Here you go, miss," the server says. "Wow, Lake Powers!" the kid, no more than seventeen, says to me through his braces. "You're a legend."

"Thanks. That means a lot," I tell him genuinely.

Then I notice that Tessa used the distraction to move past me and head farther down the counter to settle in front of the bar.

She's waiting for the bartender to come, and I'm guessing she's planning to order a pitcher of beer for the table.

"You can head to the booth and start eating, if you want."

"It's fine. I'll stay with you. I have something I want to discuss anyway," I tell her, laying down my plans.

"What can I get you?" the bartender asks.

"A pitcher of whatever you think is best and four glasses," she asks.

I turn to the bartender. "Make it three glasses," I correct.

She looks at me with a side tilt.

"I don't drink if I'm driving."

She turns to me, her left arm still resting on the bar top as she faces me straight on.

"Okay, you have my full attention. What would you like to discuss?"

"The adoption day charity that you scheduled for the end of the trip," I tell her, setting the large pizza down on the bar top, not because it's heavy but because I want my full focus on her for what I say next.

"What about it?" she asks, her guard up as I can see her shoulders tense in defense and her eyes glaze over like she already wants to be over with the conversation.

Does she think I'm going to wiggle my way loose of this event?

Not in the least.

Now I have a good reason to look forward to the day after tomorrow.

"You need to call the charity back and let them know that we'll only be there for a day. I'll have all the animals adopted by dinner."

She rolls her eyes. "You think you can get all three hundred animals adopted in one day? Not a chance."

She turns back toward the bar, shifting her weight away from me like she's closing off herself to this conversation. I'm losing her. I need to spark her interest and go for the kill.

"Want to put a wager on it?"

My lips pull into a lopsided smirk when she spins back to me instantly.

Gotcha!

"What kind of wager?" she asks, a flicker of a spark in her eyes.

Fuck, do I have this girl's number or what?

I hold back the chuckle wanting to bubble out at how easy it was to bring her back around, but I hold it in. She'll think I'm being a cocky asshole... and she has no idea just how much I'm about to be.

"I bet that I can get every single animal adopted in one day," I say, my hand gripping the rough-cut wood bar top. I can't help myself as I lean in a little closer, Tessa's soft fruity smell of strawberries and a touch of coffee filling my lungs.

I don't know if it's her shampoo or her lotion, but it's the perfect concoction to hook me in.

I'm not sure if my mouth is watering from the smell of the pizza or the delicious plan I have for her when I win this bet.

"You have over a million followers on your platform, and they're all psychos. All you'd have to do is set up a kissing booth inside the shelter and you'd be handing out puppies like bottled waters in the Sahara Desert," Tessa says, glancing over at the bartender who's still filling the pitcher of beer on tap.

"No social media, then. I won't touch it," I offer.

Tessa whips a look back at me. She has no idea how much I'd give up, for her to agree to this bet.

"Let me get this straight, you're betting that you can get every one of the three hundred animals adopted in one day without using your social media accounts?"

"Yep. And if you win, I'll give you full access to all of my social media accounts for three months. I won't touch them. You can post pictures of butterflies landing on puppies' noses, and baby seals giving Eskimo kisses to orphans for all I care."

I see her bite down on her lip, trying to stop the smile from spreading across her face. She wants this win. We both know Phil Carlton, the owner of the Hawkeyes, would shit a brick knowing that Tessa could turn my social image into the perfect player on his family-friendly team if given the chance.

And here I am, offering it on a silver platter.

This screams pay raise for Tessa and complete adoration by upper management.

"What do you want if you win?" Tessa asks, but there's no way I'm giving it up that easy.

"What? You think you'll lose?" I ask, playing on her overconfidence since she and I are currently 3-0 on our bets. Although I attest to the first two not being real bets. Even so, she's been wiping the floor with me, but that stops today.

She hesitates for a second, a small unsure growl from her throat tells me that her gut is telling her not to do it but it turns out I'm not the only cocky one standing here. She's going to do it—I can see it in her eyes and her body language as she unconsciously moves closer to me.

I put out my hand for her to shake on it.

"This deal goes away in thirty seconds. Are you going to take it?" I ask, my hand outstretched toward her, tingling in anticipation of feeling her soft palm slide against mine and locking this in without me having to reveal to her what I want if I win.

She stares down at my hand. Then I see in my peripheral the bartender walking over with the pitcher and glasses.

I pull my card back out of my back pocket and shove my card toward him to pay for the beer. "Here... thanks," I tell him quickly and then look down at Tessa who's watching the bartender walk back toward the cash register.

"If I walk away the deal is gone," I repeat. "Three... two... one..." I start counting down.

"Ok! Ok!" she yells, and pushes her hand out towards mine, but right before she does, I pull back.

Damn my sense of decency.

I need her to agree to the wager before we shake.

"Don't you want to know what you have to do if I win?" I ask.

"Ok... what?"

"You have to show me what your kink is."

She pulls back instantly and looks at me like I've lost my mind. Maybe I have. "Excuse me?" she asks, but she heard me loud and clear.

"We're going to watch porn if I win, and you have to show me how you use it."

Her jaw drops to the floor, her eyes widen, and her cheeks flush.

"Have you lost your damn mind?" she says in an angry whisper, bending in closer to me once the initial shock wears down a little, her eyes burning with fire.

She doesn't want anyone to hear us but I can't stop grinning because Tessa on the verge of nuclear eruption is fucking cute as hell.

"You can pick the movie... in fact, that's part of the deal. It has to be whatever you usually watch to get yourself off," I tell her, taking another step closer, but she takes a step back and away from me.

She stares back at me for a second, and I have no idea what she's thinking. Finally, she speaks.

"Fine," she says and then slips her hand into mine. I almost can't believe she just did. "It's not as if you've won any bets anyway. You won't win this one either." Her confidence is peaking.

Her hand is even softer than I thought and so much smaller than mine. I want to lean in and seal this bet with a kiss but I'm sure she'd slap me.

Before she can pull her hand out of mine, I make sure to cement the wager. "You're agreeing to the terms that I will get every animal adopted in one day, not using *my* social media accounts, correct?"

"That's right, and I'll be monitoring your accounts to keep you honest," she says, lifting an eyebrow in challenge as if I hadn't considered the fact she would check it.

"I don't cheat, Tessa," I tell her, pulling her just slightly closer when I say it.

I meant that I don't cheat on bets or hockey games, but really, I want her to know that's a blanket statement. Even though it shouldn't matter to me if she thinks I'm the loyal kind.

I know Tessa checks every player's social media like a damn fiend and scours the internet for any blog entries or posts for the media that might mention a player to ensure our images are kept clean to the public eye. I guess it's her job or some shit... but still.

"So, we're on? You get three months to do whatever you want with my social media accounts if I lose."

"And what will you do without your precious DMs?" she asks, wiggling her eyebrows at me.

"I don't use that shit anyway," I tell her honestly.

"Bullshit!" she chokes out in a humorless chuckle.

What the hell did her exes do to her?

She seems as untrusting as anyone I've ever met when it comes to hockey players and cheating.

"I swear to God," I tell her, my gaze pinning her with a look to make sure she sees the sincerity in my eyes.

My fingers still grip hers, not letting her pull away, but she's not trying to either.

"Okay, I'll pretend to believe you because I don't care what you do with your DMs anyway," she tells me, not making eye contact. Instead, she studies the droplets of perspiration forming on the pitcher of beer she ordered.

A beer sounds good right about now. A little something to take the edge off between us, and I'd do it if this party was being held at my house in the hills of Aspen or up in my penthouse in

Seattle, but since it's not, and I won't drink and drive, I'll skip the alcohol.

It's a hard and fast rule, and with Tessa as my passenger, I'd never risk her safety like that.

I smirk and then pull her closer. She comes willingly to my surprise, taking a step forward toward me.

I dip down close to her ear. The smell of her sweet breath from her Jolly Rancher-like drink has my mouth watering.

"I won't need those DMs with you naked on my couch."

I prepare for the possibility of a slap, but it doesn't come. Instead, Tessa's pupils flare for a split second, and she goes quiet, her breath shallow. If I hadn't been standing as close as I am now, or watching her every movement, I would have missed it.

She's turned on.

And fuck, now so I am. My cock hardens at the thought that Tessa's turned on thinking about touching herself to porn in front of me.

"Everything alright over here?" Bobby asks, surprising us both.

I don't know how I didn't see him coming to check on us from the booth. I guess I'm mesmerized by Tessa's reaction.

"Yeah," Tessa says, breaking eye contact with me and then clearing her throat. "We're all good here."

She turns away from me and spins toward Bobby.

"Can I take the pitcher for you?" he offers.

"That would be great." She nods and follows him back to the booth after he picks up the pitcher and she grabs the glasses.

I pull the pizza box back into my hand, take the card and receipt that the bartender dropped off, then we head for the booth.

CHAPTER
FIFTEEN

Tessa

I head for my room, with Lake trailing behind me. When I open the door to the guest bedroom, I stop in my tracks. Just inside my room sit ten large expensive-looking rectangular heather gray shopping bags with shimmery tissue paper darting out from the tops.

I know those bags and the store name because I hold a smaller version of it in my hand with a pair of designer jeans and a shirt that Lake bought me.

"Juniper's" reads along all ten bags as I recount each one.

"Where did all this come from?" I ask my eyebrows stitching together. I don't have to bother to look behind me, I know that Lake is standing there.

Now I know why he was whistling to himself on the way up and was walking uncharacteristically slow.

He was waiting for me to open the door and see what was inside.

"I asked Harmony to add a few things to my tab," he says, looking over my shoulder at the contents of my room. His closeness after everything tonight has my body on alert to every movement he makes now.

"A few things?" I ask dramatically, scrunching my nose. "This is not a few things. This is a completely new wardrobe. How am I supposed to get all of this home?"

"I'll pay for the extra baggage fees," he says over my shoulder, still looking in at all of the stuff.

"I can make do with what I have and for all we know, my luggage is probably on its way here now."

Lake's eyes slant down at me as if to say, "We both know you're never getting your luggage."

I can't even convince myself with the lame excuse—my clothes are never going to get here, but I really could make do for the next few days that we're still in Aspen. Chelsea would have let me borrow more items out of her closet if I asked. She tried to get me to take more before I left earlier today.

"I owed you the shopping spree that we agreed on for our last bet anyway. And I asked her to only send me the things that looked good on you. I guess a lot of shit looks good on you," he says, close behind me.

"Why would you do this for me?"

"Maybe I feel bad that you lost your wallet, your luggage and you almost stayed the night in a brothel."

Good point.

"Well, when you put it like that..." I say.

"Just wear the clothes and let me worry about getting them home for you. Or leave them here. I have a feeling you'll be back."

I turn to see him gleaming, and his hands stuffed in his pockets.

I can feel my forehead creasing in confusion at his words. "I'll be back? To Aspen? I doubt it. And why would I ever stay here even if I did?"

I'm not so sure I wouldn't come back, just next time... without Lake.

"You don't hate it here like you pretend to. I can see it. You're enjoying yourself, admit it. And you don't hate me as much as you say you do either but hell would have to freeze over before you'd acknowledge that too."

I don't say anything back because I have no idea what to say.

Yes, I like it here... more than I thought I would. Something about this place feels more like home than San Diego did, or Seattle, or my own brother's house. I haven't felt this sense of home since before my parents passed away.

I love Aspen's mountains and the scenery. I love the small-town feel and the idea of a close-nit community that showed up to see Lake. I love his sisters and his nieces.

He walks farther down to the end of the hall that leads to his bedroom, one door down from mine. He stands with his hand on the door to the master. "Good night, Tessie," he says.

I'm about to correct him but he escapes into his bedroom and closes the door before I can object to the use of that nickname.

I guess that's a fight for another day.

CHAPTER
SIXTEEN

Lake

It's a little after six in the morning, and I've already gotten in my full forty-five-minute workout. Fifteen minutes on the treadmill that sits against the back wall facing the TV mounted to the ceiling. Just enough time to get my heart rate up. Then it's thirty minutes on the All-in-one power rack. The gym isn't as big as the one in the Hawkeyes stadium, but it's big enough for four or five people to work out in here without an issue, and since I'm the only person who uses it, it's plenty big enough for me.

I begin my stretching routine that I've been working on with the Hawkeyes sports physical therapist when a text comes in from Bobby.

Bobby: Let me know when you get here this morning for setup. We need a few bigger dudes to help put up the stage for the wet T-shirt contest that you'll be judging later today.

Lake: No problem. I'll be there in an hour.

Bobby: You know this shit is going to get hits on social, right? Everyone's got a cell phone these days.

Lake: Yeah, I know.

Bobby: And Tessa is going to be cool with this? Because the quarterback from Denver will be here for the festival. We can ask him to fill in for you.

Lake: Fuck that. Tessa isn't my boss.

I text it almost more to remind myself than to inform him.

A few minutes go by with no text but the bubbles keep popping up like he's either writing a novel or he keeps changing his mind on what he's going to say.

Bobby: What does she think you're do-ing today?

Fucker.

Figures he thinks I pussed out and told Tessa some lie not to get my ass chewed. Tessa doesn't scare me.

...mostly.

> Lake: I told you... she's here instead of Cabo because I told my boss that I had a previous charity engagement to attend to. This is it.

> Bobby: You fucked up her trip to paradise so you could come to this? You're cold-hearted, man. Even I kind of want to kick you in the dick for that.

> Lake: Why? It's for a good cause. I'm sure whatever college-age girl up there who wins the wet T-shirt contest will apply her winnings to her schooling. It's practically a scholarship program.

> Bobby: You're fucked up, man. You know that, right?

I'm tempted to send him a middle finger emoji... but he's sort of right. So instead, I ignore it.

I stand up off the floor where I was stretching out my glutes and then push my phone into my pocket. I pick up the blue yoga mat that I was stretching on, roll it up, and walk over to tuck it back in the corner of my home gym, between the treadmill and the floor-to-ceiling wall mirrors on one whole side.

When I make it back up to the main floor of the house, I set off for the kitchen, wondering if Tessa is up yet with that morning scowl that's typical even when I see her in the mornings at the hockey stadium.

I always thought that the saying that seems to get printed on T-shirts and coffee mugs was a joke... an exaggeration that, mostly, women think is funny.

Coffee before Talkie.

Or some ridiculous thing like that.

But now that I've met Tessa... I'm a believer that some people do have a true co-dependency on the caffeinated shit-water.

Give me an energy drink any day over that crap.

I walk through the kitchen and try to ignore the fact that I'm a little disappointed that Tessa isn't in the kitchen yet.

I hold my breath for a second to listen for the little pitter-pattering feet of Tessa in the upstairs bedroom. Her room is situated just above the entry of the kitchen on the second floor, and her en suite bathroom is somewhere above the fridge.

If she's up... I'd hear her moving around a little, but there doesn't seem to be any movement yet.

I head for the fridge and open it up. I already know what I'm going to find... nothing.

The small amount of groceries Chelsea picked up for me before I got here have since been eaten.

I meant to go shopping yesterday but with everything going on, I got distracted.

We still have milk, a banana, and a bagel... and thank God, we still have coffee. Otherwise, the fire-breathing dragon would probably burn down my house the minute she came down the stairs and realized she couldn't get her fix.

I pull out the small blue and white container of cream cheese from the fridge and set it on the island. Then I head for the pantry that's mostly desolate besides a few canned goods that are likely expired, a massive bag of white rice that Chelsea bought for me last summer when I was living here, and the last bagel that sits all alone on one of the four evenly hung white wire shelves lining the inside of the pantry from the door to the back wall. This would make for a great pantry if you had a family of fifteen, but for a guy who only lives here during the offseason, it's overkill.

I shut the pantry door behind me and walk over to the back countertop, near the range and coffee maker, and bend down to pull the toaster out of the wooden cabinets. I set the toaster on the granite countertop, plugging it into the outlet situated behind it against the wall.

Pulling the bagel apart, I separate the top half and bottom half and then pop the top half into the toaster, leaving the other half for Tessa. Within seconds, I can smell the sweet aroma of crisping bread and onion from the everything bagel's seasoning.

My bagel finally pops up, and that's when I hear the sound of the toilet above the fridge flush.

She's awake.

I don't like the flutters of anticipation in my stomach at the idea that my sparring partner will be down at any moment, ready and willing to go another round of giving each other shit.

I smile to myself as I turn toward the toaster and pull out the top half of the bagel. It's hot to the touch but my fingers are calloused enough from gripping a hockey stick for so many years that it doesn't bother me to pull out the hunk of delicious carbs.

Tessa's footsteps echo as she comes down the staircase, and it has my senses on alert, attempting to assess the exact spatial distance between us and counting down the seconds when she and I will be back in proximity to each other once again.

Will she walk into the kitchen and give me a salty morning greeting right out of the gates? Or will she ease in by at least pretending not to be the sour morning person I already know she is?

I pick up my bagel and turn toward the kitchen opening, leaning my ass against the countertop, my right ankle crossed over my left. My left hand grips the rounded edge of the cold marble countertop as my right holds the bagel up to my mouth and I sink my teeth into the lightly crunchy but mostly soft bread.

"Good morning," I say, the second that an already scowling Tessa comes into view as she trudges into the kitchen.

Her long dark brown hair up in a high ponytail, swishing behind her.

"What's so good about it?" she fires back.

Yep, Tessa Tomlin is in the building.

"Nothing... with that attitude," I say, adjusting my ass still pressed against the countertop, and then take another bite of the toasted goodness in my hand.

She doesn't even bother to look up at me as she enters the kitchen and heads toward me, crossing the entry of the kitchen and then weaving around the island to where the coffee maker sits behind me against the dark stone backsplash.

She passes by the large commercial fridge and then finally looks up at me. "I need coffee," she says, squaring up with me and setting those mesmerizing golden eyes on me.

Are they copper in color... or honey? I don't know, but if I thought she'd let me, I'd cup her jaw in both of my hands and pull her face closer to mine, bending down to get level with her shorter height and spend a minute or two looking a little closer at them to determine.

"Are you going to move?" she asks impatiently, looking back at me through her dark mascara-coated lashes, her lips drawing a harsh straight line... no smile in sight.

She leans to her right to look past me at the coffee maker I'm unintentionally blocking for her use, then points at it.

"You're in the way," she says, her voice still a little raspy from sleep, and a frown starting to form on her strawberry ChapStick covered lips.

Why the fuck is a sleepy voice sexy? I have no damn idea.

Nothing about the way Tessa intrigues me makes any damn sense, but there it is.

Maybe because it means I had Tessa Tomlin sleeping under my roof last night... right down the hall from me.

There's a slight glow to her lips and a faint smell of strawberries from her ChapStick.

Suddenly, my lips feel unusually chapped, and an idea pops into my head to bend down and kiss her to get some of that sweet lip balm on my mouth.

Chapped lips should be a sin, and with her taking pictures tomorrow at the animal adoption event, I need to look my best.

Although, I know better than to try. I wouldn't put it past Tessa to clock me if I got any closer than we are right now.

I take another bite of my half-eaten bagel and then take a large step to my right to get out of her way, my eyes still locked on hers as I do.

"There. How's that?" I ask.

I stare back at her, chewing.

"It's only marginally better, but I suppose I can't banish you from your own kitchen," she says, stepping forward and opening up the cabinet above the coffee maker to grab a coffee pod out of the box they came in. "I thought you would be gone already."

She loads the pod into the coffee maker and then reaches up on the tips of her toes to grab a coffee mug that's just a little out of reach.

At my height, I put everything where it feels natural to me. I've never had to consider putting anything where a woman shorter than me could access it easily because I've never had plans for a woman to share this space.

I pop the last bite of my bagel into my mouth and then my ass pushes off the stone countertop as I turn over toward her, chewing my last bite. I come up directly behind her.

"Here, let me help you," I say, reaching out for a mug on the third shelf.

"It's okay, I can reach it…"

But before she can finish her sentence, I'm already reaching past her. My chest brushes against her shoulder blades as I lean into her slightly to reach the mug above her head. Her head turns back to look up at me over her shoulder, the swishing of her ponytail sending her usual smell of vanilla and strawberry in my direction. It's void of the smell of coffee, but I realize now that it's only because she hasn't had her fix yet.

That makes me smile when I think about it.

Tessa has a vice... too bad it's not me.

Wait... what the fuck?

I shake the thought and then set the mug down on the marble countertop, all under her watchful eye.

"There you go," I say, and then take a half a step back.

She looks down at the mug I placed in front of her and now I can't see her face anymore. I can't read her thoughts as she stares down at the mug for a moment and then picks it up by the handle and loads it under the coffee maker's pour spout.

"Thanks," she mutters ungratefully.

"No problem. Happy to help," I tell her.

She still doesn't look back in my direction as her perfectly manicured bright coral index finger selects the medium cup size on the machine, and then the thing hisses to life as it begins to brew.

She huffs in response to me.

I know why she's still mad at me.

Those bright-painted fingers weren't meant for Aspen in the snow. They were painted for a wild trip to Mexico to drink too much, dance half-dressed on a table in some distant Mexican bar, and lie topless on the beach with a rich asshole who thinks he's getting Tessa.

Relief hits me that Tessa is here with me instead of on some sandy beach with him.

I turn and pick up the bottom half of the bagel I left for Tessa so she would have something to eat this morning, along with the last banana. I'm leaving in a few minutes and can grab something on the way to help setup for the festival today, whereas I know Tessa said she has virtual meetings with more players from the team to see how she and Autumn can help beef up their public image.

I skewer the bagel on my index finger, the bagel hole fitting tightly around my pointer finger. I lift it right next to Tessa's face as she works diligently to concoct her version of a decent cup of coffee with milk and sugar.

"I left you the bagel's asshole."

Tessa's head spins lightning fast to look at me, a disgusted look on her face.

"Bon appetite." I gleam at her and joust the bagel at her again.

"Did you just call that the bagel's asshole?" she asks, her whole face practically squinting at the bagel and then back up at me.

"It's the bottom of the bagel, isn't it? What do you think the hole is for?" I ask. "But I'm still hungry so if you don't want it, I'll eat it."

I just about make a comment about enjoying every bite, but I think I've hit my limit based on the way her eyebrows are drawn together and the scowl across her face. I'm one more dirty joke away from getting that lava-hot coffee poured on me.

"Yum... how appetizing," she says, glaring through a sideways look.

She looks down at the bagel perched on my finger again and then reluctantly pulls the bagel off my finger. She has to give it a good tug to get it off... I've got rather large fingers, and then she sets the bagel down on the countertop next to her coffee, not bothering to look up at me again after that.

I chuckle and then walk over to my wallet sitting on the counter on the island.

"I'm headed to the ski resort this morning for the charity event." I don't look up from my wallet as I say it. I usually have a good poker face, but with Tessa, I find it a lot tougher to keep the guilt off my face. "Bobby says they need help with setup. I'll probably be there all day. You're staying home and working from the house, right?" I ask, wanting to make sure I can account that her whereabouts won't be anywhere near the festival.

The last thing I need is for Tessa to find out what's going on today.

"I have meetings all afternoon." Then she stops and turns to me, my pulse quickening at her abruptness. "Do you think I should come down and get a few photos? Seems like a missed opportunity now that I think of it," she says, her hip resting against the countertop and her foot resting atop her other foot, like a cute-ass flamingo as she takes the first sip of her coffee, sipping it slow as not to burn her mouth.

She pulls back from the mug quickly with a scowl like something bit her. Turns out it's still too hot to sip even with the large amounts of milk she added to it.

"No, it'll be fine. Bobby said there will be professional photographers there. I'll just ask them to get a few good shots and send them to you."

Like a few shots without crazed festival people in the photos or half-naked women.

Luckily, the media for this festival always downplays the shenanigans of this twenty-one or older festival held on the ski resort grounds once a year. If Tessa ever googled it, it would seem like a tame music festival from the perspective of anyone who's never attended.

This "music" festival could rival any Cancun spring break in crazy antics, if not in crowd size. The women are all dressed the same, in bikinis and thongs... or sometimes only pasties over their nipples. I've seen full body paint instead of a bikini. The only difference between the two events is that the half-dressed patrons of the event usually wear boots lined with fur along with whatever costumes, bathing suits, or other creative getups they choose to wear. And instead of sandy beaches... there are ten-person hot tubs in every corner of the festival space, which are usually the epicenter of some all-day orgies.

It gets wild, to say the least, and if Tessa finds out that my attending this festival is why she missed out on her tropical vacation with her friend, shit will hit the fan.

"Oh good! Have them email the pictures as soon as they can, will you? I have a ton of calls today so that will save me time not having to reschedule everyone."

I nod and then pick up my wallet and flip it open, pulling out my black card and flopping it onto the marble. The heavy card makes a loud slap noise when it connects with the stone top.

"I'm leaving you my credit card for gas or whatever you need."

"I told you last night...you don't need to do that," she says, looking up at me from her coffee that she's been blowing on to cool down and then over at the card lying on the counter.

"I know, but I don't know how easy I'll be to get ahold of today. I'll feel better knowing you have something to buy your way out of trouble," I admit, not meaning to seem so protective of her, but I know she has nothing since she lost her wallet and luggage all in the same day.

"Buy my way out of trouble? Like pay off a drug dealer?" she asks, pulling the coffee mug farther away from her mouth and cocks one eyebrow up almost to her hairline as if I'm the weird one.

I'm not the one whose mind goes straight to paying dangerous drug lords, but...

"No... like if you need a tow truck or something... God, you go dark, don't you?" I ask with a chuckle.

"It just seemed like an odd thing to say 'buy your way out of trouble'... and it's not like I know this rich-ass neighborhood. Maybe it's all built on blood money," she says dramatically, wiggling her eyebrow at me with a slight smirk that she tries to hide as she pulls the coffee mug up to her mouth again to test out the temperature.

The coffee has cooled enough this time, and she takes a larger sip than before.

She moans out her approval, and the sound makes a direct shot to my cock.

He gets confused and stirs for a second in my workout shorts. *That wasn't for you, buddy.*

"Well, I hadn't considered it until this very moment, but I guess if a gang member approaches you, and they take American Express... by all means, pay off whatever it takes to make them go away," I tease.

She pulls the mug from her lips, and a small smile stretches across her lips.

"That is oddly sweet of you, Lake. Thanks."

"Any time. Now eat your bagel hole and be good while I'm gone," I say, giving her a devilish grin.

She gives me a quick bratty scrunched nose look that I've seen her give Brent a million times.

The sound of the bagel popping up has her turning away from me sooner than I'd like. She sets her coffee mug down and picks the hot bagel out of the toaster, dropping it onto the marble the minute she pulls it out and burning her fingers a little.

"Ouch," she mutters to herself and then plops her index finger into her mouth quickly as if her hot mouth is going to soothe a burn.

I know something that mouth could soothe.

Shit.

"You okay?" I ask, sort of wishing she'd say no and let me come closer to investigate, but she nods that she's fine and moves on quickly, opening up the cabinet and reaching for a small plate.

I'm slightly disappointed when she reaches the plate quickly and doesn't need my help.

She grabs the knife I left on the tub of cream cheese and starts spreading the thick white dairy product on the bagel, just using the bare minimum of her fingertips to keep the bagel in place as she spreads the creamy topping.

"I will. I have an exciting day of cleanup to do and all the guys are being cool to set aside a few minutes to talk with me on their vacations," she says as she works to cover the bagel.

The excited cadence to her voice makes it seem like she's looking forward to it, which doesn't surprise me since I've always gotten the impression that Tessa likes her job. I guess it makes sense. And it's not as if she's on vacation... she's technically working this week.

"I'm going to head upstairs and shower. I'll be out of here in a few minutes, and you can get to work without distractions. I told the girls not to bother you today while you work."

"You didn't need to tell them that. I like when Chelsea and the girls come over to visit," she says, lifting the plate with the bagel and her coffee cup off the marble countertop and heading for the kitchen table. "Are they going to the festival today?" she asks, turning back to me and taking another sip of her coffee.

Turns out a few sips of caffeine really does put Tessa in a better mood.

I take note of that for another day: Bring Tessa a coffee before delivering her bad news.

Duly noted.

"No," I say quickly, and then spin around and head for the hallway. I don't need her asking any more questions.

I can feel Tessa's eyes on the back of my head as I retreat, my long legs increasing the distance between us at a rapid pace.

I climb the staircase two steps at a time, out of her watchful eye, and before I know it, I'm in my master bathroom, rinsing off the sweat from my workout and hoping I can get out of here without raising any suspicions.

CHAPTER SEVENTEEN

Tessa

After trying to internet search Lake after he left for the charity event this morning, I came up empty-handed. There isn't any accident on the wide web regarding Lake Powers and Aspen. I'm a little disappointed but also relieved. Maybe it wasn't as big of a deal as everyone makes it out to be.

"I can't believe you ended up in a makeshift brothel and they lost your luggage," Autumn says. Her eyes flash wider over our virtual call, and she leans in a little, her face taking up most of the video on my laptop.

She's wearing her hair in a short braid that's laying just slightly over her shoulder and a huge turquoise Hawkeyes hoodie that's about two sizes too big for her.

She could have bought it from the gift shop in the stadium or online, but I bet it's one of Briggs's.

"I've had better bye weeks... let me just say that." I huff, looking back over at the space in front of the coffee maker where Lake had pressed me against the counter with his body as he reached above me to help get a mug down for my coffee.

I hate the way my body reacted to him. A zing of excitement raced up my spine when his solid pecs brushed against my back. I swear I could feel the heat of his crotch radiate over my butt as he stood so close.

"I know." She frowns and breaks me from my trance, bringing my attention back to her and away from the memory of Lake. "I'm sorry this happened to you. But on the bright side, I overheard Phil telling legal to rewrite your contract with a raise on it for you to sign when you get back," she says, wiggling her eyebrows at me. "Whatever you're doing with Lake out there is working."

I can see her mom and Briggs working behind Autumn in her childhood kitchen in Walla Walla. They're both working diligently, slathering multiple pieces of bread in the background as Autumn sits at the kitchen table that's been turned into a makeshift office for the duration of our bye-week vacation. They're spending their time in the town they both grew up in only four hours from Seattle to spend time with Briggs's dad while he gets treatment.

It looks like they're making sandwiches for lunch. My stomach rumbles at the idea of eating a ham and cheese sandwich right about now.

I'd take anything at this point. After spending the entire day returning emails and getting through virtual meetings with several of the players on the Hawkeyes roster to discuss plans to get them a boost in media coverage, I've worked up an appetite. I already know there isn't anything in the fridge, so no point in looking, and unless I take the black card Lake left for me, we won't have any food for dinner tonight or breakfast tomorrow morning.

I started my day with a cup of coffee that I doctored up with a good amount of milk and a heaping scoop of sugar... probably more like a fourth of a cup, if I'm being honest. I ate the last banana that was sitting next to the fridge and reluctantly ate the bottom half of the last bagel that Lake split with me after I slathered it in the minuscule amount of cream cheese that I could scrape out of its tiny white and blue plastic tub.

It's not as if the bagel wasn't delicious... it was. I love a good everything bagel. It's the way he offered it to me when I came downstairs after I showered and got ready for my virtual face-to-face meetings, that turned a sweet gesture... us sharing the last bagel, into a cringeworthy breakfast with every bite.

Now I'll never look at another bagel hole the same way.

I look back over at the black card sitting next to the coffee maker where Lake left it for me.

"We haven't even gotten through the charity animal adoption yet. Once I get through that tomorrow, I'll feel better about my chances of getting that raise. Lake is too much of a wild card to count on any raise."

I'm tempted to tell her about the bet Lake and I entered into, but I'm too embarrassed to tell anyone that I shook knowing the terms of the bet if he won.

The chances he'll win are slim, especially since he can't use his media account, but the confidence Lake has that he's going to win has me unsure about me winning this new bet and coming out, once again, the undefeated champ. This might be the first time I lose to Lake Powers and his wager has me torn. It's inappropriate on every single level, but my sex-deprived body disagrees.

I won't admit this to anyone... but a small part of me feels a thrill at the idea of Lake winning the bet.

"You've got this in the bag. You're going to nail this and even Phil is sure of it," Autumn says, looking over her shoulder back at the kitchen. "Hey, lunch is ready. I have to go, but I'll see you back in the office in a few days, and we can go over all the players and our plans for each one when you get back?"

"Yeah. I think that's a good plan. I'll chat with you later. Tell Briggs I say hi."

"I will." She smiles back at me. "Tell Lake not to be a royal pain in the ass."

"I do... every day... but he doesn't listen," I tell her.

She snickers. "Good luck tomorrow."

"Thanks. Bye." I wave, and then she does too.

I click the end call button and then the screen disappears, showing the screen saver I put on my computer a couple of months ago of a stock photo of Cabo when I made my plans with Elliot. I look over at the large kitchen windows to see little bits of snow fluttering down and wonder how I ended up here instead of on the white sandy beaches with Elliot.

I walk over to the island where Lake left his credit card and pick it up. I walk it over to my purse and zip it into an inside pocket. Without a wallet, it's the safest place for an unlimited spend card. I hate having it on me, too much responsibility, but it's the only money I have right now and I need to eat.

I push my cell phone into my back pocket, sling my purse over my shoulder, and head for the mudroom.

It's time for some grocery shopping before my stomach goes rogue on me and starts eating my vital organs.

Pushing a cart through the store, my first objective is to get the staple items... coffee, coffee creamer, eggs, and milk. I head for the refrigerator section at the back of the store when I see the knowing blueish hue of the large commercial refrigerators beckoning me from between the cereal and the toilet paper aisle.

When I get to the back of the store, I reach for the black-framed refrigerator door, debating the dozen options for an item as simple as milk. People seem to have their preferences and it seems most people like drinking the milk they grew up with... 1%... 2%... non-fat... whole... lactose-free. The list has grown even more to other kinds like soy, almond, and other plant-based.

I pull the door open to reach for the coffee creamer while I debate what type of milk Lake would like since I can't remember what he had stocked that I drank most of in my coffee. I was too busy scowling at its lack of fat and sugar to properly douse my coffee.

"Tessa!" I hear a little girl yell.

I turn immediately to see Lake's nieces headed straight for me, Chelsea in tow farther down the toilet paper aisle.

"Girls!" I yell back, crouching down low enough for them to get their little arms around my neck for a hug. "What are you three up to?" I ask, looking down at them and then up at Chelsea as she approaches.

"I just picked them up from school," Chelsea tells me.

"Yeah! And we want to swim in the heated pool when we get back, but Uncle Lake said you're working," Lana says up to me, her eyes pleading for something she hasn't asked for yet.

"Lana, that's not how we ask."

"Are you still working? Can we come over and swim?"

"Pretty please!" Sadie says, folding her hands like a prayer and gives me big puppy dog eyes.

"Of course, you can. I'd love for you to come over and hang out with me. I was getting lonely at the house all alone."

"Really!?" they both say in unison.

"I would love it," I assure them. "Your uncle is at the charity event all day today, so we'll have the house to ourselves."

"Charity event?" Chelsea says, but I'm too engrossed with the excitement of the girls to catch on.

Both of the girls screech with joy at the prospect and I couldn't be more excited to spend some time with Lake's sister and nieces. There's something about the connection with his family. Between the girls, Chelsea, and Harmony. And even the few times I've spent chatting with his parents when they've come up to the owner's box over the time I've worked for the

Hawkeyes. There's a family dynamic here that I haven't felt in so long.

Not that my brother doesn't feel like family to me. He does... and he's the only family I have, but maybe because of the loss we suffered so young, sometimes it feels like we're hanging on to each other so tight that it doesn't feel like family, it feels more like survival... necessity, like oxygen. I don't know how to explain it any other way. But Lake's family...? They don't feel like oxygen... they feel like a warm snuggly blanket, all cuddled up on a comfy couch with a rom-com all queued up on the TV while a fireplace crackles nearby and bright fluffy snow flutters by the windows outside.

Maybe it's not just his family. Something about this place... its beauty and the calm of a small town that I've never had living in San Diego or Seattle. It feels like... home. A home I haven't known since my parents passed when I was fourteen.

"Yeah, the charity event at the ski lodge."

"What charity event?"

"The one that has every hotel room booked out for a week."

She looks at me with confusion, her eyebrows drawn together and her nose scrunched a little.

"Do you mean the Snow Dayz Music Festival?" she asks as if the idea that they are one and the same is preposterous.

I'm not sure if I should answer yes or no at this point. The severe scowl on her face says I don't think "yes" is the right answer.

"Uhh, I think so. He told our boss that he had a charity event this week and that's why he couldn't stay in town to do his charity work in Seattle. It's the whole reason I'm here... so I'm pretty sure—"

"Oh my God! I thought you knew," she says.

"What?" I ask, my heart beginning to pick up speed.

I don't like the way she's looking at me. Her eyes stare at me with severity, but I can't understand what it means. Then she looks down at the girls. "Why don't you girls go pick out some fruit for a snack to take to Uncle Lake's?" Chelsea suggests.

The produce aisle isn't far and we can see them from here but I don't think the fact that Chelsea's trying to move the girls out of earshot of us bodes well for whatever she's about to tell me.

"It's not a charity event Tessa, it's a pared-down Coachella... with less clothing, if that's even possible. They have "clothing optional" hot tubs set up in every corner of the place. It's an adult-only event."

I can't even speak. I just stare back at her like I'm frozen at this moment. I don't think I even blink for a full minute.

She stands there watching me and realizes I'm shocked into silence. Not a usual response for me.

"I mean... it's fun when you're in college..."

My eyebrows stitch together as she almost takes me down memory lane and then she bales on the idea when she sees it's about to go over like a lead balloon. "... you know what, never mind."

"I gave up Cabo for this?" I say out loud, my eyes breaking from hers, and search over the laminate flooring of the grocery store as if somehow, they will give me the answers that only Lake can.

Like what in the ever-loving hell did I ever do to him to possess him to do something like this to me?

Suddenly the idea of having a blood pact with my girlfriends is starting to sound good. I was kidding with the girls back in Seattle about killing off Lake, but now... cutting his brakes seems completely warranted.

"You gave up Cabo?! What? Why?"

"Because I need to clean up Lake's image so we can land a huge sponsor for the franchise. They're offering millions just to get their name on the stadium, and Lake convinced my boss to let him do the charity in Aspen instead of Seattle because he said he already committed to another charity."

"Oh, well then, you're really not going to like this," she says, and then shifts her weight, moving her cart a little out of the way, and steps closer, checking to make sure the girls can't hear her. "Bobby told me that the event asked Lake to come out to emcee the wet T-shirt contest today. That's what he went to help set up for this morning."

I can't help the words that come spilling from my mouth.

"That motherfucker," I say, at least low enough for the girls not to hear it.

"I'd say so." She nods, crossing her arms over her chest, and pops a hip out as her weight shifts.

"I have to go," I say, pulling my purse out of the top basket of the shopping cart, designed for small children to sit.

"Where are you going?" she asks, spinning around to watch me speed walk down the toilet paper aisle.

"To kill your brother," I say over my shoulder, loud enough for the entire grocery store to hear me.

"Okay, good luck. Let me know if you need a hand stashing the body," she yells after me.

Yep, I knew I liked her.

CHAPTER
EIGHTEEN

Tessa

It takes me almost an hour to drive ten miles to the ski lodge
and then find a parking spot a mile away with all of the traffic,
but I finally get here.

I have no idea what I'm going to do or if the tickets are sold
out, and I can't even get in, but I'll jump a fence if I have to. I'll
risk getting arrested to find Lake.

I want to say I can't believe he did this, but really... I can.

I walk up to the ticket booth and see that they still have
day passes available for today. There's no way in hell I'm using
Lake's card since I already know from the day I pick-pocketed
him that he has alerts on his phone. The last thing I need is

for him to get tipped off that I'm here. I want the element of surprise.

From their sign, it says I can buy online. I already canceled all my cards to be on the safe side, so I call my brother.

"Hey, sis, how's it—"

"I need you to buy me a ticket and send the confirmation email to my phone."

"Good to hear from you too."

"Now Brent, please. It's an emergency," I say, my voice urgent.

"Okay, okay. Text me a link to what you want me to buy. But are you okay? You don't sound okay," he asks carefully.

I love my protective brother, but right now, I just need him to hurry.

"I'm fine. I promise. I'll text you the website," I tell him, pulling up the website and sending him the URL to the exact place for him to place his order. He might end up looking more into the event after the fact, but I'll deal with him later. Right now, I just need to gain access to Lake.

"Thanks. Love you," I say and then hang up on him.

I have no idea when the wet T-shirt contest happens, but I want to be there front and center when he walks out on stage so I can see the look on his face when he realizes that I know. I also plan on getting a few blackmail photos of my own to show Sam and Phil if this entire trip goes haywire, and his whole plan was just to drag me out here.

For all I know, he's going to no-show me tomorrow. But then I would win the bet and get his social media account for three months... and not have to touch myself while he watches. That actually might not be the worst-case scenario. Except my raise is based on this trip going well, not me getting Lake's social media account.

Not even a minute later, a confirmation email comes up on my phone and a bar code pulls up to be scanned at entry.

I haven't been under twenty-one in eight years, but I have no idea how strict this place is about carding people before entry, and without a driver's license, I may still not make it in.

I walk up to one of the women layered in a huge black canvas jacket and matching pants that look wholly uncomfortable but probably warm, and a vest over the top with the word EVENT STAFF on it. She looks to be about as happy to be here as I am.

"Do you have your ticket?" the woman asks me, void of a smile or any interest.

She looks freezing and miserable from being out here all day I would guess. The end of her nose is red from the cold and her cheeks are pink.

The snow let up about an hour ago when I left the grocery store, but it's still under thirty degrees outside right now.

I show her my bar code, and she scans it. She still doesn't offer up a smile at my quick answer to her question in the way of my scannable ticket.

Her scan reader beeps and then goes green.

"Go ahead," she says, and tosses a glove-covered thumb over her shoulder to tell me I have gained entry.

I blow out a breath of relief that she didn't end up asking about my ID.

"Do you know where the wet T-shirt contest is taking place?"

She looks me up and down in a judgmental fashion. She and I are easily the most dressed individuals at this festival based on the scantily dressed individuals I see coming in and out of the event gates.

She finally looks back at my face, her eyes squinting slightly. "Through the gates... take a right... keep going until you see the stage next to the lodge," she says, not even looking at me any longer as she finishes.

Instead, she's turning toward another couple in what can only best be described as "sexy yeti" matching costumes and face paint and asks for their tickets.

"Starts in twenty minutes," she adds, not looking back at me as she scans the yetis' tickets on their phone.

I shake my head and move on. I'm not going to yuck anyone's yum. I have my own that I'd prefer not to be judged for, although you wouldn't likely see me out parading it around for everyone to see.

I weave through the makeshift walkway created by vendor tents selling beer, food, and henna tattoos, along with many other things. It's littered with lazily discarded red Solo cups and sprinkled with pieces of kettle corn all over the place.

You know your stomach has now begun to eat its own reserves when you look down longingly at a piece of popcorn on a snowy dirt floor and wonder if the ten-second rule still applies.

I keep walking, looking for a stage as I make my way through this giant place, hoping I haven't missed it yet. I want to be at the very front of the stage when he walks out, so I need to get there as soon as possible.

Then I see it. The massive lodge first, but then my eyes trail down to the left side of the building to find a temporary stage. It's large, and music is already playing through the giant black speakers on either side of the platform. Eventgoers have already started forming around the stage, red Solo cups in hand and less than a full outfit among a few dozen people who got here early to get a front-row spot.

I look to the right of the stage.

The kiosk for sign-ups.

One woman is still signing what I'm guessing is the waiver form, and I don't even think as I walk up behind her.

I can't see her face but considering how distracting her bright red bikini is, matching with fuzzy Uggs and an odd-looking penguin hat on the top of her head, I don't imagine she was aiming for people to look at her face anyway when she got ready this morning.

The dude waiting for her to fill it all out looks over at me and then looks me up and down. Taking in my huge puffy jacket, jeans, and calf-high snow boots that Chelsea let me borrow. I have ten times the amount of clothing on as the woman signing the waiver in front of me.

The man standing behind the kiosk wears an identical ensemble to the woman who scanned my ticket earlier at the entry gates. The same vest with EVENT STAFF writing on it.

I want to scold him and demand he gives this poor girl his jacket, but she doesn't even look cold... she looks plastered by the way she's swaying back and forth while trying to sign her name. A relatively easy task when you're sober.

Who's letting her do this right now?

That stage looks too dangerous for a woman who soon enough will have a large bout of dizzy spells and vertigo. My stomach turns just thinking about it. I've had my own experiences with it during my college years. I know the feeling all too well.

"Are you here to sign up?" he asks, politely but hesitantly.

I break my eyes off the woman and then look at him.

"Yes!" I say firmly without even thinking about it.

If I want to get Lake's attention, this will do it.

The woman in front of me finishes signing her waiver, and then he hands her a white T-shirt with the words Snow Dayz on the front of it.

Cute. Not.

I guess it's a festival-issued T-shirt for the contest... good advertising, only... these pictures will end up on social media, and Lake's face along with it. Then the animal shelter charity will be all for nothing. I need to get to him and stop this.

She steps back and wobbles a little like she's about to fall over. I outstretch my arms to catch her, and the guy behind the kiosk leans over the table, attempting to reach out for her too, but then she regains her footing and turns to head toward the stage, not even noticing me. Originally, I figured she's a few shots in, but now looking at her, she must be half a bottle.

He and I both look at each other like we should say something about her, but neither of us does.

I'm probably going to need a drink for this too.

"Here's the form to fill out, releasing Snow Dayz or the ski lodge of any liability relating to photographs taken by anyone in the crowd or the event staff and any liability if you fall off the stage or slip on ice... that sort of thing." He shrugs from the cold and then rubs his hands together after he passes me a wooden clipboard and a gray pen with a Snow Dayz logo on it.

Well, they're well branded. I'll give them kudos for that.

"Got it," I say, bending down over the table to complete the paperwork.

"It's a thousand-dollar cash prize if the crowd selects you as the contestant with the nicest..."

He stops himself the second I look up. Is he getting shy about exactly what his job entails all of a sudden?

Strange timing.

"Yeah... I know how this works. Not my first time," I admit.

I had my crazy days, especially in college with my girlfriends. I mean, I went to school in San Diego... one of the top-ranked party schools in the country.

His eyebrow shoots up quickly and then his lips purse. "Oh okay," he says.

I didn't realize there was a prize for this.

That's some luck for once.

That money will help get me home when I turn rubber out of this place the second I tell Lake where to cram it. I can't fly out of here because I have no ID. It's currently sitting in Seattle with my wallet, so I'll have to ask Chelsea or Harmony to help me rent a car, or I'll have to take a bus, but at this point, I'd jump in the back of a semi-truck hauling cow manure to get as far away from Lake as possible.

I guess this idea isn't so bad anyway. A thousand dollars would get me pretty far on a charter bus, and I don't think I have to show ID for that. I'll have to look into it.

The last thing I want to do is call Penelope or Brent and ask them for the money. I'll have to admit to bailing early.

I'm at least seven or eight years older than the barely twenty-one-year-old woman who was in front of me, but my tits are fabulous... I've got a shot at winning this.

"Here's the white T-shirt that must be worn without a bra to win."

I look to my left, where he places it on the table, and nod as I keep filling out the paperwork.

I finish the paperwork quickly and then push it back to him. I scoop the shirt up off the table.

"Where do I go now?" I ask.

He points at a door to the right of the stage. It's an enclosed space, unlike the stage that's open to the elements. It's a portion of the building still attached to the ski lodge. It looks like an add-on designed for the maintenance department. It's not as pretty as the lodge with rough-cut logs and siding. This part of the building is two stories of concrete. Such a lackluster design if you ask me, but I guess large amounts of snowfall require heavy-duty construction.

"Hang out in there until they call you out. There's a place to change, and it's heated until you have to walk out on stage. Lake Powers is emceeing today." He winks at me as if hearing Lake's name should make me swoon.

Make me want to clench my fists is more like it.

"That's what I'm betting on," I tell him, and flash him a fake smile and turn to walk away.

"Tessa!" I hear a voice behind me near the kiosk.

I look back to find Bobby standing next to the guy who just signed me up. He's dressed in a snowboard jacket and snow pants... the appropriate gear for this event. Someone should send out a memo.

"What are you doing?" Bobby asks, his forehead scrunched slightly as he looks at the white T-shirt in my hand.

"Looking for an easy grand. You?" I ask, my face blank as I stare back at him, trying not to give away how mad I am.

After all, he isn't the one who dragged me here under false pretenses, ruining my first true vacation in forever.

"I'm helping out at this event. Does Lake know you're here?" he asks with a poker face.

I can't tell if he knows that Lake wasn't completely honest with me or not.

"He's about to find out." I huff.

He nods with a grin. Something about the way he looks back at me tells me he knows this isn't good news for Lake, and he finds it amusing. At least someone's getting entertainment from this.

"Do you snowboard?" I ask even though I know my time to get changed is dwindling, but he's the only one I've seen in this crowd of people who looks like they belong at a ski resort.

"Yeah. I'm going to hit the slope after I help out with this last event for the day. Do you?" he asks, his lips turning up on one side in a smile like he's happy I asked.

"No, but I've always wanted to learn," I admit.

He nods, crossing his arms, and stares out at the empty stage for a second.

"Well..." he says, seeming to consider his next words, and then locks his eyes back on mine. "I'll be around later if you'd like a private lesson," he offers.

Why does Bobby have to be Lake's cousin? Why couldn't he be some cute guy who I bumped into at a coffee shop or met in line at some concert?

"I'd take you up on that, but I'm leaving after this. I just came by to tell Lake," I say with a scowl meant for Lake... not Bobby.

His cute lopsided smile flattens out a little, and he gives a tight-lipped nod.

"That's too bad. It was nice meeting you, Tessa," he says. "Let me know if you need anything."

"If you have Lake repellent handy, I'll buy your entire supply."

"Fresh out, unfortunately." He gives a soft chuckle.

"Just my luck," I smirk back and then turn around to head for the building.

"Hey, Tessa," Bobby says.

I stop and spin back around. "Yeah?" I ask.

Bobby pushes his hands deep into the pockets of his snowboard pants.

"Lake's not a bad guy."

I thought he wanted to take me out... so why is he defending Lake now?

"Okay...?"

"He's the way he is because he doesn't think he deserves to be happy."

First Harmony with this excuse, and now Bobby?

I try not to roll my eyes because, well, I like Bobby. I think we'd be friends in another life... another world. But did he come up with that junk, or is he just regurgitating the excuse he hears Lake make to the hundreds of women he leaves in his wake?

"Wow, I've never heard that one. I'll give it to you, Bobby. I've heard a lot of lines in my life for why men are nasty manholes, but I'm going to give you a 10 out of 10 for originality."

I spin around, not waiting for a rebuttal from Lake's too-loyal cousin, and see that the girls are already filing out onto the stage.

He calls out, "It's not a line," softly to himself, but I'm too busy to worry about it.

I have to hurry and get dressed, or I'll miss the whole thing.

CHAPTER NINETEEN

Tessa

When I trot up to the tall concrete building and swing open the door, a wave of heat hits me. The building is heated, thank God, and it's warm in here.

No other contestants are sitting around on the bottom floor. They all must have walked up to the second story. I find a little changing spot, which feels silly, considering everyone within view of the stage will be able to see our breasts. What's the point of modesty while changing into a barely-there white T-shirt?

I pull off my many layers of jackets and long sleeves as I hear a male announcer's voice come over the microphone. It's not Lake, it's someone else.

I try to listen but the delay and echo from inside the bland gray concrete walls of this attached building to the main portion of the large ski lodge makes it tough. However, I can't miss when the announcer finally calls out the name Lake Powers, and the crowd erupts.

I get my shirt in place and still feel overdressed in a pair of designer jeans and boots, but the point is not how I'm dressed. The main point is to catch Lake in action. I make sure my phone is in my back pocket to ensure I get a few shots of him at his "charity event." I'm sure Sam will find this interesting.

Finally, I hear Lake's voice come over the speaker, and I know I'm out of time. I rush out behind the changing room and haul butt up the staircase toward the second floor where the contestants are walking out on stage.

The warm building is somewhat cooler on the second floor with a large overhead door similar to a large garage door that is wide open for people on stage to flow in and out of it but it's not bad if the winter breeze isn't blowing through.

A cold whip of wind flies past me. Cool bits of wet weather cling to the tiny hairs on my arm and I fold my forearms over each other to keep me warmer.

My nipples are hardening into an uncomfortable state as I glance out onto the stage, hidden behind the protective walls of the building.

I see six women in varying stages of drunkenness standing in a line waving back at the crowd, dancing in place, or swaying to the music playing over the loudspeakers as they stand on the stage, facing out. All six of them turn to send flirtatious smiles at Lake to their left. He's standing at the end of the stage and a good ten feet from them, near where the control station table is sitting and where the music is probably streaming from.

I take out my phone and start taking a few shots that I can show Sam of the "charity event" that Lake couldn't miss.

Once I've taken enough pictures to show as evidence, i slide my phone back into my pocket.

Lake looks hot as hell in a pair of dark-wash jeans, black boots, and a long black peacoat with the collar flared up against his neck, the buttons undone as if the cold barely registers with him.

Why is that so freaking attractive?

Guys that don't seem to notice freezing temperatures... oh right, because I have a thing for players who make their living on a block of ice.

I really should consider hypnosis just like some people do to quit smoking. Maybe they could help me eliminate my own nasty habit...

Hot hockey players.

His ashy-blond hair is styled in that slightly disheveled way that I don't want to admit always looks so damn sexy on him.

He smiles back at them and then faces the crowd and gives a small wave. I don't like the flash of jealousy that bubbles up in my belly. I hate this man... more than ever for what he did to me. There is no way I would wish him on my worst enemy. So being jealous of a group of women who he'd only ever give one night and then toss them aside like a used napkin doesn't make sense.

"It's cold out here, folks, so let's get this event on the road," the announcer standing next to Lake says. "Can we get the guys with the buckets of water out here?" he asks toward whoever is in charge of the actual water.

From the corner of my eye, I see Bobby come from the back of the stage near Lake. There must be a staircase that also comes from behind the stage for the announcer, Lake, and anyone else who needs to adjust the music or lighting on stage.

He walks over to Lake and whispers something close to his ear. Lake's eyebrows furrow and his jaw tightens as he looks out to the crowd before him while he listens to what Bobby has to say. Within seconds, Lake's head whips over in my direction.

I hear loud multiple sets of footsteps behind me, walking up the stairs of the building. I turn my head to find seven guys, each not much older than twenty-one, cresting over the staircase one by one, carrying a five-gallon bucket of water with steam billowing from the top.

At least the water will be warm.

I watch as they pass by me and head out to the stage with their buckets toward the contestants.

If I don't make a move now, I'll miss my shot.

The announcer gives Lake the mic. He's now on as the emcee.

That's my cue to walk out on stage, and the second I take my first step out from behind the building, Lake sees me and shoves the mic against Bobby's chest, abandoning his post to take long forceful steps toward me. He shakes his head as if to warn me not to take another step, but he isn't going to deter me.

He's moving quickly across the stage like a missile headed for destruction. The look on his face... his eyes squinting, his eyebrows downturned, and a deep frown on his face... he's not happy. Good, that makes the two of us.

Serves him right.

I take several more steps out onto the stage, trying my best to ignore the freezing temperatures and not let it show on my face. The second Lake reaches me, I expect we're about to have an argument in front of this entire crowd of people. I clench my fists in preparation, but he doesn't say a word, instead, he grips around my waist and hoists me up over his shoulder, without breaking his stride.

"Oof," I mutter.

His quick motion knocks a little wind out of me as he slings me over his shoulder.

He doesn't even falter with the additional weight of me bound up over the left side of his shoulder, carrying me off like some archaic caveman.

"Put me down." I squeak out my demand.

"No," he growls.

His left hand holds me in place by the back of my right thigh and his touch has me thinking how easy it would be for him to spank me.

For God's sake Tessa, don't think of that now.

His forceful steps bounce me against him as my ponytail smacks involuntarily against his back and I lay upside down, my right hand holding me off his back a little so that I don't face-plant into a wall of muscle and spine.

I can't even imagine how this must look to the crowd of people.

Hopefully they're all too drunk to notice.

"Lake!" I yell louder this time.

I try to squirm out of his hold but there is always the possibility that if I'm successful, he'll end up dropping me... maybe headfirst.

"Stop squirming. I'm not putting you down until we're inside. They can see you," he says gruffly, and then slaps my left butt cheek that's practically resting against his face.

My center squeezes at the sharp radiating sting caused by my butt cheeks already being cold and the fact that Lake just slapped my ass.

"Ouch! Lake!" I say, kicking back and forth.

I know I'm going to have a Lake-sized handprint on my butt when I get home.

"You earned it, Tessa. Keep it up and I'll give you more," he threatens, and I hate how much I hope he's a man of his word.

But why does he care if anyone notices me in the line of other women on stage?

"So what if they can see me?" I demand.

"Your shirt is see-through," he seethes.

We pass back through the entrance of the gray concrete second story that I had exited not more than a minute ago, me still hanging over his left shoulder.

"That's the idea, genius," I fire back.

"I don't like it."

"Oh, so you can do it but I can't? Nice double standard," I retort, speaking to his back.

I start to feel the blood rushing to my face at this point so I push up against his back a little more aggressively and it gives me a chance to look back.

"More like none of those dicks out there deserve to see your wet tits," he mutters to himself.

I'm about to ask him to clarify exactly *who* gets to see them then when I hear a tapping on the microphone and push myself up against Lake to find the announcer watching Lake as he retreats into the building with me slung over him.

"It seems as though Lake is helping a festival patron who is in distress. Let's give Lake Powers a round of applause for being a decent guy and then also give a warm welcome to the Quarterback for the Denver Heroes, Branson Huckley who will be taking over the emceeing of this event."

The crowd erupts and I watch, my vision shaking while Lake continues to walk us farther into the building, as Branson takes to the stage, a good-looking guy for all intents and purposes but he doesn't have anything on Lake.

He finally sets me down directly in front of a load-bearing wall in the middle of the room. He blocks my view of the crowd and my ability to get past him much at all.

My butt brushes up against the wall that he sets me in front of as he blocks me from heading back for the stage.

I peak past him at the opening where I can still see the stage and the contestants but it's too dark in here for anyone to see us all that well from the outside.

His eyes bare down on me standing at arm's length.

"What are you doing here?" he growls.

His voice is deep and raspy. Probably from working all morning in the dry cold climate... although was he working to help set up anything? Or was that all a lie too?

I glower at him and my lips purse. I'm trying to keep in the profanity I'd like to yell at him. I don't want to lose control. Lake isn't worth it and we still have to find a way to work together after this trip from hell is over. I like my job and there is no way I'm going to put in my notice, and Lake just renewed with the Hawkeyes for a record-breaking contract amount for the next three years.

"Just thought I should get a few photos of your charitable giving. I think Sam would be interested in learning about the charity you're so passionate about. Don't you think?" I say sarcastically.

"You can't be up here. Go home," he demands.

He takes another step closer to me and I'm starting to feel slightly caged in, a door to a storage closet to my left and the staircase down to the first floor to my right are my options to flee. Not that I'm scared of him but the intensity of his stare feels like he might actually decide to carry me all the way out of the event and set me back outside of the event gates.

I won't let him win.

He's a big guy and he's used to getting his way but not today.

I'm done being corralled by hockey player assholes that think they can push me around, intimidate me, cheat on me... hit me.

San Diego was the last time. I made a promise to myself when I told my brother I wanted out of Southern California. I didn't tell him the gory details, just that I needed some new scenery and was done working for the San Diego Blue Devils hockey franchise where I held the same job that I now hold with the Hawkeyes. He hates the Blue Devils so he was more than happy to poach me and bring me to Seattle. Sam and Phil were happy too.

Ironically, it's the same team that Lake played for before being traded to the Hawkeyes four years ago. I started working for the Blue Devils a few months after Lake left so I was lucky enough not to have had to work with him back then too.

Brent told me to come live with him and got me a job with the Hawkeyes. I left my old life behind and never looked back. Lake is the last man who I'll let take me back there again.

No more hockey players... never again.

"I have just as much right to be out here as any other person on this stage," I argue, glancing past him at the six women still on stage.

I see Bobby shoot a look toward the building and in our direction, as he gently pulls the woman who was standing in front of me at the signup kiosk off the stage and hands her over to two people at the top of the staircase. They look like paramedics.

Good, I'm glad someone has some sense around here to get that girl off the stage before she hurts herself... or falls off the platform and hits someone else.

"I don't want you here," he snarls, his eyes darting down to my nipples poking through the white T-shirt and the color of my areolas showing through the thin, light fabric.

"Good thing I don't give a shit what you want," I say, turning up my nose at him.

I might as well not be wearing a shirt at all. He can see everything.

When his eyes reach back up to mine, I can see the arousal in his dilated pupils. He lets out a breath that tickles the baby hairs around my face that have come loose from my ponytail over the course of the day.

Heat flashes low in my belly at his reaction and his intense stare, warming the apex between my thighs that's been neglected by a man for far too long. Too bad Lake Powers is the last man getting anywhere near my aching center.

He can stare all he wants; he's already seen my nipples when I took off my hoodie in his walk-in closet the night he brought me back to his house after I ended up in a sex motel because of him. The memory of what he's done to me and my canceled vacation comes flooding back, hardening my heart to him again. I wish I can say that it also dries up my dampening excitement but of course, it doesn't. I'm as wet as ever, which just pisses me off more.

Off in the distance, I hear the announcer give the instruction for the buckets of water to be splashed on the contestants. And then a second later, I hear the shrieks and then the giggles that follow as the women on stage all get drenched.

The quarterback comes over the microphone to facilitate the voting for which woman will win the wet T-shirt contest and then I'm brought back to remembering why I'm here, who forced me here, and the fact that if I hadn't shown up, Lake would be out there helping vote on the best rack on stage.

I hope he got an eye full of my breasts because it's the last time he'll ever see them. I'll make sure of it this time.

I try to sidestep and walk past him back out toward the stage to get in line with the other five women with one fewer participant who Bobby is hopefully taking to some well-padded drunk tank to rest it off.

Lake's hand reaches out and grips my right arm, stopping my progress.

It's not an aggressive hold like I experienced too many times from my ex. It's solid and steadfast but there's also something protective in it, just like the owner of the hand wrapped around me. The same man who made sure to leave me half the bagel and the last banana to make sure I didn't go hungry, and who took me to his sister's shop and bought me practically an entire year's worth of clothing.

"If you think I'm going to let any of those assholes out there see you dripping wet with your tits out for them to ogle... you're crazy," he says, his voice gravelly and low.

I try to speak but I can't.

Did he just say "ogle"?

His hand is warm against my bare skin and even though the sharp bite from the cold has riddled my body in goosebumps ever since I stepped out onto the stage in only a T-shirt and a pair of jeans and boots, it's the shivers from being in his grasp that has me painfully aware of what Lake Powers' presence does to me.

"What is wrong with you?" I demand a little breathless.

He takes another step, the tips of his boots butting up against mine.

"I told you, Tessa, I'm not letting anyone see what should belong to me..." He winces slightly like he didn't mean to say that out loud.

"What *should* belong to you, Lake?" I jab, pushing my hands against his chest but he doesn't budge.

I don't belong to anyone, least of all a one-night-stand-only hockey player manhole who's a relationship pariah and who's responsible for my missing luggage, lost wallet, and all the other myriad of bad luck I've had over the last week.

My challenge to his unfinished statement should have him retreating but instead of moving back, he gets closer, leaning in and bracing his left hand against the wall behind me, above the right side of my head, his jaw clenching as his eyes hood. His mouth opens just slightly, and as he glances down at my jaw, his right hand comes up softly and brushes over it as gently as a feather.

"Should I show you what should belong to me, Tessie?" he whispers, our noses so close they could almost touch.

His eyes zero in on me and I know that I'm not getting out of here unkissed.

When I don't respond, he wraps his right hand around the base of my skull and his left around my waist and then drops his mouth to mine, pushing my body up against the concrete wall with his own.

My hands cling to the open lapels of his peacoat. I'm not pulling him closer but I'm not pushing him away either, I'm just trying to keep my head above water because this kiss could take me under, gasping for breath and wanting to drown in him when I know I shouldn't.

His mouth is so warm, his body against me like a heating blanket. Any coldness I felt before evaporates and in its place are tingles of excitement and anticipation.

I should tell him off for the way he makes assumptions about what I want and who I want. I should squeeze past him and run down the staircase, escaping this situation altogether. I don't like the way my body wants him. It's all so wrong.

It reminds me of exactly who I'm kissing.

I have to do something... I have to stop this, even though there's nothing I want more at this moment than him. But that's the old me... the weaker me. Whose knees go weak for a man in skates.

I pull my hands off his peacoat and flatten my hands against his chest, giving him a shove. He pulls off my mouth, his lips red from our kiss, his pupils wide with lust.

My senses tune out all other noise besides the sound of our breathing. I stare back into his eyes. There's an offer in them but one I can't take him up on.

Suddenly, the bucket brigade of empty buckets of water passes by us as the guys wielding them chatter about which practically naked woman should have won and the excitement around Branson Huckley being here for the festival. In my peripheral, I only see five guys pass by. Where did the sixth and seventh one go without me and the drunk girl to dump their water on?

"Oh... there you are." A kid no more than twenty-one years old stops to the left of us.

I barely even look at him before he pulls back his full bucket and douses me with water just like the women on stage.

I let out a yelp as the water hits me harder than I expect and I stumble back into the wall, the lukewarm water soaking me from top to bottom. The top of my head and my back are the only things that don't get drenched.

"Oh my God," I say, my arms outstretched to the sides as I look down to find my white T-shirt is now... wet, as it was intended to be, but I'm no thousand dollars richer and closer to getting a ticket out of here.

"You fucking idiot." Lake growls, and turns to the guy, shoving him.

The surprised bucket-carrying jerk slips on the water, his feet coming fully up over his head as his back hits the floor before anything else.

A loud thud from the kid and his bucket echo through the building.

"Shit, I'm sorry," the guy chokes out, lying flat on his back.

Lake looks down at me just long enough to see that I'm soaked and then slides his left arm around me protectively and pulls my wet body against him to cover me from anyone seeing.

"Don't you ever touch her again or I'll beat the living fuck out of you, do you understand?"

The guy looks terrified sprawled out on the ground. He can't be more than twenty-one or twenty-two, a whole decade younger than Lake. Too young to die for his stupidity under the hands of the Hawkeyes' Left-Wing superstar.

The kid nods. "I'm so sorry, Mr. Powers... I... I thought she was a contestant," he stutters while trying to get to his feet and then turns toward the staircase and practically throws himself down the steps to get away from a pissed off Lake as fast as possible and then scampers off.

Lake looks back down at me, pulling away from me just enough to see that my shirt is completely wet... and completely see-through.

"Shit," he mutters, his tongue darting out to lick his lips. "You look...cold," he whispers, his eyes fixed on my hardening nipples.

"I am." My teeth chatter.

I feel cold in some places and warm in others as his eyes darken with arousal as his eyes drift over me.

"Then here. Let me warm you up," he says, and without warning he bends down and nuzzles into my breast, his hands gripping my hips and pulling me against him, his mouth dipping down and latching onto my left breast, sucking down on me instantly.

"Ohh..." I moan out in instant gratification.

My hands wrap around the back of his neck, holding him closer to me.

This is a bad idea, anyone can see us, but there is no part of me that can say no to him. His tongue is swirling around my cold nub and with every flick of it, he's warming every inch of me.

He pulls me into his arms, tightening them around me, and then lifts me, my thighs instinctively wrapping around his waist.

I can still faintly hear the competition still going on so I know no one will be headed this way for a second but even if they were, I wouldn't tell Lake to stop.

Not yet.

With my eyelids fluttering closed to focus on the feeling of him, I can't see much but I feel Lake's body jerk toward the left and I hear the broom closet door open.

Lake pulls me off the wall, his mouth still suctioned against me, and walks us both into the closet, closing the door behind us.

"Where the fuck is the lock?" I hear him mutter against my left breast as he feels around the door for a way to lock us in here so no one catches us.

"I don't know. I don't care," I tell him, too blinded by need at this moment to take a second to make sure no one interrupts us.

"Me either. I just want to take care of you," he says, abandoning the front of the broom closet and heads for the only bare space of wall.

It's warmer in here but my skin is still cool from the once lukewarm water turned ice cold.

The feeling of his warm mouth against my cold skin and the way his tongue swirls around my hard nub... I wish I could deny him the satisfaction of knowing he's making me feel this good but I can't control it. I let out a whimper that I can't hold back.

His hands slide over my hips and trail up my back, pulling me closer as he nuzzles his face against my breast even harder.

"Lake..." I whisper in a breathy voice.

He lets out a groan. He's enjoying this too.

His lips tighten around my nipple as he applies more pressure. Then I feel the slight sharp pain of Lake's teeth as they gently slide against the fabric around my nipple and create a zing of tingles that shoot down to my clit, making it pulsate with need.

I whimper at the pleasure and pain as my hands trail over his strong shoulders and up his long neck until my fingers find his hair and run through it, gripping and holding him in place... right where I need him.

"This is the only thing I've been able to think about since the second I saw you standing out on that stage," he admits.

"This is why you pulled me off the platform?" I ask.

He nods and then shifts his mouth from my left breast and slides his face to my right, baring down the second he gets it in his mouth. My fingers stay clenched in his hair.

"This is what I've been thinking about doing since I pulled you out of that motel," he admits.

Since the motel?!

Another moan breaks through my lips at the sensation of his mouth taking care of both needing nipples and his confession, knowing he's wanted me this whole time.

I can feel his excitement through his jeans too. The hard rod in his pants tells me that I'm not the only one getting worked up over his sucking and nibbling as he slides his hard length between us.

He begins to rock into me slowly. He's testing out the waters to make sure I want it and how could I possibly say no even though I should? It feels too good to stop him now.

His thrusts increase and he presses me into the drywall a little more aggressively than the time before as he dry humps me into submission.

He lets me slide down his body just a little as his mouth moves up my chest and then over my neck.

He kisses and sucks his way up my body until his lips press against my jaw and before I can register it, his mouth is on mine again.

He's kissing me and I'm kissing him back. His full lips on me are soft but dominating. His tongue licks a line over my lips and I open in response, letting him taste me like I'm dying for him too.

Our mouths lock as our tongues dip and dive into one another's. Lake nibbles down on my lip and I whimper again at the sharp sting of it.

"You like that?" he asks, wolfishly, his voice deep and low.

"Yes," I admit, my voice not more than a breathy whisper.

There's a short silence as he continues to thrust against me, controlling my mouth and making me wetter as his bulge rubs me harder. Then finally he speaks again.

"Are you on birth control?" he says, his voice laboring slightly as he increases speed and pressure against me.

Uh, what?

I'm not sure how to answer. I'm a sexually active woman, even if I haven't been as of recently, and I still like to keep my affairs in order should the moment arise but sex with Lake is out of the question. Sex with any hockey player is off the menu and he already knows this. Not to mention that I'm not interested in a one-night stand with Lake and that's all he offers women.

"Umm, yeah, but..."

"I don't have a condom on me," he says without offering any other explanation, keeping his perfect rhythm.

"Okay...?"

"I don't fuck in Aspen, so I don't bother carrying any in my wallet ... but I'm clean, I swear. I haven't been with anyone since before my last checkup over three weeks ago."

Pump the brakes. What?!

I have so many questions.

For starters, why don't you have sex in Aspen? Are you related to all the women in this small town or something? And why haven't you had sex in over three weeks when I know you have women throwing themselves at you nightly?

And why are you offering me unprotected sex in a broom closet when you know I won't sleep with hockey players anyway, least of all without a condom?

I need to put an end to this. It's getting out of hand. Fantasy be damned, this just isn't worth it.

"I think we got a little carried away," I say, reluctantly pulling my fingers out of his blond hair.

I unlock my legs from around his waist and attempt to pull them under me to safely dismount his body but Lake senses I'm pulling away and grips both of his hands around the outside of my thighs and stops me from dismounting.

"Wait, hold on. What did I do?" he asks.

His eyebrows knit together like he's truly confused about why I'm pulling away.

"I told you, I don't get involved with hockey players anymore. This was a moment of clouded judgment," I say plainly.

He shakes his head, not agreeing with me.

"I know you feel the tension between us. We both need this," he says, searching my eyes.

We both need this? That's quite the assumption.

"Need what?" I ask.

"To get this out of our system. One time."

Figures... one time.

"One time? That seems to be your motto, doesn't it? At least you're consistent, I suppose," I say, pushing my legs back down again. This time, he releases me but slowly like he doesn't really want to, his hands gliding along my outer thighs as I slip down farther from his body, his hands securing around my hips to make sure I'm stable as my feet hit the floor.

"What are you talking about?" he asks, an edge to his voice, his eyes locked on to me.

"Your one-night-only rule. It's a well-known fact. And something that I've even heard you mention before."

He makes a scoffing noise and stares up at the stack of paper towels on the shelf above my head for a moment. Then he rests his hands low on his hips. His intense stare comes back down on me.

"Are you seriously mad that I'm not interested in a relationship with anyone? You just said that you don't date hockey players."

"Exactly," I say firmly.

"Exactly what?" he asks, shifting his weight from the left to the right leg.

"That having sex together is a bad idea," I say, crossing my arms over my chest to close myself off even more.

"Tessa, I know you can feel the sexual friction between us, and it's fucking maddening. We need to let out a little steam or this thing is going to blow up."

A bomb. His analogy is spot-on.

That's exactly what this is. A ticking time bomb that will take out everything in its wake once detonated.

"I don't feel the same way."

"Liar," he says, watching me. "Once is all we need. I know you need this as bad as I do."

I look toward the exit, considering sliding out past him and exiting this conversation. The more he talks about how we both need to screw each other silly to get past this growing tension, the more I'm starting to want it to, but it will only bring *him* relief... I can be sure, that for me, it will be the opposite.

In theory, I'm okay with one night, but what happens when the very next night, I see the gossip blogs post a photo of him taking a new girl home after a game or after we all leave the bar after a win?

I can't allow myself to break my oath to myself or do something when I'm not sure if I can live with the regret.

I can't risk it.

"You're wrong about what I need. What I need is for you to finish the charity event tomorrow so I can go home and forget this trip ever happened."

He stares down at me, searching my face for authenticity. His poker face doesn't tell me what he's thinking but the lack of smile tells me this isn't going the way he wants it to.

Then he takes a step back, and I lose his body heat.

It's not cold in the broom closet like it was outside but a chill still runs over me as he retreats from the stand he tried to make.

I hear the jiggling of a metal handle, and I jump a little in surprise, my heart skipping a beat. Lake steps closer to me and slides his left hand around me, making sure to cover my see-through shirt with his body as his head turns toward the intruder. My hands grip onto him to keep my breasts hidden behind him.

The storage door opens, and the janitor is standing there in a pair of overalls, a puffy jacket, and a wool beanie.

He jumps a little when he sees us. He wasn't expecting two people to be inside.

"Oh sorry," he says, seeing us inside.

He pulls the door back against himself when he realizes that there's more than just rolls of toilet paper and bleach behind the door. "I was just getting a mop. I'll, uh... I'll come back," he tells us, and then backs up.

"No, no!" I stop him.

The presence of another person will keep me from changing my mind. "I was just leaving," I tell him, squeezing past Lake and quickly covering my see-through top with my folded arms, making a quick exit past the janitor and out the door.

"Wait! Take my coat," Lake yells from the closet, but I'm already halfway down the stairs and headed for my jacket I left on the first floor.

I hear Bobby stop Lake, giving me the extra time to escape down the stairs and out of the building.

CHAPTER TWENTY

Lake

I walk out of the broom closet, tempted to chase after Tessa, but I know that won't help things.

I know I'm not the only one feeling this. I could feel her damp heat through her jeans as I rocked into her against the concrete wall. She wanted what I was offering her no matter what she says. However, offering her unprotected sex wasn't my best move. What I told her is true, though, I don't bring condoms to Aspen.

This is my hometown, and after the accident that happened the week after I got recruited to the San Diego Blue Devils, I don't want to cause this town any more grief.

I poke my head out from the broom closet, after the janitor left it open, grabbing his mop and speeding out of there after Tessa left.

The women from the contest are all now inside, covered in navy blue towels with the Snowy Dayz logo on them, getting selfies with Denver's QB. Everyone seems to be in a good mood and distracted. Bobby snaps a few shots for everyone and then spots me.

I step out of the closet and head for the staircase, hoping no one stops me for photos. I'm not in the best mood, and I still have a boner that didn't get the memo that Tessa rejected us and fled our joint space to get away from me.

"Lake..." Bobby says at the top of the stairs behind me, his steps slapping through the water that's still present from where that kid dumped five gallons over Tessa.

I don't stop my descent down the staircase because I don't want to get pulled into the group upstairs. If I make eye contact with anyone from the contest or event staff, I'll feel obligated to head back up and make an appearance.

Right now, I need to wrap my head around what just happened between Tessa and me. And also, what didn't happen?

"Hey, Lake, hold up, man," Bobby says again as soon as I clear the bottom of the stairs.

I turn right toward the large gray steel door with an illuminated EXIT sign above it.

I glance around for Tessa, just in case I get lucky and she had a change of heart, realizing that leaving like that was dramatic, but there is no sign of her.

"Yeah. What?" I say over my shoulder toward him.

"Can you stop a minute?" he asks, jogging behind me to catch up.

I stop, and he just about runs into the back of me. I turn halfway around, still eyeing the door. I need to get out of here. Go for a drive... or... I don't know, something.

I can still smell Tessa's strawberry lip balm in my mouth and her vanilla essence on my shirt. She's all over me, and nowhere near me, all at the same time.

"What is it?" I ask, tucking my hands in my pocket to keep my clenching fists from being obvious.

I'm not mad at him; I'm mad at myself.

I handled that situation with Tessa as poorly as I could have but I'm not used to having to try. I'm not used to being turned down, either. It's not a good excuse; it's just the only one I have.

"What happened with Tessa? I saw you carry her off stage. The announcer froze, but Branson Huckley was close by, so I tossed him on stage in your place."

My eyes cast down to the concrete floor. I feel bad that I put them out like that. It wasn't professional of me, but when I saw Tessa step out on the platform, all I could see was red. And the only thought I had was. *"Get her somewhere safe and warm, where no one but you can see her."*

"Shit, I'm sorry, Bobby," I tell him, running a hand through my hair.

The memory of Tessa's hands running through it a minute ago and the sounds she made for me echo through my head. I shake them loose.

"I didn't mean to flake like that... I..." I pull my hands out of my pockets and outstretch them flat toward him as if my lame excuse is all I have to offer for my poor professionalism.

"You tossed her over your shoulder and hauled ass off stage in two seconds flat. I think you know exactly what you were thinking. And if you don't... I sure as hell do." A slight uptick to one side of his mouth forms.

"Christ... she drives me fucking insane," I say, wiping my hands over my face. "I brought her here to teach her a lesson, but it feels like I'm the one getting the brunt of it."

He chuckles. "It was a shit plan to begin with, and now that I've met her... I know you never stood a chance."

"A chance to make her miserable? I still have time."

"Nah, man." He shakes his head and smiles. "But you'll figure it out. Are you headed back home to find her?" he asks, looking past me out the exit door window as if he's looking to see if she's still around too.

The thought that he asked her out still eats at me, but she's not mine to claim, and he can offer her things I can't. Like a real relationship and a future.

I promised Shawna that I'd never be happy with anyone else. That I'd never build a life since she no longer can.

"No, there's nothing in that house waiting for me." I Resolve myself to the idea that there isn't. Tessa doesn't want me, and I can't have her. It's that simple. "I need to clear my head and get back on track."

He looks down at his shoes and shakes his head with a sigh. "What is it with you and always having to do things the hard way?"

"I don't know. It's just hardwired," I joke with a lopsided grin.

"Okay, so what are you going to do?" he asks.

I look at the snow gear he has on, and I get an idea. Bobby always comes prepared. "You got any backup gear? I could use some fresh powder snowboarding right about now."

He grins. "Yeah, I have a second pair of gear I keep in my duffel. Come on, let's get you out on the slopes," he says, pulling me with him toward the exit and patting my shoulder.

In another thirty minutes, I'm dressed in Bobby's backups with a snowboard from the rental shop and I'm sitting on the lift, hoping that this little R&R of shredding down a mountainside will seal back up what broke loose on the stage and in that closet.

I hope at least for Tessa's sake I can get this back under control. I don't want to be the asshole who hurts her again.

It's almost eleven o'clock when I get home. Bobby went home after a couple of hours, but I stayed into the night, riding when the ski lodge turned on music and disco lights off the top story.

It was all lost on me because the only thing I could think about was how in the hell am I going to keep my hands off Tessa now that I know what it feels like to kiss her, to have her thighs squeeze around my waist, to hear her moan her pleasure against my ear, and twirl her tongue against mine.

This magnetic draw I've felt toward her over the past four years since I stupidly added her to my bucket list before knowing that she's Brent Tomlin's little sister, has to be severed.

I've done a damn good job of keeping Tessa at arm's length ever since. Always making her job harder has worked to make sure Tessa despises me.

At first, it worked. I started disliking her because she couldn't stand me and my social media account and media coverage where I did everything wrong and kept her running to put out fires. Then soon enough, I started getting off on the way she hates me. I started living for the moments that she'd storm in looking for me to chew me a new one.

It's the only time I could get her to focus her attention one hundred percent on me while still keeping her at arm's length. It's the only time I could stare down into those warm fiery eyes and feel her heat.

I got too close this time. That's why the bet is so smart.

No physical touch. No penetration. No promise of anything more.

I walk through the mudroom door and hit the garage door button. I hear the sound of the garage door engage as it slowly closes, and then I close the door to the house behind me and lock it.

I turn left and hang up my keys, then kick off my boots, seeing Tessa's boots laying in more disarray than usual. I can already imagine Tessa walking in a few hours before me and yanking off her boots angrily... cursing me as she did.

I walk through the mudroom and then down the hall, passing the massive empty living room, wishing for some reason that Tessa was out here, reading a book on the U-shaped couch with the fireplace roaring. I know better than to want that. I already made my game plan on the snowy mountain as I skied more slopes than I have in years.

I headed toward the kitchen, which has a small light that I keep on all night in case I need to come down for a glass of water or something. Another bout of disappointment hits when she's not in there either, not that I thought she would be.

I pass by without entering and head up the staircase gently since my impromptu snowboard session will mean I'll probably have Jell-O legs tomorrow.

I'm in good shape, and I put in a lot of time skating on the ice, but snowboarding uses different muscles, and I spent more hours on the slopes than I ever do on any given day on the ice.

Tomorrow, standing on concrete floors all day helping with the adoption day at the pound isn't going to be pretty, to put it lightly. But if everything goes the way I plan, tomorrow will serve the bigger purpose of permanently getting Tessa-inspired fantasies out of my "shower time."

Sore hamstrings, calves, and glutes for one day is worth it to save me from blue balls for another four years.

When I reach the top of the stairs, I walk down the second-story hallway, headed for my room. My eyes are glued on the guest bedroom Tessa is staying in. I assumed she'd be asleep this late, but a small blue illumination glows under the door. She's got to be on her phone or tablet. There's no TV in her room.

Maybe clearing the air is a good idea.

I could apologize for dragging her out to Aspen for a wet T-shirt contest, although I would have easily canceled that, I didn't care about it. It was all to make Tessa give up her Cabo trip.

I inhale and then knock on her door lightly.

"Tessa," I say softly. "You awake?"

No answer.

"Hey Tessie," I say again. "You in there?"

But no answer.

I hear a click, and then the blue glow goes dark.

She heard me, but she's choosing to ignore me. That's fair, I suppose.

"I'm heading to bed, but if you decide you want to talk, just come in... anytime. Okay?"

She can ignore me now, but she can't ignore me tomorrow.

And tomorrow night, she's mine.

For the first time and the last.

CHAPTER
TWENTY-ONE

Tessa

I wake up to the sound of my alarm. I'm too exhausted to get up, but it's after seven in the morning, far later than I usually do.

I slept like crap last night after not being able to turn off my brain to what Lake offered me.

And I feel so wrong for enjoying every second of it.

He's the enemy, and the last thing he should be responsible for is bringing me pleasure.

It was still light out when I stormed out of that festival, but as the night grew on, and Lake didn't come home, I couldn't stop imagining that Lake found someone else. Maybe one of the other wet T-shirt contest girls took him up on his offer for sex after I left.

Maybe it was a damn orgy. I have no idea, and my mind went wild with it.

When he knocked on my door sometime after eleven o'clock, it took all of my self-control not to jump up off the bed and run to the guest bedroom door and fling it open. I have so many questions about what we both gave in to at that moment and what we almost did—having unprotected sex in a broom closet in a ski lodge when neither of us can stand the other.

I couldn't bring myself to do it. Instead, I stayed perfectly still when he knocked all three times.

Now, I haul myself out of bed. I shower and brush my teeth. My original plan was to do my usual light makeup for casual days around the house or running errands. I bite down on my lip as I debate doing a full face since I know I'll see Lake today at the animal shelter.

I shouldn't want to look pretty for Lake today. It's an animal shelter where no photos will even be taken of me.

Instead, I should be looking for ways to spike his bottled water and make his death look like an accident.

After my makeup is complete and I'm dressed, I slip down to the kitchen. I had plans to make myself a coffee and breakfast before this long day starts, but since I left the grocery store yesterday with no food, nothing is in the fridge.

The coffee shop that I met Lake at after he dropped me off at Chelsea's shop looked like it had some amazing breakfast sandwiches and yummy coffee specials. Today is going to be a long day and with the impending results of the bet hours from now... I need some liquid courage in the form of a double shot of espresso. Actually, I'll need a triple this morning and an egg and bacon croissant breakfast sandwich... to go.

My mouth begins to water. I check my phone, and sure enough, if I leave right now, I can make it to the coffee shop and still make it to the animal shelter with time to spare.

I grab my laptop bag off the kitchen table first and then pull the keys for the Jeep off the hanging rack and then shut and lock the mudroom door as I leave.

My thoughts of yesterday plague me as I drive.

What happened to Lake last night, and what happened to him this morning? Did he go again to his ultra-secret morning appointment he's had almost every day since we've been here? The one he doesn't want to tell me about?

I pass by the grocery store on my way into town to the coffee shop, but just before I get there, I notice a black Porsche parked in the parking lot of an older-looking building.

The building is large but lacks much in the way of signage except for a sign that says Women's Shelter near the door. I don't know this town well enough, so I have no idea how many black Porsches there are in this town. In Seattle, that car is a dime a dozen.

I slow down a bit since no one is driving behind me until I come up to a sandwich board.

Hot Breakfast from 6-9 a.m.

All are Welcome

It's a women's shelter at night and a soup kitchen during the day? It must be since they're serving food while the people standing in line are holding backpacks and sleeping bags. Is this where Lake has been coming every morning to volunteer?

No way.

Not possible.

That Porsche must belong to someone else, or Lake is in a different building.

I find a parking spot on the curb and pull in, cutting the engine and then slowly slipping out. I have no idea what I'm going to find at this point.

Lake is usually very giving of his time and money whenever Penelope puts out signup sheets for giving back through the Hawkeyes brand. He was the first to sign up for skating with kids for our last fundraiser, and he's always up for signing things to give out for silent auctions when we get request from non-profits asking the team for items. But volunteering at a soup kitchen day after day...? It just doesn't make any sense.

I walk around the Jeep and to the concrete walkway that runs along many storefronts along the busy street that leads into town.

I eye the sandwich board and then look down at my phone for the time. There's only thirty minutes left for the hot breakfast, and I have no idea if Lake is even helping or if he will still be here this late.

I walk up to the solid door with a small window at the top of it. I push up on my tiptoes, and to my surprise, I see Lake in a Henley and an athletic brand baseball cap, one with zero affiliation with the Hawkeyes or any company he endorses. He's not standing behind the buffet line, though. He's sitting with someone, his hand on their shoulder like he's trying to console them or encourage them... I'm not sure which.

I step back as I hear someone approaching behind me wanting to enter the building.

"Oh sorry," I tell them. "Go on in."

The older woman with a small cane smiles up at me as I open the door for her to enter, using the door to shield me in case Lake spots me.

What the hell is he doing here? Why is he giving up so much of his time? And why in God's name am I just now hearing about this? We could have gone this route instead of the pet adoption, and we'd already be on our way home... I wouldn't even have had to come at all.

I want to follow the elderly woman into the building and demand that Lake explains this all to me, but will he be pissed that I showed up here? Will he think I followed him here like a creeper?

I need him to show up and do the pet adoption. The best option is to let this go and not tell him I know until after we get through the adoption event today.

Uck... and if I lose this bet, who knows what tonight will look like. My stomach does a summersault at the thought of what Lake wants if he wins the bet.

I back away from the door farther and turn to leave. There's a reason that Lake didn't want me to know about this, and I wonder if that meeting he had a few days ago was regarding this too.

Hmm.

I mull over the possibilities while I get back in the Jeep and head for the coffee shop. I only have twenty minutes to get my food and coffee, eat it, and get to the animal shelter.

Lake

"Aw, he's so cute. Hold him up, and I'll get a picture," one of the women from the wet T-shirt contest says as I pick up one of the golden retriever puppies from the litter. I'm sitting on the ground, crisscross applesauce with the four women I bribed to show up today.

I hold up the little buddle of yellow fur and pose with him for a shot.

"Perfect," she says, not looking up at me as she works to write a caption.

"Who's cuter? Vote now," the blonde says, her fingers doing the work quickly.

"How about this one?" another contestant from yesterday says, handing me what looks to be a one or two-year-old brindle wiener dog.

Her fingers start working overtime as she captions the photo on her social media.

"Come down and adopt a wiener." She and the three other women I convinced to come down here to help spread the news about this event with their social media accounts all giggle.

All four of them have their heads down as they seem to be answering comments from people asking where to find us or what kind of animals are available when I see Tessa walk in and bypass the long line of people who were waiting at the door this morning before the shelter opened. I asked all four women to send out a notification that I would be here this morning. I thought they were too drunk to have heard me after I went looking for them after the R&R I got snowboarding.

I came up with a plan to make sure that I win this thing. I can't lose. Tonight is the night that after four years, since the first time I saw her in the stands not knowing who she was, I'll finally get Tessa off my mind.

I swear I can still taste her on my tongue from last night. And goddammit, I need another hit like a fucking addict.

My offer was simple: show up today and I'll guarantee two things if they help me reach three hundred adoptions. One, viral posts of a hockey player kissing puppies, and two, free tickets to the Hawkeyes game next month in Denver... plus I'll introduce them to a few of the single guys on the team because I have no interest in puck bunnies at the moment. My taste has become singular, and until I get my fill, I don't see that changing.

She smiles and stops at the front desk, not seeing me and the four women who met me here, tucked in the back of the animal shelter.

The deal was that I couldn't use my social media, but nothing was said about using someone else's.

With the number of people waiting in line to adopt, the shelter's manager, Becky, only lets two to three people come to the back at a time to meet the animals.

I watch as Tessa makes an introduction with Becky—an older woman with kind eyes and a graying ponytail under a baseball cap. I could tell from the moment I met her this morning that she cares about this place and is grateful for us coming in to help these animals find new homes. Then the manager tells Tessa to follow her to the back where I'm waiting.

I try to wipe the smirk off my face. I can't wait to see her reaction when she sees my workaround for social media.

The second Tessa walks around to the back portion of the room, our eyes meet, and then within seconds, her attention gets taken up by the four women surrounding me, covered in puppies.

Tessa scowls but tries to recover the look and cover it up.

"This is our back room where all the animals are for people to view them. Once a person has been cleared to adopt, we'll let them come back and see if any of these wonderful animals feel like a good connection, then we handle all of the paperwork up front," Becky details for Tessa.

Tessa turns to Becky, giving her back to me intentionally.

"This all looks great. It would seem that there is going to be a good turn-out," Tessa tells her, looking back in the direction they came in at the line of people out the door, most with clipboards in their hands filling out the applications.

"I have every reason to believe we're going to hit our goal!" Becky practically squeals with delight.

"Oh, okay... what's the goal?" Tessa asks.

Becky looks over at me with a smile. "Mr. Powers over here told me three hundred animals by the end of today." She turns back to Tessa. "We don't even have three hundred adoptions a year, so that is a huge number for us. I already called a couple of the shelters in the counties over and they are busing over more animals that need homes." Her eyes twinkle back at Tessa.

Tessa's head spins to look over her shoulder, and her eyes dart straight to mine. Her honey-golden eyes turn dark amber, and I can't stop my cock from stirring.

"Can I have a minute alone please?" she tells me, her eyes pinned on me.

That's fine. It's the only place I want them to be anyway. Mad, happy... turned on, I don't care, I just always want her eyes on me.

"Yeah," I say.

"I'll leave you to it. They're very busy in the front, and they could use a hand."

"Could you use me too?" Tessa asks her.

She's not going to be back here with me? I don't like that at all. I expected to work closely with Tessa today.

"We could use you, but wouldn't you rather be back here to get photos of Lake and the shelter animals?"

Tessa looks over at the wet T-shirt contestants that are now dressed more appropriately for January in Aspen and shakes her head. "No, that won't be necessary. Lake brought in a few *extra* hands."

She says the word "extra" as if those hands are meant to do something more than make social media posts and play with puppies. My instinct is to correct her, but the slight look of jealousy on her face is something I keep seeing on repeat and works toward my goal for tonight.

As I look over her beautiful features, I realize she's wearing more makeup than usual. And her hair is down in that long waving way I like it instead of in a ponytail or messy bun, the way she's worn it every day since we got here. Did she do that for me?

"Perfect! I'll put you to work whenever you're done," Becky tells Tessa.

I get up off the floor where I'm sitting in a sea of dogs and carefully step out of the pen, leaving the other four women to take care of the puppies. They barely seem to even notice me going.

Women and puppies... I don't get it.

I follow Tessa as she just about stomps off, her hips swaying side to side with irritation. Damn, I like watching her walk away when she's pissed.

Instead of leading me back out to the lobby where I'll undoubtedly get mobbed by fans, she hangs a quick right and into a quiet hallway where no one can see us.

"What the hell is that?" Tessa says, spinning around and pointing out toward my "extra" hands.

"It's good publicity for the shelter. I thought we were supposed to get animals adopted... now we have a line out the door. How can you be upset about this?" I ask, leaning down to see if I can smell her coffee and strawberry essence.

Her lips look soft like she just applied her ChapStick, and I'm tempted to adopt all three hundred animals for myself if it means I could bend down and run my tongue over her full bottom lip again.

"You think I'm going to buy that? You're cheating!" she angrily whispers at me, her eyes glaring behind me to make sure no one listens to our conversation.

"I'm not cheating. I'm not using my social media. The girls are only posting to their accounts... It just so happens that their posts are going viral," I say, inching closer to her.

"I wouldn't have agreed to this bet if I had known that you're capable of cheating. What did you have to offer them last night? A ride on the Magic Stick?" she asks, her words dripping with jealousy.

"Are you kidding?" I ask.

If she only knew that there is no one I want more than I want her.

"Do you think I'm an idiot? You didn't come home until late last night," she says, and I can hear the disappointment in her voice.

"That's what you thought I was doing last night?" I ask.

She turns her body slightly away from me to block me out.

"No... I... just forget it," she says, looking away like she's feeling self-conscious.

"I'm not going to forget it," I tell her, catching her line of vision. "I was snowboarding, that's it. I asked them to come and offered to introduce them to some hockey players if they showed up for a game. I sure as hell didn't give them or anyone else a ride on the Magic Stick last night... or any night that we've been here."

"It's none of my business even if you did," she says, her eyes cast down to her shoes.

I can see it in her body language. She's trying to pretend she doesn't care who I'm with... or who texts me... but she does.

"Ok... so why then are your cheeks red?" I ask.

She doesn't step back to create more space between us. She's letting me inch closer and isn't stopping me.

The instinct to wrap my arms around her and pull her close tingles through my fingers, but even though she's letting me close, I've pissed her off too much for her to let me get away with that. It's been a long time since I've ever wanted that type of physical connection, and it has me questioning what I'm doing with Tessa. I should back away now, but I can't bring myself to do it.

"Well... I..."

She's got nothing to argue at this point. I didn't do anything wrong except outplay her. She's not happy about it, but there's nothing she can do about it.

A bet is a bet.

CHAPTER
TWENTY-TWO

Tessa

I can't believe the nerve of this guy!

"Tessa, I have you all set up at a desk to take applications when you're ready," Becky says, not noticing the body language of our heated standoff.

Instead, she leans to her left at the end of the hall to see past Lake and smiles at me.

She does seem like a sweet soul, and what she is doing here should be applauded, taking care of animals who need love and care until they can find safe homes. She's just not exactly catching me at the best time to receive a smile in return, but I plaster on one anyway, happy to at least be getting away from Lake.

"This isn't over," I say under my breath to him as I walk around him and back out to the hall.

He spins around and follows me.

"I sure as hell hope not."

I can almost hear the smirk in his reply, and I'm tempted to stop dead in my tracks and trip him up by letting him run into me... but then we'd have to touch, and right now, after seeing the girls from yesterday's contest here this morning, I have zero interest in having any physical contact with him, ever.

I walk over to the front desk to two other younger women dressed in T-shirts with the shelter's name on the front. They must work here or volunteer.

They're handing out clipboards with paperwork and receiving filled-out paperwork faster than their arms can handle.

The manager and I jump in, and I grab a huge stack of clipboards with new applications on them. I start walking down the long line of people that stretches out the door and out the glass double door front entrance of the building. The crowd now wraps around the side of the building, and luckily, the snow has stopped, and a little sunshine is peeking through the clouds, or we'd lose them all.

Wait... shouldn't I want to lose them?

I'm stuck in the dilemma of wanting this to be a huge success with big media attention that my bosses will see back at home, and wanting Lake to fail... or at least hit two-hundred-and-ninety-nine adoptions.

The longer this crowded line gets, the more likely Lake is to win.

I hear the chatter of people in line, mostly female...shocker, and mostly in their early to mid-twenties, a few years younger than me. But there are also a handful of guys in Powers #12 jerseys.

"Can you believe we're going to meet Lake Powers?"

"I'm going to grab his ass."

"Do we get selfies with Lake and the animal we adopt?"

Hmm, actually, that's a great idea for exposure because that could turn into a huge social media reach if we get a hashtag going.

My brain won't turn off all the ways we could use this to our benefit as people are physically pull clipboards out of my hands as I walk past.

This puts me in an uncomfortable position because the more I encourage this, the more likely I'll end up on Lake's couch with my own fingers between my thighs while he watches.

I start heading back toward the entry of the building to get more clipboards when someone reaches out. A dainty hand with blue nail polish gently wraps around my bicep to stop me.

I look over to find a small group of teenage girls with braids in all varied starting points on their heads and big puffy jackets with fur along the rim all huddled together.

"Yes?"

"Is Lake Powers, left-wing for the Hawkeyes, really in there?" the leader of their pack asks me, her eyebrows lifted in question.

Several people all turn to look at me too, wondering the same question.

"Yep, and he's holding a teacup chihuahua."

A uniform "aw" breaks out among the group.

"Is that wiener dog I saw in that girl's story still available for adoption?" someone calls out from the crowd, but I can't determine its exact location as I search through the sea of people.

"Which wiener?" someone else tosses out as a joke.

"I'll adopt them both. I'll be Lake Powers's mommy," another woman calls out.

The crowd erupts with laughter.

I snicker to myself as I turn back toward my original destination of the glass doors of the shelter.

I walk through the doors and up the long line of people waiting inside.

I seek out the hockey player in the back room and catch Lake helping one of the male shelter employees put out kibble for the animals and fill their water bowls. The women he brought seem more interested in reapplying lipstick or scrolling through their feeds when I survey the entire scene.

This part of Lake is still new to me. Volunteering at the women's shelter this morning, and now helping the staff with their daily tasks when he doesn't need to do anything but snap a few photos with the animals.

I swing around the front desk to grab more clipboards but there aren't any left.

"Can we set up a photo op with Lake for every person who adopts an animal before they leave and ask them to post it to their social media with the same hashtag? If these people are local, it's more likely we can get more people to come in and adopt the animals," I tell Becky.

"That's a great idea." She looks back at the two girls as they're busy getting through the paperwork that continues to get handed in at an alarming rate. "Let's make sure no one leaves without a selfie."

They both nod, one pulling applications off the clipboards and reloading them while the other seems to be tallying off the animals already adopted.

"What's the number, girls?" Becky asks.

"Fifty-one," the girl tallying up the numbers says back.

The manager walks up to a whiteboard hanging behind the oak front desk and writes the number up on the board:

51

"That's a good start," she says, pushing the cap back on the dry eraser marker.

My stomach flips when I look at the number. Three hundred seems more attainable now that we're down one-sixth of the total goal.

I get back to handing out applications, occasionally looking back to see Lake talking with people looking at animals to adopt, and taking selfies with people who have found their match.

When Lake isn't looking, I snap a few candid shots with him and some of the animals and post them up on the Hawkeyes website and social media accounts.

A couple of hours later, the crowd still hasn't dwindled, and the manager keeps updating the number every half hour. At least one other shelter has shown up with both animals for adoption and a few more helping hands for the front desk and the back, helping prospective families find their perfect match, whether it's a dog, cat, or even a few potbelly pigs.

I watch as she walks back to the whiteboard after helping a family find a sweet three-year-old beagle. The little girl whose family adopted the beagle beams from ear to ear as she leads her new best friend out of the door by his leash. Becky reaches for the black dry-erase marker. The temptation to knock the dry-erase marker out of her hand so that she can't increase the number is strong, but I fight it.

I pretend not to care as I watch through the corner of my eye while she swipes the old number away and changes it:

134

Ugh, but the number of people walking in has to slow down... it just has to.

My attention catches on something in the back room and I turn to find Lake looking at the number change. Then his eyes settle on mine, focused and determined with a slight glint in them.

I divert my attention back down to sliding a new application into the clipboard and slipping a pen under the metal flap. Then I walk back down the line of people waiting, armed with ten new sparkly applications.

Lake offers to order lunch for the employees and volunteers. We each alternate taking fifteen minutes to scarf down the food, everyone agreeing to take a short lunch since we have so many people here to adopt, but Lake never takes his lunch.

I come back out of the break room, having taken the last lunch spot to make sure that everyone who was here before me got their lunch, and then I look back up at the whiteboard:

242

My heart lodges into my throat.

It's only been six hours since this place has opened. How is that possible?

Lake walks out to the main lobby, and everyone standing in line almost hyperventilates. It's the first time I've seen him leave the back room.

He turns to one of the girls standing at the front desk.

"How many more people do we have in line?" he asks, his fingers drumming on the desk with a hint of nervous energy.

"Oh… uh… I'm not sure," she says, attempting to count all the applications that people have been turning in but have not yet left with an animal.

Lake flashes a look at me and then trudges to the double glass doors. He pushes one of the glass doors open and pops his head out to see how many people are still wrapped around the building.

"There are still a lot out there," he says with a satisfied smile.

"If you have to leave early, we understand Mr. Powers. We're just grateful for what you've done here. So many animals are going to have their very own homes tonight," Becky says.

"Oh no. I'm staying till the very end. We have to make that goal," he says, sending a wink my way.

A flutter of nerves hits me… where did that come from?

There's no way the idea of losing is exciting… is it? That the idea of being alone in Lake's living room with him while we do something a little dirty together is the real reason I'm checking the numbers.

I'm torn, that's what it is.

"Well, in that case, I'll adjust the number after every adoption so we keep you up to date. How about that?" she asks with a smile.

"That would be great. I think Tessa would like to be in the know at all times as well. Right, Tessie?" he asks, using my nickname.

My lip twists to the side as I bite down on it to keep myself from saying something I shouldn't. He sees it in my eyes and grins.

We all get back to our tasks, and Becky becomes a permanent fixture of the whiteboard, standing in solitude with a black dry-erase marker, the fingers of her left hand now black with marker all over them from continually wiping off an old number in favor of an updated one.

With each minute that passes, a new person or family walks out with an adopted animal and a smile on their face. I don't dare to look up. I can't take the ever-turning sensation in my stomach as I know the numbers are climbing faster and faster. The gap between how many animals have been adopted and the goal of three hundred is closing quickly.

We only have an hour until the shelter closes for the night and still have a line wrapped around the outside of the store. Losing the bet would be a hit to my pride but the wager I'll have to pay up tonight has my belly filling with butterflies or bumble bees... I wish I knew which one.

I can't help the nagging part of my brain that begs me to look up. It's like a car accident... too tempting not to rubberneck at the carnage of my poor decision that allowed me to fall into Lake's trap.

I was being cocky.

I'm woman enough to admit it.

And he played on it.

Lured me in, and I took the bait.

Loud cheering rings out near the whiteboard. In my periphery, I see the three volunteers behind the desk and the manager jumping up and down.

My stomach turns, and I seek out the black marker to find my fate.

311

The numbers practically scream out at me. It's not close enough to ask for a recall, and with people still in the back, a crowd still waiting their turn, and another twenty minutes left on the clock... I'm done for, but I can't decide if I'm relieved or not.

Maybe I want this too.

I turn to find Lake already staring at me, something feral glimmering in his eyes.

I walk over to the desk, putting down the last clipboards that I needed to hand out. I force a smile when the manager sends me an air high-five. I return it because I can't be rude to her. This is a big day for this shelter and these animals.

I need a minute to process how I feel about this. I turn slowly, not wanting anyone to know that my feelings are mixed.

I head for the long, lonely hallway again, seeking a moment alone and out of sight of anyone.

Once I know no one is following me and I'm farther down the hallway, tucked out of view, I lean my back against the wall, my head falling back and my eyes fluttering closed as I take a cleansing breath.

Within seconds, I hear the sound of someone approaching. No!

Please go away!

I can only imagine that it must be Becky following me to discuss the momentous feat of giving over three hundred animals new homes today... some kind of record, I'm sure, but I can't discuss that now. I just need a minute to wrap my mind around losing this bet and the payoff to Lake later tonight.

Now that the results are in, and the bet is over, the worst part of the whole thing is that I'm not dreading it like I should be.

Maybe a part of me agrees with Lake. That this thing between us is building like a volcano, and the longer we let it fester, the bigger it will blow. Maybe it is time to let off a little steam.

"Are you planning on running?" a deep timbre echoes through the walls.

It's not the manager... it's Lake.

Shivers shoot down my arms at the sound of his voice, and my eyelids pop open to find him inching ever so closely to me.

He doesn't stop until we're toe-to-toe.

His attention flashes back down the hallway from where he came to make sure the coast is clear while my eyes stay focused on him.

"Why would I run? I always make good on my bets," I tell him.

"Are you ready to make good on your bet tonight?" he asks but he doesn't have the cocky smile I expect.

His expression is unreadable as he searches my face for something.

He's asking a question, and he wants the actual answer.

Unfortunately, I don't have it.

"If that's what you still want," I tell him, giving him the opportunity to give us an out.

"You'll let me change it?" he says curiously.

"Maybe..."

Now it's my turn to check down the hall to make sure no one is coming.

Lake leans in closer. My head whips back toward him.

"Then I want something else."

When I don't speak, he continues.

"Why won't you date hockey players? I want to know who hurt you."

What?!

No, I won't tell him that. He'll tell my brother and then my brother will do something stupid that could cost Brent too much. And I don't trust Lake not to retaliate either.

How protective Lake is... he might do something if he knows who it was.

"No, I don't accept the change."

"Why not? This should be music to your ears to get out of our original bet. Why won't you tell me?"

"Because you play them next week."

"He's a Blue Devil?" Lake asks, his eyebrows raised, and his eyes widen. "Now you have to tell me who he is."

"No."

"Why?" he says, inching closer, his hands smoothing over my hips with a soft grip to anchor me to him.

I shouldn't like the way his touch calms me. I shouldn't like this intimate moment between us. He feels more like a protective boyfriend than the mortal enemy I've had for the past year and a half.

A part of me wants to curl into him and let him protect me from everything. The loss of my parents and the ex who has me running toward Elliot, a man who I know is safe, but isn't the man I want.

Lake's pleading to know, but now I'm even more sure that he'll do something stupid when he plays them in two weeks.

I can't tell him, but the longer we stand here and he looks at me like that... like he'd light the whole world on fire for me... I need to break from this moment before I confess it all.

"Let it go, Lake... I have," I say.

"Pardon the interruption..." Becky says. "Lake, we'd like to get a group photo with the staff before you go, if you don't mind."

Becky gives me the distraction I need, and I slip out behind Lake

"Whoa, Tessa, hold on."

He tries to reach for my wrist, but I narrowly escape into the main lobby as a mob of fans crowd Lake. He tries to follow me out but gets stuck with people asking for selfies and autographs. I turn around quickly when I realize he can't chase after me now with fans needing his attention.

It gives me just enough time to snap a few photos of Lake, surrounded by the animal shelter volunteers, that I'll post on the official team social account.

Then I call, "I'll see you back at the house," and scurry out the door and into the Jeep.

I twist the key in the ignition, and the Jeep revs to life. Within minutes, I pull out of the parking lot, and I watch in my rearview mirror as Lake finally makes it out to the curb of the shelter, panting from trying to make it through the crowd and sporting a frown.

He won't chase after me. He still has a building full of fans and ten more minutes left on his charity work. Turns out, he's the true professional here since I just ran with my tail between my legs.

CHAPTER TWENTY-THREE

Lake

"Lake! Can I get a picture?"

"Will you sign my jersey?"

People crowd around me the second I chase Tessa out to the lobby.

I watch as more people block my exit toward her, and I can't push past them, even though physically, I could. But these are my fans. People who have traveled great distances to come to see me. The kind of people who buy my jerseys and pay steep ticket prices to watch me play. I can't disregard them and leave them in the lurch to chase after a woman who doesn't want to be chased.

I tell the manager that I won't be returning to the back room anymore, since I already exceeded the adoption number that I set out for.

I excuse the four women who came to my aid today and let them know that I'll have tickets waiting for them at will-call next month in Denver and then I take the next hour to sign everything that my fans push at me. From taking selfies with eighty-year-old grandmothers to kissing the foreheads of half a dozen babies, I get through the line and then thank the manager for opening her shelter up to us and take a group picture with all of the volunteers and staff at the shelter.

I pull into the garage fifteen minutes later and close the garage door behind me.

"Tessa?" I call out as I step through the mudroom, after discarding my keys and shoes. "You here?" I ask, but I already saw the Jeep, so I know she's here.

I take several steps into the house, heading toward the kitchen.

"Tessa?" I ask.

The hallway begins to open into the living room with every step I take.

"In here." I hear her voice almost monotone and void of interest.

I take the last few steps until I'm standing in the opening of the great room, the large windows showing a picturesque view of Aspen outside of my house. The sun starts to set behind the mountains. I shift my attention to the left to find the large TV on and Tessa's head peaking up over the far side of the U-shaped couch. I can only see her from the top of her head to her chin as I step into the giant living room.

With every step I take, Tessa's beautiful face becomes closer and her reserved expression doesn't give me much to go on. I have no idea what she's thinking right now. She almost seems as though she's come to terms with her fate. That's not what I was hoping for when I made this bet. I wanted her to realize how badly she wants this too but instead, her eyes are void of that amber fire and I'd give anything to get it back.

I round the couch and then stop dead in my tracks when I see Tessa's full body laid out on the far end of the couch, is sprawled out for my view.

She's in nothing but the blush-colored bra she wore when I brought her home and flashed me in my walk-in closet. Hugged tight against her curvy hips is a matching blush thong.

My cock instantly gets a semi at the vision in front of me. She's a fucking knock-out, not that I thought she wouldn't be. She's a wet dream in a down jacket and a pair of jeans, or even in the business attire she wears to work with those fuck-me heels.

Anything Tessa wears has had me imagining taking it all off her for the past four years. It's been an excruciating wait to get here, and I tried like hell to do anything to put a bigger gap between us but it didn't hold.

"What are you doing?" I ask, trying to force down a swallow.

She caught me off guard, I'll give her that.

"Making good on my loss," she says with a sultrier voice than she probably meant, or maybe I'm imagining it because everything about her is sexy.

I hate that she used the word loss, as if only one of us is benefiting from tonight. I have to believe that deep down, she knows this is mutually beneficial.

"I told you... you don't have to do this. Just give me a name. You don't even have to tell me what he did."

She shakes her head as I walk around to the middle of the couch, headed toward her. My vision glides over the see-through material of her bra that gives me an almost completely unobstructed view of those dark peach-colored nipples that are hard in the coolness of the room and her matching thong that has my eyes pinned to the soft curves where the cleft between her thighs starts.

My fingers itch to trail over the lacy scalloped edges of her thong, where the soft lace meets her buttery-tanned skin. And my mouth waters at the thought of sucking her pussy clean of all the arousal her body can make for me.

I know that tan skin isn't meant for me. She spent hours under the UVA rays of a tanning bed for another man, but I won't let that stop me from using it tonight to feed my craving.

"Stop!" Tessa says, holding up her hand, her full breast jiggling a little at her abrupt movement. "Don't come any closer. That wasn't part of the deal."

I stop as requested, halfway down to the other side of the couch toward her.

"What wasn't part of the deal?" I ask.

"You touching me. That wasn't part of it," she clarifies, her palm still outstretched.

"How did you know I planned to touch you?"

Her hand falls on her left thigh and I'm envious of her fingertips getting to touch that silky smooth skin.

Her eyes search back and forth between mine.

"I can see it in your eyes," she says, reading me like a book. "You were planning on doing more than watching."

Nope, not a book.

The woman has telepathy, but I know what we bet, I wouldn't have taken it past that unless she let me.

"You can watch from over there," she says, pointing at the opposite side of the couch.

I smirk at her and then turn around toward the way I came, walking back over to where she banished me.

"Just remember... I gave you an out," I remind her.

"It wasn't a real option."

"Why not?"

"Because you would have done something stupid to him... losing the Hawkeyes their shot at the Stanley Cup."

"Is the Stanley Cup really the thing you're worried about?" I ask, grabbing the remote control off the coffee table as I go.

She shrugs, keeping her eyes on the black screen of the TV that hasn't been turned on yet.

I discreetly unbutton the top of my jeans to give my hardening erection some growing room—he doesn't fit in my jeans once he expands to full length. I keep walking until my shins hit the couch and then lift my left leg to flop onto the couch with my right foot still on the ground, still fully clothed.

There's a silence on her end once I settle in and it has me curious as to what's going on in that brain of hers.

I turn my head to find her giving my body a full scan as I lay on the couch. When our eyes meet, I see the stunning golden hue of Tessa's irises.

I make a vow to myself here and now. I'll do anything to keep that color in her eyes when she looks at me.

CHAPTER TWENTY-FOUR

Tessa

"Can you take off your clothes?" I ask.

I scan Lake across the couch from me, fully dressed with his jeans unbuttoned and an impressive bulge running from the crotch of his jeans up to the very top of his waistband. I have a feeling that if he lifts his shirt up, I'll see a significant amount of his tip peeking out to greet me.

I'm unsure of Lake's length in inches but I know I've never been with a man whose erection supersedes the top of his jeans before.

My core squeezes at the sight of him but I do my best to seem unfazed. I'll follow through with the bet because I lost, even if

I think it was rigged. I'll do this one last thing and then I'm out of here. I'll pack my minimal clothes into my laptop bag and hitchhike if I have to, and then I'll spend the entire trip back planning how I'll get even.

"You want me naked?" he asks, jumping up off the couch quickly and pulling his shirt off.

And there it is... the crown of Lake's cock pushing past the top of his jeans. He looks as hard as steel.

"Well, I'm laying here with practically nothing on and you're dressed for a blizzard," I tell him.

He scoffs. "If you think this is what I'd wear then you've never had to dress for a blizzard before. But I'm not complaining," he says, unzipping his pants and then pushes them down to the floor, his cock only covered by his boxer briefs that might as well not even be there. I can see everything through the thin material. "I'll take it all off if you want," he says, hooking his thumbs through the last shred of clothing he has on. His underwear.

"No!" I say, waving out a hand at him.

Seeing him completely uncovered would probably be my breaking point and I would no longer be able to stay on my side of the living room.

I'd be straddling him on his side of the couch in seconds, lowering myself on his length to finally feel the filling of a real man inside me after so many months of lackluster silicone toys that only barely scratch the surface.

I need the stretch from his erection with the bulging that runs along the length.

I need his body heat warming me from the inside.

I need to squeeze his thick cock when I climax.

I need to feel him pulsate inside me when he comes loose and rails into me to chase his own.

He stops for a second and then pulls his thumbs out of his waistband.

He sees me bite down on my lower lip just slightly at the thought of skipping the porn and going for what I really want even though I know better. A one-night stand will only leave me wanting more.

"Are you sure? Because I'm more than happy to lay naked for your viewing pleasure if it helps you get off. Or even better yet, I could come over there and warm you up while you watch," he says, standing tall and proud... and oh so cocky, just like the filthy player he is.

That was my mistake—licking my lips let him see that I'm not unaffected even though I did a good job to start but I couldn't follow through. Those glacier-blue eyes unravel my self-control.

There is no way I'm letting him come any closer than the other side of the couch. The last thing I need is Lake "warming" me... whatever that entails.

"That won't be necessary. Keep your boxers on, lay down, and shut up," I demand, breaking eye contact and staring back at the blank screen of the TV, trying my hardest to stay still and in my seat and not race to him and collide in a heap of need. This is what's gotten me in trouble in the past. Not looking before I leap into the arms of a hockey player.

Luckily, I've spent the best part of a year and a half watching Lake, and I know exactly what pitfalls await me if I ever dared.

The biggest one?

An empty bed in the morning and then a career-long sentence of misery watching Lake take home endless one-night stands.

I can't.

I won't.

Yet still, my clit radiates with need at the idea of it and my panties increase in dampness the longer Lake stands facing me with that monster in his shorts.

"Alright, fine," he says, turning toward the TV and pointing the remote at the receiver to turn it on. "Just remember, my offer still stands if you change your mind." He winks.

I roll my eyes for good measure, and he snickers as he pulls up the search engine for his smart TV.

"So, what's it going to be?" he asks.

"I don't care, just pick something," I tell him, adjusting the waistband of my thong.

He looks back over at me, his eyes taking turns between my face, my breasts, and my panties as he speaks. "That wasn't the deal. The deal was that you tell me your kink and I watch you enjoy it."

Damn it.

Couldn't I at least bypass this one thing?

He stands there, his thumb on the ready to start typing in anything my heart desires.

"Come on. If you want this over so badly just call it out."

"Tell me yours first?" I ask.

"Nice try. You're just going to ditto it and not give me the real answer," he says. "I want the dirty honest truth, Tessie. What do you like?" he asks.

I shake the thought.

I can't go there.

"I like watching surprise ménage."

Lake's eyebrows shoot to his forehead.

"What?" he chokes out.

"What?" I echo back as if what I said isn't that unheard of.

"You like watching couples have a threesome?" he asks, his jaw going slack at my confession.

"Not couples. I just like when three people end up in the same place at the same time without knowing one another and then randomly they all join in. Nothing's planned and there's no infidelity at play."

He lets out a chuckle.

"Lake! I just told you a very vulnerable thing that I've never told another soul and you're laughing at me," I scold.

"No... shit... no." He tries to wipe the dumb smile off his face. "I'm not laughing, I swear. I just wasn't expecting you to like threesomes since you claim hockey players are all cheaters. Seems like you wouldn't be into sharing."

Sharing?

Hey now... who said anything about me being into sharing?

"I'm not into sharing. I could never do it with someone I'm dating. I just like the fantasy of three people getting stuck in a hotel and somehow all getting the same key to the same room with no other vacancies... or a weird castaway situation where three people get stuck on a remote island and have to use each other for body heat."

Lake sucks in his lower lip to wet it and then smirks... I've said too much.

"You know what, never mind. I like missionary-style married couples," I say crossing my arms over my breasts and slightly crossing my right leg over my left to cover myself a little under his watchful eye.

I feel more exposed now than I have ever in my life. Why do I let him do this to me?

"Whoa, whoa, hold on," he says, taking two sideways steps toward me still pointing the remote at the TV. "I'm sorry, I didn't mean to make you feel weird about it. That's fucking hot and I'm down for watching that. It's just not what I thought you'd say considering the reason you say you won't date hockey players anymore."

"I don't watch porn that much. Only when I'm single and need a little inspiration." Why the hell am I telling him this?! "But I like the plot of it."

"Like the one about the mailman I caught you watching?" he says over his shoulder as his fingers work to search for a movie to fit my preferences. "What do you like about it then?"

"I don't know... guys can be so cocky at times. I sort of like the idea of them becoming overwhelmed with two women to satisfy at the same time."

Lake's still listening as he nods but he's engrossed in finding a film. It doesn't take long because soon enough, he cues up a film.

"How about this one?" he says. "It's right up your alley. A rideshare driver's app goes haywire and double books two separate bookings at the same time. Now he'll have to make sure he delivers two fully satisfied customers. He won't settle for anything less than a five-star review."

Lake reads the movie's plot to me.

"That will work," I tell him, a little self-conscious but I'll have to shake that loose because there's no turning back now.

The movie starts up and Lake walks back over to his side of the couch. He takes a seat and leans back.

We share a look and then I decide that for me to get through this, I'm going to avoid eye contact from here on out.

The film doesn't mess around and within minutes the driver is pulled over in his car waiting for both of his 'riders' to show up.

It's a new film and must have had a decent budget because the cinematography is actually really good and I already find myself wanting to bite down on my fingernails in anticipation for when things really get down.

I don't have to wait long because before I know it, one of the women in the back seat reaches around the driver's waist and slides her hands into his pants as he's driving while the other woman climbs into the passenger seat in the front and unzips his pants, bending over the armrest.

My right hand begins to smooth over my belly and my fingertips duck under the waistband of my thong as I bite down softly on the inside of my cheek to keep back the moan that wants to slip past my lips. I won't give Lake the satisfaction of hearing my sounds.

He doesn't deserve them.

"What kind of ride are you looking for down there, princess?" the driver says gruffly to the woman sitting in the passenger seat.

"From the looks of it, a thick one," she says back.

"Well then, you'd better climb on because you're about to *arrive* at your final destination," he tells her.

The dialogue is cheesy but the visual is doing its job. I reach down farther into my panties and slide a finger through my folds. I'm dripping wet. But it's not just from this film. Seeing Lake's hard cock react to my mostly naked body did most of the groundwork to get me here, and the fact that he's still watching me from his spot across the couch and not watching a second of the TV, has me wishing it could be his fingers between my thighs instead of mine.

I watch as the scene continues to build, the driver pulling over and all three of the actors climbing into the back of the car, limbs, and clothing flailing everywhere. The noises all of them are making egg me on as I dip a finger inside my aching center, but it needs something so much bigger than my finger. My body craves Lake.

I try to shake the feeling by adding a second finger, my two fingers softly hooking and stroking toward the spot I know will give me the result I need, an orgasm. But two fingers aren't going to get me there, not with how much my body wants Lake's girth.

I add a third finger, the added stretch causing me to arch into my own hand, my eyelids fluttering closed as I tune out the film, it's not what I want anymore... it's not what I need.

I need him.

I see him behind my eyelids. The moment in the club, the look on his face heated and headed straight for me. The time in the locker room when Briggs made him drop his towel and I got my first glimpse of Lake completely naked. And the time he sucked on my nipples in the broom closet and offered to put me out of my misery against the wall next to the commercial grade bleach and the mountain of toilet paper rolls.

Through every single moment, the thing that has me coming back is the look in his eyes. He has a panty-dropping smile that's tried and true, thoroughly tested in the field, but the way he looks at me, as if he's trying to study the color of my irises when he doesn't think I'll notice, has my heart thumping an extra beat for him.

It shouldn't.

Of all the organs in my body, it's my heart that has the most scars, the most damage from men like Lake.

When will it learn?

When will I?

My fingers gain speed but still stay at a steady pace, the tips of my toes beginning to curl as I chase after my climax. It's so close now.

It's about to break, I can feel the knowing signs of a self-induced orgasm.

I can still hear the background sounds of the actors panting on the screen and I can hear Lake's breathing become heavier as he watches me.

I let out a moan that I can't force back. It's a desperate plea that echoes into the grandeur of Lake's vaulted ceilings.

My body pulsates, and I free-fall off the cliff.

"Lake!" I whimper out as I come.

My eyelids dart open, and I think I'm going to pass out from the name I called out as I came.

Maybe he didn't hear me.

My neck swivels to see if somehow, miraculously, maybe he got bored and left, but after I blink a few times to clear the blur from having them closed, I find Lake staring right back at me.

"Did you just say my name?" he asks, his eyes wide and his nostrils flared. He's already pushing off the couch and headed for me.

He doesn't really need me to answer that, does he?

"No..." I try in vain to convince him.

His long legs eat up the distance between us anyway and before I can stop him, he's standing a few feet from me.

I pull my hand out from beneath my thong and between my thighs to slow him but the second he reaches me, his long fingers slide around my much daintier wrist and pull my fingers up to his mouth. My shoulder blade comes off the couch since his much taller height is further than my short arm can reach.

"You got off thinking about me, Tessie. So in that case, the least you can do is give me a taste," he says, and then slowly guides my three fingers into his mouth. He bares down on them, licking and sucking them clean. His tongue swirling around each finger to get every drop of arousal left for him to consume.

I watch him above me, all six feet plus of hard muscle as more hot need drips out of me. Even after that orgasm, I'm not the least bit sated with him hovering over me as he sucks on my fingers, his heavy cock bobbing against his boxer shorts, a mere two feet from my face as I lay on the couch. The thin material can't seem to contain his full God-given gift that's pressing against his stomach, almost to his belly button.

He hums his approval at the taste of me on his tongue. A visceral sound passes through my lips as his Adam's apple bobs with each swallow he takes of his saliva mixed with my arousal.

He's enjoying every minute of it and I don't think I can take another second more before I beg him to take me. I have to keep strong.... keep from giving in when I know I'll only regret it later when our one night is over.

Finally, he pulls my fingers from his mouth.

"You taste as good as I thought you would." His eyes cast down and survey my entire body with hooded eyes. "I've waited four years for this," he says, under his breath.

"Four years?" I ask, sitting on my elbows.

His eyes reach back up to mine.

"I've wanted you since the first time I saw you on opening day four years ago."

All this time and he's never said anything.

CHAPTER TWENTY-FIVE

Lake

I kneel on the couch cushion, getting closer to her. She watches my every move as I bend over her, my hands planting above both of her shoulders and my knees straddling either side of her thighs. I hover above her, our eyes not shifting away from one another.

This is how I want her... under me.

"Lake, this is a mistake," she says, her hands flat against my chest, bracing herself against me to get some space between us. I won't force myself on her. If she tells me to back off, I will, right now. But unless she utters the words, I need her to tell me that I'm making this all up in my head... that I'm reading her all wrong because everything up to this moment tells me that Tessa wants me as bad as I want her.

"No, that's not true," I tell her, shaking my head. "Nothing about you... me... us, will ever be a mistake. Can't you see that?" I ask, begging her to see what is clear as day to me now.

Her hands soften against my chest. She's not pushing back anymore but the pressure of her fingertips still warm my bare chest. Her amber-colored eyes reach up to mine. Her eyebrows stitch together. She wasn't expecting me to say that. This might be the first time Tessa doesn't know what to say and I'm going to take advantage of it.

"I'll do anything you ask of me... anything at all, just please, don't ask me to leave," I plead.

This is it—this is all the fight I have left. I can't push her to see it. I can't force her to want me back or be willing to see where this goes. She has to want this too.

She just keeps staring back at me without uttering a word.

I need to know what she's thinking. I need this woman who has no filter and no lack of vocabulary to put me in my place when she deems it necessary.

I need her to speak so I can start breathing again.

"Please say something Tessie... anything," I beg, leaning closer.

This might be the last moment she lets me be this close after what just happened on this couch a moment ago.

She sucks in her bottom lip slowly as she stares back at me, still without a word being uttered. I barely catch the subtle move but when her full lip slips slowly out behind her bright white teeth, my eyes divert from hers and land on her sweet wet mouth.

"Lake…"

"Yeah?"

"Kiss me."

Finally, that's the green light I've been waiting for.

I move my left knee between her thighs, coaxing them to open wide for me so that I can slip between them. She gives in, watching my every movement.

I press my throbbing bulge against her and I lay my body along hers. My lips come down and press to her sweet mouth. The heat and need are instant. No matter what angle I attempt, no matter how hard I kiss her… it's not fucking enough.

I grip her thighs tighter in my hands and her arms wrap around my neck. This feels like déjà vu from the broom closet, except this time when I press my cock against her wetness, there's barely a millimeter of fabric between us, and being on top of her gives us a completely different angle.

Her heat radiates through her panties, and I can feel my boxer briefs begin to soak with her need for me. Nothing in this world has ever felt better.

She lets out a soft whimper when I thrust her into the couch cushion. Pressing my erection tight to her clit but not penetrating.

My cock is a heat-seeking missile and I'm incapable of stopping at this point unless she tells me to. My dick is determined to bury himself deep inside her and by the sounds Tessa's making, I think she wants that too.

I slip my tongue into her mouth, loving the way the tip of her tongue greets me eagerly on contact.

Tessa is so responsive to everything I'm giving her. She's not pushing me away anymore and I think this might finally be the moment when we're both in agreement of where we're headed... this night doesn't end until I've had her in every way I've fantasized about for four years.

I came prepared this time, stopping off at the store after I left the animal shelter and bought condoms. I tucked one condom into my jeans before I walked into the house. I didn't know what to expect tonight but I had hope that this might happen. That she'd give up her no-hockey-player rule and finally let me be with her.

"Condom," I say simply against her mouth to gauge her reaction.

She moans into our kiss, and I take that as my answer.

My jeans are on the other side of this large couch but I won't disconnect from her for a second.

I lift her into my arms and carry her to the other side of the couch, bending down and pulling the condom from my jeans as we go.

I lay her back down on the couch and drop the condom above her head on the cushions.

I stare down at her for a second, her beautiful silky hair splayed out over my couch as I kneel between her thighs.

Fuck, I've had dreams about this more times than I can count since I first laid eyes on Tessa. Now she's half-naked waiting for me, her eyes locked on mine, right where I want them from this day forward.

I reach for the unopened condom and pick it up. Her eyes narrow on the foil wrapper.

It's not as if I expected anything with Tessa tonight but offering her unprotected sex yesterday was reckless and obviously unacceptable in her eyes. I get it... I've never offered it before Tessa and I have zero plans to ever offer it again.

"You have condoms?" she asks. "I thought you said you don't sleep around in Aspen."

"I don't," I say. "This is only for you."

"Just the one because of your one-night-stand rule...?"

I shake my head to stop her. "Not with you Tessa. One night won't be enough," I say. "I have a full box in the car and I plan to use every last one on you."

I lean down and brush my lips against hers gently, not sealing them together yet. Instead, I tease her softly. I want her begging for me. Soon her eyelashes flutter closed and she lets out a breath that shakes with anticipation.

She won't have to wait much longer. I'm here to give her anything and everything she could ever ask for.

I'm going to worship her body in a way no man ever has before.

"Please..." she whispers.

It's the sweetest sound I've ever heard, and I want her to say it over and over again. To whisper it against my ear as I drive into her.

I reach under her back and unclasp her bra. Her full breasts spill out from their lacy pink confines. They're a little more than a handful with just the right pear shape. Nothing about Tessa is fake. Not her attitude and sure as hell not her breasts. They're fucking perfect and I swear my cock grows thicker at the image of them to the point where my erection is throbbing almost painfully, begging for release inside of her.

She watches my every move, content to let me do whatever I please with her.

I drop the bra to the floor and then hook my fingers into her thong. I need her naked and splayed out for me. I study her every curve, every delicious inch of her skin as I uncover her, like a present, just for me.

Holy shit.

Tessa completely bare and naked is a site I'm unworthy to witness.

"They're probably not as big as you're used to," she says softly.

I look up to find Tessa avoiding my eye contact.

What the fuck?

"Who told you that? Whoever made you feel less?"

Does she have a complex about her body?

Her?!

The damage I'm going to do to the motherfucker who shook her confidence before I could get to her is going to get sent to the ER. His broken jaw will never have a chance to speak a single negative word to her again.

"Look at me," I tell her.

She still avoids me. "Tessa..."

She finally looks up.

I pull her hand off the couch and place it on my raging cock. That gets her attention, and she watches me cup her hand over my rock-hard cock, her mouth dropping open. I'm not sure if it's because of my boldness or because she wasn't expecting how big I feel in her hand. I'm hoping for the latter.

"I've never been this fucking hard in my entire life. I've never wanted anyone the way I want you. There is nothing about you I'd change. Not a thing."

She's in a league of her own and I'm the lucky bastard who she's letting touch her. There's nothing I wouldn't give to secure my spot to be the *only* lucky bastard that ever gets to.

I let go of her hand and she takes it back, nodding like she believes what I'm saying... now I'm going to show her.

Tessa

Feeling Lake's cock in my hand for the first time sent a thrill through my belly.

His pelvis presses me tight into the couch while his arms keep him hovering above me. I moan at the feel of his bulge pressing against my sensitive clit.

I've already come once and with everything he just admitted, I'm wetter than I've ever been. It feels like it's been days of foreplay and my body is thrumming with the need to have a Lake created orgasm.

He dips down and takes my left nipple into his mouth, while his other hand cups my other breasts and begins to knead it while he rubs his bulge against me.

Now there's only his boxers between us and I wish there was nothing.

"Lake, I need it," I admit, finally giving in fully to what we both want.

"You need what, Tessie? Say it out loud and I'll give it to you."

"I need you inside of me."

He presses against me harder, and I whimper when he bares down on my breast and presses his cock against me as tight as he can. He likes that idea too.

I could come just like this, with Lake rubbing my clit against his fabric-covered erection, but I don't want to. I want to feel his girth... I want to be taken by him in only the way Lake Powers can do it.

I grip the condom in his hand and pull it out. He lets me.

He watches, his eyes fixed on mine as I rip the condom package open with my teeth.

"Christ," he mutters watching me tear the packaging myself and pull the rubber from its foil wrapping.

"Do you want to put it on?" he asks.

"Yes," I tell him simply.

He nods and pushes his body off mine. He does a full plank with one hand, pushing his boxers down with one hand. The image of him suspended above me has me soaking the couch cushion under me.

He holds himself and watches me patiently, waiting for me to roll the rubber over him. I slide the condom over his tip and then roll it down his thick shaft, my thumb following the feeling of the deep vein that runs along the side of it.

My hand skims up and down once to make sure it's secure.

He groans at my movement and his jaw clenches.

"Shit..." he mutters, shaking his head. "If you keep that up this is going to be embarrassing for me."

A small giggle bubbles out of me. I didn't mean for it to, but having this effect on Lake is the sexiest thing I've ever witnessed.

He smiles down at my giggle and then his body slowly collapses back onto mine and he pushes a strand of hair off my face. It's so much more caring than I knew Lake could be.

"This is about you tonight. Tell me what you want... what you like. Ok?" he says, reaching between us and sliding his rubber-covered tip through my arousal, lubricating himself but holding back.

I give him a nod to his nonverbal request to enter me.

He licks his lips and then presses against me.

I arch my back immediately at the overwhelming girth of his tip demanding entry. I moan as I grip his shoulder to steady myself. My body tingles everywhere at the first touch of pressure to my opening. This is what I need... I've been starving for all this time and now I'm finally being fed. Fed by a man that has changed the way I see him since we arrived in Aspen.

He's not the man I thought I knew, he's so different here. The Aspen version of Lake is the one I could fall for and that scares me, but ignoring it isn't an option anymore. He wants more than one night and I can't deny him, I'm not strong enough to resist.

His right hand grips my hip to hold me in place. I grip the back of his neck, my hands folded over one another while our eyes lock.

He rocks into me, entering me inch by inch slowly, trying to give my body time to stretch to his size.

I whimper at the pain and pressure of his size. He bends down and seals our lips, consuming the noises I make for him.

He's so big but I'm so wet. He slides in even with so much resistance from my tight body that hasn't had a man in so long.

"You're so damn tight. Am I hurting you?" he asks, a flash of concern in his eyes.

"No, keep going. Don't stop," I tell him, loving every minute of Lake's touch.

With each advance he makes inside me, he glides over the sensitive spot that's already buzzing with need since my climax on the couch earlier.

Lake's worried about his performance but I'm not so sure my body won't erupt within seconds with the way his cock works me already.

Magic Stick has a whole new meaning to me now.

Lake advances into me again. Each buck becomes wilder. He's losing more and more control the deeper he gets, and so am I.

"Goddamn it..." he growls, his eyes hooded, his breathing becoming more labored.

Seeing Lake falling apart above me has my body coating him in more wet arousal. His blue eyes brighten above me, and his blonde hair becomes more disheveled... he's so beautiful when he fucks and if I had known how good it would be, I wouldn't have been able to resist this long.

I grip around his neck tighter, and he presses against me harder in response. He wants me closer just like I want him. His lips lock down on mine. He kisses me with more passion than he has before... more passion than any man has ever kissed me with.

I rock against him too, begging him for more pressure... more speed.

He's hitting all the right spots and my body is veering toward combustion.

"Lake... I'm..." I breathe out.

"Come, Tessie. I want to feel you grip me. Come on my cock," he demands.

"Keep going," I say against our kiss. "I'm almost there," I tell him.

He abandons my lips and dips down to pull my nipple into his mouth.

I whimper at the sharp feel of his teeth sliding across my sensitive nub. I can feel the heat build in my belly as my orgasm threatens to release.

I can barely speak as Lake's tempo increase and his thick cocks hits the spot over and over again.

He drives into me again and again until I'm a puddle of need.

"Go Lake... go..." I beg.

He thrust again, biting down on my nipple one last time and my body erupts.

I scream out his name as I fall over the cliff. Lake holds me tighter, securing me to him as I pulsate over his cock. Squeezing him continuously.

Lake doesn't back down as he keeps the tempo. He's waiting for me to recover but I can hear the grunts and groans as he tries to keep it together.

My eyes open finally to see him watching me.

"I've never witnessed anything as beautiful as you coming," He says, thrusting into me again and again.

I smile up at him for a moment, but I can see the pain on his face... he needs release too.

"Come in me," I tell him.

"Fuck..." he whispers and then kisses me again.

His lips don't pull off mine as he rails into me, once, twice, and then a third time until he groans into my mouth as he unloads himself into the condom buried inside of me.

His face buries into the side of my neck as he pumps a few more times slowly as he comes down off his own climax.

He peppers my neck with light kisses as he breathes through his orgasm and I hold on tight to him still, not ready for us to separate.

A switch just flipped, and I have no idea how I'm going to turn it back off but with his promise to use the whole box of condoms on me... maybe I can enjoy tonight and worry about that another day.

Tonight... I just want to be Lake's.

Chapter
Twenty-Six

Lake

I stay inside Tessa for as long as I possibly can and then after we both clean up and I discard my condom, I lay back down on the couch and pull her over my chest.

She giggles when I do it and fuck, I've only heard Tessa giggle twice in the time I've known her and both have been tonight, on the couch with me. I hope that means something.

Her left hand soothes over my chest while she lies on her side against me in the crook of my arm, her breast pressed against my chest, and I'm already addicted to the feel of it. She's choosing to touch me, and it feels too fucking good to have this version of Tessa.

Her index finger glides down the scar over my left shoulder and she stops for a second and looks at it. I don't look up to see her face, I already know the frown I'll find if I look at her now. I know when someone sees the scar and debates asking about it. Instead, I stare up at the timber beams in the two-story vaulted ceiling. I turned her down last time, but I have my own unsavory question I want to ask.

"You want to know about the scar?" I ask, finally looking over at her.

"Yes," she says softly, still analyzing the mark that's the only physical evidence I have of the worst day of my life.

I don't want to tell her, she may never look at me again... she may jump off this couch and leave me when she hears, but I have to take that risk because I need to know who hurt her.

"I'll make you deal. I'll tell you about my scars if you tell me about your scars. All I want in return is a name," I tell her, trying to lessen what information she thinks she needs to divulge.

"How did you know he left a scar?" she asks, gingerly touching a spot towards the back of her head underneath her hair... as if there's no way I could have seen it.

I haven't. I didn't know there was a scar hidden beneath her hair.

"Wait! He left an actual scar?" I ask, my voice rising higher than I wanted.

I lift my head immediately trying to get a look at the scar but there's no chance I'll see it under all that hair.

I pull her closer against me instinctively as if I can protect her now from what he did to her in the past.

I can't.

I know that.

But I can level the playing field, and I can make him pay for what he did.

Now the name isn't all I need. I need to know what the asshole did to her.

"It...it was an accident," she says, trying to defend the piece of shit.

"He laid a hand on you?" I ask, my concern increasing.

There's a flash of fear in her eyes but not for herself, she's worried I might do something with this information... and she'd be right.

"It was a long time ago, Lake. I got out. I left. We no longer work for the same team and now I'm in Seattle."

"Does Brent know about this?" I ask, trying to get my voice under control.

She's not going to tell me anymore if she thinks I'll do damage to the guy. I have to make her believe this is for information purposes only.

"No, I didn't tell Brent because I quit my job the next day and Brent offered me a place to stay and a new job. Brent would end up serving twenty to life if I told him."

She's right. Brent would kill him.

If there's one thing I know about Brent, it's that he'd do anything for Tessa. She's more than just his baby sister... she's the only immediate family he has left.

My blood begins to boil at the idea of any of my old team-mates landing a hand on Tessa, but I can't imagine any of them doing it. Well, except one..

"Who was it? Who hit you?" I say, as softly as I muster.

"It was an argument... he was drunk. He shoved me and I fell against the kitchen island... he didn't mean it," she adds quickly, pleading her case.

Bullshit again.

"Who. Was. It?" I ask again trying not to look like I'm about to rip a grown man to shreds with my bare hands.

I don't want to be anything like the dick who hurt her but an animalistic need to even the score with this guy and teach him that he fucked with the wrong woman, builds in my gut.

I can feel her heart rate increasing. She's feeling cornered and interrogated but the more she tells me the more her answer is merely a formality.

I already know who it is. There are a lot of new guys who've joined the team since I was there but I still know it well enough to know he's the only one capable... and has prior history with other women... all hearsay, but I believe he's capable.

Noah Sinclair.

"It won't do anyone any good." she tries to argue.

"Like hell it won't. He needs to be taught a lesson by someone his own size."

There's a glossiness to her eyes now like she's trying to keep the welling of tears at bay. I'm making her relive the memory of it and I hate that I'm bringing it all back to the surface. But if this is the reason she won't date hockey players, then I need to rectify it if I ever want a shot with her. "Why won't you tell me who it is?"

"I already told you... you play them head-to-head this season."

Yeah, we do.

"Good."

"No Lake, not good. You'll get in a fight. You'll get suspended and we can't have that. The team needs you in order to make it to the championship this year. He's not worth giving that up."

"Protecting you is worth everything. Even a championship." I tell her gliding my thumb over her cheek and brushing her dark locks that have fallen in front of her face, back behind her ears.

My arm pulls her up closer and I bend down to meet her lips. I kiss her, pressing my mouth to hers— she kisses me back.

My body thrums with a need for her and only her. My cock hardens uncomfortably thick, needing to bury into her again and show her everything I can give her. Things I swore I'd never give another soul.

I have to slow this down. I promised to tell her about my scar, both visible and the one buried deep.

I pull back from our kiss and glance down at her swollen lips, her eyelashes fluttering back open.

I don't want to tell her this part because I'm not sure how she's going to feel about me after.

Will she blame me like I blame myself?

Will she pull herself out of my arms and never want to see me again?

I wouldn't fault her but I hope she doesn't.

I know I don't deserve her and if I could work up the strength to push her away like I have for the last four years, I would, but now that I've tasted her, held her, I'm no longer strong enough to walk away.

"I guess I have to hold up my end of the deal," I say.

She stays quiet and watches me carefully. There's curiosity in her eyes as they scan over the tattoo that I got to mask the mark left behind by the seat belt.

It seems so odd to me that people miss it since it feels like a red beacon calling me out and telling my greatest sin.

I roll my thumb over the softness of her jawline. I want to remember every smooth edge of her face, every soft curve of her body lying against me. I want to memorize the way her heart beats against mine and the faint smell of strawberries on her breath from her lip balm because after I tell her everything, she may never let me touch her again.

I relax my arm and she goes with it, sinking back down against my arm and my rib cage. I can't look at her when I tell this story. It's been years since I've had to, and I was hoping never to have to again but the moment demands it.

She told me about her ex... or mostly about him. I need to hold up my end of the bargain.

She shifts her position and pushes up to rest her chin on top of her hand as her head towers just slightly over me.

She wants to be close and there's something comforting in that. I want her close too.

"When I was a senior in high school, I got drafted as a rookie to the San Diego Blue Devils farm team."

She nods as if she already knows.

"You knew that?"

"A lot about you is only an internet click away. I search all of the players regularly to see what people are putting on the internet about them. Getting drafted out of high school is impressive. I might have looked you up." She smirks.

"Oh right." I give a small grin.

I like that she looked me up but with the heaviness I'm about to unload, I can't enjoy that tidbit of information.

"In high school, I had a girlfriend named Shawna. Bobby and I both fought to win her over from freshman year on, but she ended up picking me our junior year. I still to this day don't know why she picked me. Bobby's a better person than I am," I say, my eyes fixed on the ceiling.

"Don't say that. You're a good person, Lake. Look at what you did with the animals today and with the woman's shelter." She interjects with a softness in her voice."

"How do you know about the women's shelter?" I ask, a little surprised.

I know I never said anything about it to her.

"I might have seen you this morning when I was getting coffee down the street."

I just nod. I'm sure from her outside view, I looked like a saint, but that's not the truth.

"Just wait until you hear it all before you make that assumption, ok?"

"Ok." She nods against her hand still on my chest.

"Shawna didn't grow up in the best situation. She never met her dad, and her mom was a drunk. A few days after I got drafted a storm blew in and Shawna hadn't seen her mom in days; she was worried and asked me to drive her around to find her. The weather was fine when we left but soon, the weather turned. I didn't think anything of it. After all, we grew up in these types of storms."

Tessa's eyes narrow on me and I see her gulp down. She's already reading into how this goes.

"We got in her small red sedan she loved so much. I had a four-wheel drive truck at the time that handled better in the snow but she loved that damn car because, after years in foster care, it was the first time she owned something all for herself."

"She was in foster care?" Tessa asks, sadness for Shawna's upbringing flashing in her eyes.

I guess foster care could have been an option for Tessa too if Brent hadn't been old enough to be her guardian when their parents died, although Brent mentioned a grandmother and a great uncle too.

Tessa knows something about losing parents. Something that I've never known since my parents are still very active in me and my sisters' lives and have been married for almost forty years. A rarity, I know.

"She ended up in foster care at thirteen when her mom's addiction got to the point where she was blacking out and not coming home for long periods."

"That's heartbreaking."

"She got a better deal than most. A widow from one of the churches in this small community took her in. When her mom would clean up, she'd show up to try to get back in Shawna's good graces. It was easy to do, Shawna was always quick to forgive," I say, grimacing at the memory of driving up to Shawna's foster house and seeing her mom's barely working car in the driveway.

Shawna would be so excited to tell me about all the things her mom was promising her and then we'd fight when I begged her not to believe anything her mom said. She'd accuse me of not being supportive or that I lacked compassion for her mother's illness since I had a charmed life with two parents.

After our fights, sometimes Shawna would go days without talking to me... until her mom would inevitably take off in the dead of night or the break of day before Shawna got out of bed, not saying goodbye but taking whatever babysitting money Shawna had saved up out of a coffee can she always kept it in. She'd try to hide it in different places each time but her mom would find it somehow.

I'd spend the next day or two at her foster mother's house holding Shawna and letting her cry. It was always the same thing, except each time, I hated her birth mother more and more. It started feeling like the wedge between us grew with each visit because as my hate for her mom increased, Shawna's fear for her mother's wellbeing increased too.

"So, what happened?" Tessa asks.

"We shouldn't have been out that late with the snow advisory warning but she wanted to find her mom, so I drove her a few towns over to make sure her mom got into a shelter for the night."

"Did you find her mom?"

"Nope," I say, grinding my teeth at the thought of what we sacrificed for that woman who turned out to be warming herself in a crack house while her daughter lay dying on the side of the road.

"When we were only a few miles out from her foster mom's house, the roads got worse. A truck a lot bigger than our car, spun out in front of us..."

"Oh no..." Tessa says, her eyes almost pleading with me to change the outcome.

But no matter how many times I've tried, the outcome still remains.

"It hit you?" she asks.

"No, we overcorrected to avoid the collision and her car left the road and rammed into the tree on the passenger side."

"Lake..." she says, sitting up further to look at me and my eyes cast back up at the rafters to avoid hers.

There's so much about telling this story that I hate, but the pity people feel for me might be the worst of it. No one should feel sorry for me. I survived and if we would have collided with that truck, it would have been me on the gurney when the paramedics left that night and not Shawna.

"Shawna died on impact. She didn't even have a chance," I tell her, still staring up at the ceiling.

No matter how many years go by, I still remember calling out her name in the darkness of that lonely highway after we hit the tree. I remember begging her to be ok but she never responded to any of my pleas. Then I remember being pulled out of the car by the driver of the other vehicle who had called 911 already.

I begged him to pull her out too, my shoulder dislocated and broken, an injury that still requires that I tape it up before a game to keep from dislocating it. A large laceration from the seat belt had cut across my shoulder from the impact.

He ran over to open her door but then came back without her. He said he shouldn't move her because it looked like a neck injury. He said he didn't want to make it worse and that we should wait for the EMTs but somehow I knew, he had already checked her pulse.

I knew it right then.

She wouldn't be ok.

The tears didn't come right away... I was in shock.

But they eventually came, and they fell hard the second the sound from the ambulance rang through the trees and the mountains of the lonely highway with only the two of us out there, alone in the dark.

"She was beautiful and the kindest person I've ever met. She had so much to give to this world. It should have been me instead," I admit.

Tessa rolls her body further onto mine and then pushes up to straddle my stomach.

"Don't talk like that. You have survivor's guilt, that's normal but to say that this world would be better off with her instead of you is something you can't know for sure."

I brush off her words. Survivor's guilt doesn't even begin to describe it.

"The shelters were her idea. It was her senior project. She wanted to make sure that no matter what town her mom ended up in Colorado, she'd have a place to stay... along with anyone else who needed a safe place for the night."

"That's why you do it?" she asks, her eyes soft.

"I made her a promise the day of her funeral that I'd put shelters all over Colorado to make sure that she still lived on in some way. That she could rest easy knowing her mother would have a place to go. And then I promised her that I'd never move on."

"Never move on from what?"

"At her funeral, I promised her that I'd never be happy with anyone else since she no longer can be. And I thought I could do it. I thought I could keep my promise... and then I saw the most beautiful woman I've ever seen standing in the stands four years ago... wearing Ryker's jersey, and I've been struggling to keep that promise."

Tessa lets out a breath, the only sound in this room aside from the wind blowing against the large windows of my living room.

"I didn't know Shawna but from what you tell me... I think she'd want you to be happy."

"I don't want to betray my promise to her but I can't resist you anymore either," I say, sliding my hand softly over her cheek as she hovers above me.

"Then don't resist," she says softly.

She leans down and presses her lips on mine. She's giving me a chance. I can feel her doubt in me melting away through our kiss.

CHAPTER
TWENTY-SEVEN

Tessa

I wake up to the feeling of being wrapped up in strong arms. The feeling of Lake behind me and his morning wood.

"Good morning," he says, talking against my neck.

He leans in and presses a warm, soft kiss to my shoulder.

"Morning," I say, a stupid smile on my face thinking back on every toe-curling moment of last night.

Lake lifts up his head and peers over at me.

"Is Tessa Tomlin smiling before she even gets her first cup of coffee for the day? This must be some kind of fluke, or the world just turned on its axis."

I chuckle, bringing the blanket up to my mouth to hide my morning breath... and my sex-drunk smile.

"I think last night had a lot to do with it," I tell him, snuggling back against him to feel his hard cock against my lower back and the top of my butt crack.

I like that he kept it warming between my cheeks last night.

"Keeping you regularly satisfied is how to keep a smile on your face? Duly noted," he says.

I chuckle. Regular sex with Lake sounds too good.

"What do you have planned for today?" I ask, trying to change the subject because I'm about to start blushing if he calls me out anymore for being a happy morning person when I'm getting sex consistently.

"I have my last volunteer day this morning with the women's shelter before we head home in a couple of days. What about you?"

"I was thinking about working from the coffee shop today just to change it up. I might even walk over and help Chelsea with the inventory."

"That sounds nice. How about I meet you at the coffee shop after I finish helping with the breakfast rush?"

"You want to meet me at the coffee shop? Like a coffee date?" I ask.

"Yeah." He smiles. "Like a coffee date."

My stomach flips at how quickly he agrees.

"That sounds fun. I'd love that."

"Okay, I have to go. The shelter opens in thirty minutes, and I stayed in bed too long because I didn't want to leave."

My cheeks heat with a blush I can't avoid. I never thought I'd see this side of Lake.

Lake

It's only thirty minutes until I'm done with the breakfast rush for the shelter when my phone buzzes in my pocket for the fourth time.

It's not unusual for me to get multiple calls this close together, but four is a lot back-to-back, and it has me concerned that it might be Tessa or Chelsea and the girls.

I reach down to pull out my phone and see that it says Chelsea on the caller ID.

"Hey, I have to take this. Can you cover for me? It might be an emergency," I tell one of the other volunteers who nods when I hold up my phone.

He gets back to work as soon as I walk away and helps dish out the applesauce and chocolate milk boxes, not a tough feat.

"Hello?" I say once I'm several feet away.

"Where are you!?" my sister demands.

"I'm at the shelter. Why?"

"Because there's a rager at your house and there are drunk half-naked people in the heated pool and your nieces are home viewing this," Chelsea says, the irritation in her voice escalating.

A party at my house? What the fuck?

"I'm not throwing any party. I have no idea why there are people at my house."

"Well, then I'm going over there to kick them all out."

"Whoa, just hold on. Don't go in without me."

"Why? I'm a single mother with two pre-teen daughters. I'm scarier than anything those drunk frat kids have ever seen."

She makes a valid point. Chelsea can be scary.

"Fine, go in. But don't make any enemies until I get there and try to find out how the fuckers got in."

"The code to your house is the jersey number, Lake... it's not complex."

I ignore her. Easy code or not, someone thinking they can use my house for a party isn't my fault.

"Keep the girls in your house. I'm on my way," I tell her.

I find the supervisor and tell them I have an emergency and have to go and then I jump into my Porsche and get to my house as fast as I can.

I think to call Tessa and find out if she's there, but since I saw my Jeep at the coffee shop, I know she isn't.

With everything she thinks about me and my reputation, the last thing I want her to see is yet another reason she might not want to give me a shot.

No, I need to try to clean this one up as best I can before she sees it.

I shoot her a quick text.

Lake: Something came up. I can't meet you right now.

I set my phone in the cup holder and haul ass up to the house.

I walk into my house, and sure enough, there are at least forty people. The crowd must have grown.

I look for Chelsea over the crowd. My height is an advantage for this.

When I spot her in the kitchen, I walk over to find a pissed-off Chelsea talking to some guy who Bobby and I went to school with.

He looks too drunk to remember his own name, let alone who invited him to this party.

"Who told you there was a party here?" she demands again, her hands on her hips and she gives him a scowl.

"Chill out, buzzkill... who invited you?" he asks, slurring his words a little.

"If you don't get out, I'm calling the cops," my sister threatens.

"Hey now, no need to go that extreme," he says, and then sees me headed toward them. "Lake, my man! You got to get this chick out of here," he says, gesturing with a full cup of beer that ends up splashing all over my sister.

My sister jumps back. "Are you kidding me?" she yells at him.

"What the fuck, man?" I yell at him.

My sister pulls the hem of her shirt out and away from her so that the cheap beer doesn't touch her skin.

"Dude, this chick is being a bitch—"

I barely let him utter the words and my fist flies, connecting with his nose. Blood immediately runs out of his nose and over the left side of his lip.

"Get all your fucking friends and get the fuck out of my house before I call the cops," I tell him. "Here, come on, Chelsea, let's get you a new shirt, and then we'll kick them all out and call the cops."

Chelsea follows me up the staircase.

Tessa

It's been over an hour since Lake said that something came up. I texted back to see if I should wait, but I never heard back. I decided to stay and work since the coffee shop is warm and snuggly.

I like watching the light snowflakes fall from the large bay windows of the shop.

As I'm packing up my things, I get a call.

Bobby calling...

Weird. He's never called me before even though I gave him my number at the pizza parlor when he asked for a date.

"Hi, Bobby."

"Hey, Tessa. Are you home right now?" he asks, his voice urgent.

"No why?"

"I got a call from one of Lake's neighbors saying that there's a party going on at the house. They didn't even know Lake was back yet, so they called me since Chelsea isn't answering either."

Hmm, that's weird.

"I was just about ready to head back. I can see what's going on."

"Are you with Lake?" he asks.

"No. He texted me earlier, though, and said something came up and he couldn't meet me for coffee."

"I've tried him half a dozen times. I'm headed to Lake's, so I'll meet you there," Bobby says.

I decide to call Lake myself a few times to see if I can get through but no luck.

Ten minutes later, I pull up to the house and there is no room to park anywhere near the house with cars piled up everywhere. I park and then walk in, looking for Lake's car, but I don't see it. Maybe it's in the garage?

I walk in the front doors and find half-naked women being chased by half-naked men... this feels like déjà vu from the festival earlier this week.

I see Bobby over by the kitchen having a heated conversation with some of the party-goers.

"Well, if you don't know who called the party, where is Lake?" Bobby asks.

"I don't know, man," some guy with a backward hat says and then walks off.

"You looking for Lake?" another guy says. He walks over with what looks like a bloodied nose he just got to stop with a piece of paper towel shoved up his nose, but he keeps taking drinks from his red Solo cup even though he looks drunk enough.

"Pete," Bobby says, obviously recognizing the guy. "Yeah... have you seen Lake?"

"Sure have. The dick coldcocked me and then took some girl up to his bedroom trying to get her shirt off."

"What?" I interject, taking a step forward.

Bobby puts out his arm to block me from walking any closer, like he doesn't want me anywhere near Pete.

"Yeah, he told her to take off her top upstairs in his closet."

The blood in my veins begins to boil, and Bobby sees it start. Now I know what "came up" ... his worthless dick when he got a booty call from someone else.

"Just hold on a second, Tessa, don't lose your head. We don't have all the information, and Pete here is fucking drunk," Bobby says, giving Pete a raised eyebrow.

"I don't know, man. She was hot as shit, and they looked like they knew each other if you know what I mean." Pete gives a little wink, but he's so drunk that it looks a little more like a weird tic than a wink.

"I don't, asshole, and shut the fuck up," Bobby says, trying to shoo him away from me.

"I don't want to hear this," I say, close enough for only Bobby to hear.

He turns to me and bends down lower, cutting Pete off from our conversation.

"We have no idea. The woman could be anyone for any reason. Don't make assumptions until we talk to him."

Too late. Assumptions have been made based on my experience with men who make their living skating on ice and my experience seeing Lake firsthand.

"Do you still want that date, Bobby? Otherwise, I'm leaving town now," I tell him.

"Don't do this, Tessa," Bobby says, reaching out and gently clutching my right arm. "He's changing. It's the first time I've seen him like this in fifteen years. Hold out for him. It'll be worth it, I swear."

"Date or no date, Bobby?" I say, ignoring his plea.

Even though I think it's clear by the way he's pushing me toward Lake, there's no future between Bobby and me besides friendship.

He ponders his options for a moment and pulls his hand off my arm. He comes to terms with the fact that I'm not going to be persuaded.

"How about coffee?" he asks.

It's a compromise. I'll take it. Anything at this point to get out of this house and have a distraction, even though I should just bribe someone in the house to take me to Seattle or at least to a bus station.

I nod and turn to leave back out the front door. I don't want to be here when Lake finally comes down with swollen lips, a satisfied smile, and whatever girl he must keep steady here in Aspen.

No sex in Aspen, my ass.

I knew that was a load of shit. How many more things has he been lying about?

I'm not sticking around to find out.

Goddamn hockey players.

The snowstorm that was picking up as I left the coffee shop is now dropping thick clumps of snowflakes the size of silver dollars outside, and the temperature feels as though it's dropped another five degrees.

"Let's take my truck," Bobby offers, following closely behind me. "It might get icy out there."

Now knowing Lake's story with Shawna and my lack of experience driving in cold conditions being from Southern California, I take him up on the offer.

I walk to the Jeep and pull out the computer bag that I left in there when I first arrived, along with my purse that I had all locked up. They are the only two things I have to have before I leave town.

He opens my door like a gentleman to make sure I don't slip on the flat black running board of his electric-blue four-door pickup.

I slide in, and then I click the butt warmer on the inside panel for me even though the truck is still warm since he must have just barely beat me here.

My emotions pull in different directions sitting in the passenger side of Bobby's truck while he walks, slowly, around the front, staring back at the front door like he's hoping Lake will walk out any second with a full explanation that he assumes I'll buy. Part of me doesn't want to leave the place I know Lake still occupies, but the other part of me, the angry green goblin deep inside me, hopes he suffers from some sort of erectile dysfunction and the woman he has upstairs broadcasts it to every puck bunny blogger on the face of the planet.

Yes, I'll have to deal with the media frenzy of it, but that's the kind of workload right now that I'd happily take on. Not that I'd enjoy having to read the intimate details... but at this point of my career in pro sports... you read a lot of "Too Much Information" from women who like to kiss and tell.

After this coffee date with Bobby, I'll find my way out of this town before the storm gets worse.

Lake

"Why are all of the clothes still in bags?" Chelsea asks.

Chelsea had a better idea to raid Tessa's closet instead of mine. After all, Tessa hasn't worn any of the clothing from my sisters' store anyway, so Chelsea might as well.

"She's being stubborn."

My sister smirks back up at me while digging through the clothes and then pulls out a T-shirt and a sweater that she hand-picked out for Tessa days ago.

A few thousand dollars' worth. Not that I'm complaining. I'd say it was worth it if Tessa would wear any of it, but now the idea of her keeping it all here for when she and I come back and forth for vacations and the offseason, assuming she'll want to live here with me in the offseason, works fine for me.

I'm just about ready to grab her bags and haul them to my primary closet and drop them in there for her to organize when my sister laughs.

"What?" I ask.

"It's just interesting coming from you. One of the most stubborn people I've ever met. Maybe you finally met your match," she tells me with a lifted brow.

"Maybe," I say back.

Chelsea's back straightens immediately, and a glint of excitement flashes in her eyes.

"Wait... are you two... dating?" she asks, her head cocked like a puppy dog as if the word dating and me don't mix.

She's never known me to date a woman in over fifteen years. This might come as a shock to her, but the smile across her lips says she's happy about it.

"We agreed to talk this morning at the coffee shop, but then you called, and I headed straight here."

"I stopped you from finalizing a relationship with Tessa this morning. Are you insane?" she yells. "You should have just told me to call Dorian down at the sheriff's office. He would have just driven up and turned on his lights out front... everyone would have bolted."

"You seemed distressed and on a suicide mission. I had to get up here before you did something stupid... like get a beer spilled on you."

"It was an accident." Her eyes flare.

She spins toward the en suite of Tessa's room with a set of clothing with the tags still on them.

"Was it, though?" I call after her.

She flips me the bird.

"Call Tessa now. Get her up here. And call Dorian. I left my phone at home with the girls in case they needed me. I told them to call you."

I don't want to call Tessa and have her see this mess, but she's probably wondering where I am, and I'm surprised she hasn't called or texted to check-in.

I go to reach for my phone and feel that it's missing.

Shit, I left it in the car.

"I must have left my phone in my car," I call out at the shut door of the bathroom. "I'm going downstairs to get it."

"Ok," she calls out.

On my way out of Tessa's room, I pass a couple trying to find an open room.

"Whoa, Lake Powers, I'm your biggest—"

"Get the fuck out of my house. I didn't invite you here," I threatened.

The guy grips the woman's hand, and they spin around quickly, hurrying back down the stairs.

"And tell all your friends too," I call after them.

When I finally reach the Porsche, I duck in and retrieve my cell phone.

13 missed calls.

4 from Tessa.

7 from Bobby.

2 from my neighbor.

Shit.

I stand back up and close my door and then something catches my eye parked a good distance away.

My Jeep, with no Tessa in it.

Fuck... is she inside?

I call her quickly, but she rejects the call.

What the hell?

I try her again. Maybe it was a fluke.

She rejects it again.

Is she really that mad about the party?

Or maybe she's mad that I didn't show up at the coffee shop?

I send her a text.

Lake: Where are you? Answer your phone.

She still doesn't respond.

Lake: I'm sorry I didn't show up at the coffee shop. There was an emergency at the house.

Nothing again.

Finally, I call Bobby since I missed seven calls from him.

"There you are, man! Where have you been? Your neighbor called and couldn't get ahold of you or Chelsea."

"I'm still at the house. Chelsea left her phone with the girls when she came over to disband the party, and I left my phone in the car. Are you here?" I ask, looking over the tops of vehicles for his blue truck.

"No, I left a little while ago."

"Did you see Tessa?"

There's a short silence on the phone, and I hear the clinking of silverware and plates like he's at a restaurant.

"Yeah... I did, and she's with me."

"What?" I ask, the unmistakable sound of jealousy in my voice.

Why the hell would she be with Bobby right now?

"Why?" I ask, not able to hide my concern.

"I called her when I couldn't get ahold of you. She met me at the house, and Pete told us that you were upstairs with a woman."

I hear Tessa whisper a scold at him, *"Don't tell him. It doesn't matter."*

"A woman?" I ask, still not sure why it's a problem... it was my sister.

"He said that you took a beautiful woman upstairs with intentions to..."

"Shut it, Bobby," Tessa says loud and clear.

Oh fuck...

She thinks I took a woman up to my room and messed around with her like all of her cheating exes.

"Bobby, where are you? I'm heading your way."

I'm not explaining this to Tessa through Bobby's phone. She has a history of unfaithful boyfriends, but I'm not one of them. She needs to hear it straight from me.

"Don't you dare," I hear Tessa tell him.

"I can't give you that information, Lake. Bye," he says, and then hangs up.

What the actual hell just happened?

Not even a minute later, a ding hits my phone.

> Bobby: The coffee shop. Come quick.
> She might make a run for it.

I jump in my Porsche and dial the sheriff's office. My buddy Dorian from high school agrees to come down and park by the house with his lights on. That should be enough to scare them away.

Then I ask him to check on my sister and make sure she's not pulling out some girl's weave. He'll do it. He's had a crush on her since we were in middle school.

I ask him to go upstairs too and get a picture of my sister holding up her stained beer shirt. I have a feeling I'm going to need hard evidence to clear my name.

Could this day get any fucking worse?

CHAPTER TWENTY-EIGHT

Tessa

I grip both hands around the piping-hot toffee butter latte that the barista just brought me. It's a soothing feeling having something warm in my hands, with the snow falling even faster.

The barista tells us that they're going to close early before the roads get too bad, but she says we have an hour while they close all the machines and clean the kitchen.

Bobby pulls a sip off his black coffee, and I'll never understand how anyone can drink coffee without at least cream... although if I was deserted on an island, I'd make do and count my blessings even if I was only left with coffee beans to chew on.

Okay... so it's a real addiction, but I won't apologize for it.

And the fact that Lake doesn't drink it should have tipped me off that he's untrustworthy.

"How did he find us?" I ask Bobby.

Turns out, Bobby might not be trustworthy either. I should have figured he'd side with blood over me.

"Please hear him out. I know Lake better than most and he has feelings for you. He wouldn't fuck this up."

"You can't know that. And there is a string of women who would tell you different about Lake."

I give him a side-eye. He knows exactly what I mean. He can't be ignorant of Lake's reputation as a hockey *player*.

"None of them he's ever been serious about. I don't know what happened upstairs, but I promise you, whoever she was, he didn't touch her. Pete was wrong."

"Why do you care so much?" I ask.

"Because this town didn't just lose Shawna that day and I think you're the only thing that can bring Lake back."

The chimes above the door ring as Lake pushes through the glass storefront entry. I don't look up at him. Instead, I pull my drink up to my lips and take a sip of my latte, hoping somehow that it calms my nerves. There's a little shake of my hands, but not enough for anyone but me to notice at this point.

"Tessa," Lake says, now standing over me to my left.

His voice is low and smooth like he's trying not to spook a wild animal.

"What?" I say, setting my coffee cup down and wiping the little bit of lip balm with my lip print on the rim.

"I came here to take you back home."

"Your house isn't my home."

"That's exactly what we need to talk about. I want to change that."

I turn and glare back up at him.

"You think I'll ever want to sleep in the same bed that you—"

He steps closer and cuts me off. "It was my sister," he says, shaking his head. He slides his phone onto the table with a picture of Chelsea in the shirt I tried on at her shop while she holds up a T-shirt with her boutique's logo on it, covered in a beer-colored wet stain.

"A kid Bobby and I went to school with dumped a beer on her when she tried to kick them all out."

I look back at the photo and then up at him.

"Did you break his nose too?" I ask, wondering if the idiot with the paper towel shoved up his nose had it coming.

"Yeah, I did."

"You're not supposed to hit people. They could charge you for assault," I remind him.

"He wouldn't want the cops poking around, trust me." He nods at Bobby like they both know there won't be an issue.

"You took Chelsea upstairs?"

"I went up to find her one of my shirts, but she went through the stuff I bought you from her store instead. I think she's a little offended you're not wearing any of it."

"It was your sister?" I ask again, staring down at the picture again.

It's not a serious question since I can see the evidence in front of my face, I just need to work out the mind screw of what I thought had happened. This isn't what I expected.

Lake steps forward and then bends one knee to the ground and pulls my left hand off his cell phone and holds it in his. His warm fingers clutching mine and the nearness of him has my full attention.

I turn to him. He's so much taller than me that I barely have to look down at him taking a knee while I stay seated in my wooden café chair.

"Today didn't go the way I planned, and I wish that I hadn't put off what I wanted to say on our coffee shop date when I could have said it with you in my arms this morning."

Bobby shifts in his chair and then decides to bus our table of items to have an excuse to bypass another man laying out his feelings.

"I need to know something," he says, his steely-blue eyes gazing back into mine. "If the stupid house party hadn't happened, and no drunk idiot misidentified my sister because there was never anyone to head upstairs with, in the first place... and I had shown up at the coffee shop to have the coffee date as we planned... would you have agreed to date me?"

What? Is he being serious?

"Date you?"

"Yeah... exclusively. No more billionaires from college. Or any other asshole who's had a crush on you since eternity. Just me."

My heart gallops at his question.

Would I date him?

I definitely considered it this morning while lying against him in bed. And when's the last time he's asked a woman that?

I already know the answers—that's why I know this is rare. Maybe Bobby's right... maybe something is changing in Lake. I've certainly seen a side of Lake while being in Aspen that I've never seen before.

"What would you have said?" he asks again.

My right hand fiddles with his as I contemplate his question.

If the last couple of hours hadn't happened, I would have jumped into his arms and kissed him. I would have felt privileged and lucky for Lake to give up his one-night-stand rule for me. Who wouldn't?

I can't hold what happened today against him, though, and I need to try to erase it from my memory. No matter how many times I've promised myself I wouldn't fall for another hockey player, I can't help that I have yet again, and I have to trust Lake not to hurt me like he swore he wouldn't.

I need to see this through and know once and for all if all of this blazing chemistry between us has been there all along because we were always meant to be more than enemies.

"I would have told you that I want that too," I tell him.

"You would have?" His lips curve up on one side in a hopeful lopsided grin. "And how about now?"

"My feelings since this morning haven't changed. I still want to try, but I'm scared."

"I know. But I promise you that everything is going to be okay."

I nod, my lower lip sliding between my teeth due to nerves.

A wide smile stretches across his face, and he loops his right hand around the back of my neck and pushes up off his knee, plastering his lips against mine.

We share a long-awaited kiss. His mouth is warm and inviting with the cold storm sweeping in.

I want nothing more than to cuddle up tonight under the blankets with him and watch the snowfall. The idea of being snowed in with Lake by morning sounds like a small piece of heaven that I'd be happy to indulge in.

He pulls his mouth off mine.

"Can we go home now? We still have a lot to talk about, but it looks like this place is closing down early, and I don't like the idea of you out in this weather. I want to get you home where it's safe."

Home... I like the sound of it now.

"Home sounds good." I nod, and we both stand.

Lake and I walk out of the coffee shop while Bobby buses my coffee cup for me. He tells us to take off and that he'll walk to the back and let the staff know we're leaving so they can get out of here.

Lake opens the front door for me, and I walk out first, the snow coming down so hard that Lake wraps an arm over my shoulder to keep me from slipping. The man handles icy surfaces very well. An occupational hazard, I suppose.

Within minutes, Lake has me sitting on the passenger side, and then he jumps in the driver's side and starts the ignition of the Porsche.

He pulls out of the parking spot and heads for home, driving at exactly the speed limit and not a single MPH over.

Lake starts talking and asking questions about our new relationship, and the fact that he wants to discuss it is already a promising sign.

"We should probably tell HR as soon as we get home next week," he says.

"Are you okay with PDA at work because I'm not sure I'll be able to keep my hands to myself?"

"You're going to burn Ryker's jersey and wear mine now, right?"

I answer them all quickly as we discuss how life will work now with our new relationship. We haven't discussed ground rules yet, but that can wait until tomorrow. Tonight, I just want to use up those condoms he promised me.

We're a little over ten minutes in with five more minutes until home when he asks a question I didn't think we were ready for.

"Where do you want to live in the offseason?"

"The offseason?"

"The hockey season will be over for me here in a couple of months if we don't make the finals. Then I usually head home for Aspen."

"Oh...well, I work all year for the Hawkeyes. I don't have an offseason," I remind him.

"Shoot right... I didn't think of that," he says, his hands twisting lightly over the steering wheel as he thinks through the issue.

"Could you work remotely for those few months?"

I try to bite back the stupid grin at the idea that Lake is already making plans for the future with me.

"I can ask, but with Autumn now on the team, it's nice when she and I can be in the office together at the same time," I admit. "But maybe I could split my time?" I tell him.

He reaches out his right hand and grips my left hand, pulling it up to his mouth and kissing the inside of it.

He turns to me and smiles.

"We'll work it out, Tessie. I'm not worried." His thick raspy voice tickles my ears.

I love the sound of his voice.

And now I have to admit that when he says "Tessie," my heart squeezes a little.

"Yeah, we will," I say, turning to look out the windshield when all of a sudden, a deer darts out in front of us.

"Lake!" I shout.

He drops my hand and grips the steering wheel with both hands.

"Hold on," he yells, letting off the gas, but it's too late. The lack of visibility from the snow didn't give us enough time.

I let out a shriek and grip the door handle on my right and the middle console to my left as the Porsche slams into the deer, the impact tossing the deer up onto the windshield and cracking the entire thing into a million pieces. My head hits the dashboard, the airbags deploying a second too late, and the deer's momentum tosses it like a rag doll up over the car.

"Fuck!" Lake says, steering the sliding car and keeping us on the road.

The car slides almost sideways, still in our traffic lane, and then stops as it hits where the deer landed on the road.

My forehead stings. A few shards of glass must have come loose from the mangled windshield. The rest seems to be held together by the thick film coating on the glass.

Warm blood streams down from my forehead over my eyebrow. It drops on my cheek.

"Tessa! Tessa!" Lake yells, slamming the car in park, and rips off his seat belt, practically clawing to get halfway over the center console to get his hands on either side of my jaw to turn me toward him to look at me.

"Are you ok? Jesus! Please tell me you're okay?" he says, his eyes searching all over my face and then down my body, looking for obvious wounds.

I place my hands on either of his wrists, squeezing in the hope my touch will settle him. "I'm okay, Lake. I'm fine, I just..." I say, reaching up to touch the stinging wet spot on my forehead.

"You're bleeding," he says, his voice wobbling.

I can feel his pulse where my hand wraps around his wrist, and it's pumping faster than mine.

I bring my hand back down to see the color of the liquid coating my fingers that I just wiped off my head. It's a bright red and a decent amount although not enough to be concerned about. It's a bad glass cut, and that's all.

I don't think I have a concussion, but bad whiplash and a giant goose egg where I hit my head will probably start forming in the next little bit if it hasn't already.

"I think it's from the glass," I say, turning my head to look at the airbags that have blood on them, probably from the blood left on the vehicle's dash.

He looks back at the windshield. "Shit."

Then he looks back at me.

"We need to get you an ambulance," he says with wide eyes and urgency in his voice. "You need a hospital."

"Lake, I'm fine. It's just a cut," I tell him, trying to put his mind at ease.

Lake lets go of my jaw and pushes back into his seat, searching his pockets feverishly until he finds his phone still in the cup holder.

He picks it up, his hands with a slight shake to them as he dials quickly and plasters the phone to his ear.

It's adrenaline.

I've never seen Lake shaken up before. Not during a bad fight on the ice. Not after Ryker went to the hospital earlier this season from a blow on the ice by an opposing player. Not even when they're down multiple goals with mere minutes left in the period, and the pressure is on to make some goals.

Lake Powers is notoriously unshakable.

"Lake... I'm fine," I tell him, gripping his right bicep with my hands to insist that he not worry.

He looks down at me, but the worry in his eyes doesn't lessen.

I can hear the 911 dispatcher on the other line faintly as I keep my hands on his arm.

"911 dispatcher, what's your emergency?"

"We hit a deer on the highway in my car, and my girlfriend is hurt! Send someone now, please!" His desperate plea distracts me from enjoying the fact that he just called me his girlfriend.

There's fear in his voice. I can hear it, and now when I think about how Lake was on this same highway fifteen years ago with a different woman and different results, I suddenly understand what's happening.

I need to calm him.

I need to reassure him.

I run my hand back and forth over his arm in an attempt to soothe him, but it doesn't feel like it's working as his body still feels tense.

"I'm dispatching help now. They're on their way. Now stay on the line with me so I can get a little more information to give them. Where are you exactly?"

Lake looks around for a second, squinting through the broken glass.

"Mile marker fifteen is, uh... maybe, thirty feet from us. She hit her head pretty bad, she...she's bleeding. Tell them to hurry," he says, a little fluster in his voice.

He looks back down at the gash I assume is open on my forehead.

"I shouldn't have done this," he says under his breath.

"You shouldn't have done what?" I ask, but his eyes almost seem glazed over like he can't hear anything I'm saying.

I feel almost like some kind of ghost he can see but can't hear.

"Is your girlfriend coherent? How bad is the bleeding?" the dispatcher asks.

"She's awake, but she's bleeding badly."

I shake my head at him. That's not true.

More like I'm alert and the bleeding is average for slicing skin across glass shards. He's making it sound worse than it is.

She continues to ask follow-up questions to keep him on the line until the paramedics arrive. She asks him to walk her through the event, and she asks him if I'm sleepy or if I can remember the names of the last three presidents.

"Lake, I promise... I'm fine." I try again.

All of a sudden, flashing red and yellow lights from the ambulance show through the rearview mirror. They're still half a mile away, but I'm surprised they made it here this fast in this weather.

"I see the lights. They're here," Lake tells her.

"Okay, I'm going to let the paramedics take it from here so I can field more incoming calls."

"Thank you," Lake says, and then hangs up.

Before I can talk to him, there's a paramedic yanking open my door.

"Hello, ma'am. We received a call that you were in an accident. We're here to help."

Lake

I stand a few feet away from the police to file a report. After ruling out that I was driving while tired or intoxicated, they ask me questions to put together a report I'll need to send to my insurance agent to get the Porsche fixed.

It's fucking freezing, the snow is still falling, although not as hard as before, but the wind has picked up.

I check back over my shoulder every few minutes to make sure Tessa isn't cold, but they have her inside the ambulance and covered in one of those foil blankets as they shine a light in her eye to check for a concussion.

"Alright, I'm taking this information back to the station. Call in a couple of days and I'll have an accident report for you to give to your insurance agent if they need one."

"Thanks."

He nods and turns to leave.

I see a new set of headlights in the distance. The sun is still in the sky but with the dark storm clouds, the visibility is as if the sun has set, and it's harder to see than it should be at this time of day. I'm not sure if it will be someone I know, but the last thing I want is someone from Aspen seeing me on the side of the road in a car accident... again.

The closer it gets, the faster it seems to drive.

It pulls off the road the second it gets close enough.

The driver's door swings open, and I see Bobby jump out.

"What the fuck happened?" he yells, running toward me.

He doesn't miss the dead deer lying behind my Porsche as he looks past me.

"Holy shit, dude! Are you guys okay?" he asks, gripping both of my arms and taking a quick scan to see if I have any obvious wounds.

"I'm fine... I'm always fine. But Tessa..." I tell him, the guilt of hurting yet another woman I care about making it hard to fucking swallow let alone stand vertically on my two feet.

"Tessa?" he asks, looking past me at her.

One of the two EMTs walks over to us, the other staying with Tessa. He pulls off his gloves as he walks up.

"Your girlfriend's going to be okay..."

I slide my hands in my pockets and lightly kick the imaginary gravel on the icy shoulder of the road.

"She's just a friend," I tell him.

"Oh, uh, the report said... you know what, never mind," the EMT says, shaking it off.

It's probably not a relevant part of his report.

I can feel Bobby's and Tessa's eyes on me.

"How is she?" Bobby asks him.

"She suffered a hit to the head and whiplash, but the gash on her head should heal up without stitches. All in all, she's going to be alright. She'll be sore tomorrow, though."

Bobby nods. "Thanks for your help today," he tells the EMT.

"We're going to pack up and head out. She's safe to go home. Just have her ice that goose egg tonight."

I nod and look over at her.

She stares back at me, her lips flatlined and a dullness to her eyes.

I look back at Bobby.

"Can you take her home?" I ask.

"What? Why?" Bobby asks, his eyes furrowed and searching mine.

"I'll wait for the tow truck—"

"No, I'll wait for the tow truck. You take your girlfriend home," he says, turning away from me to head for Tessa.

I grip his jacket, and he stops to give me his attention again.

"Take her home, Bobby. I need a minute."

His lips purse as he studies me.

"You're about one minute away from blowing this all to shit."

"Maybe that's what I deserve. I made a promise, and I broke it. This is a reminder."

A reminder that I don't get to have Tessa. This is karma coming back to warn me that if I step out of line, I'll pay for it.

"That's bullshit, and you know it. Shawna wouldn't want you miserable. You think she'd have wanted you to end up miserable with a laundry list of STDs?" he asks, taking a step closer.

I know Tessa can hear this conversation, but maybe she should.

"You made a promise to a ghost... a ghost you made up in your head. This isn't about you making it up to Shawna... this is about you punishing yourself for something out of your control," he says, lifting his hand and planting it on my shoulder, coming eye to eye with me as if we haven't had this same conversation a million times before.

"She should have picked you. You're a better driver. It wouldn't have happened if you had been the one driving her," I tell him.

"That's bullshit, and we both know it."

"Just take her home, Bobby."

I know what he's trying to do, but seeing Tessa like she is... in that ambulance, the only way to protect her is to stay away.

I'm jinxed.

He shakes his head.

"Fine. But the tow truck will be here in less than five minutes, and you're less than ten minutes from home. That gives you about thirty minutes tops to get your head right and your ass back to that house before your world implodes," he says, his voice deep and low so that Tessa doesn't hear.

Bobby walks over and puts an arm around Tessa, pulling her with him. She goes with him, not looking back at me, until the last second when he helps her up into his truck.

The sadness in her eyes that flickers to a look of disappointment says it all. She knows this is over.

And so do I.

CHAPTER TWENTY-NINE

Tessa

Neither of us says a word as Bobby drives me to a house that I left this morning blissfully unaware of how quickly my world would crumble before the sun even sets.

Right now, my room at the Royal Inn sounds pretty damn amazing compared to the loneliness of an empty mountain mansion while I wait for Lake to return.

The snow still lightly falls on the glittery white blanketed roads but only barely as Bobby's truck handles the road smoothly without any trouble. I hold the ice pack that the EMT gave me to the right side of my forehead, where they gave me a butterfly wound closure bandage.

"He's going to come back around. Have faith," Bobby says, breaking the somber silence.

If I hear Bobby tell me one more time to keep giving Lake more rope, only for him to hang me with, I'll definitely consider blocking him from all forms of social media in the future.

"I'm not sure who you're trying to convince. Me or you," I tell him, not bothering with trying not to hurt his feelings.

At this point, I feel more like Bobby's sacrificial lamb, willing to give any victim up to Lake, hoping it will magically heal him from the loss he's faced.

If anyone can understand losing someone you love at such a young age, and so tragically, it's me. I can't fault Lake for the damage it has done to him, the emotional and physical scars it left, or the fact that it's caused him to push love away in hopes he'll never get hurt or hurt someone else.

It sounds like he made her a promise never to move on because she no longer can, but I know the real reason he doesn't let another woman get close. He's worried that he won't survive the pain of a second loss. I know the very same fear.

What I can fault him for is not knowing his limitations. However, I knew mine too, and just like him, I ignored the failsafe I put in place to make sure I didn't fall for a player again. I made a promise to myself, just as Lake did, and we both broke those promises that were designed to protect us from this kind of hurt again.

I guess some lessons are determined to be learned more than once.

Bobby parks under the large, covered entry of Lake's house and turns to me.

"How much do you know about the accident?"

"Enough, I guess."

"Did he tell you that Shawna jerked the wheel?" he asks, his left wrist resting against his steering wheel.

"What...? No."

Lake left that part out.

"The other driver veered back out of the lane just in time, but Shawna panicked and gripped the steering wheel, yanking them off the road. They wouldn't have collided with the other truck like he claims would have happened."

"He claimed he wouldn't have made it."

Why... why would he leave that out?

"She begged him to drive her that night, wanted to take her car instead of his truck when he knew they shouldn't be out in that storm. She gripped the steering wheel out of pure instinct. The other driver saw it happen," he says with a sigh. "He blames himself, but he's not to blame for that night... no one is. It was all an accident."

He doesn't say anything else, and I'm speechless.

He gets out of the truck and comes to my side to open the door, helping me out. My head is starting to pound, and I only have one hand to help me get out since my other is clutching the ice pack.

"Here, let me help you," he says, pulling the door open and then carefully gripping my elbow as I take slow steps out of his truck.

"Thank you for bringing me back."

"Anytime. I'm glad you're okay."

FILTHY SCORE   373

"Me too," I say, and then look past him down the drive, willing Lake to show up all of a sudden in the tow truck to tell me that he made a mistake by not taking me home instead of Bobby.

Instead, the road is pitch dark, other than the lights of Bobby's truck as it runs idle.

"Do you want me to wait with you until Lake gets back?" he asks as if he knows that Lake will be back within a short time.

I want to believe him.

I want to think that Lake is going to come to his senses and show up in the next ten minutes with some massive eighties movie grand gesture and we'll fall back into bed together and not leave those Egyptian cotton sheets until we have to leave for home.

I know he's not.

"No, thank you, Bobby. If I need anything, I'll call Chelsea since she's right next door."

He turns to glance over at Chelsea's house, her lights still on all over the house.

"Ok." He nods, seemingly feeling better about agreeing to leave since I have someone nearby I can call.

We exchange our goodbyes, and Bobby heads back to his truck, and I input the code to the house and duck inside. Bobby waits until I close and lock Lake's front door and then I hear Bobby's truck rev up to life and drive off the property.

The minute I open the door, I'm surprised to find it clean and smelling of pine sol.

Who could have done all of this that quickly?

I head for the kitchen in search of a new colder ice pack and I notice that the keg is no longer in the house and everything has been wiped clean in here as well. Then I hear the side door to the kitchen open. Lake's security system is designed with a different chime depending on when each door to the house opens.

I hold my breath for a second to hear the sounds coming from the kitchen,

Is it a burglar?

The thought of that puts me on alert and I clutch my cell phone in my hand, readying it to call Bobby immediately and get him back here. A few seconds later, the sweet sound of two little girls fills the kitchen with giggles and even though I have bandages and an ice pack on my head, I'm still happy to have some company.

I debate pulling the ice pack away from my forehead so as to not frighten the girls. But the bloody bandage might do a worse job so I forge ahead with a clean white ice pack to block the head wound.

"Hello, this is a nice surprise," I say in the entryway of the kitchen.

"Tessa!" the two girls yell and then run for me, a backpack on each of their backs and a rolled-up sleeping bag under one arm.

"To what do I owe this surprise?" I ask.

They both look at my ice pack for a second but neither seem surprised. How could that be?

"Mom said that you got a little cut on your forehead and that we're coming over to have a sleepover and make you feel better, isn't that awesome?" Lana says, bouncing up and down.

"Uncle Lake called and said you need company tonight because you had a bad night. What happened to your head?" Sadie asks, wide-eyed.

"It's no big thing, sweetie but I'm so happy you're here to keep me company," I say, not wanting to alarm them.

Then I glance up at Chelsea when the girls seem content with my answer.

"Yep, Uncle Lake said that he's got a lot to do and won't be home tonight, right?" she asks the girls, both still hugging me on either side. "He wanted to make sure Tessa has us looking after her," Chelsea says to the girls but it feels more like she's informing me of the situation unfolding in front of my eyes.

"Yeah! And Uncle Lake said we could make a tent fort in his living room tonight." The girls jump with glee, releasing me and then head straight for the living room.

Once they're out of earshot, I shoot Chelsea a look.

She walks up to me, double-checking that the girls are too far off to hear us.

"Let's wait until the girls are settled, then we can talk about what happened just now," she says, staring at the ice pack I still have pressed to my forehead. "And you might need a new dressing on that cut too."

"Ok but who cleaned the house?" I ask as I follow her to the living room where the girls are already building a fort in front of the TV with chairs and blankets.

"I had the sheriff demand that all the uninvited houseguests lick this house clean, or they would all be arrested for breaking and entering."

I laugh for a second at how much that sounds like something Chelsea would do even with my limited time with her.

As we help the girls get settled, it all hits me fast. Lake isn't coming back tonight. He sent his sister and his nieces to babysit me... or maybe spy on me to make sure I don't leave. I don't know what his true motive is, but whatever it is, I'm blowing it all to shit.

I give Chelsea a nod to meet me upstairs, and a few minutes later, she joins me in the spare room I've been staying in as I pack up the very few things I care to take.

When she walks in, she can tell that something has changed.

"What are you doing?" she asks, seeing me pack the few things I have into my laptop bag.

"I'm leaving."

"What? When... how?"

"I'm leaving now before the storm gets too bad and I get stuck here."

"Tessa you can't leave, you just got in a car accident tonight. You need to rest and you don't need to be out in these conditions."

"I'm leaving. So you have two options... be a good friend and help me donate all of these amazing clothes to Lake's shelter, or sit there and watch me pack? Either way, I'm taking Lake's Jeep and I'm leaving. If Lake can't bother to show up tonight to babysit me himself—"

"We're not here to babysit. He just didn't want you alone after the accident. He told me everything. I'm so happy you're both okay."

He told you everything? Like how he made Bobby take me home, and not him.

"Are we okay? Lake doesn't seem okay at all."

Chelsea steps forward into the room and starts shifting things in the Juniper store bags she gave me using Lake's money.

"Tonight, really threw him. He got scared. He just needs a minute."

"A minute?" My eyebrows stitch together as if she can't be buying her own bullshit. "Well, he'll get all the minutes he wants."

"He loves you, Tessa. I can see it."

Not her too.

I turn to her, an I-give-no-fucks look on my face because I need her to understand something that Bobby can't seem to either.

"I'm not here to fix Lake. I have my own issues and I don't need his too. Either help me pack or get out," I tell her.

I don't like snapping at her but this is about as much as I can take. Leaving Aspen and closing the door on what could have almost been with Lake, is hard enough.

Her lips twist in thought and then she turns to head toward the door but instead of walking out of the doors like I think she's going to, she closes us in.

"Okay... Let's do this."

Lake

I wake up on the kitchen floor of the soup kitchen, the smell of coffee hitting me. It smells like Tessa and I feel sick for what I did last night.

I came to the women's shelter yesterday after the tow truck took the Porsche. I stuck to the separate cafeteria space that isn't connected to the women's clinic that's on the other half of the building.

I don't really know why I came here. Maybe I was intending on making amends with Shawna for trying to move on with Tessa or maybe I came here to finally close the door on that chapter of my life.

The look on Tessa's face when she took one last look at me, and Bobby's words that I made a deal with a ghost, all swirled around in my head last night as I couldn't find rest until the early morning. But by five am, the soup kitchen manager started the coffee and then promptly kicked me out.

"You look like shit, man. Go home," he said, kicking my boot this morning after he started the batch of coffee.

I woke to the smell thinking it was Tessa, and when it wasn't, I knew in that moment... I never want to wake up another morning without her.

Little did I know... I had a rude awakening waiting back at home for me.

"What the fuck do you mean she's gone, Chelsea?" I say, my hands planted on my kitchen island.

I stare at the back of Chelsea's head as she starts breakfast for the girls.

"Watch your language around the girls, Uncle Lake," my sister says.

We're back in my kitchen. It's morning, but time is a blur right now. My neck is killing me from falling asleep on the floor of the shelter's kitchens last night, only my jacket as a pillow after I brewed a pot of coffee... just to smell her.

Yeah, that was a little weird, but it was a weird night.

"She packed her things, got in the Jeep, and left last night."

"Why didn't you tell me? I thought you were coming over to watch her?"

"If you're about to blame me for the way you handled last night with Tessa, you'd better rethink that right now."

"I can't believe you let her leave... in this weather," I tell her, referring to the storm that started back up early this morning. We now have multiple feet of snow on the ground.

"You act as if I had a choice. She's just as stubborn as you and holding her against her will is considered kidnapping, last I heard."

I shoot a text out to her, but it comes back as undeliverable. I try a second time but it comes back the same. I pull up her number and try to call but it says that the call can't be completed.

She blocked me?!

What the fuck!

"She blocked me." I hold up my phone.

"And you deserve it."

"This is serious. She could be stuck on the side of the road or worse."

"She made it through the storm before it got bad last night. She made it to Idaho. She's only six or seven hours from home by now."

"What? How do you know that?"

"She's been updating me," Chelsea says.

"She drove the entire night?"

"Yeah, we talked over the phone for a good part of it. I didn't want her to fall asleep while she was driving."

"Tell her to pull over at the nearest hotel. I'll pay for a room for her so she can get some sleep at least."

"She asked me not to tell you anything."

"Chelsea, for the love of God, you better tell me everything."

"Nope," she says, flipping her hair as she spins around. She heads for the living room where my nieces eat cereal they brought from home and watch cartoons on the big TV while still sitting in their tent forts.

I pull up the airlines and quickly work to book a flight, but when I attempt to select my flight, I see the red lettering.

Weather Cancellation.

It's on everything.

I go to the weather report and see that the roads out of town are closed due to snow. There's no way out of here that gets me to Seattle.

My phone tingles with a charge on my black card. It's a fuel charge in Boise, Idaho. Chelsea might not tell me where she is but at least she'll leave me a trail to know where her route takes her. It doesn't solve the biggest problem...

I'm stuck in Aspen, and Tessa is hundreds of miles away from me.

CHAPTER THIRTY

Lake

A few days later, I'm back home. I drove by Brent's house, but I'm too chickenshit to knock on his door uninvited. I have no idea what she told him, and since everyone's first day back is today, I haven't seen Brent or Tessa since I got home.

I don't see my Jeep parked out front, but she must have it parked in the four-car garage since Chelsea, at the very least, confirmed that Tessa made it back.

I walk into the Hawkeyes conference room. The whole team, coaching staff, and corporate are all here to discuss the new merger that Phil signed with the big sponsor he was trying to win over.

Tessa's little stunt worked. Our adoption numbers were a record, and it got huge news coverage that the new sponsorship wanted to use it to its advantage as well.

Tessa can block me and avoid me all she wants any other time, but she won't be able to avoid me here.

I take a seat in the large conference room.

Lines of padded metal chairs make up three rows for more seating. People are still streaming in but mostly everyone is here and people are taking their seats, only... someone is very obviously missing from the group.

"If everyone can find their seats, we'll get started on this exciting news," Sam Roberts announces, standing in front of everyone.

People start scurrying from the craft table with disposable coffee cups, muffins, and bagels, looking for a spot to sit.

Briggs and Autumn come over and sit next to me.

"How was Walla Walla and your dad?" I ask Briggs.

"Seeing everyone was good," he says, clutching Autumn's left hand in his right, playing with the engagement ring. "The doctors are happy with their results, but there's still a long road ahead."

I nod, then take a sip from my large water bottle.

Why the hell can't Tessa live in The Commons like the rest of us? It would be so much easier to "accidentally" bump into her if we lived in the same apartment building.

"How was Aspen?" he asks.

Autumn inches a little closer toward Briggs as if she wants to hear the answer more than he does. I guess I should have expected that the first thing Tessa did when she got home was to update her friends with all the shit that went down between us last week.

"It went pretty fucking good, I'd say, since the adoption blowout snatched the win with the new sponsorship."

"Yeah... it must have," Briggs says, unconvincingly.

He knows.

I bet Autumn told him.

Autumn gives him an elbow to the arm, and he turns to her and whispers, "What? How could I have said that any different."

She lets out a little huff at her new fiancé.

I scan the room again, looking for the leggy brunette probably a tight-ass pencil skirt somewhere around here.

Instead, I notice Penelope, who wears an uncharacteristic scowl pointed at me.

What the hell is that for?

I didn't do anything to Penelope... This must be Tessa-related too.

"Ok, is everyone ready?" Sam asks.

I take a quick look again and still no Tessa.

"Sir," I ask, getting our GM's attention. "We're missing someone." I intentionally avoid saying her name out loud.

"We are?" Sam asks, looking for himself. "Who? I think everyone's here."

"Tessa Tomlin," I say.

"She's in Cabo," a voice says from behind me. I look back to find Brent was the one who said it.

"Cabo?" I ask him, and then my head swivels back to Sam, waiting for someone to explain why she's in Cabo this week.

She just got back from Aspen. When was this planned?

Confusion and dread hit me that maybe she was always planning this.

"After the massive success from you and Tessa's efforts this past week, Phil agreed to give Tessa this week off since she missed her bye week vacation helping out the team. She knows someone who has a penthouse down there, I think," Sam adds, his light blue eyes watching me under his usual Hawkeyes ball cap.

Does he know what happened between Tessa and me in Aspen? I don't think so. Not unless Tessa told him. Yet Penelope is his daughter. The information that Tessa told Penelope may have spilled out. Or Sam might have just figured it out on his own. He tends to know everything before anyone else.

Wait... Cabo... Penthouse.

Goddammit...Elliot.

She went with the "safe" guy from college?

My stomach begins to churn thinking about them together on the white sandy beaches of Mexico and spending the night together in his penthouse.

I've seen Tessa naked. There's no way he could keep his hands to himself. I wouldn't... I didn't, and now I drove her to someone else.

I have to stop this from happening.

I have to beg her for forgiveness.

Sam might fine me for missing the meeting and for missing practice tomorrow, which is inevitable, but I'll pay whatever fine they want to throw at me to get to Tessa and convince her to come home with me.

I stand, not meaning to make a scene, but eyes are on me now that I'm the only person standing beside Sam.

"Sir, an emergency just came up. I have to go," I tell him with urgency.

I look over at Penelope because if anyone knows Tessa's travel arrangements, it's her.

"An emergency?" Sam echoes.

Penelope stands far off to the left of her dad, sitting with a laptop taking meeting minutes. Her fingers stop typing, and she stares back at me with a frown.

She's not happy with me. I get it.

"I'll explain later, but I have to go now," I tell Sam with haste. I spin around and take quick steps to the large conference room door.

I feel Penelope's small stature behind me the second I reach the door and exit the conference room.

"Lake, hold on," she says.

Looking over my shoulder, I see her close the door behind her, cutting out everyone in the conference room and blocking their ability to hear us. I see beady eyes from rubberneckers watching after us right before she pulls the heavy dark mahogany conference room door closed, closing off their view.

I spin around to get the answer I need.

"Where's she staying, Penelope?"

Penelope turns to me, releasing the large handle on the door.

"You're not exactly in a place to demand answers."

"I need to know where she's staying. I need to stop her from making a mistake. Where's his penthouse?"

I see a devilish smirk try to break through her lips, but she reins it in. She's enjoying my suffering, meaning that Tessa painted me as... well, the dickhead who hurt her.

Maybe I do deserve Penelope's reaction, but time's wasting. The longer she holds out on giving the information, the more time that dick gets to touch Tessa.

My fists clench at my sides at the image of another man's hands on Tessa's silky skin.

The sounds she made for me in my bed echo through my head, and the idea that those sounds could be filling his penthouse right now makes me want to punch a hole through the drywall of this hallway.

"I was really rooting for you Lake when she told me what was happening in Aspen. You were so close," she says, shaking her head at me. "And now, she has someone who's willing to do anything to be with her."

"He's the safe bet."

"He's a better bet," she counters.

Shit, maybe she's right, but I'm too selfish not to try to get her back.

"If you can't offer her everything... then don't screw this up for her. He might just be the guy to make her happy."

Fuck that, that guy should be me.

"I need to tell her that I'm sorry... actually, I need to tell her a lot of things, but she blocked me."

"I know." She frowns. "But you deserved it."

I won't argue with that.

"Then you also know my only option is to show up and tell her in person."

She shifts from one leg to the other. I can hear the meeting getting underway with Sam's voice booming inside. She knows she should be in there taking notes and not out here with me.

"I can't give you the hotel name. It's girl code."

I clench my jaw. She's not going to help me.

She bites down on the inside of her lip for a second and debates telling me something. I can see it in her eyes. A part of her wants to see Tessa and me together still.

"What?"

She takes in a deep sigh.

"I didn't give you this idea if anyone asks, ok?"

"Yeah, Ok." I agree quickly, inching closer, about ready to grab her by the shoulders to keep her attention on me and block out all distractions of the meeting behind us until she tells me.

"She tends to post pictures and tag her location on social media."

Yeah! She does. Brilliant.

A huge smile breaks across my lips. A loophole where Penelope doesn't get in trouble with Tessa.

I grip Penelope and pull her in for a bear hug, pulling her to my chest.

"Thank you. I won't forget this," I tell her against her hair. She's so much shorter that I have to bend my head a little.

She's like the little sister I never had... and never wanted either. Two older sisters are enough of a shit show, even though I love Chelsea and Harmony—we've become close as we've gotten older.

"Just don't fuck it up this time." I hear her muffled voice against my Hawkeyes team jacket.

Did Penelope Roberts just curse?

I let out a little chuckle and release her.

"I owe you... big!" I tell her.

Then I turn and start running down the hallway, headed for the elevator to get me back down from the corporate offices to the main lobby of the stadium.

Forty-five minutes in traffic and I'm pulling into the long-stay parking lot of the airport when I get a text from Penelope. I couldn't book a flight since I was driving, and I'll have to run to the counter and hope something is going out right now.

Seattle is a big airport and flights are going out all the time.

> **Penelope:** Got you a flight. Nonstop. Leaves in fifty minutes. RUN to TSA.

> **Penelope:** I booked you in coach by the lavatory… you don't deserve anything better.

I'm too damn happy to have a flight booked to give a shit. I'd ride on the wing of the plane at this point if that's what it took to get me there.

> **Lake:** Send me your Christmas wish list. You're getting it all.

> **Penelope:** There's only one thing on my wish list. A happy best friend.

I wish I could guarantee that.

> **Lake:** How about a Lamborghini instead?

I'm kidding… sort of.

I run through the airport, using the easy kiosk to print my ticket. I don't have any luggage to check so I grab my boarding pass and race to TSA. The line is ridiculous and after getting a wheelchair to the back of the leg by a twelve-year-old with a broken leg... who is a Blue Devils fan, based on the logo on his hoodie, and the lady in front of me with a dozen more electronic devices than any one human should ever own, I get through TSA with fifteen minutes before takeoff. The gate has to be closed, there's no way I'm going to make it.

But I have to try because all of the other flights are booked solid. I don't know how Penelope even got me this one. If somehow this pans out, I'm buying Penelope a house for Christmas, I don't care what she says.

I run full speed down the hall, grateful for all the drills we've been running lately. My cardiovascular system is conditioned perfectly for this moment.

I see the gate and the gate attendant starting to close the door.

"Wait! Wait!" I yell about a hundred feet from her. "That's my flight."

Her head whips over to see me.

"Are you Lake Powers?" She squints.

She's a younger woman with her red hair in a tight bun and a navy-blue airline uniform. "Oh! You are," she says, opening the door back up.

She presses the button to her radio but keeps her eyes glimmering back at me and tells the crew that they have one more passenger coming through.

The person on the other end doesn't seem happy at first so she responds, "Trust me... you'll want this passenger." She winks, then gives my body a once-over as she takes my boarding pass and scans it through the reader.

"You're all set, Mr. Powers. Good luck in the playoffs," she says in a sultry voice.

It's wasted on me. There's only one woman I want and I'm about to lose her... for good this time.

"Thanks," I say quickly and then jet down the gangway toward the open aircraft door.

I find my seat with everyone staring back at me.

There're a few gasps from people who know who I am but there are plenty of people who couldn't give a shit who I am and are pissed about the oversized dude making them late to make their connections... except we're all headed nonstop to Cabo. Shouldn't everyone be happy?

Three hours after sitting next to the kid with the broken leg who finds new ways to call me a traitor for leaving the Blue Devils, we finally land. I don't want to break the kid's heart and tell him that I was traded because the team was having money troubles and had to offload some of their better and more expensive players to keep the franchise afloat.

He doesn't need to hear that even though crushing his spirit right now might make my calves feel better after all the bruising he caused in the TSA line.

After I've hopped into the rideshare on the airport sidewalk, I pull out my phone.

Sure enough, there's a photo Tessa took sitting on a sunbathing chair from the tops of her thighs down on a white sandy beach, a Mai Tai in her hand, her coral-coated toes laid out and covered with bits of sand around the edges of her feet. She must have been walking barefoot on the beach.

My fingers itch to run up those tanned legs. To pull her against me and beg her to forgive me for everything I've ever done to push her away for all these years.

The one thing I don't see that has me hopeful is a set of hairy legs sitting next to her.

Maybe he's getting food or a refill on their drinks... or maybe he's the asshole taking the picture.

Suddenly, I can't get there fast enough.

> There's no tag on the photo though and her caption doesn't say enough but it does make me feel like shit.

"My decompression station from the worst week."
Fuck—I did that.

I look through the comments and sure enough, I see a comment from Penelope about an hour ago.

Penelope: Looks nice. Where are you?
Tessa: In front of the Grand Island Resort in a cabana.
Scratch that, Penelope's getting two houses.

I give the driver the name of the resort, and within no time, he's pulling up to the resort. I jump out before the car even stops.

"That was fast, man. I'll give you a great review," I tell him over my shoulder as I haul ass up to the main sliding glass doors of the resort.

I act like I'm already staying here and keep my head down. These places usually only let people who stay here out on their private beaches.

I dodge around staff and make it out to the beach, headed straight for the white cabanas.

Shit, there are a lot.

I start walking the perimeter, peeking over the cabanas like a creeper, but most of them are empty. It's a nice day to be in the ocean.

After checking about twenty, I start getting discouraged, until finally, I walk up to a cabana where I can only see her feet. They're painted a familiar orange-pink hue.

Tessa

"Hi, Tessa."

My heart just about jumps from my chest. I had just fallen asleep on this damn sunbathing chair. The first real sleep I've had in the days since I left Aspen.

I know that voice, but there's no way it's...

Lake Powers at my feet in all his gorgeousness. Why can't he be uglier?

A couple of women in barely-there bikinis walk by, giving Lake's backside a look, and I must turn green with jealousy.

I shouldn't be jealous or at least, I should get used to it. This is just the start of watching Lake with other women after what happened in Aspen.

"What are you doing here?" I demand.

"You blocked me."

"And you thought stalking me would be a good idea?" I ask.

I hate that my heart skips at the thought that he flew all the way here to see me. Or... I think he did.

"Yes, because we need to talk."

"No, we don't. You had enough time to come talk to me when you sent your sister and nieces to come watch me like a bunch of puppy sitters."

"That's not what that was," he says, stepping closer to the end of my lounge chair.

"Oh really? What time did you come home, then?" I ask, crossing my arms over my breasts since they seem to be catching his attention and my nipples harden under his gaze.

He doesn't deserve to see them, and I hate the goosebumps trickling down my spine at the memory of the way his tongue swirled over them.

"You already know what time. I'm sure my sister told you everything."

I lick my lips, tasting the sweet pineapple from my drink, the warm wind kicking up and sweeping over my stomach and tousling Lake's perfect blond hair that I had gripped between my fingers only a few nights ago.

"Why are you here?"

"Because you're making a mistake."

Cocky jerk.

"Is that right? Because I think the only mistake I've made was breaking my own rules with you last week."

He rounds the chair and comes closer, bending down to a closer eye level next to my chair.

"He's your safety net, and we both know it. He won't make you happy."

"Who are you talking about?" I ask, my face scrunching at his comment.

"Elliot. You didn't date him in college because you already knew that he can't handle you, not like I can."

How dare he say that about Elliot?

He doesn't even know him.

How dare Lake tromp into my vacation to put down a man I have known for years and who let me use his penthouse this week while he's back at home working. Especially after everything Lake put me through. I won't let him get away with this.

"Elliot isn't a mistake. And he's a hell of a lot better a man than you are."

Lake pushes forward, his hands gripping the lounge chair as he leans in closer to me.

"He probably is a better man than me, but any decision you make, that doesn't put you and I together, is a mistake," he says, his eyes searching mine. "Please, Tessa, don't fuck him."

My hand swings back and slaps him across the face. It was an out-of-body experience, and even though he deserved it, I can't believe I did it. I've fantasized about hitting Lake over the time I've worked for the Hawkeyes, but I'd never hit a coworker. I've never slapped any man. Not even Noah.

But something about Lake begging me not to physically be with someone else after his history with women just unleashes something in me.

Maybe it's more because he lured me into a trap. Making me fall for him in Aspen. He gave me so much hope, only to rip it from me before I ever got to truly feel it.

He robbed me of the happiness I could almost taste and now tells me not to move on.

I hate him and I try to keep the angry tears from falling.

I'll do that alone in the penthouse later tonight while I video chat the girls and tell them what happened. Only after I order every dessert item on the room service menu.

Lake

She diverts her attention from me and stares down at the sand on her chair and then folds her arms protectively over her chest.

I don't even know what to say, but I lean back farther from her. I pushed her too hard, and I deserved that slap. Begging her not to sleep with him was a step too far. It's not even what I meant to say but I got tongue-tied... probably because I haven't put my feelings out there for a woman in years. And even though I doubt she'll hear it now... I have to at least tell her. I have to know that she knows how I feel about her, even if she turns me down.

"Tessa... I'm sorry. I never meant to fall for you, but I don't believe I was ever meant to make it out of this life without loving you." Her eyes jet up to mine at my confession. "I fought it for so damn long that I'm not exactly sure when I started, but I think it was the minute I saw you in the stands during my first home game."

"How can you say that and leave me like you did? You made your cousin take me home and you sent your sister to babysit me. It should have been you," she says, her voice shaky with emotion.

Tessa is always solid. She rarely shows when she's shaken. I hurt her, badly, and I'll never forgive myself for failing her like I did and not coming home the night of the accident.

I take a step forward. I'd rather she lay into me and cut me apart than cut me out.

"I know, Tessie."

"Don't call me that!" she barks.

"I'm sorry," I say, taking the same step back.

"And don't tell me you love me when you leave me to be taken home by someone else," she demands.

"You're right. I fucked up. I should have taken you home and held you all night. I should have—"

Then a shadow enters the cabana before I finish my thought, and I don't have to guess who it is.

A man a few years younger than me stands in the entrance in a tropical shirt and pair of khaki shorts and his chalky brown hair brushed back.

Who the fuck dresses like that.

I guess the guy who gets Tessa does.

I stand, trying to make myself look intimidating. It doesn't take a lot. He's smaller than me in height, but he looks like he surfs or something with some muscle on him.

I want to yell at him to get the fuck out. I want to pick her up in a cradle hold and move her to somewhere no one can see us so that she can yell and scream and hit me again if she wants until she's too tired to fight anymore. Then maybe she'll finally hear me out.

I want to prove to her that I'm sorry and I'll do anything to win her back.

"Hi," she says to the man out in front of us, smiling back at him.

"You're Lake Powers?" Elliot says to me, a little star-struck if I'm not mistaken.

That's a small consolation but not enough.

"Yeah," I say, trying to ignore him in hopes he'll get the hint to leave us alone, but he paid for this cabana, so I guess that he's not going to leave me alone with the woman he's wanted for years.

I know the feeling.

"He was just leaving," she says, scowling up at me.

Her eyes are threatening, and I already pushed my luck with her.

It's time to retreat.

I said what I came to say. What happens next is up to her. I can't will this to happen, and I can't keep pushing through the pain like I know to do on the ice where the only option is to make the goal, at any cost.

I can't break her to make her mine. She has to come because she wants me too.

"Okay," I say, walking backward toward Elliot and away from her. Her eyes cast down to her thighs as she pretends to pick at the nail polish on her hand. She's not watching me leave. She's done, and I have the red mark on my face to prove it.

She's done.

I lost her.

"Take care of her," I say softly to Elliot as I walk out.

"Will do, sir," he says.

That was weird.

Tessa

He left.

Because I asked him to, but it doesn't hurt any less.

"Here you are, ma'am. Sorry for the inconvenience. We didn't know that Mr. Copeland was sending anyone to his private family penthouse this week, but everything is stocked per his request. Here is the key, and I will be your private butler while you're here."

"Thank you," I say, reaching forward, and taking the key from him.

"Will Mr. Powers be staying with you this week?"

"No!" I yell at him by accident.

I think I startled the butler as he jumps back a little.

Elliot took it well when I told him that I'm not in the head-space to date anyone. He asked if Lake had anything to do with it. He put together that Lake sabotaged my trip with him and the fact that I was noncommittal to rescheduling with him to Cabo as a sign.

Then when I told him that Aspen was a bust, he offered his penthouse to me so I could be alone somewhere warm. I wouldn't want to hurt him if the butler told Elliot that Lake came to Cabo, and we used his penthouse as a lovers' reunion or something.

"I'm sorry. I just mean that Lake will not be joining me. Thank you though."

"As you wish, let me know if there is anything else I can get you," he says with a guarded smile and then leaves.

Now all I want to do is go home.

CHAPTER THIRTY-ONE

Lake

It's been almost a week since I left Tessa in Cabo with Elliot, and I haven't heard a single word.

Neither Autumn, Penelope, or Isla will give me any indication of what's going on over there, and Tessa stopped posting to her social media.

Tonight, we play the Blue Devils, and there's one person, in particular, I'm anxious to get face-to-face with.

Noah.

She asked me not to do anything to him when she told me about him pushing her into his kitchen island, and I agreed. And since I'm in the doghouse, I'll play as nice as I can, but if he gives me any excuse to ram him against the plexiglass, I'll make it my mission to make sure it hurts.

I walk out of the physical therapist's room, all taped up and ready to play.

I take a left down the hall, hoping to get a glimpse of Tessa in her office since I heard she got back into town last night and will be at tonight's game.

I hear a voice I haven't heard in a while, but I know it well enough to know it belongs to the asshole I'm playing tonight.

"What? You're not going to wear my jersey while I'm here." He laughs.

"Get lost, Noah. We're not together anymore."

"Oh, I know. There's been more than enough women to take your place."

I finally spot them in the far-right corner near the break room. He has her almost corralled in the corner with no way out.

"Good, then you can go back to them," she says, trying to squeeze past him, but he grips her arm.

I see red the second he puts his hands on her. I'm close enough now to see his fingertips biting into her arm.

"Ouch, don't touch me."

"Hey! Let her go, Noah!" I say, picking up my pace.

The second I reach him, I wrap my hands around his shoulders to pull him back.

He swings around and looks at me, fire burning in his eyes, and shoves my chest back.

I take one step but he's not strong enough to get more from me.

"Get the fuck off me, Lake. Know your damn place."

"You're in my house now, asshole," I tell him. "And you'll learn some damn respect for women," I threatened, stepping forward.

He does too, and our chests practically bump against one another.

"Stop this! Knock it off." Tessa begs, trying to pull Noah's arm back since she's still blocked a little behind him, but he doesn't budge, and neither do I.

"Some respect, huh? I've seen you at work, Lake. You've got less respect for women than I do."

That's bullshit and he knows it. I've never hit a woman.

"Noah, stop this. You have a game to play," Tessa says, finally getting between us and trying to push us apart.

I wrap an arm around her waist and pull her back, her dress swaying with the movement. She always dresses professionally for special media events and since we're getting closer to the playoffs, the house is packed with cameras. I'm an idiot who hoped she'd be here in my jersey.

"Tessa, leave," I bark, sliding her back.

"Not a chance. You have a game. Both of you need to stop this," she demands once I set her down on her heels.

"Oh, I see. Lake's fucking my leftovers." Noah smirks. "Tessa, you're no better than a damn puck slut." He smirks, looking at her to my left and behind me.

"Don't you ever talk about her like that, you motherfuck-er—"

I reach back to hit him, and he does the same, but before either of our fists fly, Ryker gets ahold of me and Kaenan grabs Noah, pulling us apart.

They must have heard us from the locker room.

"I'm leaving! I'm leaving!" he says, trying to get out of Kaenan's hold.

Kaenan finally lets him go but gives him a good shove.

"Get back to your side. Save it for the ice," Kaenan says.

"Fuck you, Altman," Noah practically spits.

"Good luck with your hockey whore, Lake," Noah calls out as he turns to leave, but he doesn't make it far before Kaenan reaches back and coldcocks Noah in the back of the head.

The captain of the Blue Devils rushes in with another player. Both are new guys from the team that's only half the team it used to be. I never played with these two, but the looks on their faces say they're tired of cleaning up Noah's messes.

I've been there.

"We're getting him out of here," the captain says and then they pull Noah out.

"Are you okay?" Ryker asks Tessa. "What the hell happened? Why was he back here?"

She turns to him as he looks her over in assessment.

"It was a misunderstanding, but I'm fine."

She doesn't look fine. She looks shaken up.

"Go back to getting ready. You're supposed to be on the ice soon. I'm sorry you had to get involved."

Ryker and Kaenan look at me and then at each other.

"Okay, let us know if you need anything," Kaenan tells her.

"You okay, Lake?" Ryker asks.

I nod, not taking my eyes off Tessa.

The guys both leave and head back to the locker room. Ryker eyes us right before he walks back through the door.

He knows something is up.

I take steps toward her, wanting nothing more than to pull her into me and protect her, but when I put out my hands, she smacks them away.

"I told you not to get involved. It's over. He's just being Noah," she says, her dark amber eyes blazing into mine.

"There is no way I'll ever let him put his hands on you, Tessa. Never," I say, locking my eyes with hers.

She might not be mine anymore, but I'll protect her forever. Even if I have to do it watching from the sidelines.

She shakes her head in annoyance.

"That was highly inappropriate of you to get in a fight with an opposing player off the ice."

"He grabbed you and had you cornered. What was I supposed to do?"

"Be a damn professional," she says, her hands on her hips.

"You're taking this too far. I would have done it if it was Penelope or Isla too. No one treats any woman like that in front of me. What would you rather I do?"

"Forget you know me, Lake," she says, and then spins around and heads for her office, slamming the door as she gets through.

I'll never win.

This is a losing game.

But I'm a glutton for punishment.

Tessa

I watch from the owner's box where we're wining and dining the media. It's also warmer up here than my brother's season tickets, and I wore a dress since I knew I'd be the media's personal tour guide tonight. As the game starts, I try everything I can to shake off what happened downstairs.

We're into the first period with a couple of goals made on each side.

Noah gets put into the game finally even though he's usually a starter. Maybe that hit from Kaenan rocked him too hard and he needed a minute. Or maybe the coaching staff made him sit it out for getting in a fight with a Hawkeyes player before the game. Whatever it was, he's on the ice now. His eyes are on Lake, and Lake's eyes are on him.

I bite down on my thumbnail. No one else in this room is privy to what just happened down by the lockers.

I watch as the puck drops. Lake doesn't go for the puck at all. Instead, he and Noah collide on the ice like two magnets, shoving one another.

"What the hell is going on?!" Sam yells at the glass.

A second later, Lake yanks Noah over and slams him against the plexiglass. Fists fly as Lake rips off Noah's helmet, both brawling, but Lake is getting the better end with his bare fists against Noah's face.

Lake's a better fighter on the ice, and Noah's better at running his mouth.

"Did Lake go straight for the attack?" someone asks.

Before I can even blink, Noah's face is bleeding, but I'm too far up to tell from where, and the jumbotron can't get a good visual.

The refs start blowing their whistles, and Noah falls to the ice with Lake on top of him, still hitting him. Both teams jump over the wall and collide to pull Noah and Lake away from each other.

The refs are going crazy, and all the coaches have also jumped onto the ice to pull their players out of the carnage.

"Lake just beat the shit out of that player," someone from legal says.

"Oh my God!" Penelope and Autumn look at me in question.

Isla pulls Berkeley away from the window, so she doesn't witness it all.

"Why did Lake attack him like that?" Autumn asks, looking between us all as if one of us has the answer.

Technically, one of us does.

Lake

My fists are itching the second Noah comes out onto the ice.

I hear Ryker give me a warning.

"Play nice, Powers."

"I always do," I tell him.

We get in our formation on the ice. Ryker, our center, Briggs, our right-wing, Brent's position behind me, Kaenan behind Briggs, and Seven as our goalie. Noah hunches, knees bent and in striking position, our eyes locked. Neither of us is interested in playing a game.

We're playing for something wholly more important.

Tessa.

I'll probably get thrown out of the game for this, and as selfish as it is for me to get pulled off the ice when we're so close to the playoffs, nothing matters more than Tessa anymore.

Nothing.

The second the puck drops, Noah and I skate full speed at one another.

We collide in the middle of the ice as I shove him as hard as I can. He snaps back like a rubber band, pushing me back and grips my jersey, anchoring himself to me.

"You like sloppy seconds, Lake?" he barks.

"Shut the fuck up. She's always been too damn good for you," I say, shoving him again, but his grip is tight.

I reach for his helmet, but he blocks it.

"I'd say we could share, but she's too damn mouthy for me. I had to shut her up," he says with a devilish grin.

He knows where to hit me the hardest. Anywhere that has anything to do with hurting Tessa.

Fire rages in my stomach, and steam builds in my helmet as anger builds so fast that I almost think I might black out.

I send a punch low to his stomach where I know he doesn't have any padding. He's too slow to stop my fists, and I hear an "Oof" whirl past his lips.

He hits me against the helmet, knocking my neck to the right, but it's not a hard enough hit.

I grip his jersey and shove him into the plexiglass not far away from us. It knocks the wind out of him a little and the crowd starts roaring down at us.

"If you ever touch her again, I'll kill you," I warn him.

"I don't have to hurt her anymore. You'll fuck her up better than I ever could."

And that's when I lose it and yank off his helmet and my gloves.

I swing over and over, only hearing the sound of my fist against the bone of his cheek but not feeling the pain.

Whap!

Whap!

Whap!

It's all I hear pinging off the sideboards next to us as my fist connects with his face until finally multiple hands reach around me and pull me off him.

He's bloody by the time I look down, and a ref yells to get me off the ice.

They skate me to the box and push me through it. Coach Bex barely looks at me.

"You're done for the day, Powers, and probably for the season. I don't want to fucking look at you. Sit in the locker room until the end of the game," he says, not making eye contact with me.

"Yes, Coach," I say.

"You're dismissed," he scowls, facing out at the ice.

I walk past him and out of the home team player bench. I knew this might be my fate if I went through with it, but I'd do it all the same again.

Actually, I would have settled this in the team hallway if Ryker and Kaenan hadn't shown up.

I walk to the locker room, fans from our side cheering and fans from the other side booing in equal measure.

I head through the locker room door opening and trudge to my locker, my helmet and gloves still on the ice.

I pull off my shoulder pads and jersey and drop them to the ground next to my locker. I sit down, unlacing my hockey skates, and yank them off. I pull down the pads off my legs next, until I'm only in my boxers and then I pull on my team sweats. I'd better get comfortable for the shit show coming my way.

My thoughts run to Tessa, who's probably standing up in the owner's box fuming along with Sam and Phil. I'm sure she's pissed that all her hard work in Aspen all went to waste... the cleaner image she tried to create with the animal adoption shot to hell. And after our conversation in the hallway before the game, I know she's going to be pissed about this. Noah had it coming, though, professionalism or not. That asshole can't be allowed to get away with it.

I hear the locker room door open while I start wiping down my face and hands from the fight but the clicking of heels has me turning to see who's coming through it.

Tessa.

Time to face the music.

"What are you doing in here?"

"I saw what happened out on the ice."

I shake my head. Of course, she did. I couldn't get that lucky.

She heads straight for me, her eyes fired up. She's mad, and I'm about to get the brunt of her anger.

"I know you're mad," I say, shifting my weight from one leg to the other, waiting for her to tear into me.

"I'm mad?" she says, the dress that stops at her calves and fits the rest of her perfectly, swooshing as she comes closer.

"I know you think I was unprofessional... that I shouldn't have hit him, but fuck Tessa, what he did to you today... what might have happened if I hadn't shown up—"

Tessa takes one last step and the way she's coming in full speed I half expect her to slap me again.

In one full fluid motion, Tessa wraps her right hand around the back of my neck and pulls my mouth down against hers.

The taste of strawberries fills my senses, and I'm home, it's the only way to describe it.

I don't know what I did to deserve her sweet lips against mine again, but I grip her waist and pull her against me, changing the position of the way I lay my mouth on hers.

We kiss in a feverish frenzy as if this might be the last time, and for me... it might be the last time she lets me kiss her.

I pull her up against me and she wraps her legs around my waist. I walk her to the lockers, pressing her back to it, my cock hardening under her. She opens her mouth for me, and I don't waste a second to dip my tongue in to taste her.

She moans, wrapping her arms around me tighter and pulls me even closer. It's hard to imagine being any closer to her, but I can think of one other way we could be.

My cock twitches at the idea of sinking inside of Tessa's tight body.

I don't want to alert her to the fact that she just jumped me, but I don't know what's happening, and my cock is coming up with ideas on what she and I should be doing.

"What's happening, Tessa?" I ask into her mouth.

"I can't believe you did that for me," she says back, in between our kiss. "Sam said you could get suspended for the rest of the season," she tells me breathless and needy.

Hearing her say that even Sam thinks I might get suspended hits me, but not hard enough to hurt now that I have Tessa back in my arms.

"I didn't protect you once, and I won't miss my chance to protect you ever again. You may no longer be mine, but I'll never let anyone hurt you again."

I'll take any punishment they want to dish out if this is the reward for finally putting Noah back in his place. Getting Tessa's hot little body in my hands one last time.

Someone should have beat the shit out of Noah a long time ago.

"I didn't go to Cabo with Elliot. I went to Cabo alone to get over you," she admits, and then her tongue dips back into my mouth.

Wait, what?

I pull my lips off her for a second, and she sees the question in my eyes.

"He just let me use his penthouse, and I let you believe that the butler bringing me my room key was him."

"Why?"

"Did you miss the part where I said I went to get over you?" she asks, dipping in to kiss me again.

I take her kiss because I'm a fucking hungry man for her, and she's the only thing that feeds me.

"Did you succeed?" I ask against her needy mouth.

"No. And I don't think I ever will," she admits.

That's what I've been waiting a week to hear.

I press my kiss into her further as I rock against the thin layer of her dress against my black athletic sweats. I press her into the lockers, feeling the heat radiate through her panties and onto my athletic sweats.

Thank God I had already pulled off my hockey gear before she walked in.

"Harder," she whispers against my ear.

Yes. Fuck yes.

I add more pressure between her thighs, and her sweet little moans start to pass through her lips and fill the locker room.

"You can have anything you want, Tessie, just tell me," I say, pulling my mouth off her lips to kiss the side of her neck, sucking deeply on her delicious skin.

"Then I want you," her sultry voice says against my ear.

Her right hand slithers between us and pushes past the waistband of my sweatpants.

I take a surprised inhale the second her fingertips touch my tip. I wasn't expecting this.

Her right hand slides down the length of my throbbing erection over and over, and if she keeps this up, I'll come in her hand quicker than is acceptable.

There is nothing better in this world than the feel of Tessa's hand gripping me... besides Tessa's pussy gripping me.

"What are you going to do with that?" I ask against her neck.

"Sit on it," she tells me.

"Jesus," I growl against her shoulder, gently biting down on her silky soft skin.

She moans at the feeling of my teeth against her skin.

Tessa lets go of my cock and pulls her hand out of my pants. I miss her grip immediately, but then she reaches between us and pushes my pants far enough down my ass that my cock is free to drive into her. She pulls her hem up between us and slides her panties to the side.

I watch between us as she does. I can't see much, but I can feel her actions as I hold her up against me.

A realization hits me at the worst time.

"Shit, I don't have condoms in the locker room," I admit, disappointed at the missed opportunity.

"I'm on birth control," she tells me, eyeing me carefully.

"You're sure?"

I haven't been with anyone since well before her, and I've never been bare with anyone, ever.

She nods. "If you are."

"Yeah. I've never been more sure of anything in my life."

I'm clean, and an accidental baby with Tessa would be a happy surprise, not that I'm angling for it right now, but I want everything with Tessa even though all she's offering me right now is sex.

She reaches down and grips me again, positioning me right under her.

The second my tip feels the warm wetness at her entrance, I let out a breath I didn't realize I'd been holding in since I showed up at my house in Aspen to find Tessa gone.

Any of my teammates or coaches could walk in right now, but I don't give a shit. My body is taking over, and I couldn't stop myself from taking Tessa, even if the whole stadium was watching.

I press into her, and her whimper sounds like heaven. I ease her onto me slowly, trying not to hurt her as my tip coats in her arousal. Her tight channel has my jaw clenching, trying to do anything but come in seconds.

I can last. I'm usually a champ, but there's no condom between us, and the animalistic need to fill her with my cum has me seeing stars at the sensation of being squeezed tighter in her warm pussy with every inch I press in.

"Lake..." she moans, tightening around my neck to give herself more leverage.

"I'm not letting go this time Tessa, you're mine," I say, thrusting into her deeper.

Claiming her.

"Say it again," she whimpers.

"You're mine, Tessie." I grunt again, my advances inside her increasing with ferocity.

Her fingernails dig into my back as she holds on. I love the desperation of her need for me.

"Harder... please!" she begs, taking all of me as I bottom out inside her. Every last inch of me fills the woman I love.

"Oh God..." she cries out.

"Take all of me," I demand.

I can feel more of her wetness coat my cock at my demand.

"Right there... oh," she tells me at the position.

I'm hitting the spot where she needs me, and I know she just needs a little more.

I thrust harder into her, her body clenching around me. She's about to come, just a little more.

"No one will ever fuck you as good as I will, Tessie. Now take my cock and come. I want to feel that pussy choke me."

Her thighs grip me, and her face burrows into my neck as she tries to muffle her scream.

My hands grip her perfect ass tighter as I use my cock to get her off, thrusting into her harder each time.

Her tight muscles around me pulsate, and nothing has ever felt better as Tessa comes on my cock, muffling my name against my shoulder.

I can't hold on anymore. I've held out for as long as I can.

I hear the buzzer ring out for the period ending, and I know we're about to have company.

I keep my momentum going, thrusting in and out of her, and she holds on to me.

My balls tighten, and I know my orgasm is imminent.

"Come in me, Lake," she begs.

That's it. I can't deny her any longer.

I come. White-hot heat pools from my body and fills her full of me. My cock pulsates over and over inside her as I come. My own release takes over as I try to ride the wave as it passes through my body.

Fuck... I've never needed someone this bad.

"Jesus... that was..."

She lets out a small chuckle against my neck when I can't finish my train of thought.

I pull her closer, my mouth to her ear.

It might be a cliché moment to tell her, but I don't give a shit. She's in my hands and a captive audience.

"I love you, Tessa."

She pulls her head up, and her gaze locks on mine. I took her by surprise. "I thought I knew what love was before I met you. I thought I had it once and lost it. But this, with you... I know now that I've only ever been in love with one woman in my life. I've only ever been in love with you."

A smile slowly breaks across her lips, like she sees sincerity in my eyes.

"I love you too," she says, her eyes flickering with warm honey.

"Wait for me tonight? I might be here getting my ass chewed after media."

She nods.

"I'm taking you home tonight."

Then I hear the sound of players leaving the bench, and I put her down quickly, smoothing over the dress and then slap her ass as she runs out the door of the locker room, her heels clicking as she does. I pull up my own boxers and sweats that hung high on my thighs from where Tessa pushed them down and then I adjust my erection as best I can. I don't know if the guys heard her leave, but I don't care and none of them mention anything. They're all on a high of their own... a winner's high.

We won the game.

No matter what happens tonight with the coach...

Tessa is worth it all.

CHAPTER
THIRTY-TWO

One year later – Bye week
Lake

Sitting in this cabana, I play with Tessa's engagement ring on her left hand while we watch the waves crash on the beaches of Cabo and smirk to myself at where we were this same time last year.

Now we're planning a wedding.

Turns out Tessa left the locker room and went straight up to Sam and told him everything that Noah had done in their relationship and what he was trying to do in the locker room earlier that day. Ryker and Kaenan witnessed it and backed up her story about Noah showing up on the home team side to cause trouble. Sam was able to negotiate a two-game suspension instead of the rest of the season, although Noah ended up benched for the rest of their season.

This last offseason, Tessa and I got engaged in Aspen with my nieces' help.

Tessa got approved to work from our house in Aspen during the offseason and helps part-time at the coffee house and at my sister's shop, just to make friends.

I still help out most mornings at the soup kitchen and have been pitching in where I can with the animal shelter too, going down once a month and helping drive up adoptions.

The renovations for the Denver women's shelter finished a few months ago and Bobby has been keeping an eye on things for me during the season since we've been back in Seattle since hockey season started.

"Can I get you two anything else?" the butler for the penthouse asks.

I rented our own. No way I was going to let Tessa ask Elliot for his, but we did end up with the same butler.

"Yeah, can I get a beer? You want a Mai Tai?" I ask her.

She's enthralled by some hockey romance book that Penelope and Autumn recommend she read and barely even looks up at me from whatever chapter has her attention.

I asked her why she needs that when she has the real thing, but she says the spice in the books are addictive.

It seems like it's been making her hornier than usual, so I'm totally on board.

I told her to buy every last damn book she wants.

"No, nothing for me," she says, barely lifting her head from her device.

"You don't want a piña colada or raspberry lemon drop?" I ask.

I wouldn't usually push her to drink but she typically likes something while we're on vacation.

She looks over at me.

"I can't drink," she says, her eyes locked on mine.

"I'll go get you that drink, sir," the butler says, speeding away as if he walked in on something private.

"What do you mean you can't drink? Are you feeling ill?"

"Sure... you could say that, but it's more like... I'm pregnant."

"What?!" I say, jumping out of the lounge chair and reaching for her. "We're pregnant?"

I know she wanted the wedding first, but I don't care which one comes first. I want it all.

"Do we need to go home?" I say immediately. This is my first baby and I have no idea what the hell we're supposed to do but I think she's supposed to see someone about this, right?

"I can book a flight now. We can leave and go see an OB-GYN or whatever you need."

"No." She smiles and shakes her head. "We have a while before that. I took the test the night before we left, but I wanted to surprise you. I had a baby jersey getting made up online. You kind of ruined it," she teases, but she looks a little serious too.

"Shit, I'm sorry," I say, squeezing her hand.

"It's fine," she says, eyeing me with a hopeful smile. "Are you happy about this?" she asks carefully.

"I've never been happier in my life," I tell her and then bend down and kiss her.

The END

Want to keep reading?
Continue the series with Book 3 BRUTAL SCORE!
To be in the KNOW about all the NEWS, subscribe to Kenna King's newsletter so you don't miss a thing click HEREfor digital readers, OR check out the website to sign up at www.ken naking.com

SCAN ME

Thank you for reading and supporting my writing habit ;). If you missed any of the other books in the series, you can find the series in Author Central.
Feel free to reach out via email (kenna@kennaking.com) or Instagram (@kennakingbooks)! I love hearing from you.